HORNS OF DILEMMA

SEVENTH BOOK IN THE BRIGANDSHAW CHRONICLES

PETER RIMMER

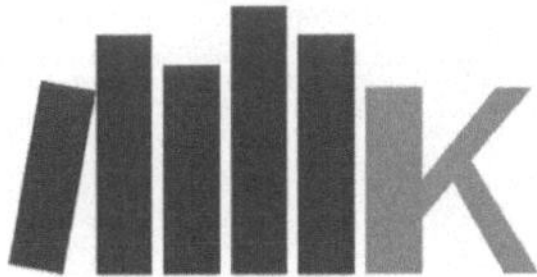

ABOUT PETER RIMMER

~

Peter Rimmer was born in London, England, and grew up in the south of the city where he went to school. After the Second World War, aged eighteen, he joined the Royal Air Force, reaching the rank of Pilot Officer before he was nineteen. At the end of his National Service, he sailed for Africa to grow tobacco in what was then Rhodesia, now Zimbabwe.

The years went by and Peter found himself in Johannesburg where he established an insurance brokering company. Over 2% of the companies listed on the Johannesburg Stock Exchange were clients of Rimmer Associates. He opened branches in the United States of America, Australia and Hong Kong and travelled extensively between them.

Having lived a reclusive life on his beloved smallholding in Knysna, South Africa, for over 25 years, Peter passed away in July 2018. He has left an enormous legacy of unpublished work for his family to release over the coming years, and not only they but also his readers from around the world will sorely miss him. Peter Rimmer was 81 years old.

ALSO BY PETER RIMMER

The Brigandshaw Chronicles
The Rise and Fall of the Anglo Saxon Empire
Book 1 - Echoes from the Past
Book 2 - Elephant Walk
Book 3 - Mad Dogs and Englishmen
Book 4 - To the Manor Born
Book 5 - On the Brink of Tears
Book 6 - Treason If You Lose
Book 7 - Horns of Dilemma
Book 8 - Lady Come Home
Book 9 - The Best of Times
Book 10 - Full Circle
Book 11 - Leopards Never Change Their Spots
Book 12 - Look Before You Leap
Book 13 - The Game of Life
Book 14 - Scattered to the Wind
Book 15 - When Friends Become Lovers

Standalone Novels
All Our Yesterdays
Cry of the Fish Eagle
Just the Memory of Love
Vultures in the Wind
In the Beginning of the Night
The Big River

~

The Asian Sagas
Bend with the Wind (Book 1)
Each to His Own (Book 2)

~

The Pioneers
Morgandale (Book 1)
Carregan's Catch (Book 2)

~

Novella
Second Beach

HORNS OF DILEMMA

Copyright © Peter Rimmer 2020

First published in Great Britain in January 2020 by

KAMBA PUBLISHING, United Kingdom

10 9 8 7 6 5 4 3 2 1

PART 1

SEPTEMBER 1946 – SINS OF THE FATHER

1

———

hen the front doorbell rang at the four-storey townhouse in Piccadilly, the house of the Honourable Barnaby St Clair, Smithers got up from the couch he was resting on in his small room on the first floor. Smithers had worked for Barnaby's brother Merlin for years until Merlin inherited the family title and left London to live in the country. When Edward, Barnaby's valet, retired to live with his sister in Brighton, Barnaby had offered Smithers the job, saving Smithers the unwelcome prospect of living in the old, cold manor house at Purbeck, far from any of Smithers's friends, all of whom were in service. It was Smithers's job once a week to check in on the flat in Park Lane, used by Lord St Clair on the rare occasions he came up to London from Dorset. The new arrangement had proved convenient for everyone. After the war, young men who wished to enter a life of service were nowhere to be found. For Smithers, it had cured his loneliness. At the age of sixty-four he was not a man who liked change. The doorbell rang again, whoever it was keeping a thumb on the button.

"Don't be so impatient," muttered Smithers, slipping on his shoes. It was the end of summer, and the trees across Piccadilly in Park Lane were lush with foliage. On the top of the steps that led up to the front door, Smithers could see a young man through the window. The man was hatless, and dressed in a blue blazer with a crest unrecognisable to him.

He was half turned towards where Smithers stood looking into the street.

"Where have I seen that face before?" said Smithers to himself.

"Will you answer the door, Smithers?" shouted Barnaby St Clair from the lounge on the second floor. "Whoever it is, I'm not in."

"Right you are, sir."

"You can bring me some more tea, then I'm going out."

Unlike his brother Merlin, a man who never raised his voice, Smithers's new employer liked to shout. At the door when Smithers pulled it open, the young man turned round and smiled. Smithers thought him in his late teens, the face nicely tanned as if the man had been in the tropics and just returned to England.

"I wish to see Mr St Clair."

"The Honourable Barnaby St Clair is not at home, sir."

"I just heard him shout at you, Smithers."

"Who shall I say is calling?"

"Frank."

"Frank who, sir?"

"That's what I've come to find out."

TURNING his back on the open door, Frank Brigandshaw walked back down the steps to the pavement where Brian Tobin was waiting.

"Isn't he coming out?"

"He'll come out if the story is true. Curiosity. All men are conceited. He'll want to have a look, if nothing else."

"There's a man peering down from a second-floor window."

"What does he look like?

"A bit like you, come to think of it." Brian was grinning, enjoying what he thought was a joke. "How long do we wait?"

"If the Honourable doesn't come down for a chat there won't be any point standing around."

"Why don't you turn round and have a look at him, Frank? After this, are we going to visit your mother?"

"What for? We've plenty of money."

"Then why did you come here? I thought you were going to ask him for money."

Frank turned round and looked up at the window.

"Do you feel anything inside?" asked Brian sarcastically.

"Not a bloody thing. Sod him. Look at that. Smithers just closed the front door."

When Frank looked up, the face at the window had gone.

"That settles it," said Brian.

"I think not. If he has nothing to hide, why didn't he come down instead of staring from behind the window? You always know who your mother is, Brian. It's your father you're never quite sure about. Let's go and walk through the park. After the boat trip my body craves exercise. So here we are in London. Twenty and footloose. Marvellous."

"Where are we going to stay tonight?"

"The cases are quite fine at the station in the left luggage office. Let the day take us. Be adventurous. I'll bet that gave him a fright if nothing else."

"Don't you want to see your brothers and sister?"

"Not particularly. Anthony was all right. The rest are a pain in the arse."

"Does your mother even know you're in England?"

"Of course she doesn't. When the money runs out we'll get worried. Let's enjoy ourselves. Girls, girls and more girls."

"Thought you had enough of them trying to score out on the boat. You're still a virgin."

"So are you. You never get enough of looking at girls. How long have we been out of the valley?"

"About four months. You know, I miss it."

"So do I. If there had been girls in the Zambezi Valley we'd still be there."

"Dad says once you've been in the bush you always want to return."

When the door clicked shut, Barnaby St Clair went back to the window. After staring until the two boys were out of sight, Barnaby picked up the telephone and gave the operator the number of Harry Brigandshaw's house in Surrey. Harry answered the phone.

"Did you know Frank's in London?"

"The last time I spoke to my sister on the farm he had taken young Josiah to shoot crocodiles in the Zambezi Valley. The river's swarming with them. They were going to cure the skins and sell the underbellies to a chap in Salisbury. Old friend of mine. He sells the crocodile leather to the Italians. They make very expensive shoes. How are you, Barnaby?"

"He's just been here! Told Smithers I was out. He knows, Harry."

"How could he? Nobody told him."

"There are people who delight in passing on unpleasant information."

"So you didn't speak to him? Probably trying to extract money. Runs in the blood, Barnaby."

"I never extracted money in my life! What are we going to do?"

"Let it alone. As we have done for the last twenty years. I did everything I could for Frank. Do you want me to tell Tina? He'll come down to Hastings Court. Young lads always run out of money. Don't you remember? I seem to recall there was something about mess funds in Cairo going missing on your watch. Why they asked you to resign your commission. Why is England so grey now the war is over? You'd think they'd be celebrating the Labour government, rather than moaning. If Attlee gets his way we're all going to get free spectacles. I wonder how Winston Churchill feels right now having been dumped after winning the war? ... So Frank finally came home now they won't call him up in the army to fight."

"They're talking about a year's National Service. The British Army on the Rhine needs men. Did he get his school certificate? He'll need that to apply for a National Service commission."

"Oh yes. Top marks from Bishops. Had him going to Cape Town university before he ran away into the bush with Brian Tobin. Was Brian with him?"

"There was another young lad. I watched them from the second-floor window."

"Did he see you?"

"Probably. Smithers will be discreet."

"We agreed, all of us, to leave the matter where it stands. So far as I am concerned, he's my son. He won't like the idea of his National Service. I read it was two years. Not a bad idea. Knock some sense into him. You never know with youngsters what they're up to. I've got two more of them, don't forget. Is it raining in London?"

"Not at the moment."

"Let sleeping dogs lie, Barnaby. Leave it alone."

"Thought you'd like to know."

"Thank you. Always nice talking to you."

· · ·

When they reached Piccadilly Circus, Frank bought the *Evening Standard* to look for somewhere to live. Their boat had docked at Tilbury in the early hours of the morning. Frank had not known what to expect by confronting Barnaby St Clair. Either they took the train from Waterloo and on to Hastings Court with all the boredom of family life, or they stretched their money as far as possible. In the 'smalls' there were cheap rooms to let in Soho, round the corner from where they were standing watching the traffic go round the Shaftesbury Memorial. Frank counted eleven whores before they made up their minds to have a look at one of the rooms. One of the whores, a woman older than his mother, had called Brian 'Duckie' and asked him if he wanted to have a good time.

"What are we going to do, Frank, when our money runs out?"

"Oh, they'll catch up with us. That look down from the upper window said the rumours are right. I remember the first time it happened. I was still in short pants. Lady St Clair came across me in the woods and got a surprise. She called me Barnaby. Must have drifted back thirty years in her mind. Old people do that. They daydream. I was staying with Mum's parents when I told them I'd seen an old lady who called me Barnaby. I knew something was wrong. Ever since, Barnaby has been in the shadows. Nothing properly spoken. Too many people stopping their conversations when I was around. You'll meet the rest of them. Bad news travels fast. By tomorrow, half of my relatives will know I'm back in England. We'll take a room and sit it out. See what happens. There's a jazz club in Oxford Street according to the paper. Let's rent a room for a month and enjoy ourselves before the shit hits the fan. That one whore wasn't bad looking. The one with her foot up against the wall staring at me. I can see her black knickers. There's a good time. We can try and look for a way to make money."

"Get a job, Frank? I'd prefer to get back on the boat and go and shoot crocodiles."

"Girls, Brian. There are no girls in the Zambezi Valley. I want a fuck."

"Go and ask her."

"Not till we've somewhere to stay. My balls are cracking just looking at her knickers."

2

On the following Friday night, Beth Brigandshaw and Nancy Longhurst were standing in the queue outside 101 Oxford Street dressed in flared skirts and sleeveless turtleneck sweaters a size too small, waiting to go in. Three in front of them was a young man their own age carrying an instrument case.

"What's he doing in the queue if he's playing in the band?" said Nancy.

They were both staring at the back of the man's neck when he turned round and smiled. Beth's father had once told her staring at an enemy pilot from the rear caused him to turn round. That there were senses built into the mind other than the five accepted by common experiences. Somehow, the face was familiar to Beth from a long time before.

"He's coming back," whispered Nancy. "He's gorgeous."

"Any man who looks at you is gorgeous," Beth whispered back, racking her brains as to why the man's face was familiar.

There were thirty to forty people waiting in the street to pay their shilling entrance to the basement jazz club that had opened a month before. It was the girls' third time at the London club, their one splurge of the week. Were it not for Beth's father paying half the rent of their two-bedroom flat in South Kensington neither of them would have been able to afford to live in London on their salaries as secretaries. They had spent two years together at the same secretarial college before finding themselves jobs. For Beth, living at Hastings Court and commuting up to London every day was a nightmare. The train station at Leatherhead was too far to walk or ride a bicycle in the dark. Instead of having to take his daughter to the station in the morning and collect her at night, something her father said at the age of twenty-one was nonsense, he had helped them find the smallest flat in a good area and subsidised the rent, giving both Beth and Nancy their freedom. Nancy's parents had no money to spare after the war. The arrangement suited both of them.

"You're Beth Brigandshaw," said the young man with the case. "Paul Crookshank. Your brother busted my nose when my family spent Christmas with you in 1939 at Hastings Court. Before the Phoney War turned nasty."

"Well, I'll be blowed. What are the chances queuing up to get into a jazz club? What's in the case?"

"My clarinet. I'm hoping they'll ask me to jam with the band. This your first time, Beth?"

"Our third. Nancy's my flatmate."

"You have a flat in London?"

"Father helps. Now I remember. Didn't your father go down at Dunkirk? Oh, I'm sorry, Paul, I didn't mean to. My father speaks so highly of yours. They met when Dad flew the Short flying boat on a test flight to Lake Constance in Switzerland. He went to see your mother after the war. Doesn't she live in the Isle of Wight? We were both kids that Christmas. You had a fight with Frank. We kids were all in the nursery at the Court with Mary Ross meant to be looking after us. Mother was furious with Frank. Not my favourite brother."

"I was sorry to hear about Anthony. Do you mind if I sit with you at the same table when we get into the club? What do you think of Freddie Marble on trombone? I'm surprised I didn't recognise you before. When I turned round you were looking straight at me as if you knew who I was. Only then did it twig."

"What are you doing in London?"

"Working for an insurance company. Deadly dull. I get my pension in forty-four years' time if I don't die of boredom. Do you two have jobs?"

"Secretaries. Equally dull. Our only refuge is the club on Friday nights."

"Same as me. I'm a frustrated musician. Music scholarship at Brighton College where they taught me the clarinet. Short Brothers put me through school after Dad went down with his boat. It was his fourteenth trip to the beaches to pull off the troops. German dive bomber got them with a direct hit. It's so nice to meet you both. Don't have many friends in London."

"How long have you been working at the insurance company?"

"A month. The queue's beginning to shift."

"What were you doing before that?"

"I was in the army. Saw a bit of action in Burma. Then they posted the regiment to Germany. Part of the occupation forces."

"Were you a regular?"

"Conscripted when I was eighteen."

"What was Burma like?" asked Nancy, who had hung on every one of his words.

"Hot. The jungle was hot. So were the Japs. Thank God that's all over."

"Did you kill anyone?"

"Only one. We were ambushed. That man's face as I shot him with my .303 is going to stay with me the rest of my life."

"But he was trying to kill you."

"Only because he was told to, we were all told to... I'd pay your shillings if I had enough money. Insurance clerks are rather poorly paid, I'm afraid."

"Don't be silly," said Beth. "We can still sit together if we can find ourselves a table."

"Or we can stand. Once the band starts you can't hear much else. Oh, this is fun. I so remember that Christmas. Mum and Dad were so happy."

"What happened to your younger brother? I seem to remember there were two of you."

"He's at home in the cottage with Mum at the moment. On leave. Jeremy is still in the navy. Three-year short service commission. Not much chance of promotion. You need to go through Dartmouth to get on in the navy."

"What's he going to do?"

"Bit like me, really. Hobson's choice. Get a job in a bank or an insurance company. Spend the rest of our lives paying off a mortgage. The usual thing. I've been racking my brains. Here we go. That's the sound of Benjie Appleton on the trumpet. You can smell the heat coming up the stairs with the music."

"Have you asked them if you can play?" said Beth.

"Not yet. I hope one of the band will recognise my clarinet case."

"From a music scholarship to traditional jazz. Isn't that a jump?"

"I was in the school orchestra. Doesn't matter how you learn to play."

"Have you been in a band?"

"Not yet. I play along with the records in my room. Landlady complains. I have the top room. Try and practise when she's out. I know all the band's music from playing along with their records. Just a hope, bringing the clarinet. You have to hope sometimes in life. Listen to that. They're really swinging tonight. Can you two jive? Good, we'll have a go."

"Never jived with a man," said Nancy. "We girls have to dance together when we come on our own."

"Not tonight, Nancy. I'll bet you're good at it."

Instead of answering, Nancy gave him one of her smiles that said she was good at more than just dancing. Then they all went down the stairs into the basement where they found a table right at the back. Paul put down his instrument case. Behind them was a counter for drinks and snacks. None of the drinks were alcoholic. With their eyes on the band playing up on the stand under the lights, their feet began tapping in time under the table. All of them were smiling as the New Orleans-style music pulsed through the cavernous room. On the other side of the long basement, in front of the bandstand, people were dancing. Along the wall others were standing, tapping their feet in time to the music. The air was thick with tobacco smoke. When Paul looked back from studying the band, Nancy was watching him, making him blush like a schoolboy. They were lucky to get a table. The jazz club was as full as it was ever going to get. Beth sat back to enjoy herself. Nancy and Paul went off to jive. A man she had never seen before sat down at her table.

"They've just gone to dance."

"There are four chairs. Do you mind?"

"Be my guest."

"Aren't they good, the band, I mean? Your first time?"

"Third, actually."

"What's in the case?"

"A clarinet. Paul wants to jam with the band."

"Why doesn't he ask them?"

"He's shy."

"Is he any good?"

"I can't hear you." For Beth, trying to talk to a complete stranger over the noise from the band was absurd.

. . .

FRANK BRIGANDSHAW HAD SEEN his sister a minute before she sat down at the table. He and Brian Tobin had arrived early, not knowing what to expect on their first visit. Neither of them had been in a jazz club before.

"Don't turn round but my bloody sister just walked in. This town's too small. What's she doing in London on a Friday night? Quite sophisticated in her old age. The bloke with her looks familiar."

"Why don't you go and talk to her?"

"Not until I've worked out what to do."

"Do you scheme all the time, Frank?"

"All the time. It's the only way to get on in life without having to work too hard. A casual meeting in a dance club leaves me at a disadvantage. I like to be in control. The other two are getting up to dance. Now look at that. Another blighter's sat down next to Beth."

"Won't she see you if you stare?"

"She's talking to the blighter. Good. They're getting up to dance, if you can call this dancing. We'll go out round the back."

"Are we leaving?"

"Of course we are. She must be living in town. That could be interesting. Free accommodation. We don't want a brush-off in public. Too easy."

"We took the room for a month."

"Bugger. She's seen me. You must remember Beth from when we were at school in Cape Town? She's dumped the blighter and is coming over."

"How long have you been back in England, Frank?" demanded Beth. She had to shout above the band to make herself heard. Frank just leaned back in his chair.

"Don't you say how nice it is to see me, sis?"

"Don't call me sis."

"Who's the blighter?"

"I have no idea."

"Really, Beth. You're beginning to behave just like our mother."

"Does she know you're here?"

"Not yet. I went to see a man living in a very nice townhouse opposite Green Park in Piccadilly. Chap wouldn't come to the door. Saw me through a second-floor window. Oh, he knew, I'll take a bet he was on the phone to Hastings Court before Brian and I were down the street. You do remember Brian Tobin?"

"Wasn't he one of your fellow bullies at school? You had an extortion racket involving new boys, if I remember. They paid you to stop themselves being bullied."

"A man has to make a living. Was that Paul Crookshank you came in with? He has grown. Last time I saw him he was lying on his back with a busted nose."

"Where are you staying?"

"In a cheap room in Soho."

"Do you have any money? I won't ask if you have a job."

"A little, my big sister. Crocodile hunting in the Zambezi Valley. Grandmother Manderville must have told you."

"Why didn't you stay?"

"No girls. Who's the chick dancing with Crookshank?"

"Keep your hands off Nancy."

"Would you like to join us?"

"Not particularly."

"The blighter's still waiting for you. Go and dance. I'll find out where you live. You do know who lives in that Piccadilly townhouse, don't you, Beth? I was going to ask him if he was my father. Servant called Smithers answered the door. Surly brute. Isn't life fun when you have a rich man's secret? Poor Mother. Now off you go and dance with the blighter."

"I can't hear you, Frank. Call Mother or I'll never talk to you again."

"That's tempting, sis."

"You really are a shit."

Brian Tobin gave Beth a big smile, hoping for a moment she was going to slap her brother's face. The band was so loud the two of them had been shouting at each other at the top of their voices. No one seemed to care so far as Brian could see, looking at the surrounding tables.

"So now we don't have to go after all," he said to Frank when they were alone.

"Shut up, Brian."

"That's what we need. Another scam like those frightened kids. She looks so pretty when she gets mad. There are three girls watching us, Frank. The place is humming. I'm so horny they have no idea. Oh, good. The music's stopped. You keep the table. I'll go and chat to the girls. One has the biggest pair of tits I ever saw on such a nice young girl. Better than that whore. Did you really, Frank?"

"A man has to start somewhere. This is fun. Nothing to start a good evening like a verbal fight among siblings."

"She really doesn't like you, Frank. Do you know that?"

"Shut up, Brian."

"It will be my pleasure. Back in a sec."

THE CLARINET CASE was still alone on the table. The four chairs were empty. Beth supposed there were unwritten rules. She had ignored the leery look of Brian Tobin dancing with a full-busted girl. She had never liked him since the day he kicked their cat on a weekend visit to the Bishopscourt house they stayed in while their father remained in London at the Air Ministry during the war. Young Brian liked to hurt anything smaller than himself. The man Frank called the blighter had followed her back to the empty table.

"We'd better introduce ourselves," he said. "What was all that about? Do you know those two men? With the band playing I couldn't hear what you were saying. I could see you were shouting. You don't mind me joining you? I'm on my own in London. On my own pretty much everywhere, come to think of it. Missed the war that killed Dad by a month. They'd called me up of course. Did my square-bashing at Aldershot. Kenneth Grahame. No relation of course to 'the' Kenneth Grahame. Mother says I gabble a lot when I'm nervous. Never been so forward in my life. Here come your friends. I can get you all a bottle of fizzy Tizer if that will be all right? Way to introduce myself. Hello, you two. Purloined her, I'm afraid. Don't know her name. Kenneth Grahame is my name."

"Was that Frank you were having a shouting match with, Beth? Don't you want him to join us? Just because he bloodied my nose as a kid doesn't mean he can't join us. I'm Paul Crookshank. Your dancing partner is Beth Brigandshaw. This is Nancy Longhurst. They share a flat together in South Kensington. Did I hear about a bottle of Tizer? That would be nice. Sorry, I'm a bit broke."

"Aren't we all after the war? No one seems to have any money, just as well with everything rationed. Thanks for the dance, Beth. You're good at jiving."

"He's my brother."

"Who?"

"The man I was shouting at. Frank and I never liked each other."

"Where'd he get the suntan?"

"In Rhodesia. Crocodile hunting. They like to kill animals, those two."

"The skins must be worth something."

"What they've been living off, I suppose. Never asked Dad for money. Frank dodged the war. He dodges everything that isn't to his advantage. Always on the take, never gives."

"What a horrible way to live," said Kenneth Grahame, putting the bottles of Tizer on the table next to the clarinet case. "Just one more thing to do. I know Benjie Appleton. We were at Eton together. Strange for an Old Etonian to play trumpet in a jazz band. The war's changed everything. In the next break I'll tell him you have a clarinet you'd like to play. They will often let chaps join the band for a set."

"Now that is lucky," said Paul.

"Not as lucky as me. I met Beth. I don't have any brothers or sisters. You're lucky, Beth."

"Anthony was killed in the war. The rest are all right. It's just Frank."

Kenneth Grahame smiled twice at Beth as they listened to the music; with the band in full swing it was too much strain to talk. It was nice not to be on his own. Standing on the side, moving his weight from one foot to the other as the evening progressed. Trying to think of something to do with the rest of his life. During the war there had been no point in trying to think, the evil day of reckoning put off one way or the other. The war, when it came to Kenneth, had taken the decision out of his hands and placed it in the lap of the gods. He was broke, like the rest of his family. Schooling had been paid for from his grandfather's trust which was finished. Cleaned out by school fees. Kenneth had a good classical education, as he liked to say. And nothing much else. Nothing that could be turned into money. He had given up wearing his Old Etonian tie. With it, people expected him to be rich. When they found out he was poor they mostly lost interest in Kenneth Grahame. The old school tie was all about connections. Connections that could be turned into money.

When the band stopped playing, Kenneth excused himself. They had drunk their glasses of Tizer. No one suggested another. The man had said he was broke. Everyone was broke. The new Labour government had brought in taxes to redistribute what was left of the wealth. It was either suffer in silence or get on the boat to Australia. Or America. He preferred to stay where he was and hope for a miracle. Kenneth had read somewhere it was good public relations to let one of the fans play along with the band. Made the band more down to earth. When he asked Benjie Appleton they told him to send Paul along. He had never met the trumpeter, this leader of the band. He had seen him only once at school. A year's age difference or a different house made most of them strangers.

"He can play behind the bandstand at first. So we can hear him. After five minutes, if we don't ask him up he must go. Do I know you?"

"Not really. We were at the same school."

"Really?"

When Kenneth told Paul Crookshank he could play in the next set, Paul was visibly excited.

"Behind the bandstand. Off the dais. If you squeak the clarinet you're out. After five minutes, if they ignore you just fade away."

"Thank you so much. Do you know him well?"

"Never met him, actually. Eton's a big school. Good luck."

"I can't thank you enough. My lifelong dream has been to play in a regular jazz band. Look after the girls while I'm playing. I want you all here when I come back. Even if it is with my tail between my legs. My mother says you've got to try in life."

Kenneth watched Paul go, clutching the case that had been on the table. When the band struck up again Paul was out of sight behind the drums. They all listened hard for the high strains of his clarinet. Beth thought she heard something. Kenneth still did not know anything about her. He had found out Paul Crookshank worked for the Contingency Insurance Company in Billiter Street. Again he smiled at her and left it at that. As he told himself again, it was nice not to be on his own.

"They're drowning him out," she said, leaning close to his ear.

"Probably," said Kenneth leaning close, taking the chance to smell her perfume. It was *Lily of the Valley*.

Kenneth was expecting Paul back at the table any minute when he saw they were making room for him up on the stand. A little while later the band gave Paul a solo all to himself. Kenneth smiled his broadest smile. Paul Crookshank could play when the other instruments fed themselves back into the piece, the man he had met at the table was as much a part of the band as the rest of them. It had been nice to help. Kenneth liked helping other people, expecting nothing in return. His mother had told him from a small boy, giving with expectations was not giving at all.

The last set finished at half past nine when Paul Crookshank rejoined them at the table. Everyone was getting up to go to catch the Tube to the big London railway stations and the last trains to the suburbs. Only those with somewhere to stay in the heart of London had the time to linger. Paul was flushed, elated with his playing. No one at the other tables took any notice of him. He was not the first to be invited to play along with a band. To them he was just another clarinet player for whom they had paid a shilling at the door.

"Did they ask you to come back?" Kenneth asked him.

"No one said a word. Jazz men don't talk very much. The only talk they do is with their instruments."

"I'll have to hurry. I live in Wimbledon with my mother."

"Where do you work?"

"I don't. Not yet. Still have a bit from my last army pay. Beth, Nancy, Paul, it was so nice meeting you. Thank you for the company."

"Thanks for getting me to play with the band."

"Glad I could help. Got to dash to get to Waterloo on time."

Then he left as quickly as he had come, leaving Beth about to say something. When she gave a quick look around there was no sign of her brother Frank or Brian Tobin.

"Must have been to see the Honourable Barnaby St Clair," she said to herself. Everyone in the family knew Frank had a different father to the rest of them. No one talked about it out loud. Beth had never dared bring up the subject with her mother. Now the cat was about to get let out of the bag.

"Paul, we must keep in touch. Why don't we all go down to Hastings Court next weekend? Dad would love to see you. Dad's going to be in town on Saturday morning. Mother likes to shop. We can all drive back in the car. Save the train fare. Does that sound all right, Nancy?"

"Sounds wonderful. Just look at this. It's raining. Better make a dash for the Tube station. Why does it always rain in England?"

She would have asked Kenneth Grahame had she known him better. Wimbledon was on the way to Hastings Court. One minute he was there, the next he was gone.

"That chap really did me a favour," said Paul.

"You play well," said Nancy.

"Thanks. Come on, we'd better run for it."

. . .

FIFTY YARDS back on the opposite side of Oxford Street, the girl with the large breasts slapped Brian Tobin with considerable force across the side of his face, making a sound like a pistol shot. Then she brought up her knee into his groin with the same malice aforethought. The few people in the street turned to look at the commotion. Beth had stopped in her tracks, smiling with satisfaction when she saw what was happening. Neither of them had seen her, their immediate problem being closer at hand. When Brian looked up from clutching his groin, she waved at him before turning with the others to run from the rain, more of a drizzle than a downpour.

"What you done that for?" she heard Brian Tobin say before they were out of earshot.

"No one gropes my tits without my permission. Who do you think you are? And you can't dance. Go back to where you came from. Now bugger off."

Frank, having taken a step back from the brief fracas, began to laugh.

"What are you laughing at? The bitch kneed me in the balls."

"Told you whores were less trouble. They take their money with gratitude. Really, Brian. What were you doing? Can't you see the street lights? Never mind, old chap. You get five points for trying. Bloody good clap she gave you round the face."

"The face stings. The balls hurt."

"Poor old Brian. Can you walk? Good chap. It's not far to Soho. If your balls are still cracking, we can find you a whore in Piccadilly."

"I'm going to get that woman one of these days."

"Which one are you talking about? I hope it wasn't my sister. I saw her give you a wave. Really, Brian, what a spectacle. No wonder Beth was laughing at you. Where's your sense of humour?"

"She was damn common."

"They all behave the same in bed."

"How do you know? You only had one whore."

"Just what I heard. There's a pub over there. Closes at ten-thirty. Would you like me to buy you a drink, old chap? Think you could do with it."

"I'm going home to bed."

"Probably wise. I think your dancing partner went in the ladies' bar with her friends. Oh well. Can't win them all. Better than being slapped by the tail of a crocodile. At least your girlfriend didn't try and kill you. You'll feel better in the morning."

3

At six-forty the next evening, Frank Brigandshaw and Brian Tobin stepped out of a London taxi, dressed in their best finery, into Bond Street. Their black bow ties and starched white shirts were immaculate, befitting their appearance of two gentlemen. The sapphire studs in Frank's shirt had been sent to him for his eighteenth birthday by his mother. Both their dress suits had been made for them by the same Indian tailor in Salisbury. Soon after, Frank made his bolt from Cape Town to avoid going home to England on the boat and the prospect of being conscripted into the British Army and sent to war. Frank's grandmother had thrown a party for her grandson's eighteenth birthday at Meikles Hotel and paid for the new clothing. When Brian's father refused to send him money from the Tobin family cattle ranch outside Bulawayo, Grandmother Manderville had paid for his dress suit as well. Frank had spent weeks charming his grandmother and Aunt Madge while they stayed on Elephant Walk before getting off into the bush with young Josiah Makoni, the only son of Tembo and Princess. Tembo, the bossboy of the farm, had been there since his youth and as a man was just as important as Ralph Madgwick, the farm manager. So far as Frank could understand, young Josiah knew his way round the bush which was the reason Aunty Madge had told Frank to take the boy on their journey into the Zambezi Valley. Being conscious of the origin of their finery made Frank think of the farm and young Josiah, making him smile: there was something about Rhodesia.

"Leave this to me, Brian. My word, you look handsome."

Then they stepped into the art gallery that was throwing the exhibition. The gallery was half full of well-dressed men and women. Just as Frank had hoped. A woman in her forties, beautifully decked out in a long skirt, smiled at Frank, holding out her hand for his invitation, just as Frank had rehearsed. The taxi they had taken from just round the corner had gone off with the minimum fare and no tip: Frank believed in conserving his money. For Frank, flashing his money required a purpose.

"My father, Colonel Harry Brigandshaw, sent us in his stead. Your invitation, I'm afraid, is still at Hastings Court, the estate that has been in our family for centuries. You may remember my father from when he disappeared on a pioneer flight from Africa in a flying boat. All over the press. In those days the family owned Colonial Shipping before we invested in America. I have rather a good eye for art. Why Father sent me. We need something new at the Court."

"How nice of you to come."

"Yes, I suppose it is. My word, this does look jolly."

"Would you care for a glass of wine?"

"Most definitely. Frank Brigandshaw, my friend Brian Tobin. Back from Africa. Crocodile hunting."

"My word."

"So good to be back in civilisation."

When they were out of earshot, sipping their wine, surreptitiously looking for a mark while appearing to look at the paintings, Frank gave out a small giggle.

"She'd never heard of Harry Brigandshaw. Amazing what you can do with a little bullshit."

"The crocodile hunting went a bit far."

"How are your balls, Brian? We're here to chat up rich women."

"They'll all be married."

"So what? Two tall, handsome young men with rich suntans are hard to find in London. Flirt with your eyes. Don't look down their dresses."

"You really can put on a plummy accent when you try."

"You have to go to the right school. Bishops was only part of my education. You're the bloody Colonial. Do you know, I rather think I can still see her finger marks."

"Shut up, Frank."

"Cheers, old boy. This wine is quite delightful. The French must have hidden it from the Germans. There's one on her own over there. Let's move along. There's work to be done. Our money's running out."

"Do you know anything about paintings?"

"They hang on the wall. At Hastings Court they are all Manderville ancestors. Dark pictures with eyes watching you from the dead. Gives me the creeps."

"Are they worth anything? Some family portraits were done by famous artists. You should have a look. What on earth is this? All squares and triangular eyes. Now that gives me the creeps."

"Actually, that's a Picasso," said the woman on her own. "You look a bit like fish out of water. What are you two doing here? Can you find me another glass of wine? My husband hates art galleries so I came on my own. How did you get an invitation?"

"We didn't," said Frank, grinning.

"You're all dressed up."

"We were walking down Bond Street this morning and looked in the window. There was a rather smart stand announcing the launch of the exhibition tonight. Don't tell the woman at the door. Said Father had an invite. We came for the wine and the company of sophisticated women. We're just back from Africa, matter of fact. Just off the boat."

"That much I might believe. Your skins have beautiful colour."

"Please get the lady a glass of wine, Brian. My name is Frank Brigandshaw. My friend is Brian Tobin."

"Constance Whitaker. My friends call me Connie. Are you related to the famous Colonel Brigandshaw? Africa and the name Brigandshaw are quite synonymous... Oh, don't be silly. I overheard your little speech at the door. Fascinating what young men will do for a drink these days. Would you like to go out to supper? Frederick is away on business, so boring. Money, you know. He's very rich. Quite a bit older than me. I get bored on my own. Why I attend the galleries. Thank you, Brian. You are very sweet to get me the wine. You can both come to supper. Such fun. Don't worry, I'll be discreet. Slip you some money so you can pay the bill without being embarrassed. Everyone's broke after the war. Does your family really live at a place called Hastings Court? Fancy name for a house. I think of Hastings as a town on the south coast."

"The first of my ancestors to arrive in England fought at the Battle of Hastings, with William the Conqueror."

"Not the Brigandshaws, surely?"

"The Mandervilles, Connie. Connie is such a lovely name. Supper would be lovely, I'm starving."

"We'll have to look interested for half an hour and then make our escape. The Mandervilles are a very old name in England. Are they really your ancestors?"

"Quite frankly, I'm not sure. Why I'm here in London, trying to find out who I am."

"Why don't you tell me over supper? I'm a very good listener, Frank. You look like a young aristocrat. That much I'll say."

"It's either the Mandervilles or the St Clairs. Both came over with the Conqueror."

"I know a Barnaby St Clair. The Honourable Barnaby St Clair. His father was a baron. Likes young girls, I'm afraid. Never married."

"I think he's my father."

"Oh, my goodness. This is going to be a lovely supper. There's nothing juicier than a good bit of scandal. He's very rich."

"I went round to see him when we came off the boat. He wouldn't come to the door."

"After supper, we can go back to the flat. Would you like that, Frank?"

"Very much, Connie."

"The wonderful part about life is you never know what's going to happen next. You don't think I'm a little old?"

"Perfect. Beautiful and perfect."

"What did I hear you were just doing in Africa?"

"Hunting crocodiles for their skins."

"How exciting. Much more fun than dull old London."

"In the Zambezi Valley, there are no beautiful women to meet at the opening night of an art exhibition... Is this really Picasso?"

"Probably not. There were a lot of imitators... What happened to your face, Brian?"

"Don't ask him."

When they left the Bond Street gallery, Brian Tobin made an excuse that he had a prior engagement. The two of them had been working together for a long time and knew the drill. In his finery and patent leather shoes, Brian walked all the way back to his room in Soho, smiling at every whore on the way. If there were any monetary spoils, they would split them afterwards. For the first time all day his balls stopped aching from the kick in his crotch.

. . .

CONNIE WHITAKER WAS forty-one years old and her life was a mess when they sat down at their table in the Café Monet, a short walk from the Bond Street art gallery. Around the walls of the restaurant were prints of the artist's works. The place was less than half full, in between the early diners eating before the West End shows and the ones who ate afterwards. The very rich were still rich, it was only the average man suffering the consequences of war and the new socialist taxes meant to placate the masses. Frederick, her husband, had shifted most of his money into a numbered Swiss bank account before the war had started. She was twenty-three years younger than her husband and childless.

She had seen Frank when he came in the door, as well aware as Mrs Walters that the two young men did not have an invitation. Still, her interest had been piqued by their brief conversation at the door. It had made her smile as it made Mrs Walters too, after she let the two young men in to drink a free glass of wine: having spent so much time dressing up for it, the boys deserved to come in. Frank was probably the best-looking young man the women had seen in years; his rich, dark suntan against the stiff white shirt having something to do with the appeal. He looked to Connie so damn healthy. So damn virile in contrast to poor old Frederick, who hadn't got it up in months despite some futile efforts in trying.

Looking the first time at Frank as he professed to study the Picasso, Connie had known they both had what the other one wanted: his youth and her money. Drifting towards him along the gallery wall had been more simple than she had hoped. They both expected each other. She had only heard of Barnaby St Clair from the papers and the *Tatler* magazine. Probably much like young Frank, smiling at her now so sweetly over the dinner table, ordering the food and the wine with surprising knowledge and confidence, making Connie think she had picked up a professional which really did not matter. At least for a brief while her life would not be boring.

"The money is in your pocket," she said softly across the table, her dress unintentionally dropping open. Frank's eyes almost bolted out of his head. "How long have you been hunting crocodiles, I think it was, in Africa?"

"Two years, on and off. I didn't want to get my head blown off when I turned eighteen. The rest of them had gone back to England after Anthony was shot down."

"I'm sorry. For a moment I had the wrong idea."

"Only half the wrong idea. We're broke."

"Was Brian in on the game?"

"We were at school together in Cape Town. Brian's a Rhodesian."

"So you came for a free glass of wine and what else you could find."

"You learn to live on your wits when you are broke."

"What about your parents? Won't they help? Those sapphires in your shirt are real."

"Eighteenth birthday present from Mother."

"How old are you, Frank, if you don't mind me asking?"

"How old are you, Connie, if you don't mind me asking?"

They both laughed. They were both smiling directly into each other's eyes. The man sitting on the stool at the white piano began to play a medley from Noël Coward's West End shows.

"I don't expect to get change."

"How much did you slip in my pocket?"

"Ten pounds."

"My goodness. Where is it we go after this?"

"He's away. The flat's in South Kensington. My husband never liked living in the country."

"Won't he mind me going to his house?"

"He won't find out. It's a big block of flats. There's a long corridor to the front doors. No one watches the corridor at night."

"Would he do anything if he found out?"

"Like divorcing me? Probably."

"Would that matter?"

"He's an old man, Frank. I gave him what he wanted. I gave him my youth when it counted. When we're young we think it will last forever. Both his professed love and my youth. He wanted my body."

"Why did you marry him?"

"Because he was rich. All that nonsense about living on love is a load of rubbish. Everything we need in life requires money. Everything, Frank. Let's just forget who we are and enjoy ourselves. If we get a bit tight it doesn't matter. Let's pretend tonight nothing matters. Except the two of us at this table... Would you like to dance?"

"I would love to dance."

"Are you any good?"

"Let's find out, shall we?"

When they left the restaurant, Frank found them an empty taxi that had just discarded a theatre party outside the door. The patrons came in, all in evening dress. Inside the Café Monet, Frank had paid the bill without having to show a ration card. Connie was right. Money could buy anything. She gave the cab driver her address in South Kensington, an address Frank committed to memory. The woman was almost panting for sex after Frank had pushed his leg between her thighs on the dance floor when she pulled him close. There were four pounds and change still in his pocket. Dancing, something Beth had taught him in Cape Town when he was still at school, was one thing. Making love for the first time, despite the whore story to confuse Brian, quite another. Deliberately, Frank drank his wine slowly, concentrating on Connie.

He got out of the cab when the taxi stopped at the address in South Kensington and opened her door. Then he got back in the taxi, leaving Connie on the pavement.

"Aren't you coming up?"

"You're a married woman, Connie. I could never take advantage."

"Aren't I going to see you again?"

"Who knows? Ships in the night, Connie."

"Where do you live?"

"In a room in Soho without carpets."

"Can't I come to Soho?"

"Not tonight, Connie. It's been a lovely evening. A lovely surprise. Please don't tell Mrs Walters I lied to her."

"I thought, Frank..."

"Goodnight, Connie. Soho, driver."

"What's the address, cock?"

Loudly, Frank gave the address of the room where he had paid a month's rent. When he looked back, Connie was still standing under the street light. Even at this distance, Frank recognised her forlorn look of disappointment. Then the cab driver turned into Kensington High Street, heading for Piccadilly and Soho.

When Frank tapped on Brian's door, his friend was still awake, his dress suit neatly folded on the one chair in the room. Their rooms were next to each other.

"What happened? Aren't you early?"

"She swallowed the hook so far down her throat she'll never get it out. Never quite give them what they want until they are desperate. In some book I read."

"Are you going to see her again? She had nice tits when she leaned forward."

"She must have heard me give my address to the cab driver. I gave it loud enough. I can remember hers. Let's wait and see. Meanwhile we've got four quid and change."

"You're bad, Frank."

"We're bad, Brian. How are your balls?"

"Why didn't you take what was on offer?"

"I want more than a fuck. She's rich. Or the old husband is rich. Do you know he's twenty-three years older than Connie? Dirty old bugger. Now he's going to pay for the fucks he had when he married her. Can't get it up anymore. I'm going to make him really pay. Swiss bank account before the war. Moved his money out of harm's way. Must have a fortune. We have youth and looks, old boy. The sky's the limit. To hell with my sister. We're going to make our way on our own. Said she knew the Honourable Barnaby, which was a lie. Why do people always lie to you when they want something? Read his name in the papers, I should think. People say what they think you want to hear."

"You really are a bastard."

"Probably, old cock, but it's fun. What we're trying to find out for certain. The rules don't apply to me. They broke the rules the day I was conceived. I'm going to get some sleep. It's hard work keeping your wits about you. There's two quid, Brian. Outside there are whores a-plenty. The world's full of whores. Why I didn't fuck her. I want a lot more than a fancy supper and two quid."

"You really think I'm going out now to find a whore?"

"Poor old Brian. Your trouble is, you don't know what you want."

"Oh, I do. They slap my face when I try and get it. What's on the menu tomorrow?"

"Another day, Brian. Another day. I thought we'd take a stroll up Piccadilly. Try and spot my father. Keep the Honourable on his toes. The world indeed is our oyster. And you are right, old boy. She does have nice tits. Get some sleep. Keep your strength up. I've contributed a couple of quid. Now it's your turn. Tomorrow's Sunday. We should go to church. Make ourselves out to be nice young boys instead of wolves in sheep's clothing. I like church music. We were both in the choir at Bishops before our voices broke. How we first met. In the choir."

"Do you think God would approve what we are doing?"

"Takes all types to make the world. We are all God's children according to the Archbishop of Cape Town. Darwin had a better theory. Survival of the fittest."

"Where do we find a church?"

"Listen for the bells. You can ask God's forgiveness for fondling that girl's tits. When we're rich, she'll come running, or someone like her. They want to mate with the best."

"You really can talk a lot of garbage."

"Wine, women and song. And church on Sunday. Can't go wrong if you touch all the bases."

"I have a good idea. Why don't we watch the Honourable's front door from across Green Park and follow him to eleven o'clock matins?"

"You think he goes to church?"

"Can only find out. You can fix him with a stare from the back pew. You can sing your heart out."

4

———————

*A*fter the euphoria of playing in the band on Friday night, Monday working was an anti-climax for Paul Crookshank sitting at his desk at the Contingency Insurance Company. After two weeks in the mail department, opening letters and sorting them into the various departments with the help of the old woman who ran the desk where the post was delivered, they had put him in the claims department for six months. The idea was to move him from one department to the next as part of his managerial training programme. One day, if he was lucky, he would become head of the marine department, the only part of insurance in which Paul showed any interest. If he could not sail a boat he at least could insure them, a rationale from his mother when Paul agreed to take the job, his wages just enough to pay Mrs Bigglesworth two guineas a week for his digs in Holland Park and feed himself by cooking his food on the two-ring gas stove that stood in the alcove of his room.

Major Pilkington-Jones, retired, was sitting in the chair reserved for claimants on the other side of his desk for the fourth time in two weeks. Major Pilkington-Jones was a freelance claims assessor specialising in antiques, augmenting the army pension he had told Paul would not keep a fly alive. After the new Labour government of Clement Attlee had slapped punitive taxes on landowners at pre-war property valuations, there had been a spate of fires in English country houses, the claim forms reaching Paul who handed them over to the major to ultimately recommend the amount of payment to be paid by the insurance company. The major, Paul had been informed on their first meeting, was an expert on the value of antiques, even charred ones. The problem of charred antiques was rife. Every second owner of a country house was unable to pay the new taxes. No one in England, according to the major, had any money to buy the old paintings and artefacts that had been in the old homes, sometimes for centuries. It was easier to insure their old relics at their pre-war value and have them burn.

"Another arson attack, young Paul?"

"Don't ask me. They all look the same."

"You looked far away when I came in?"

"Played clarinet in Benjie Appleton's band on Friday night and met an old friend with her flatmate."

"And the friend was a girl?"

"How did you know?"

"I may be old, Paul Crookshank, but I still recognise that faraway look that tells me you were thinking of a beautiful young woman."

"We're going down to her father's estate on the weekend."

"Is he also broke? I don't want to hear of a fire just after you leave, young man. You do know half these claims you give me are fraudulent?"

"Quite the reverse. Invested heavily in America before the war. Owns a tobacco farm in Rhodesia. Without enough dollars we can only buy our tobacco from the few Rhodesian farmers that have put in a crop. Beth says they're making a fortune. Colonel Brigandshaw knew my father before my father went down at Dunkirk. His fourteenth visit to the beaches to pull off the troops."

"I'm sorry... Beth's a nice name. Pity these people putting in wrongful claims had not tried to ship their antiques to America. America's rich after the war. Many of them. They pay a fortune for something really old with a history. If I was twenty years younger, I'd stop this caper with the insurance companies, buy up all these antiques the old families are being forced to sell and ship them to America. Set up a shop in New York or one of those big American cities. I'm too old. Anyway, I don't have the capital to buy in England and wait to sell the antiques in America."

"But do you know what's worth buying?"

"Antiques have been my hobby all my life. Brought some lovely pieces back from China and India, one of the advantages of being in the regular army. Posted all over the place. Very exotic. Quite happy the way

I am, thank you. Always be content with what you've got, young man. Now, let me see what you've got for me today. My word! This is a big one. Burnt the old house to the ground. Either his lordship is really desperate or the fire got away from him. Amateur arsonists. I hate amateurs. Any kind of amateurs. Make sure you know what you are doing, I say, or keep out of it."

"Could I buy you a drink after work, Major?"

"You don't have any money. I'll buy you one if you like, young man. Could do with the company, matter of fact. Like a good chinwag. Get a bit loud in my old age. Never married. Never in one place long enough! There's a price to pay for everything. What do you have in mind? Young people never do anything without a reason."

"An idea, just an idea. If I don't get out of being an insurance clerk I'm going to go nuts."

"Why not play your music?"

"There's no money in jazz. So if a person could ship English antiques to America, that person could make a fortune?"

"Most likely. Never been there, of course. By the time I joined the British Army, America was no longer a colony."

Paul, looking up from the claim file he had opened for the burned down house, found the old man's eyes looking at him. They were twinkling. An amused smile at the corner of the major's mouth. Paul had the feeling his leg was being pulled.

"I'll go down to the ruin on Wednesday," said Major Pilkington-Jones, getting back to business. "Set it up for me, Paul. Shall we say five o'clock tonight outside the door? You'll know a good place to drink. Go to my club when I fancy a drink, which isn't very often. Can't afford it as much as I'd like. And they're all so old in the Cavalry Club. I have a better idea. Meet me outside the club at six. One hundred and twenty-seven Piccadilly. Opposite Green Park. Next to the RAF Club. The drinks are cheaper. Bit of young blood will do 'em good. Don't be late. At least the Germans didn't manage to bomb the club. I'll go and see the manager with this claim. He'll want to know what he's up against. Could be a big one if we can't prove arson."

"How can you prove arson? How can you prove the fire was set deliberately by the owner?"

"Very difficult with these old places. They are a fire hazard before anyone tries to burn them down. Dry rot in the timbers. Half of the old houses in England are falling down. A bit like England these days. Oh well. We're going to get a national health service, so the government says. Take them years to put that in place I'll bet. I'll be dead by then. Governments are much better at taking than giving. What they like is a nice fat bureaucracy. Jobs for the boys."

Paul smiled at the old man who smiled back at him. The major had a habit of going off a bit. Paul told himself he would have to ask someone which end of Piccadilly was one hundred and twenty-seven. Then, his mind wandering from the piles of paper on his desk, he thought of Nancy Longhurst and the happy prospect of a weekend at Hastings Court. And this time brother Frank would not be there to spoil it by bloodying his nose. Paul, so far as he could recollect, had never struck another thing in his life. Not even a cat or a dog. Something in which he had never seen the point.

"Daydreaming, Crookshank? You'll never learn the business if you sit daydreaming all day," said the manager. "This time we want to prove his lordship burned down his house."

"Isn't that going to be difficult, sir? I was just thinking about the same claim. Thinking what we could do to get out of the claim."

"Good man. Have you thought of anything?"

"Not yet, sir."

Smiling at the gullibility of the manager as the man walked away having been told what he wanted to hear, Paul went back to daydreaming about Nancy Longhurst. After lunch, when Paul answered his telephone, he was happy to find the caller did not wish to talk about insurance.

"It's Kenneth Grahame, Paul. Do you remember me?"

"Of course I do, Kenneth. I'm still on cloud nine after playing with Benjie Appleton. You have no idea what a favour you did me on Friday. I can almost bear looking at insurance claim forms this Monday."

"This time, could you do me a favour?"

"Anything you want, old chap. Anything."

"Could you give me the address of Beth Brigandshaw? Better still, her telephone number. Should have asked her on Friday but I forgot. Frankly, I find it difficult to ask girls for their phone number. Probably won't use it. Just like to think I could if I plucked up enough courage."

"I can give you her father's phone number in Surrey. We're all going down to Hastings Court for the weekend. Why don't you join us? I'm sure Beth won't mind. We're meeting her father with the car in town on Saturday morning."

"I can't just pitch up. You can't invite yourself for a weekend."

"When you left in such a hurry Beth was rather upset. Said she would have invited you when we all decided about the weekend."

"Did she really?"

"I owe you that favour."

"Can we all fit in the car?"

"It's a big one. Believe me. Mrs Brigandshaw will be with us on this journey down. She comes up to town every now and again to shop."

"I'd prefer to ask Beth first."

"I'll phone her father and get her number in the South Kensington flat."

When Paul walked up the steps to the entrance of the Cavalry Club it was exactly six o'clock. Apart from an old man in some kind of livery there was no one to be seen. Except for the muffled sound of traffic when the door closed behind him, Paul could hear not a sound. There was no sign of Major Pilkington-Jones. About to turn round and go out of the door with his tail between his legs, he found the old man in livery staring at him, barring his way.

"Mr Crookshank, sir? The major is waiting for you in the Long Room. Please come this way. Have you been in the club before, sir?"

"No I haven't," said Paul, knowing the man knew that just as well as he did. "I was in the Royal Army Service Corps. Second Lieutenant. Burma. Not exactly a cavalry regiment."

"As an officer, you will know the rules. You see, we don't allow other ranks in the club. Even as guests. Women, of course, have never graced the portals of the Cavalry and Guards Club. Rules, sir. We all have to comply with the rules. If you open that door and go inside you will find the major waiting. One of our older members. Did you know he fought in the South African war under General Kitchener? Received the Distinguished Service Order so I am told."

The room contained a series of small tables surrounded by the most enormous leather armchairs Paul had ever seen. Major Pilkington-Jones was watching him from one of these chairs, a broad smile on his face. A mess steward was standing just inside the door, balancing an empty silver tray on the palm of his right hand. On the low table in front of the major was a half-finished pint of beer. Paul felt it was like being back in the officers' mess in Rangoon just before the Americans dropped their bombs on Hiroshima and Nagasaki, finishing the war with Japan. After the ambush when Paul had killed the Japanese soldier, a memory that constantly haunted him, they had sent what was left of his unit back to Rangoon. Paul had been shot in the side by the man he had subsequently killed, the bullet going right through his body. The medical orderly had kept him alive in the back of his own truck on the return journey. He could still feel the wound when he leaned over, compressing his stomach. He had been lucky, they had told him in the hospital. Luckier, he remembered, than the Japanese soldier.

The major signalled Paul to join him at the table. The steward went across, standing next to the major.

"What will you have, Paul? You don't mind me calling you Paul?"

"Isn't that against the rules?" smiled Paul, thinking it his turn to pull the major's leg. "Same as you, sir."

"Hear that, Bonner? Now sit down and tell me what this is all about. My curiosity doesn't usually get the better of me."

"If I could get the finance, would you, sir, be willing in the course of your freelance work to buy some of the antiques you were talking about? I would then go with them to America and sell them to rich Americans, making, hopefully, the huge profit you were talking about in the office."

"How would you be able to convince your American buyer that what you were selling was the genuine article?"

"I thought you could write something out, sir. A certificate of authenticity we could guarantee with an insurance policy. So if they buy something they can prove is a fake they get their money back."

"Would someone insure my word?"

"We take your word for it when we pay out a claim. Mr Hudson, the manager of the Contingency, might agree to write such a policy. Or we can go to Lloyd's. Lloyd's are always boasting they will insure any risk. All we would have to do is make sure we tell the buyer exactly what he is getting. You and I split the profit. After expenses are deducted, of course. Yours and mine."

"You'd have to lose your job."

"And become a client if Mr Hudson underwrites our policy."

"Where are you going to find the capital to start this venture?"

"I have someone in mind."

"Why would he do it for you?"

"He owes my late father a favour."

"Interesting. Is he rich?"

"Very rich."

"It's normally more difficult to part the rich from their money than the poor."

"I can only ask him."

"When are you seeing him?"

"This weekend."

Major Pilkington-Jones sank back into his leather chair. From behind the major from a similar chair with its back to them, Paul thought he could hear the faint sounds of someone snoring. When the pint of beer was put down in front of him, the major silently signing the card offered him by the steward, he was too intimidated to sit back in his chair for fear of sinking too far into the old, soft leather. The major was watching him, the same slight humour in his eyes. Paul raised his pint mug to the major and drank a gulp of beer, wiping his face free of the froth with the back of his hand. Still the major did not move. From the chair behind came the sound of fluting, followed by a brief choking as whoever it was woke up. Paul could see nothing behind the high back of the black leather chair. The steward went across and leaned down, his head out of sight, before going away with what Paul expected was an order from the invisible man. The major watched the steward all the way to the door, the empty tray tapping the man's thigh as he walked.

"Can a man start a new life at the age of sixty-eight?"

"I don't see why not."

"Make some money before you're dead, Bertie," said a voice from the chair behind them. It seemed to Paul, the invisible man had not been asleep after all.

"Thought you were dead, Lachlan."

"Not yet. People often think I've dozed off. They should light the fire in the summer. Always bloody cold in this room."

"Coal rationing. We'll run out halfway through winter if we burn coal in summer."

"Thought the war was over. Sorry to interrupt. Wish I was sixty-eight."

"Will you think about it, sir?" said Paul.

"Of course he will."

"How old is he?" mouthed Paul.

"Ninety-one."

"I'm ninety-two tomorrow!"

When Paul left the Cavalry Club on his way back to the room he rented from Mrs Bigglesworth in Holland Park, he had in place one leg of his grand plan to regain his sanity. The major had agreed to do the buying and authenticate the pieces he bought. As Paul cooked two sausages on the gas ring in the alcove of his room, his mind was not playing the clarinet with the Benjie Appleton band for the first time all day. Despite having a look when he got up to go, he had still not seen the man whose ninety-second birthday was on the morrow. Like Kenneth Grahame for getting him in the band, Paul would like to have thanked the old man for helping to make up the major's mind. On the second ring, two peeled potatoes were boiling, the slice of cabbage to go in at the last moment. His mother had always insisted they ate green vegetables, a habit Paul had found difficult to change once he was living on his own. The next big hurdle was the insurance policy to put in place before he was driven down to Surrey on the weekend. Even the brief thought of Nancy Longhurst failed to push his mind off track. Instead of working his whole life paying off a house mortgage, he was going to be rich.

They had each drunk two pints of beer enjoying each other's company. After their agreement in principle to ship British antiques to America, Paul had guided the major's conversation back to the Anglo-Boer War when the major was a young man. There was no sound from the chair behind them as Major Pilkington-Jones happily regaled Paul with his exploits in South Africa. Twice, the steward had brought a drink to the invisible man, ensconced in his big black leather armchair, the height of the back level with a man's belly button.

When the potatoes and cabbage were cooked, Paul sat at his small wooden table next to the big window, and wolfed down his supper, hungry as usual.

"One step at a time," he said out loud to himself as he took the dirty plate out of his room to the communal bathroom where he did the washing up. He was whistling happily as he went.

"IT's why we call ourselves the Contingency Insurance Company, Crookshank," said Mr Hudson the next day. "We insure all contingencies. What kind of rate do you have in mind?"

"One per cent of the value of the antiques."

"He's honest, isn't he?"

"As honest as the day comes. If he wasn't sure of what it was, why would he buy the piece in the first place? Anyway, it's his word against the word of the buyer if someone complains. But why should they?

What's the difference when you walk into some antique shop in New York?"

"Then why do you need our insurance policy?"

"People like something official. Your policy, sir, will make the major's customers feel comfortable."

"Very well. We'll give it a try. Why did Major Pilkington-Jones not come to me himself?"

"He's very busy with his lordship's burned-out mansion. There should be considerable premium when the goods are shipped to America. We, of course, will insure the risk of damage to the antiques in transit as well as their authenticity. Considerable premium I should imagine, sir."

"Are you looking for a commission, Crookshank?"

"Of course not, sir. Just doing my job."

That evening, with his stomach full of scrambled eggs on toast and his mind back to thinking of Nancy Longhurst in her turtleneck sweater deliberately tight across her chest, Paul took the Tube from Holland Park to South Kensington. Beth answered the doorbell at the flat.

"Is Nancy at home?"

"We don't have anywhere else to go during the week," said Beth, giving Paul a knowing look. "How did you know our address?"

"I phoned your father, Beth."

"Why didn't you phone? We do have a telephone, Paul. Father insisted. Did you tell him you are coming down for the weekend?"

"Before I could mention your kind invitation, Beth, your father invited me. He wants to know all about Mother and Jeremy. Your father is a very kind man. Hello, Nancy. Lovely to see you again. Beth, I asked your dad if I could squeeze a friend of mine into the car."

"Who's your friend, Paul? You didn't say you had a girlfriend."

"Kenneth Grahame."

"Is he coming? How do you know where he lives?"

"Kenneth remembered I worked at the Contingency Insurance Company and gave me a ring."

"Why, Paul?"

"He wanted to see you again."

Watching Beth not saying a word, Paul could see her mind was off on a wander.

"We can all go for a walk in the woods with the dogs. Won't you come in? We've eaten supper, I'm afraid. I can make you a cup of tea. We were only saying how well you played the clarinet on Friday. You didn't tell Father I'd seen Frank?"

"Of course not. It's none of my business. Will he be at Hastings Court?"

"He's disappeared back into thin air. Poor Frank. It can't be easy."

"Would your father be upset if I made him a business proposition?"

"Why don't you ask him? He can only say no. If it's a good one he'll be delighted. Since the war ended, and with it Father's job at the Air Ministry, he's been bored out of his mind. Driving Mother nuts at home all day. He's got nothing to do. What do you have in mind, Paul? I know nothing about business but we can both listen. You'll have to make it pretty simple. Just hang on until I've made the tea. Why don't you go into our little lounge and chat with Nancy? Nancy, stop grinning. I told you Paul would find a way to come round."

"How perceptive you are, Miss Brigandshaw. Can't be long. Have to rise and shine early for work in the morning."

"The last Tube leaves at eleven in your direction."

"That'll be fine."

While Beth went into the small kitchen, Paul followed Nancy into the lounge. She was swinging her hips the way she had done on the Friday night, the view from the back as enticing as the front. It was all getting better and better.

"Can we pick up Kenneth on our way through Wimbledon in the car?" said Paul when Beth brought in the tea. "It's on the way to Leatherhead."

5

———————

By Friday afternoon, their confidence waning with only four quid from their scams, Brian Tobin said he wanted to go back to Rhodesia, to the twenty-thousand-acre cattle ranch fifty miles from Bulawayo that had been his family's home since before the Boer War.

"The saying goes, Frank, you marry it, inherit it or work it from scratch. I'm not good at a hard day's work. Neither are you. The Honourable doesn't go to church on Sundays as we found out snooping around Green Park. Your sister has ignored you and Mrs Whitaker has likely forgotten you exist. You missed your chances. I suggest at the end of our month in these rooms you take a train to Leatherhead and I take the boat back to Africa while I still have the money for a ticket. Instead of charming strangers we should charm our families. Play the prodigal son. My mother will fall for it and so will yours. We've tried our luck and lost. The winter's coming. Little gas heaters are not going to warm these rooms."

"Where's your spirit, Brian? We haven't been here two weeks. Maybe I should go and knock on Connie's door."

"And have it slammed in your face like Smithers. Breeding beef cattle could be worse."

"There aren't any women in Rhodesia. Certainly not in the bush."

"We're not doing any better here. The nearest I've got to a woman is a slap round the face. And you fucked a whore."

"I didn't. Just said I did."

"So Connie didn't come onto you either?"

"Oh, she did that."

"Why do you lie so much, Frank?"

"I'm going out for a walk. I'll think of something. Go home if you want. I'm not going home repentant just yet."

"It hasn't turned out the way we expected."

"Nothing ever does, Brian old cock."

Outside in the street, the smells of cooking were pervasive, making Frank more hungry than usual. Looking at the girls down the street, he went on his aimless way trying not to think of the conversation with Brian Tobin. All he needed was one good break. One leg up the ladder. One bit of luck. Taking the same route he had gone on the Sunday to see if the Honourable went to church, once in Piccadilly Frank crossed the road and walked on up into Green Park and the beckoning trees, some of whose leaves were turning colour getting ready for the autumn. Finding the same wooden park bench he sat himself down, his back to the house he had called on the previous week. The squirrels were more interested than the people in the park, making him bored and restless. Frank hated not getting his own way. He got up and looked round at the home across the street where no one was looking out of the windows. A dog on a long leash sniffed at his leg. Instinctively, Frank kicked out at the dog, not even thinking, making the animal yelp.

"Why'd you do that to Misty?" snapped an old woman from inside a fur coat. Brian had been right. The winter was coming.

"He was going to piss on my trousers."

"How vulgar. You should learn some manners, young man. Didn't your mother teach you how to behave?"

The dog, standing off, barked at him making Frank step forward, the dog pulling back to hide behind its mistress's legs, tangling her in the leash. Laughing at the woman, Frank walked out of the park. A taxi with its 'For Hire' sign on was going up Piccadilly slowly. Frank waved it down. Giving the cabbie Mrs Whitaker's address in South Kensington, Frank sat back in his seat, holding onto the strap by the window. Kicking the dog had been highly satisfying. At that moment, Frank did not care if the husband was at home. For once in his life he was at his wits' end.

Five minutes later, using some of her two quid, Frank paid off the driver and walked into her block of flats and up two flights of stairs, ignoring the lift. She was right. It was a long corridor. He could see people down below coming out of the underground. It was rush hour and people were on their way home for the night. Then he saw his sister with the girl she had been with the previous Friday night. Changing his mind, Frank ran back down the corridor, down the two flights of stairs and into the street, in time to meet Beth walking towards him from the other direction.

"Frank! You look a mess. Are you looking for me?"

"Why would I do that?"

"I live down the street."

"I was visiting a woman, matter of fact."

"Oh, yes. What was her name?"

"Connie Whitaker."

"We're all driving down to Hastings Court tomorrow. If we can squeeze you in the car, you can come with us. Mum's in town to do her shopping. Where's that horrible Brian?"

"He's going back to Rhodesia."

"Thank God for small mercies. Follow on and I'll cook you supper. Are you hungry? You always were."

"Starving, Beth. Where are they staying?"

"The Savoy. Mother always insists on the Savoy."

"Do they know I'm back?"

"Not to my knowledge. Have you got any money?"

"A bit."

"Good. Go over to that off licence while we wait and buy us a bottle of whisky. Family reunions go off better when we are all a bit pissed."

"Really, sis!"

"Shut up, Frank."

"Get me a bottle of sherry," said Nancy, getting a good look at Frank.

When Frank came out of the small liquor store with his purchases in a strong brown paper bag, the two girls were still waiting on the pavement, the rush hour traffic flowing past. Smiling his best smile, turning on the charm, Frank took his sister's arm.

"Lead on, kind lady," he said, squeezing her arm, his mind racing. Once again for Frank, the game was on. When he looked up at the woman coming straight at him from the other direction, he realised it was Connie Whitaker on her way home.

"Frank. What a lovely surprise. Were you coming to see me?"

"Connie, this is my sister, Beth. She lives down the road."

"How nice for you," said Connie, sourly.

Beth, looking from one to the other, started to laugh.

"Will you be home tomorrow morning, Connie? Say eleven o'clock. We can drink some tea."

Leaving Mrs Whitaker standing with her mouth open, Frank marched on, Beth in one hand, the two bottles of liquor in the strong, brown bag in the other.

"So you won't be driving down to Hastings Court?"

"Not tomorrow, Beth. You said there wasn't much room left in the car."

"You're incorrigible. Where did you meet her?"

"At the opening of an art exhibition in Bond Street. We met studying a Picasso."

"Isn't she married?"

"Of course she is. Her husband's away on business. Much, much older than Connie. She took me out to dinner after the launch of the art exhibition. Darling little restaurant called Café Monet, frightfully expensive. She's lonely. Well, you know I don't have much to do. So there it is. What do you think, Nancy?"

"Disgusting."

"We all have different ways of doing things."

"If you weren't my brother I'd leave you right here in the street."

"Don't forget the booze, darling... I was just kidding. So you're going home for the weekend tomorrow? That should be lovely. Have they repaired the bomb damage to the Court?"

"As a matter of fact we have."

"Jolly good. Don't get mad at me, Beth. Why do we always get off on the wrong foot? It's just so lovely to see you again."

"Then come with us tomorrow."

"Oh I can't. I promised to take tea with Connie."

"She didn't even answer your suggestion."

WHILE FRANK WAS POURING Nancy a glass of South African sherry, Barnaby St Clair was slumped in his armchair on the second floor of his Piccadilly townhouse waiting for his guest. The boy was haunting him. Every day since Sunday, Barnaby had spotted Frank sitting on the same bench in Green Park on the opposite side of the road from his second-floor window. By standing far back in the room away from the window, the bench still clearly visible through his racing glasses once the focus was adjusted for the distance, he had seen the boy without being seen. What he was going to do he had no idea. It was all very well for people to pass round a rumour that he was the boy's natural father but where was the proof, he asked himself. Frank wasn't Harry's son, that was for certain. Harry had been away too long on his farm in Rhodesia, leaving Tina at Hastings Court with the children, when Frank was conceived. But, as he asked himself time after time, was he the only one to take advantage of Harry Brigandshaw's long absence in Africa to seduce Harry's wife? They had only done it once in the bushes between Purbeck Manor, his family home, and the railway cottage, where Tina had gone with the children on a visit to her parents. Likely, she had known he was down in Dorset on a visit. Was the rumour about Frank Tina's way to get back at him for walking away from their long affair, refusing to marry her? They had been lovers for years when Barnaby walked away. And why had Tina married the man first married to Barnaby's sister, Lucinda, before she died? Was that another way to spite him? The boy had obviously heard the rumour, found out he was rich, and decided to try his luck. What were the chances of himself and Harry being Tina's only lovers? Knowing Tina the way he did, the answer was clearly nil. The girl was insatiable, every man an involuntary target for those bedroom eyes. Every man sucked in by her magnetic sex appeal that had only recently flown out of the window. If he knew for certain, he might accept the boy if that was what Harry wanted. Make Frank the heir to his considerable fortune. Give him a substantial allowance to put him on his feet. But how could he know the boy wasn't some other sod's bastard, some other by-blow under some other bush by some other man who had momentarily taken her sexual fancy? It was all a nightmare come back to haunt him, right across the road, right in front of his house where the boy's face leapt out at him through his binoculars.

When Smithers finally announced Harry Brigandshaw, Barnaby still had no idea what the hell he was going to do.

"Thanks for coming round, Harry. Want a drink? Thought it better than coming to the Savoy if you see what I mean. He was here just now. Over on that wooden bench in the park. Kicked an old lady's dog that was trying to piss on his boots. Heard the dog's yelp through the window right across the traffic, he kicked the damn thing so hard. Didn't see me.

After the first time he came round, I watch the park through the glasses so he can't see I'm standing in the room. Told Smithers to keep away from the windows, make it look as if we had gone away."

"Where is he now?" said Harry, half amused at Barnaby's conversation.

"Went off towards Knightsbridge in a taxi."

"I'll have a drink."

"Did you tell your wife why you were coming?"

"I did, as a matter of fact."

"Is there any way we can prove one way or the other Frank is my son? Have you ever asked Tina directly?"

"For years we avoided the obvious for Frank's sake. I know he's not one of mine, Barnaby."

"Are we ever sure of our father? They all swear sweet innocence. We always think our parents are saints. No one ever imagines their parents having sex, for goodness sake. The kind of thought the mind instantly blocks out."

"Did he look all right?"

"Thin. Good suntan. What was he doing?"

"Hunting crocodiles with a schoolfriend. Cheers, old boy. You look a bit off colour. Anything wrong?"

"That bloody boy. He's haunting me."

"You should have let Smithers bring him up the first time. Tina's dressing to go out for dinner. Takes her a lot longer these days to beautify herself."

"How is she?"

"She's Tina. I don't think she ever changed."

"That's what worries me."

"Why don't you ask her face to face if you are the father? I don't mind. I just did what was best at the time for Frank. Whatever happened it wasn't his fault."

"Don't be bloody silly. Of course she'll say he's mine."

"So you did sleep with her?"

"Once, after you were married. No one was sure if you were going to leave Elephant Walk and come back to England. And Tina wasn't going back to Africa."

"I wouldn't have done were it not for the children. We're picking up Beth from her flat at nine o'clock tomorrow morning. Driving them down to Hastings Court. Why doesn't Frank phone his mother? It's one thing to run away from his family to avoid getting called up in the army to war. But why keep up all the nonsense now the war's over and he's back in England?"

"Bloody mess. Cheers."

"Life's a bloody mess. I'm bored, Barnaby. Nothing to do. A man has to work or there is no point in his life. Don't you get bored?"

"I have my interests. Promoting West End shows. Promoting singers. Playing the stock market. It's not so much fun when you're rich. The adrenaline pumps up better when you might lose everything. That went down quickly. Want another one?"

"Don't mind if I do. Came in a taxi. She'll be another hour before she's ready to go out to dinner. There's a cabaret at the Mayfair. So what are we going to do, Barnaby?"

"Was Tina pregnant with Anthony when you married her?" said Barnaby, angling the conversation away from himself.

"She was. Followed me to Elephant Walk after we had our affair on the boat. Oh, don't give me any of that shit. Anthony was mine. Don't you think Frank's the spitting image of you as a young man? Anthony was of me. Flew aeroplanes. All the same things."

"Through the glasses I could see you in Frank, Harry. And half a dozen other men."

"Well, I'm not going to ask her. She's my wife, I have to live with her. Who's the current girlfriend?"

"I don't have one in particular. They come and go once you get over youth's fixations. In the end they all seem much the same. Rather a shame, actually. I envy a man who falls in love forever. Never met one, of course. What would we do without the church forcing us to stay with our wives?"

"I love Tina, Barnaby. You have to take the good with the bad. No one is perfect. We're a family. Including Frank. Why wouldn't he leave well alone? I'll talk to him when I find him."

"That's some comfort. Cheers again."

"Your good health. Going to be a cold winter. The leaves on those trees over in the park are brown too early. Do you mind if I use your phone? I have an idea. After Knightsbridge is South Kensington where Beth lives."

"How would he know her address?"

"God only knows."

. . .

WHEN BETH ANSWERED the phone in her flat she was almost caught off guard. The one thing Beth hated was getting involved in other people's problems, becoming the one to take some of the blame.

"Why on earth would Frank be in my flat, Father! Last I heard he was murdering crocodiles in the Zambezi Valley so rich women can parade around showing off their crocodile shoes, or is it men who wear crocodile shoes?"

"The cow has the same problem, Beth. I'm with Barnaby St Clair. Frank's back in England. For some reason called on Barnaby. Not a word to me or your mother. Nine o'clock tomorrow?"

"Do you mind driving through Wimbledon? Met a nice man at the jazz club. Old Etonian. Doesn't have a job or much money as a matter of fact. Lives with his mother. Said we'd pick him up on the way through Wimbledon. You don't mind?"

"How many more do you want to fit in the car? Paul Crookshank's phoned for your address. Felt I had to invite him, and agreed too that your friend could come along."

"He'll be here at nine tomorrow. See you then. How's Mother?"

"Beautifying herself up at the Savoy. We're going to dinner at the Mayfair."

As usual, neither of them said goodbye when the conversation finished.

"That was Father, Frank. They're onto you. Mother's alone at the Savoy. Do you want to give her a ring?"

"Thanks for not saying anything. What am I going to do if I come home? Sit on my arse all day. I'm not trained for anything. Have no particular bent I can think of. Look at you. You're some man's secretary. Isn't that boring?"

"Matter of fact, not. Some of the time, maybe. You have to do something. Dad only chips in a bit for the rent. Wants me to be independent."

"You complain at me picking up women. What about you? Is it the blighter you're taking home to Mummy?"

"At least he isn't married and the same age as Mummy."

"Connie is a lot younger than our mother."

"Not much, Frank. Mark my words. You'd better go if you don't want Father to find you. He has a sixth sense. Wouldn't be surprised if he doesn't come round. Said he always knew when a German aircraft was on his tail in the Great War, long before he saw the German."

"Enjoy the sherry, Nancy. At least you'll all be gone when I come round to visit Connie. I saw you from her second-floor corridor and ran down into the street."

"Be careful, Frank. There are enough problems in life without making them."

When Frank left in a hurry, Nancy and Beth had a good giggle.

"At least I've got a bottle of sherry," said Nancy. "I wonder how he knew I liked sweet sherry?"

"Because you're a woman. That boy's going to get into terrible trouble one of these days. Hope I'm not around to pick up the pieces."

"What's it all about, Beth?"

"Frank thinks Barnaby St Clair is his father."

"Could that be true?"

"Probably."

"Wow, skeletons in the Brigandshaw cupboard."

"Every family has skeletons if you go back far enough. Best not to rattle them. Just what my brother is trying to do. Why can't he be happy with what he's got? He's young, he's healthy, my father is rich. What else does he want? What difference does it make?"

"Everyone wants to know who they are. And that starts with our parents. If he wasn't such a nasty piece of work I'd find him very attractive."

"Think of Paul, Nancy," Beth said wearily. "He'll be here at nine tomorrow."

"Does Kenneth know when to expect us?"

"Told him to wait. Pour yourself another sherry. I'm going to have another drop of Frank's scotch."

THE NEXT DAY Paul Crookshank arrived at the flat at half past eight so as not to miss his lift. When they got in the car, the back was the size of a bus. The plush back seat had enough room for three people to sit side by side and stretch their feet. Two folding seats hinged down behind the front seats to make room for two more people. The back of the car reminded Paul of a London taxi. A glass partition slid shut across the top of the front seat when the chauffeur was driving. It was nice to be rich, Paul told himself. When they had gone down in the lift, Mrs

Brigandshaw had given her daughter a look that appeared to Paul to be akin to jealousy. Beth had touched his arm when they glanced at each other, making Paul's heart flutter. Nancy gave them the same look which was more understandable in her. He was Nancy's date for the weekend, Kenneth Grahame, waiting in Wimbledon, meant for Beth. Then they were off with Paul sinking back in the plush seat between the two girls, his knees touching both of them. Again Mrs Brigandshaw gave her daughter the same look when she craned round to look at them in the back seat. Paul smiled at Mrs Brigandshaw to make sure she would be on his side when he asked Mr Brigandshaw to put up money to finance his exports to America: the wife, it was said, had as much say as the man when it came to spending the family money. Maybe the woman did not like the idea of any man getting too close to her daughter. There was still so much to learn since he came back from the war.

Kenneth Grahame was waiting for them out in his mother's small driveway. There was no sign of Mrs Grahame. Kenneth was carrying a small grip which Mr Brigandshaw put in the boot. As much in deference to Mrs Brigandshaw, Paul changed to a dickey seat next to Kenneth, riding with his back to the engine. In a train it usually made him feel sick. Kenneth looked as nervous as the first night at the jazz club. For an Old Etonian he was not very sure of himself. This time Mrs Brigandshaw gave Kenneth a look without any trace of jealousy. Wrongly, Mrs Brigandshaw thought Kenneth no threat to her daughter. All women were a mystery to Paul, including mothers.

ONCE OUT OF the built-up area they drove fast, only slowing to turn in at the grand entrance at the bottom of the long driveway that took them through an avenue of tall trees to the old house with its crenellated battlements. Hastings Court brooded where it stood in the September sunshine, taking no notice of the car. To Paul, as on his first visit when he was thirteen years old, the house had a life and presence of its own: the look of an ancient who knew more than anyone alive. The small upper windows, blinking in the sun, looked at them with blinded eyes as they all disembarked from the car. Dogs came at them from everywhere.

"You must be Dorian," Paul said to a young man who ran down the steps and kissed his mother.

"I'm Kim. I'm the youngest of the brood. Dorian's in the village playing cricket. Down from Oxford for the vacs. I'm not very good at ball games. You're Paul Crookshank. Frank hit you on the nose. Don't you have a brother called Jeremy nearer my age? We go back to school next week. Did you go to boarding school?"

"Brighton College."

"Jolly good. They sent me to Cranleigh. Twenty miles from here. Too far to cycle. I hate boarding school."

"So did I."

"Were you in the war?"

"Burma."

"Did you see any action? I missed the war. What did you buy, Mother? I want to see everything. Hello. Who are you?"

"Kenneth Grahame."

"Were you at boarding school?"

"Yes I was."

"Good. Well, not boarding school. I like people visiting. It's always fun when there are people around. Dad's going to put the car in the garage. When the chauffeur left to go to war, we didn't replace him. I wish I'd gone to war. Being the youngest I miss out on everything. Come on, I'll help you with the luggage."

"Better help your mother, Kim."

"Of course. Can't do everything. What's in this huge bag, Mother?"

"A new dress."

"Wear it tonight and I'll tell you what I think of it. Come on, everyone. Lunch is ready. I'm starving."

"It's only eleven o'clock," said Beth.

"Then I'll have to wait."

"Did you miss breakfast?"

"Whatever for?"

WHEN THEY ATE lunch it was in a small room with French windows looking out onto the lawn. The doors were closed against a cold wind. The lawn was at the back of the house with big cedar trees on the far side of the lawn. Two of the dogs sat under the dining room table. On the surface everything was polite. Underneath, Paul could still feel the tension that had been with them since they got in the car. There were far fewer servants than the time before, when Frank bloodied his nose. One old woman they called Mrs Craddock. Only when they went for a walk did he find out what was going on. Once, at lunch, he had brought up the subject of business. Mentioned Major Pilkington-Jones. No one took any notice. No one was interested. The only conversation was trivial, most of it the boy Kim prattling on to his mother. It seemed to Paul the two were close to each other.

There was a fork in the footpath deep in the trees. Paul had been doing his best to charm Nancy Longhurst. For some reason it was hard going. Only when he looked around and found he was alone with her did he realise Kenneth and Beth had gone their separate ways into the woods. It was quiet among the trees. The birds were singing. The dogs had gone off with Kenneth and Beth.

"What's going on, or is it my imagination?" he said to Nancy.

"Frank, Paul. It's all about Frank. How someone who isn't even there can ruin everything for everyone beats me. They are all thinking of Frank in London. Not daring to say a word."

"Why does Mrs Brigandshaw look at me like that?"

"She's jealous of Beth. She's jealous of me. She hates not being able to grab your attention and hold on. Beth says she was quite something with this man when she was young. Beth says she's lost it. Hates it. Hates anyone, including her own daughter, who has it. Combine that with Frank hanging over their heads and it isn't much fun. To have so much money and have so little. Beth's words, not mine. If you want to talk business to Mr Brigandshaw, wait until you're alone. Those pregnant pauses at lunch were quite something. Who's Major Pilkington-Jones?"

"The man who's going to make me rich, get me out of the insurance company." Sensing he had said too much, Paul walked on, racking his brains for something to say to Nancy that she would find interesting.

"Go on, Paul. Why did you stop?" she said fifty yards down the woodland path.

"Business is always boring."

"Not if it's going to make you a fortune. Tell me what you're up to. Women aren't all stupid when it comes to money. They did teach something at that secretarial college."

So he told her. All of it. Including the missing link: the money he was hoping to get from Mr Brigandshaw to start his export business to America.

NANCY LONGHURST HAD BEEN TOLD by her mother that if she wished to catch herself a good husband she should be a good listener. That men liked to talk. About themselves. About what they were going to do in life. Talking to convince themselves as much as to convince the person listening. Her mother said the trick was to look wrapped in the conversation only opening the mouth to keep the story flowing. What Nancy knew about goods-in-transit insurance was absolutely nil. And she hoped it would stay that way. Men, according to her mother, liked to boast how rich they were going to be. It was part of the subconscious nesting, the man offering the woman a safe haven to have her kids, when all the time he was consciously trying to talk her into bed. Mrs Longhurst had once said money on the table was the only money worth looking at. Paul had his ideas. Kenneth Grahame had his Old Etonian tie, a tie meant to smack of family money, something that wasn't apparent to Nancy in the small Wimbledon driveway on the way down from town. But her mother's cynical lecture was not working. By the time Paul described the old man of ninety-two, she was rooting for the antique business as much as the invisible man in his black armchair. They had found a bench under an oak tree. The tops of the roots of the tree were swelling out of the ground with thick green moss between them. By the time she was *oohing* and *aahing* she had her eyes on the soft moss, wondering what it would feel like under her back. She had to force herself to sit tight on the wooden bench, her mind sliding away from the prospect of so much money to something more important for the moment. Lately, Nancy had found herself wanting more than she was getting from the mere presence of good-looking men. Right now she was having trouble not doing something about it. As a start, she put her hand on Paul's knee, to say how much she liked his prospects, stopping the poor boy in full flight. Were it not for the sound of barking dogs coming their way they would have done it right there under the trees.

"Damn these dogs," she said only half under her breath.

Then they were laughing, the earlier tension of the day flown away.

"What are you two talking about?" said Beth, coming through the trees into the glade. Behind her were the dogs and Kenneth Grahame. "That's my favourite spot on the whole estate. My father says it's always been special to the family for some reason I'm not sure about. They say that the tree has been here as long as the Mandervilles, my grandmother's ancestors. The cold wind doesn't get in here through the trees. It's a little world of its own. Kenneth's been making me laugh. He's so much fun. What have you two been talking about?"

"Making money. Paul has a wonderful idea for how to make lots and lots of money. He wants to talk to your father."

"Dad has a small office in London with a woman called Katherine. They are both looking for something to do with the office. Katherine was Father's secretary at the Air Ministry during the war. Our main family business is in America."

"I don't believe it," said Nancy. "Paul's whole business centres on America."

"My cousin Tinus runs the American office from New York. He married the film star, Genevieve."

"My word, how exciting. There you are, Paul. You have the wonderful idea and Mr Brigandshaw has an office in London doing nothing."

"I'll put in a word for you, Paul," said Beth. "Was that what Major Pilkington-Jones was all about at lunchtime? Maybe you could give Frank a job and stop him trawling the streets of London for rich, middle-aged women."

"I don't like Frank, Beth," said Paul Crookshank.

"Neither does anyone else. If you two giggling lovebirds can bear our company again, why don't we walk up to Headley Heath? There's an ancient witches' circle with a flat stone in the middle. If you sit on the stone, Paul, you can make a wish. Tinus did it during the war and he came out safely. Maybe your business idea needs the luck of the fairies."

"Can I sit on it as well?" said Nancy, innocently.

"You can, Nancy, though somehow I don't think you need the help of the fairies for what you're after... Come on. The dogs like the walk. Thanks to the dogs we found where you two were hiding."

WHEN PAUL MADE his presentation after tea, Harry Brigandshaw said not a word. Not one interruption. The one-sided conversation ended in a long, uncomfortable silence making Paul feel a fool. It was said parting rich men from their money was difficult. Now, in his naivety, he had proved the theory right. The fairies or witches, whichever they were, were not on his side. The prospect of his life with a mortgage, sitting behind his desk at the Contingency Insurance Company, loomed back large in his mind. What was left of the weekend at Hastings Court suddenly looked a long time. Luckily no one else in the family had heard his sales pitch.

They were in a room on their own sitting next to the fire, the cold east wind still blowing outside. Not sure whether he should get up from his chair and leave the room, Paul endured the endless silence. All through his monologue, Mr Brigandshaw had engaged his eyes, not once looking away, not once smiling, not once showing Paul any emotion. No wonder, he thought, the man had shot down twenty-three enemy aircraft in the Great War. Just the look would have made Paul bale out, not that they had parachutes in those days. Wondering whether to bring up his dead father for protection, Paul, paralysed, kept quiet. Then the man in the chair opposite looked away towards the fire, a glowing fire of coals, red at the centre. Mr Brigandshaw picked up the brass tongs and put coal on the fire, one lump of black coal after the other.

"You're only looking one way, Paul," he said at last, putting the tongs back on the little stand next to the miniature shovel. Next to that was a copper-coloured brush with black bristles. Mesmerised, it was Paul's turn not to say a word. "You're only thinking of buying the antiques from the British perspective. Of the need for the old families to realise some of their assets for cash, whatever the price. You're not looking at it from the buyer's point of view. From what the Americans would buy from our old country estates if it were offered them. What looks good in some baronial hall might look out of place in a modern Manhattan apartment. In America they have interior decorators. Women, often, who look at the furnishings of an apartment from every perspective. From the paint on the walls, then hanging curtains, the paintings, the furniture, to artwork on the shelves and the tables. I don't see the stuffed head of a Scottish stag on a Manhattan wall. Not ones the size of those in our Great Hall here at Hastings Court. What we need is an American to tell Major Pilkington-Jones what to buy. Then we'll make money. We have to offer the American buyer what would fit into his apartment, not what the major thinks is a good buy."

"So what do you think of my idea, sir?"

"I'd like to meet Major Pilkington-Jones first. Something tells me I'm going to like the man. Was that chap really ninety-two?"

"Said he was. So you think…"

"That you have a first-class idea. It'll help the poor sods being crushed by the new property tax. Earn the country dollars. And make us some money in the process. Not to say, give me and Katherine something to do. I'll mention it to Tinus on the phone. He's my nephew. My sister's son. He's an American now. What we need is one of those American interior decorators who knows what they're doing. Then the game's on. Well, this is a surprise. I thought you were after my daughter."

"So what do I do next, sir?"

"Bring the major to my under-utilised office in the city. Set up a meeting, young Paul. Get the ball rolling. That chap Hudson will definitely insure the antiques' authenticity you say? For one per cent of the value? That's the key to it, Paul. People like a guarantee when they're buying something they know nothing about. If they think what they're indulging themselves with is going to be worth double in ten years, they'll call it an investment. Should be easier to sell the antiques as an investment. You'll have to go to America of course. Tinus and Genevieve will look after you. You were here with Tinus when my son punched your nose. The only thing you did wrong that day was not giving him a clout back. You were much bigger than him."

"I was in your house, sir. My father would have belted me much harder if I'd made it into a fight."

"He was a good man your father. How's your mother? What's Jeremy doing with his life? We lose touch too quickly. Why I'm so glad to have you in my house. To do business together. Repay your father's favour when he let me fly the Short Sunderland to Lake Constance in Switzerland. Still remember that trip. Good memories are precious. Come on then. Better join the rest of them. Sherry is served in the lounge at six o'clock. Sort of tradition at Hastings Court. When you get older you rather like keeping up traditions. Connects one's life. Continuity. The older we get, the less we like change."

From despair to elation in ten minutes. Life, Paul thought, was indeed strange. A whole new vista, full of excitement, was running out in front of him as he followed Harry Brigandshaw to the lounge.

He was smiling, happy and confident when Harry gave him a glass of sherry, before announcing they were going into business.

"Well done, Paul," said Nancy, taking his hand. The hand was warm and promising. "Later, you and I will celebrate. There's nothing better than winning."

Beth, standing with Kenneth Grahame, both holding glasses of sherry, raised hers to Paul.

"Kenneth, do you know anything about antiques?" Paul said to him.

"No more than the next man."

"I may have something for you."

"Getting me to Beth and Hastings Court was more than enough of a thank you."

"No. This time it's business."

"What do you have in mind?"

"You'll have to wear your Old Etonian tie. If all goes to plan, you'll be doing a tour of the stately homes of England. That tie should get us in the door."

"It's about all I've got to offer, I'm afraid. They gave me a first-class classical education at Eton and not much else. After my father was killed we didn't have any money for me to go to university and learn something practical. Death duty took a chunk. When my mother gets the little income from the estate she pays nine shillings and sixpence in the pound in income tax. On all of it, from the very first pound of her income. They call it unearned income tax. Bit of a bugger really. I've ended up with half an education."

"They can take away your money but they can't take away your brains, old chap," said Paul. "It's a new world. A whole new world after the war. England's changed forever. Every man for himself. America is where the money's going to be made in the next half of the twentieth century."

"What's America got to do with our stately homes?"

"Everything."

For all intents and purposes, Connie Whitaker's life had come to an end until she met Frank at the launch of the Bond Street art exhibition. She and Frederick had largely lost interest in each other. She was no longer the twenty-year-old with everything to offer, he no longer the much older man-about-town, rich, good looking in the way of greying, chisel-faced older men who knew exactly how to behave with women. He had swept her off her feet in every sense of the word, only marrying her when she refused to go to bed with him without a wedding ring on her finger.

Everyone at the time had said no woman would ever convince Frederick Whitaker to get married. It was not even the idea of having children that appealed to him. He wanted her young body. Badly. Wondering if his great success with young women had finally come to an end.

It was a step up the social and financial ladder for Connie, trading her youth for his wealth and position in life. As Connie King she was nothing. As Mrs Whitaker she had a future far beyond her expectations. As much as anyone, her parents had pushed her into the marriage. He was a 'catch' according to her father, a clerk in the Ministry of Works, that only came to a woman once in a lifetime. Looking only at the immediate future, encouraged by all her friends' envy at her luck, she had married the man, twenty-three years older than herself, a man whose veneer of charm and worldliness changed the moment they were married and on their own. He was a brutal lover, enjoying the pain he inflicted tearing out her virginity. On the outside, to the rest of the world and Frederick's business associates, theirs was the perfect marriage. He had done her the favour, taking her instantly from the lower classes to a place alongside the rich and famous. All she had to do was look well dressed and pretty. And keep her mouth shut until she was spoken to. To never offer an opinion of her own. Always to listen. To tell Frederick's friends, when she said anything at all, how wonderful they were. How clever to be so rich. How lucky she was to be in their company, most of them well past middle age with big bellies and bald heads. Eyes that leered at her, some of them going as far as licking their lips at the young, nubile body sitting with them at the table.

They had never had any children, for which Connie was thankful. Had she signed his lawyer's prenuptial contract he would have divorced her in the first five years. Frederick hated the idea of giving away his money to someone no longer of interest. For Frederick, it was cheaper to stay married to Connie, go back to his old bachelor life, bring her out for business when he needed to, ignore her in the South Kensington flat except when he'd had too many drinks. All in the hope she would do something stupid and give him the grounds for a divorce that would not cost him part of his fortune. Alone, life for Connie was hard, her only hope a divorce which Frederick took delight in not giving her unless she agreed to take nothing in return. To put up with so much for nothing seemed absurd. What she wanted was a lover on the quiet, so quiet Frederick would never hear a word.

When Frank made his appearance at her door at eleven o'clock on the Saturday morning, she had a few ideas for both of them. Frederick was still away in Scotland, shooting grouse. He never said when he would return. Sometimes weeks went by. Telling Frank her husband was away on business had been simpler than telling him the truth. Because it would not do his image any good among his so-called friends. There was always enough money in the bank to run the flat and buy herself the best of London clothes. She was a kept woman with a wedding ring. Only Dorothy Dent, her only friend and confidante, shared her new expectations.

Dorothy, as requested, had opened the door to Frank.

"You must be Frank. Come in. My name is Dorothy. I'm Connie's best friend. How nice of you to come round. Tea, is it? Morning tea. I always say morning tea in a nice large breakfast cup is the best of the day. Connie! Your young man has arrived. You are right, he's delicious. What a wonderful story Connie has told me. You must have had the most adorable evening at the Café Monet. Rhodesia? Where is Rhodesia? We were looking on the map for an island off Madagascar. Nowhere to be found. If you don't eat him up, Connie, I'll eat him up myself. I'll have just one cup of tea with your adorable man. Then I'll be off. My word, if Frederick hears about this he will be jealous. If old men his age are capable of being jealous. Tea for three. Come in, Frank. Don't look so dumbstruck. You are at the right address. You know, in this life you never know quite what's going to happen next. You don't have a friend hidden away by any luck?"

"Dorothy, you say? Hello. And I do have a friend from Rhodesia, a British colony in southern Africa. Right in the centre. On the Zambezi River."

"Where you were crocodile hunting."

"You are well informed. Does Connie tell you everything?"

"What's his name? Your friend, the crocodile hunter? That was what Connie failed to remember from when you all met in the gallery."

"Brian Tobin. My crocodile-hunting partner."

"How exciting. Do you hunt anything other than crocodiles?"

"Sometimes, Dorothy. Now, where is Connie?"

"Here I am."

"You look even more beautiful than I remember," said Frank.

"This is fun," said Dorothy. "Can we send for Brian in a taxi?"

"I don't see why not," said Frank.

"Then I'll stay for more than tea," said Dorothy, giving her most seductive laugh, smoothing Frank's suntanned face with the tips of her fingers.

The two best friends had a plan should Frederick return unannounced. With one so young, Frank would become Dorothy's long-lost nephew from Rhodesia.

When the taxi returned with Brian Tobin, Dorothy's eyes grew bigger. Then they all left the flat to go out to lunch.

By the time Paul Crookshank was taking his second glass of South African sherry both Brian and Frank had lost their virginities. From lunch in a quiet restaurant they had gone back slightly tiddly to Dorothy Dent's sumptuous flat, compliments of her second husband. At the time, before the war, Dorothy Dent, actress and singer, had received one of the largest divorce settlements in England.

PART 2

APRIL TO JUNE 1947 – GIRLS, GIRLS, GIRLS

1

———————

*E*arly in the following spring, soon after the snowdrops came up in Mrs Bigglesworth's garden in Holland Park, Paul Crookshank was watching three wooden crates being loaded by crane onto a vessel at Tilbury Docks. It had taken Major Pilkington-Jones, with the help of Kenneth Grahame and himself, four months of searching to buy the antiques. The SS *Kentucky* was sailing for America with a full cargo and twelve passengers the following day. One of the passengers was to be Paul.

The following dawn, in a flurry of rain, Paul set sail for America. He was alone. Too early in the day to expect anyone to see him off on the most important journey of his life. The weekend at Hastings Court seemed a lifetime ago. Everything he had once been had changed.

"You have to look after the detail, young Paul," Harry Brigandshaw had said to him the previous week. "In the detail is success or failure. Don't take your eye off those antiques until they are sold. See them on and off the boat. Behave like a mother hen. It's a pain in the arse but it works. Never trust other people with your problems. They say they care but they don't. Have a word with the crane drivers at both ends. Give them a fiver if you can. Tinus will meet you in New York. He has a young girl in mind to help you sell the content of those crates. Jeanne Pétain is an interior decorator and an artist. Instead of telling the people what they should do with their apartments, she paints pictures on canvas so they see what they are getting before they put down their money. What we want is your antiques painted into her pictures. She works freelance for the big stores, receiving a commission on everything of theirs she sells. We want her to do work for us. She's French. Living in America since before the war. If she likes what she sees in your crates you are in business. You will have eliminated the antique shops. Gone straight to the buyers. We will be able to sell antiques to the whole of New York."

When his ship sailed down to the Thames estuary and into the English Channel the only accent Paul heard was American. Looking at the shores of England he wondered if he would find again what he left behind.

PAUL SAID it was like picking among the graves of the dead. From one old house to the other it was all the same. Crumbling brick. Threadbare carpets. The smell of damp, ancient decay. Old people with sad eyes not sure what was happening to them. With homes as old as England's history, for three generations they had been slowly running out of money. Mostly all they had was what Paul saw. The crumbling old home and the furniture inside. The shrunken surrounding estate now barely a hundred acres, the rest of the land long ago sold in a desperate attempt to hang onto the family home. A horse or two. Sometimes not a car in the stables. It was, as Major Pilkington-Jones remarked sadly, a picture of the new England exhausted by two world wars. Shell shocked. Not knowing what to do with the wolves of change howling at their doors. The end of an era. Probably, as the major said sadly, the end of an empire.

"It all began in rural England," said the major in their Bedford truck a month into the odyssey. "The young sons of the aristocracy went out to conquer an empire for the rest of us. First America. Then India. Then Africa. The greatest empire the world has ever known. Now fading away right in front of our eyes. India goes this year. America went nearly two hundred years ago. Africa will go. Malaya. Ceylon. The Caribbean. Even half of Ireland divorced England. The Union will collapse leaving a small island race to paddle its own canoe. Look at all these old homes we've visited in search of something we can buy of value. They're all decaying. Like the empire. Sad in some ways. Invigorating in another. Evolution. Nothing stays the same. You either grow or you die. Only the strong survive. If you only look back there's no excitement. You see, people don't like to see another man with more possessions than himself. No one wishes to feel inferior. To be looked at as a lower class. In those old days when the empire was expanding it did not matter. Now, British Socialism is the beginning of power to the ordinary man. One man or woman, one vote. Total equality. They want to destroy class. When they succeed, as they will, they'll find themselves ruled by a different class of rich people. A few clever men through history have known how to manipulate the masses. We, on our journey round England, are helping the masses kill off the upper class, for better or for worse, by buying up their last possessions of any worth. Some day in the future your new man of wealth will buy these old homes, bring them back to their old glory and pretend to themselves they are aristocrats. Fortunately, I shall be long dead by then. You, Paul and Kenneth, will see what happens, I'm afraid. If you could put all the antiques in the back of our lorry into a warehouse and lock the door for fifty years, you'd have money to renovate that old pile back there. Two of those paintings are masterpieces. No one can ever paint them again. Their rarity will make them priceless. Not the five hundred quid we just paid for them. Now they will go to America. Lost to this little island forever."

"What else could we do?"

"Nothing, Kenneth. 'Tis the price of progress. The wages of war. I feel sorry for that old gent in his old, threadbare tweeds who has no idea what is happening to him. Or why. Stuck out in the country all his life, answering only the trumpets of war, the new world has passed him by. Left him behind. All he has left to do is die, taking with him his ancient name and half the history of England. Thank God I'm old. It pains me."

"But what can we do?"

"Drive on to the next one, boys, and see what we can find. You two still have a whole life up ahead of you. It's my turn to drive. Before this great venture I never drove a lorry in my life. How full are we, Paul?"

"About half full, sir."

"Good. We'll fill this army surplus lorry to its canvas. I love the English countryside except for the weather. Those old homes are as cold as charity. Wouldn't live in 'em if you paid me. Prefer the tropics myself. If England had had a good climate we never would have had an empire. Everyone would have stayed at home. Do you know, that chap Gandhi doesn't want to be prime minister of India? Going to let someone else do the work. Good luck to them all. One day not too far away, India will be more important in the world than England. They have our laws. They have our system of parliamentary government. They have our language. Loved it in India. Loved the people. Rich and colourful... Can we stop at a nice country pub on our way and have lunch? ... Empires come and go like people. It's the way of human life. What doesn't change is my desire for a damn good lunch. They don't have a shortage in the depths of the countryside. No ration books required. Wonderful. What would we have done without Harry Brigandshaw and his money? His grandfather started as a common seaman. Became the captain of a ship. From his share of the plunder in distant trade, bought himself his first ship. Why they called him the Pirate to his dying day. No one to this day is sure how he made that first money. Colonial Shipping belonged to the old Pirate. Left it all to his grandson Harry. When Harry went missing in the Congo jungle on his pioneer flight down the rivers and lakes of Africa in one of the first seaplanes, it was in all the papers. Again, in the papers when he walked out of the jungle three years later. The Brigandshaws before the Pirate were shrimp fishermen. On the Lancastrian coast. Simple fisher folk. Now look at them. Amazing what a lot of money and a few generations can do for a family. Neither Hastings Court nor its antiques will be sold for another generation or two. When the Brigandshaws married the ancient family of Mandervilles they brought new money to Hastings Court. New, invigorating blood to a tired old family. Harry, brought up in the wilds of Rhodesia, looks at these old possessions as an opportunity. As he should do. Not doing anyone any good collecting dust, not even used, looked at or appreciated. The ravages of time. Rejuvenation of youth. You have taken your chance to build yourselves a new life. Build it well. Helping you in your venture has given me a new lease of life. Gentlemen, I feel ten years younger. And hungry."

Standing with his hands on the rail of the ship in the cold of the morning, Paul thought back to the very beginning. To Nancy Longhurst. To making his wish in the witches' circle on Headley Heath. To when he took the chance of his lifetime and gave up his career in insurance with all its security and certainty of some kind of a mundane future with very little risk. To the moment when he threw it all in the ring and went for his life at full throttle.

THE DAY after Harry Brigandshaw announced his financial backing over a glass of sherry in the lounge of Hastings Court with its crenellated battlements and ancient history, he had gone back to Mrs Bigglesworth's small room that he rented and taken one, last deep breath before taking the plunge. That next day he told Mr Hudson he was leaving the Contingency Insurance Company, no longer its clerk. On the flat stone in the witches' circle it had come to him. To cut his ties with security. To burn his boats. To have no going back. The fear of insecurity spurring him on, replacing the lethargy and inertia of an insurance company security.

When Paul brought the major to the office in Holborn to meet with Harry Brigandshaw and cement the deal, he told them both he had resigned his job, he was so certain of what he was doing. For Kenneth Grahame, with his Old Etonian tie, it made little difference as he hadn't had a job since his demob from the army after the war.

The first concrete part of the job was buying the five-ton Bedford lorry from the War Office, which was selling off military surplus cheap now that hostilities had ended. Something Paul knew all about from his days as a junior officer in the Royal Army Service Corps. They had brought him wounded out of the Burmese jungle in the back of a Bedford lorry, shaded by the canvas, half dead and bleeding from the ambush after Paul had killed the Japanese soldier who had shot him in the stomach. The lorries, lined up in the army barracks at Aldershot, had been going cheap, no one wanting to buy them. All through the first month Nancy Longhurst had been cheering him on, laughing, speculating, making love and being young. Only after the first buying trip with the major and Kenneth Grahame had all that come to an end. Nancy was a butterfly, flitting from one flower to the next. By then, the business was on its way, the distraction of playing his clarinet in London's basement jazz clubs less important than the job in hand. They stayed friends, the four of them. Went on head first into the rest of their lives. They were happy. Life was for living. Hedonism more important than a wife and children with a mortgage for the rest of their lives. Paul thought the war had taught all of them just how short life could be.

The confrontation with Frank came before the first field trip. The invitation had been slipped under their door when Nancy and Beth were at work. An invitation to dinner at an address in the trendy part of Chelsea where men and women wore black berets and smocks, trying to look arty. Paul by then had found the ones who looked arty usually weren't, and wondered what Frank, the crocodile hunter, was doing in that part of Chelsea. The invitation included partners which brought Paul and Kenneth into the picture, Paul voicing his opinion as to whether it was a good idea, the memory of his punched nose and Harry Brigandshaw's more recent comment on the incident, asking why he hadn't hit back, springing back into his mind. Paul disliked confrontation, preferring to walk away. Never looking for a fight, Beth, saying the two of them were only thirteen at the time, prevailed. Being more than obliged to her father by then, Paul had concurred. Beth, when she wanted something, was a difficult woman when it came to changing her mind. Frank had still not contacted their mother. Expecting an artist's garret and a bowl of soup, they were all taken aback when they walked into the flat, a place as luxurious as money could buy. On a table that Paul now recognised as Jacobean, having spent days educating himself in London's antique shops, were two bowls of flowers and places laid for six people.

"Where are your partners?" Beth had said, looking round the sumptuous room. "What's all this about, Frank? This flat can't be yours."

"Oh yes it can, sis. Brian and I have a kind benefactor."

"Do you share the place?"

"Not at all. Except with each other. Isn't it such a lovely two-bedroomed flat?"

"Oh, my God. That woman! She's rich. She's rented this flat for you."

"So's her friend. Sadly Dorothy and Connie are not available after all tonight. Frederick is in town."

"Who's Frederick?"

"Connie's husband."

"Does he know about this?"

"I hope not."

"Why haven't you phoned Mother?"

"I don't have to now. Fallen on my own feet. With a little money in the pocket London is quite pleasant. Brian was going back to Rhodesia but has changed his mind. So much better than our digs in Soho. Have you been to that awful jazz club recently? Place was full of yobs. Jazz is so common. Have a drink, sis. Cheer you up. Everything you can possibly want is in the cocktail cabinet. The food gets sent round at eight o'clock by the best restaurant in Chelsea. We prefer to eat away from the madding crowd."

"What you mean is your benefactors don't wish to be seen with you in public. When you arranged all this, Frederick, the husband, was out of town."

"A perfect arrangement don't you think? Paul Crookshank. So nice to see you again. How is your nose? Tell me, are you screwing my sister or is Kenneth?"

Beth, to even Frank's surprise, had slapped him hard across the face. It was the shortest dinner party Paul had ever attended. He could still hear Frank's mocking laughter in his mind as he stood by the ship's rail with the cold wind off the sea biting into his face.

"He's not worth it, Beth," he had said outside the small block of flats.

"He's still my brother. Frank hasn't had it easy growing up with a cloud hanging over his head."

"Got it easy enough now," Nancy had said. "What a waste. So much perfect manhood going down the drain. Let's find a restaurant. A nice cheap one. I'm hungry and I need a drink."

TURNING his back on the past and feeling lonely, Paul walked down the deck to the heavy door at the top of the stairwell, pulling it open against the cold wind. The door closed heavily behind him. A draught of hot air came up from between decks. He could smell coffee. The ship, now in the open sea, was pitching and rolling just enough to make Paul keep hold of the rail on his way down the stairs to the ship's small lounge which the bursar had called the wardroom when Paul came on board. Passengers were helping themselves to coffee from a sideboard. Armchairs and coffee tables, bolted to the deck, were spread through the low-ceilinged room. Paul had to duck his head on the way to the sideboard. There was no tea available, only coffee. Paul had deliberately shipped on an American boat to acclimatise to American ways before going ashore in New York. A man just in front of him took his coffee to a table, sat down and drank from his cup.

"Now that hit the spot," said the American.

For nowhere better to sit, Paul joined him at the table, holding onto his cup and saucer against the movement of the ship when he sat down, avoiding the man's eyes.

"Your first trip? You look nervous. Hank Westphal. From New York, New York State."

"I did go to Burma and back in a boat when I was in the army."

"Mind the coffee. It's real hot. Did you fight?"

"Just a little. Paul Crookshank. Isle of Wight. Lately of Holland Park in London. This is my first trip to America."

"What are you selling?"

"Antiques. Old paintings. That sort of stuff. Three wooden crates of samples on board. The rest are piled up in a London warehouse. No one wants antiques in England. Got no money after the war. Have to pay back you chaps for what we owe you. All those supplies to fight the war. Don't know what we would have done without them."

"What's the definition of an antique, Paul?"

"Something more than a hundred years old. Applies to furniture mostly. Silverware has a hallmark with the King's or Queen's head. Paintings have the artist's signature."

"How do you know it's all genuine? What you say it is?"

"We have the certificate of authenticity insured. If the buyer proves we are wrong they get their money back."

"Do they now?"

"Good investment."

"Is it now? Can I have a look?"

"Not now, Mr Westphal. The crates are in the ship's hold."

"Call me Hank."

"Six days, they tell me. A lot of water."

"We call it the Pond. Do you play bridge?"

"As a matter of fact, I do. When the lorries weren't on the road we had nothing to do."

"Did you kill any Japs?"

Paul gave the man a queer look and drank his coffee.

"Sorry. You're right. Killing anyone don't make no sense."

"He had shot me in the stomach."

"Purple Heart!"

"We don't give medals for wounds in England."

"What did they give you?"

"A discharge from the army in the end. After a few months in Germany, with the British Army on the Rhine. Just in for the war. Not a regular soldier."

"Now you're selling antiques?"

"That's right. What do you think? If America doesn't buy my antiques I'm buggered."

"You'll only find out when you try, Paul."

"I suppose I will."

With only twelve passengers on board the mainly cargo ship with little or no recreational facilities, Paul played bridge to while away the hours of the day. By the time they were approaching the shores of

America, the shores of the New World, Paul had won himself thirty dollars and the firm friendship of Hank Westphal. Hank was a few years older but Paul had found once he reached manhood a difference in age meant very little if there was an interest in common. Old silver, old paintings, Jacobean furniture with the major. Bridge with Hank Westphal.

WHEN THEY SAILED into New York on the Saturday morning, Paul was up with the dawn, standing at the rail, getting his first glimpse of the skyscrapers and the Statue of Liberty. A present, Paul remembered from his history lessons, from the French. A symbol of liberty, fraternity and equality from the people of France and a poke in the eye for France's old adversary, Britain, the French having backed the American Colonists against King George in the American War of Independence.

All morning, Paul waited for his crates to come up from the ship's hold, using the thirty dollars he had won at bridge to give to the crane driver on the docks. Before leaving England they had agreed for him to only phone Tinus Oosthuizen, Harry Brigandshaw's nephew and manager of the Brigandshaw New York office, when the crates were safely on the side of the dock. Apparently, in America, no one wasted time sitting around without a purpose; one of them was quite capable of seeing the precious cargo safely on the ground.

When Tinus did arrive, he was accompanied by an open truck. The three crates were again carefully lifted and put in the back of the truck by the same crane driver, Paul's thirty dollars well spent.

"I've rented lock-up space in a warehouse. Wire cage with a padlocked door. Should be safe. How are you, Paul? Long time no see. I was in the RAF by then. You were still at school. Didn't you have a fight with Frank, or something?"

"Or something," said Paul as they shook hands. "When do I get to meet Jeanne Pétain? If she doesn't like what I've brought we're stuffed."

"Be positive. Everyone is positive in America. Jeanne's waiting at the warehouse to help unpack. She's as excited as we are... Off you go, driver. Be careful. You've got a precious cargo. My friend here's hard work for six months is in the back of your truck."

Laconically, the driver waved from up in his cab, leaving Paul watching his precious crates going off on their own. They were right about America. People knew what they were doing and did not have to be told.

"Come on. My car's waiting in the parking lot. Welcome to New York. Welcome to America."

"How's business?"

"Pretty good. The meat packing business and the tobacco plantation in Virginia are our main sources of income and work. In America they call them plantations. Tobacco planters. In Rhodesia they are farms and tobacco growers. We're going to make our own brand of cigarettes. Source tobacco from Southern Rhodesia. It's half the price of American tobacco. I don't get involved with my wife's hard-earned money. Trust fund in England run by the Honourable Barnaby St Clair. Well, this is fun. Did you ever meet Genevieve, my wife? Barnaby is her uncle. Her parents were never married."

"Only up on the silver screen."

"After the first kid, young Barend, named after my father, she doesn't act on the stage or screen anymore. I've never been so happy in my life. Booked you in the hotel down the road from our flat. Nothing much. More of a boarding house, really. Genevieve doesn't like showing off her money so we stay in Brooklyn. Nice, ordinary people with hearts of gold. Jeanne found us the hotel. Where she stays on her own, she has two nice rooms she decorated herself."

"How old is Jeanne Pétain?"

"About your age. Genevieve says she should have gone into films. An artist with a beautiful face. Prefers painting the pictures. She's a creative artist. Not a performing artist like my wife was before we were married."

"How did you find her? I mean, Jeanne. I know you knew Genevieve long before she was famous."

"Genevieve got chatting in the local shop. Strange how some things that can become so important start so small."

"This all started in Benjie Appleton's jazz club in Oxford street. When I bumped into your cousin, Beth."

"Save it for Genevieve. She'll want to hear. That's my car. Get in. Not that side. In America they drive on the wrong side of the road."

When Paul arrived at the warehouse with Tinus, a young girl was waiting for them.

"Hello. I'm Jeanne. You must be Paul. Well, they have arrived. *Ooh là là*. They are such big crates. I want to tear them apart to see what you have put inside. Are there any paintings, Paul? Are they good ones?"

The way the girl said 'Paul' made Paul shiver all over. She was an elf. With two small pointed ears. Elfin, twinkling eyes. Dark, short-cropped hair. Tiny. Paul thought Jeanne not even five feet tall. He had the immediate desire to pick her up and put her in his pocket. Controlling the more primal instinct, Paul put out his hand.

"Why you look at me like that, Paul? Don't you talk? The cat got your tongue, as you English say? Why a poor cat should stop a tongue talking, I have no idea."

"Hello. I'm Paul Crookshank, Miss Pétain. In the crate marked with a B are two paintings, landscapes, by Thomas Gainsborough. Authentic, I do know. Good is up to whoever looks at them."

"You are so big and I am so small. I will let you break open the crate marked with a B. Isn't this fun? Off you go, Tinus. He is under my little wing. We have some fun, Paul. Yes? Of course. It is always fun to behold beauty. It is being able to recognise beauty that makes a person different from the rest, don't you think? You don't have any French paintings? Or Dutch? Or that Spaniard who lived in France?"

"Only English painters I'm afraid. Everything in the crates is English."

"Maybe next time you go to France and buy something French."

The crates had been taken off the back of the truck and put in the small enclosure by a fork-lift truck. They were standing in the middle of the cage waiting to be opened. Tinus left, saying they would all meet again at dinner time as his wife was preparing supper.

Paul found a tyre lever on one of the shelves that were waiting for his antiques. With his mind spinning, Paul began prising open the crates. All through the appraisal Jeanne was silent, not even an expression giving away her thoughts. The paintings were broken from their wooden packing. Pottery came out of small individual wooden boxes, the vases packed in straw. When the first crate was lying broken open in the middle of the concrete floor, the pieces placed on the shelves, Jeanne looked at her watch.

"It's five o'clock. Better we find your hotel. I have a little car. You don't drive yet in New York? Then we go see Tinus and Genevieve, it is all arranged."

"But what do you think?"

"You are too impatient. It is much too early to tell. Tomorrow we take your paintings to an art gallery and have them valued. How much you pay for a Gainsborough?"

"Five hundred pounds."

"We have much work. For me it is all about beauty. For you and Tinus it is all about profit. Whether the business will work. For me to cry at the sight of beauty will not make us a profit."

"But you did not cry."

"Oh, but I shall. Later. When I am alone. When I see all these again in my mind's eye. One by one. Remembering. This major is a very clever man. Now I must be the clever girl to help you sell your antiques for a profit. A good profit. For anything truly beautiful they must pay lots and lots of money."

"Do you have any ideas?"

"So many, Paul, you must be careful. For today, work is over. We shall play a little. All work and no play is not good. If you are a good boy I'll cook you supper one night in my little apartment. Proper, French food. A good chef is also an artist. A creative artist. I don't cook as well as I paint. But you will see. I hope you like your food. Better, I hope you like my paintings."

They found Jeanne's car in the workshop next door. Like Jeanne, the car was very small. Next to the workshop was a bakery. Across the road, other small businesses. There were so many different smells to Paul's unaccustomed nose. In Mrs Bigglesworth's house there were only the smells of good, plain English cooking. Above the ground floor rose four storeys of tenement apartments. The smell coming out of the bakery was enticing, a cross between newly baked bread and hot spices. Paul's eyes were wide open trying to take it all in. It was nothing like what he had expected to find in America. In the movies they all spoke English, lived in smart houses and drove cars the size of small buses.

"Who are all these people?" asked Paul.

People were coming by in droves at the end of a day's work. Most of them were on foot. One old man wearing a turban was riding a bicycle. Paul had seen such men in the Indian Army when he was fighting in Burma with the Royal Army Service Corps.

"It's the whole world in this part of Brooklyn. Why I like living here so much. You'll hear half the languages of the world: why we all have to learn English or we'd never be able to talk to each other."

"Where do you live?"

"Above your antiques. I'll keep a good eye on them. On the third floor. Now we have to go visit Tinus. He gets home at seven or thereabouts. The

Brigandshaw office has to be in Manhattan for prestige. Tinus thinks of himself as a bit of an investment banker. Always looking for new places to put the company money. During the war, the Tender Meat Company grew into one of the largest food packaging companies in America. Harry Brigandshaw picked up a controlling interest in the company when it was in trouble at the end of the Depression. Tinus will tell you more."

"Aren't you going to take the car?"

"What for? They only live round the corner. I was just checking with Jake my car was still working. Mostly I use the subway. The day after tomorrow I go upstate to visit a client with a big old house that badly needs decorating. So I'll need the car. There's a little place that sells Turkish coffee. Come on. We have lots of time before supper. Your little hotel is close to where Tinus and Genevieve have their apartment. We will all be living close to each other. One big family."

Having left his bags in Tinus Oosthuizen's car, Paul walked with Jeanne to the coffee shop. In this strange country everything was now happily out of his hands. Even his suitcases that he hoped to find in his hotel when someone showed him where he was going to be living.

In the morning, accompanied by Jeanne and Tinus, the real job began. If the scheme he had asked so many people to help him with was going to work, he had to know the true value of his goods.

The first call was on an art dealer, two blocks off Fifth Avenue. They had wrapped the two paintings, still in their original frames that had hung on the walls of a Surrey stately home, in brown paper. Tinus and Paul each had a painting under an arm when they walked into the shop, Jeanne Pétain taking two paces for their every one coming up behind. Paul was still mellow from his previous evening's supper party. After they finally walked him to his residential hotel at one in the morning he had slept soundly all night.

"Could you give us some idea what these are worth?" said Paul, tearing at the centre of the brown paper to reveal his painting.

The man, who seemed to be the only person in the shop, put on his glasses. Then he looked at the painting in minute detail. When Tinus proffered the second painting out of its brown paper covering, the man looked scared.

"Where'd you get them?" said he demanded sharply.

"From the Maples Mansion in England," said Paul, beginning to understand and enjoy the man's discomfort.

"And how did you get them, may I ask?" The man was in his fifties with a shiny, bald head.

Tinus laughed. The wrong thing to do. The man went to pick up his telephone that was standing on the counter.

"Are these forgeries?" he said, beginning to dial a number.

"Originals. We have a certificate of authenticity. Countersigned by a City of London Insurance Company," said Tinus, smiling.

Jeanne had wandered off to look at the paintings in the gallery with an amused smile on her face.

"Do you own these paintings?" said the man, standing on his dignity.

"We'll gladly pay you one per cent of their American value for an appraisal. They belong to my uncle, Colonel Brigandshaw. We trade as Brigandshaw Oosthuizen Inc in America. We are, among other things, the major shareholder in the Tender Meat Company. My employee here has just arrived with the paintings from England where the market for a Gainsborough is depressed to say the least."

"You don't want me to buy them?"

The man had put down the phone.

"One per cent, you say?" A slight smile turned up one corner of his mouth.

"One per cent of your valuation," confirmed Tinus.

"At a first look, thirty thousand dollars."

"For both of them?" asked Paul before he could keep his mouth shut.

"For each of them. If you require written appraisal backed by our good name, I shall require six hundred dollars."

"Could you write out your appraisal now, sir?"

"Do you have six hundred dollars?" The man was still trying to recover his dignity.

"In cash, matter of fact."

"Then let us do business."

"We will, of course, be asking six further art dealers to put their names and reputations on similar written appraisals."

"I know exactly what I am looking at. You will be wasting your money, if you ask my opinion. If I were to be wrong, no one would buy paintings from my gallery. Valuations for the purpose of insurance are part of my business. I have a reputation to maintain."

"You are most kind. Your reputation precedes you. Sir Jacob

Rosenzweig of the Rosenzweig Bank recommended you to me. Sir Jacob does not use his title in America. Tinus Oosthuizen. You are welcome to phone Sir Jacob if you require confirmation."

"That won't be necessary. The appraisal should be made out to?"

"To whom it may concern."

Outside in the street with the certificate of American valuation in Paul's pocket, the paintings back under their arms, they hailed a cab to take them to the Brigandshaw offices where the two paintings were hung on the wall. For the rest of the day Jeanne and Paul visited nine antique shops in New York, looking at their prices. Exhausted and elated at the end of the day, they finally stopped off in the street outside Jeanne's apartment. On the way they had called at a small market for her to buy the food for their supper.

"Come on. I'll show you where I live. Tonight is my turn to cook supper. Just for the two of us. While I am cooking you can look at my paintings hanging on the walls and tell me what you think. I can't make a living out of selling my own paintings. Why I work in interior design. Being an artist can be very frustrating."

"When do you have time to paint?"

"Not very often. When I have enough money I am going to live on the Florida Keys. It is an artist's paradise when the hurricanes are not blowing. It is cheap to live on the Keys. Then I will paint all day and be happy. Are you happy, Paul?"

"I am now. After today I know with your help I have a business. We must work hard so you can go to your paradise and become a famous artist."

"Come on, then. Let's show you what I have done."

On the third floor, the one-bedroom apartment was as perfect as the girl. One big room served as a lounge and dining room with an upright piano in one corner. There were doors from the big room into a bedroom, bathroom and the small kitchen. While Paul went from painting to painting, Jeanne worked away in the kitchen. Everything Paul saw in the room, including the small paintings of Brooklyn, were perfect. With the smells of French cooking wafting into the room Paul sat at the small piano and began to play. First he ran his fingers up and down the keys to find out if the piano was in tune. Then he began to play softly to himself. Small pieces of Bach. A Chopin nocturne. Gershwin lastly. Paul then began to play jazz, his mind so far away he had forgotten where he was.

"You play beautifully. I have opened a bottle of wine. To celebrate. Supper will be ready in half an hour. Please don't stop playing."

"Who plays this piano?"

"Me, but I'm not very good."

"Your paintings are quite beautiful. You have brought the surrounding area alive. So alive. They talk to me, your paintings. Of the people, all so different, and their lives."

"Thank you."

"What would you like to hear?"

"Anything. Do you play any other instrument?"

"The clarinet. It's how this all began. In a jazz club."

"Tell me. The wine is French. I hope you like it. First let us drink to a wonderful day. Do you have a girlfriend in England?"

"Not anymore."

"I am glad."

"And you, Jeanne? You must have dozens of boyfriends."

"There is Rudy. We are lovers. Just not in love. Sometimes I think we use each other. What happened to your girl?"

"She likes men in the plural."

"Some women are like that. So are most men. We can only hope to find a person to love that is just for ourselves. Mostly they don't last because we pick the wrong one for the reason of sex. Get bored with each other. So we drink and make merry. Enjoy what we have. Try not to be sad. Do you play in a band in England?"

"Sometimes. Only sometimes. There was a war."

"Did you fight, Paul?"

"In Burma. Against the Japanese. War is so sad. There are no heroics in killing a man. Enough of that. To our future business. To your paintings. To your happiness, Jeanne. And thank you. Everything is so much better than I could have imagined."

"Are you going to stay in America?"

"Not all the time. I will be going backwards and forwards when I have a better idea what to buy. How sad for the old families in England slowly running out of money. To sell those two paintings for so little when they are worth so much on the other side of the Atlantic."

"Van Gogh never sold a painting. The artist rarely gets paid. He or she is the only one who should be sad."

"I suppose so. I'm too inclined to feel sorry for people."

"It doesn't matter, really. The joy for the artist is in the painting, not in the money. There is no true joy in money. Only in art. In a lovely play. Beautiful music. A painting from the heart that talks so deeply without having to say a word. Reward enough."

"There are so many beautiful places you can go and paint and be happy."

"Oh, I'm happy, Paul, just not the same complete depth of contentment I want when I paint all day. Have you ever written any music?"

"Not yet. They gave me a music scholarship which paid for most of my school fees. After my father was killed in the war, the scholarship was more important than my music. One day, maybe. Like you. One day a small home on the shores of a lake. Or beside a forest. Just me and a girl who loves me for who I am and not what I make."

"We should be so lucky."

"Your English is so good for a French girl."

"I was thirteen when we came to America. Ten long years ago. Before the Nazis invaded France. My mother is Jewish. My father was frightened for all of us. So we came to America."

"Are they happy?"

"My parents are always happy."

"You have brothers and sisters?"

"One of each. We were the lucky ones. To avoid the war. For Europe it was all so terrible."

"Yes, I suppose it was. At the time you put up with what happens. There is nothing you can do as a young boy. When it was time, I was called up in the army. Like the rest of them. I hate war, Jeanne. I hate talking about war. Let us drink your lovely bottle of wine and be happy. Cheers, as we English say. Meeting you has been wonderful. The paintings on your walls are so lovely. The smell of your cooking is making my mouth water. I'm going to like this America. What a beautiful day we have had together. It was much more than looking to make money."

"To life, Paul."

"You are right. This wine is wonderful."

Putting the half-full glass on top of the piano where Jeanne had laid a coaster, Paul continued playing. When he turned at the end of an early Mozart, composed when Mozart was ten years old, the small table in the room had been laid for supper. Jeanne had discarded her frilly apron. She was watching him intently. Getting up and sitting down at the table without being told, Paul placed his white napkin on his lap and smiled as Jeanne placed the first dish in front of him. On a small plate were four black mussels in a rich garlic and herb sauce. The mussels, still on the half shells, had been cut loose from their beds. Jeanne gave the dish a French name Paul had never heard. The food was perfect. A second, full glass of white wine was next to his plate.

Between sips of wine and eating their food, neither of them spoke. The fish course came with a white wine sauce sprinkled with fresh parsley. Stuffed chicken breast followed the fish. A pancake finished the meal with a glass of sweet, fortified wine in a small glass. The first bottle of wine had been finished. From outside the closed window came the sounds of neighbourhood, none of the noise intrusive. They were marooned in their own private island seated round the small table. A second bottle of white wine was put on the table with the coffee. Neither of them smoked. Feeling replete and happy, Paul smiled, waiting for Jeanne to start a conversation now the food was finished. There was no tension between them, only a soft, comfortable understanding encompassed by the memory of Paul's music and Jeanne's paintings on the walls.

Slowly, carefully, drinking small sips of their wine, Paul and Jeanne told each other the simple stories of their lives. Apart from Paul's father going down in the *Seagull* off the beaches of Dunkirk and Jeanne escaping France with her Jewish mother, pre-empting her chance of being snatched by the Nazis, their lives had comprised of simple families living through life loving each other. Paul talked of Jeremy his younger brother, not knowing what next to do with his life when his stint in the Royal Navy came to an end. Pierre and Marguerite were too young to worry about a career. Both had been born in America. The father taught French and mathematics at a school in Brooklyn. It seemed everyone Paul met other than Hank Westphal lived in Brooklyn. All Paul had for Hank was a phone number he had promised to use once he had settled into his digs.

When it was time for Paul to go home it was pouring with rain outside. They were both a little drunk on their friendship and the second bottle of wine. Jeanne suggested he slept on the couch in the lounge. When their eyes would no longer stay open from a long day and digesting their food, they went quietly to bed. Gently, Jeanne closed the door to her bedroom, leaving Paul alone on the couch with a pillow and two warm rugs. Then he was asleep, dreaming of life in the Isle of Wight where he had grown up.

Jeanne woke him in the morning with the smell of fresh coffee coming from the kitchen. They smiled good morning to each other, both knowing they had found a friend.

2

By the time Jeanne Pétain was painting Paul's antique vases into her paintings to show clients what their redecorated homes would look like, Frank Brigandshaw had it all worked out. The moment Frederick Whitaker came back from one of his extended trips, the caretaker of his block of flats in South Kensington gave Frank a call from the phone booth in Kensington High Street. When the old man left, leaving Connie free to visit their luxury flat in Chelsea, the caretaker rang again. Each phone call was worth a quid to Wilson the caretaker; Dorothy Dent only visited Brian Tobin when Connie paid her visits to Frank. In between the phone calls the game was on: girls, girls, girls. Six months into their jobs as paid studs they had built up a cash reserve of their own. The scams, like Wilson at the South Kensington flat where Frank had lost his virginity to Connie, were quite simple. Every supplier to the Chelsea flat loaded their bills, paying Frank the difference after Connie or Dorothy settled the bill. If they didn't, Frank changed the supplier.

"We want to walk out of here with money in our pockets," Frank had told Brian.

"How long will all this last?"

"Who knows? Anything is better than getting a job. We've got all the women we can handle. They all think this is our flat. That both of us are rich. Girls like rich men, Brian. Why they go to bed with us. If we'd stayed in our Soho rooms none of them would look at us."

"Do you even like Connie?"

"Come off it, Brian. Don't try that one. If Dorothy wasn't footing half the bills you wouldn't look at the old bag. She's the age of your mother."

"You make it all sound dirty."

"It is dirty. We're a couple of male whores."

"How can you say that?"

"Because it's true. Only a fool denies the truth to himself. Once you face the truth it doesn't matter anymore. It's like any business. A two-way trade. We get a smart way to live. The middle-aged ladies get a young stud. Everybody is happy. Money solves all mankind's problems."

"Sometimes I can't get it up for Dorothy."

"I just imagine I'm in bed with someone else. They're all the same when the lights go out. Use your imagination. On that bloody cattle ranch outside Bulawayo, even the thought of Dorothy would turn you on. Come on, the sun's shining. Time to torment my real father."

"Why don't you knock on his door?"

"I want to make him pay me to go away. All his friends must know by now I'm Connie Whitaker's young stud. Dorothy is in the theatre. The Honourable dabbles in the theatre. I want real money, Brian. Not a few bob from the wine merchant and the grocer or from getting the plumber to send us bills for imaginary leaks in the toilet."

To Barnaby St Clair, looking out of his window an hour later, the problem was quite simple. The boy sitting on the bench in the park on the other side of Piccadilly had not had a father's guidance in the crucial teen years a boy needed it most. Frank had been fourteen in 1940 when his mother took him to South Africa with the rest of her children. Harry Brigandshaw had stayed at his post at the Air Ministry for the duration of the war. For the rest of his growing up the only parental guidance for Frank had come from his mother. A lost teenager in a strange country with a chip on his shoulder. Apart from giving him money, there was nothing Barnaby could do, even had he wanted to. Like Connie Whitaker, he believed the worst thing anyone could do for the boy was give him money, stopping him having to fend for himself. It was the old story of the fish and the fishing rod. Frank had too many fish to eat without having to learn how to catch them himself.

"Is he on the bench in the park again, sir?"

"I'm afraid so, Smithers. With his friend today."

"What are we going to do, sir?"

"Nothing. If he comes to the door I am out as usual."

"He only came once to the door. The first time." Smithers, impartial as ever, the perfect gentleman's gentleman, never offered an opinion.

"Let me know when he's gone. I want to visit the new building site. With all the bombed out sites in London a new building going up will do them good. Boost the nation's morale. After the first euphoria of victory, everyone is really down. You have to think ahead to make money, Smithers. Can't sit on your bottom in the park all day. Even when the sun is shining."

"Would you care for a cup of tea, sir?"

"The answer to all problems. A cup of tea, thank you. He only just sat down. Be another hour. So predictable. I wonder what he's thinking?"

There was no point in blaming Connie Whitaker. If it wasn't her it would have been someone else. At the boy's age, he had not been much better. For years after being forced to resign his commission at the end of the Great War for embezzling mess funds, he too had lived off his wits, with the help of the boy on the bench's mother. The two of them had made quite a pair in Africa. Tina, young, gorgeous, overwhelmingly sexy, found the mark. A rich man out in the colonies. She then introduced Barnaby by his title. Barnaby suggested they all went to dinner in the hotel dining room. Then Barnaby tapped the mark for a loan. In front of the beautiful young girl, flashing him every signal of expectation, none of them ever refused. The patter was always the same when the bill for dinner was presented.

"Sorry, old boy. Must have left my wallet in my room. How much money have you got on you? Pay you back, old chap. The pater sends me my remittance at the end of the month. What a lovely evening we are having. Look, it may be a little tricky for me until the end of the month. Could you lend me a tenner?"

Thinking back, Barnaby had to smile. The boy on the bench was a chip off the old block. By the time the mark woke up in the morning with a hangover he had paid for himself, they were gone. A free meal and ten pounds in their pocket. Never once had he returned a penny. Even when he became rich. It was the principle. If the mark fell for taking the girl to supper with a friend, hoping for something more, like Connie Whitaker, they had to pay. It was the kind of mistake no man liked to brag about afterwards. In the following years, Barnaby had smirked at a couple of them. Never once had Barnaby asked for more than what was in the man's pocket. Good days out on the road. When he was young. When Tina could make any man make a fool of himself, her sex appeal so strong. It was their game together. Part of their excitement together. Making strangers pay for their livelihood. From Salisbury, Rhodesia, to the mining camp of Johannesburg in the old Transvaal, a way of life he remembered with nostalgia as he watched their son in the park.

"Thank you, Smithers. He's up to something."

"They always are, sir. I'll let you know when he's gone."

At the end of his day, on his way down Park Lane heading for home, Barnaby told the taxi driver to turn into the circular driveway of the Dorchester Hotel. The doorman in a long red coat opened the door for him. Barnaby slipped the man a ten-shilling note before turning to pay the taxi driver. Barnaby smiled to himself. Keeping up the appearance of wealth cost money, an expensive way to have the car door opened. It was all part of the pecking order. Society's way of making the rich stand out in a crowd. Without the ten shillings, the next time the man would have ignored him: the doorman had a memory for money like an elephant.

Having paid his dues and been accepted by the liveried doorman, Barnaby strode into the lobby of the hotel. A haunt of diplomats and film stars when they stayed in London, the Dorchester was arguably the most expensive hotel in town.

The first call of the day at his building site in the City showed a marked improvement in the structure of the foundations. When completed the office block would be a major component in the 'Genevieve Trust' of which he owned five per cent, the rest owned by his niece. It had amused Barnaby to build up Genevieve's wealth by buying up bomb sites during the war. By now, she was worth more than her father, the eighteenth Lord St Clair of Purbeck. The idea of the illegitimate daughter being worth more than Barnaby's brother tickled Barnaby pink. Barnaby would have done the job for nothing. He always said being the youngest son was a pain in the arse. All he had got was an 'Honourable' to put in front of his name.

The rest of the day had been spent in a music studio listening to the latest recording of an all-girl band who had a knack of jazzing up the classics for common consumption. Over the years he had slept with every girl in the band. Now they were friends. A lucrative friendship that appealed to Barnaby's sense of humour. Like Frank, Barnaby enjoyed making money out of his women.

Going up in the lift to the second-floor bar he was thirsty for the first drink of the day. Before he could reverse direction he saw Frederick Whitaker at the end of the bar talking to Dorothy Dent. They seemed to be arguing. Before the war, when Dorothy was the toast of London, she had appeared in a revue at the Windmill Theatre. Barnaby had put up the money for the show. Seeing a group of acquaintances, he joined the side of the group, away from the argument, hiding himself as he thought from Whitaker. One of the group bought him a drink. Another slapped him on the back. It was always expensive to join a group of frauds at a bar. Most of the time he found himself left with the bill. In London, friends were expensive but often useful. The first drink of the day went down without touching the sides, as Barnaby liked to say. There were no girls in the crowd. Only men. It was too early in the day for girls. The chitchat bounced around, hopefully making him blend in with the crowd, invisible to Whitaker. At a certain level of money in London, everyone knew everyone else. He had done business with Whitaker on more than one occasion. The man was a stockbroker. Whitaker was richer than most of his competitors, having made his big money, like Barnaby, from digging up information that affected the share price of public companies before it was common knowledge. After the '29 crash, the practice of insider trading had been declared illegal. By then Barnaby and Whitaker were out of that business, their money placed safely in government bonds, long before the bottom fell out of the stock market.

The tap on his shoulder came when Barnaby was enjoying his third whisky. Turning round, he came face to face with Frederick Whitaker, the old boy's whiskers doing a dance on his upper lip. The man was positively livid.

"Your son is fornicating with my wife." The man was drunk. The bar fell icily silent. Barnaby went as white as a sheet with cold fury. Only years of experience kept his temper under control.

"I don't have a son, old chap. Never been married."

"He's your son. The whole of London knows that. You put horns on Harry Brigandshaw when he was away in Rhodesia visiting his farm."

"I don't know what you are talking about."

Barnaby's eyes were laughing in the man's face. It was far more effective than getting upset.

"You are a rotter. So is your son." The man was now shaking with rage.

"Steady, old chap. Why don't you talk to your wife? If anyone has done anything wrong it sounds like your wife."

"Come along, Frederick."

"Thank you, Dorothy. How are you?"

"I'll take him home. Connie wants a divorce. Frederick won't give her one unless she agrees to go penniless. He's threatening to cite Frank as co-respondent."

"Now that won't do, old chap. Half each, I would say. Price of marrying a girl half your age. There's a price for everything, old chap. Sorry to hear about the divorce."

"It's all your son's fault."

"That I very much doubt, from what I hear. Please don't try a swing at me. You'll fall over. Look more undignified than you do already. Remember the good times, Frederick. It always helps."

"I want to talk to you."

"When you are sober, old chap. You know my number. Doubt if I can help... Sorry about all this, fellows. The round's on me. Johnston, make it doubles."

"What was he talking about, St Clair?"

"I have no idea. There are so many rumours in London."

"Do you have a son?"

"None I ever paid for."

Everyone at the bar laughed. The tension left with Dorothy Dent leading Frederick Whitaker by the elbow out of the bar.

Thinking back an hour later as he left the bar having paid for everyone's pre-dinner drinking, Barnaby thanked his lucky stars Dorothy Dent had never been one of his women. They had both thought about an affair when she was playing the Windmill, in between her marriages, before she received the obscenely large divorce settlement from her second husband. It had been a lucky break for both of them. Dorothy was good at divorce settlements. Connie Whitaker would come out all right. Maybe even Frank, if the woman was generous.

Trying to remember what dirt he had on Frederick Whitaker, Barnaby found his way downstairs into the lobby. The liveried doorman had a taxi waiting, the door open for him to step inside, leaving behind another ten shilling note on the way. Another man, about the same age as Barnaby, was waving an umbrella at the passing traffic down Park Lane, having had to walk the circular drive from the hotel. Barnaby had seen the man in the same second-floor bar. His two ten-shilling notes did not seem too expensive after all as the taxi passed the man on the pavement. Barnaby grinned and waved.

"I want to try a new restaurant. Something with a nice little bar. Do you have any ideas?" he asked the driver.

"Always got ideas, guv."

"Somewhere with ladies. Not whores. Ladies."

"Got you, guv." The taxi driver, an old hand by the look of him, knew the protocol of saving face.

Smiling, Barnaby prepared to let his evening unfold. All taxi drivers in London had their pet bars and restaurants where they were paid by the management for bringing custom. With a few drinks under his belt he was hungry.

"Thank the Lord I never married," he said, thinking of Frederick Whitaker. The glass partition between himself had now been closed. Buying the boys drinks in the bar was one thing. Paying half his fortune to an old flame he no longer wanted quite another. Marriage! That was expensive. Poor old Whitaker. How Frank could possibly want a woman the age of Connie Whitaker also crossed his mind. It had all to do with money. Everything in life was about money, all the twaddle about love merely a way of dressing up greed to make the human race seem civilised. From love to hatred in a few short years, or jealousy, in the case of poor old Whitaker, for a young whippersnapper like Frank screwing his wife.

Barnaby began to laugh. Half Whitaker's money so astutely saved from the 1929 stock market going to a woman young enough to be his daughter. He'd bet Connie had hung out for a wedding ring when she was young and desirable. Barnaby had seen Tina, Frank's mother, on more than one occasion since she brought the children back from South Africa. Not a spark. Not a peep. Absolutely nothing. All Tina's power over men had gone. All he would have had left by now was a nagging wife, frustrated with her own irrelevance once the children had grown up. Poor Harry!

Paying the taxi driver and walking into the Soho restaurant, Barnaby wondered which was worse: being Frederick Whitaker, or Tina

Brigandshaw. Both of them wanted something they could no longer have.

"And it happens to all of us in the end," he said to himself.

The small bar with the dim light was just what he wanted. Then he looked around. The one at the end of the bar was on her own. They would both pretend for the first part of the evening she wasn't a whore. Thankful of the dim light hiding some of his age, Barnaby walked to the bar stool next to the girl.

"Can I buy you a drink?"

"Why not?"

The taxi driver, bless him, had known exactly what he wanted despite all the polite disguise. Whores, always available, were a lot less expensive than a wife. Before or after the divorce. All Barnaby wanted was company. Company without complications.

By the time he reached his home he had forgotten her name. All he had given the girl was supper. When he had left with a smile she was back on the same bar stool where he had found her. All business had its ups and downs.

In the lounge of his four-storey Piccadilly townhouse, Smithers had left the whisky decanter next to the ice bucket on the sideboard. From his years roaming around the Arabian Desert in the army during the Great War, later in Africa, he drank whisky on ice with a splash of soda from the siphon. The night cap was a ritual passed down from his father. Yawning after the whisky, he went up to bed, happy with his day. If Frank hit the newspapers in the middle of a nasty divorce, Harry's name would be dragged through the mud. Likely, Harry would not worry. He was more Rhodesian than English.

"Better warn him in the morning what's going on. Poor Harry. And it's all my fault."

When he fell asleep, he dreamed of Tina. When they were young. When life was all fun.

When he woke before the dawn, it was to the premonition that someone was in his room. He could smell a woman's perfume. His whole body was satiated. Only when he turned on the bedside lamp did he fully comprehend it was all part of a dream. Smiling, Barnaby went back to sleep, the heavy curtains drawn against the noise of the traffic down in the street. When he opened the curtains at nine o'clock in the morning, the first thing he looked for was the bench in the park, on the other side of Piccadilly. There was no one sitting on the bench. Slightly disappointed, Barnaby went to have his bath.

"Let them all find out for themselves," he said, running the bath water, deciding in the fresh light of day not to call Harry Brigandshaw. "Always better not to put in my penny's worth." Then he began to sing. He had had just enough whisky the previous night not to give himself a hangover.

3

———

*J*ust before lunch on the following Friday morning a telegram
was delivered to the Brigandshaw offices in Holborn.
"Sign here please, miss."

The young man wore goggles on the top of his head from riding a
motorcycle. Katherine took the brown envelope, her stomach giving a
lurch. During the war telegrams were never good news. The death of her
husband in 1941 had been announced in a telegram. 'We regret to advise
the death of Captain Oliver Marshbanks in a Japanese attack on
Singapore.' With her eyes full of tears at the memory, Katherine signed
the man's small book. Only when he left the reception office did she slit
open the cable with a paper knife.

There were two further small offices: one for Harry Brigandshaw
when he was in town, the other for Kenneth Grahame when he wasn't
combing the countryside for antiques with Major Pilkington-Jones.
There was talk of taking another small office for the major if the new
business in America came to anything. The door to Harry Brigandshaw's
office was closed. Had been all morning which was unusual.

"What is it, Katherine?"

"A telegram, Mr Brigandshaw."

"What's he done now, Katherine? Can it get any worse?"

"Nothing to do with Frank. It's from America. Paul Crookshank has
sold a Gainsborough for fifty thousand dollars."

"Has he now? That's just over twelve thousand pounds at the pound/dollar exchange rate. Do you know what we paid for it?"

"Five hundred pounds."

"You'd better tell Kenneth. Get a message to the major. Please close the door on your way out."

Putting down the telegram, Harry went back to the problem on hand. All morning, he had been calling friends at the Air Ministry. Pulling strings. Doing everything in his power to have Frank called up for his National Service now he knew where the boy was living. The vitriolic and threatening letter from Frederick Whitaker had arrived in the post the previous morning at Hastings Court. Tina had read the letter first, leaving her in tears.

"At least we know where he is and how he's been living," Harry had said.

"This is just horrible, Harry. Will Frank have to go to court?"

"He will if Whitaker sues him for alienating his wife's affection."

"Who is the man?"

"A stockbroker. Much older than his wife. They don't have any children. I've heard of a kept woman. Never a kept man."

"It's not funny, Harry. He's my son. How old's the woman?"

"From tittle-tattle in the clubs, about twice Frank's age. Whitaker is now an old man."

"What are you going to do?"

"I'll think of something. What's he going to get from Frank if he sues him? It's a bluff. The whole of London will be laughing at Whitaker to his face."

"Frank's only just twenty-one. Do you think this horrible man can sue you because of Frank's lack of means?"

"Probably. Have to ask my solicitor. Let me find out what it's all about. I'll go up to the office tomorrow. Do you think the army knows Frank's address in England? All boys over eighteen are required to do two years' National Service in one of the armed services. A little military discipline should sort him out."

"Can't you get him out of the country?"

"I'd like to see that boy march up and down a square for eight weeks. They don't call it square-bashing for nothing. If he's any good he can go for a commission. He can argue with us but he can't argue with the army. Basic training corporals are known to be sadistic. They like breaking young men to do what they are told. How we win wars. Discipline. That'll sort out Frank."

"Why haven't they called him up already?"

"They didn't know he was back in England, most likely. Whitaker and his wife may have done us a favour. Cheer up. At least we know he's alive and well. I'm surprised Barnaby didn't know about this."

"What do you mean?"

"Come off it, Tina. Everyone knows he's Barnaby's son. Even Whitaker. Can't hide in the sand anymore. Since the war, morals have changed. Nobody cares a damn anymore about the sanctity of marriage. The country's going to pot. People do much as they like. Like Mrs Whitaker. People want to be free to make their lives the way they want. Some say it's progress!"

"Aren't you going to see him?"

"What he's going to hear from me is going to come from a military policeman. Dorian will have to do his National Service when he comes down from Oxford. So will Kim now he's eighteen."

"Will they have to fight?"

"Very unlikely. There's trouble brewing in Korea but that's America's problem. They may get a posting to Germany. To the British Army on the Rhine. It will make a man of him, if Mrs Whitaker hasn't done so already."

Chuckling, Harry had left his wife with the letter from Frederick Whitaker still in her hands.

When the phone on his desk rang in the afternoon it was his old comrade in arms from the Royal Flying Corps, still working at the Air Ministry in intelligence. Harry had introduced him to his wife.

"How's Sarah, Ding-a-ling?"

"You sound cheerful under the circumstances."

"Boys will be boys. Don't you remember? None of us are bloody saints. We all pretend to be saints. A bit self-righteous, don't you think, to criticise youth?"

"Can't get him in the air force. Only a small RAF National Service intake. The army are going to pick him up."

"When?"

"Monday morning. How are you?"

"Getting old."

"Aren't we all? That woman really looks after me, Harry. Can't thank you enough. It's so pleasant sitting talking to Sarah. We roam back over both our lives. Keeping each other's memories company. The family?"

"Fine, apart from Frank. I wish Tina could be more content with her life. She hates getting old. Kim will be gone soon from the house when they call him up at the end of the year. There will just be the two of us at Hastings Court. With the servants. Still can't persuade Tina to live on Elephant Walk. We don't need all these trappings of wealth. Sold our first painting in America for more than twenty times what we paid for it. Ridiculous. Why does speculation always make the money and not hard work? Something wrong with the system... Thanks for your help. Make it early on Monday. Don't want Frank getting wind of the Military Police and doing a bunk for Africa. If I don't sort him out now he's going to get himself into real trouble. All those years in Cape Town without my being around to knock some sense into him."

"Wish we had kids."

"Sometimes what you wish for isn't quite what you get."

"Takes all types to make a world."

"That it does."

Having tried to talk sense into Frederick Whitaker at the Dorchester Hotel, Dorothy Dent had spent the week looking for dirt. All rich men had something to hide. The pleasure of using Brian Tobin every now and again was only part of her reason. In bed, Dorothy liked men. Out of bed she found most of them only thought of themselves. Everything they did in their lives had themselves at the centre, they rarely thought of the wants or feelings of anyone else. Particularly the women in their lives.

"She's given you the best years of her life, Frederick. What did you expect, marrying a girl twenty-three years younger than yourself? You're an old man. Connie is still sexually active. She wants children."

"From a whippersnapper?"

"She wants comforting. Sexual comforting. It's been none of my business up to now. Can't you think of Connie for once in your life? Yes, Frank is very young. It probably suits both of them. You liked young girls when you were Connie's age. Why shouldn't Connie prefer young men? At that age they aren't bitter and twisted. Let her go with a fair share of the money. She's not expecting half your fortune. Just a good living. You can afford it."

"She's not getting a penny for committing adultery."

"Haven't you on your trips, Frederick? Not now, I understand."

"What do you mean?"

"You know perfectly well. You are no longer able to satisfy your wife. Connie can't go out and look for a job. She's never worked since she was nineteen. Once you two met you swept her off her feet and stopped her going to work as a secretary."

"She can still type."

"You're jealous! Or plain bloody mean. Or both. I'm trying to help both of you before all this gets nasty."

"It's your fault. You started it. Found that damn flat in Chelsea."

"I didn't, matter of fact."

"She can have a divorce if she walks away with nothing. Now look who's come in. That's the Honourable St Clair. By all the gossip, he's Frank's father. I'll sue the lot of them."

"Leave it alone, Frederick. Barnaby's with friends. You'll only make a damn fool of yourself."

"I'm going to talk to him."

"You know what's going to happen in the end, Frederick Whitaker. You're going to end up a lonely old man. No one will want to talk to you. Do the right thing now before it's too late. You haven't slept with your poor wife in years, probably. No wonder she's having an affair."

"On my money. She's paying for that boy with my money out of her allowances."

"So that's it, is it? You're plain jealous. Nothing to do with giving Connie some of your money for putting up with you for twenty years."

"She married me for love."

"Did you, Frederick? I know a lot about men. Too much. You're all selfish. You all take what you want and give bugger all in return."

"I'm going to talk to St Clair."

"Don't do it."

"Why can't you women mind your own business?"

It never did help to reason with a man who had made up his mind. As she had warned him, the incident with Barnaby St Clair had ended with Frederick making a fool of himself and her escorting him out of the bar.

After a week of phone calls and help from her friends, Dorothy knew one thing for certain: Frederick Whitaker was a sanctimonious hypocrite. Just because he was unable to get it up with any woman over the age of twenty-five, he was going to turn his wife into the female equivalent of a eunuch, or toss her out penniless.

THAT EVENING, while Kenneth Grahame and the major were celebrating their first sale in the Cavalry Club, not far away in Park Lane, close to the Dorchester Hotel, Dorothy Dent was opening the door to her flat to confront a rattled Connie Whitaker.

"We're not going to see them tonight," said Dorothy. "Or tomorrow night. There are legal aspects, Connie. You'd better come in."

"Shouldn't we warn Frank what's brewing?"

"You think Frederick is going to go around to Chelsea and confront him? I'd think two crocodile hunters are a match for your husband in a fisticuffs. The lease of the flat is in my name. Who I let stay in my flat is none of Frederick's business. We did think this all through when we started. There's no pleasure without pain. You look as if you need a drink. Has Frederick been hitting you? Your eyes are all red."

"He'd never do that. His code of honour treats women as fragile. As possessions. They don't like busting up their precious possessions. It's worse. He won't talk to me. Not a word except to say what he's going to do to Frank. Sits in the room with me in complete silence reading the paper. As if nothing has changed. Only his eyes tell a different story. If looks could kill I would be dead. What can he do to Frank?"

"Confront the father, I suppose."

"Which one?"

"He didn't get any change out of Barnaby St Clair. And he won't. A few people I knew in the theatre said it was never a good idea to get on the wrong side of the Honourable Barnaby St Clair. Under all that aristocratic veneer is a street fighter. You know they made him resign his commission at the end of the First World War? Stolen some money. The Honourable made all the money from scratch. You know the boys are loading the household bills and pocketing the difference? The wine merchant thought I was stupid. I grew up in the East End. My la-di-da accent came out of theatre school and a lot of practice. Like father, like son. Don't you worry about Frank or Barnaby. It's Harry Brigandshaw I worry about. He's a softy. Still friends with Barnaby after Barnaby screwed his wife. And he's rich. My solicitor can't tell me whether Harry is liable for the tribulations of his son. Legally, Frank is Harry's son. That much I have cleared up. Whether Frederick is going for Harry

Brigandshaw we will only find out. Sit down, Connie, before you fall down. I also need a drink. And don't worry. We are going to win. You are not walking out of this after twenty years empty-handed. At our age we need money more than ever to enjoy ourselves." Dorothy went to the sideboard and poured them both a drink. "Drink that. It's a stiff one."

"Shouldn't Frank get out and go back to Rhodesia? Before this all catches up with him? I can give him the boat fare."

"Why would he want to run away? It'll all blow over when Frederick sees sense."

"Frederick never sees sense unless it suits him."

"He's jealous. He's old. Had his day. Should sit in a rocking chair and smile back on his life. Revenge on Frank is all so petty. I can't find anything to put over him. He's too damn discreet. He has the odd young floozy but leaves no trace I can find. In business he's honest. We want someone to make him see you have given him so much for nothing in return. What's he going to do with all that money when he dies?"

"Don't wish that on him. The last twenty years haven't been all bad. I just want what's fair. Enough to live on. I don't want your kind of money, Dot."

"Why not? Money's security. Money's power. I'm going to use some of my money to get what's due to you. It doesn't have to stop with Frank and Brian. There are plenty of fish in the sea. As two rich divorcees we can still have lots of fun before we get too old."

"You think so? Don't you think we should at least give them a ring?"

"They've got what they want. They also have a price to pay. When we don't go round they're not alone. I'll bet that much."

"You think so?"

"You're too naïve. You trust people. Never trust anyone when it comes to money or fidelity. In their eyes we're a couple of rich old bags."

"He says he loves me."

"Of course he does. It's part of his job."

"Life is so complicated."

"Do you want to spend the rest of your life with Frederick and still find yourself out on the street?"

"He can't do that if we're married."

"Didn't he put his money in a Swiss bank before the war to hide it from whichever country won? What's to stop him hiding it from you? What do you know about money and Swiss bank accounts? We've got to get it out of him."

"It's all so mercenary."

"Too damn right it is. Swallow the rest and I'll pour you another one."

"You're so kind to me, Dot."

"You're my friend. We have fun. What are friends for?"

THEY HAD supper and then it was time to go. Staying the night was not an option. Connie knew it was wrong to make an important decision when she had had a couple of drinks. But she had made up her mind. Ruining her own life was bad enough. Destroying Frank in a vindictive court case would alienate him from his family for the rest of his life.

They both went downstairs to find her a taxi. Frederick was at home. Now it did not matter what happened with the rest of her life.

"What are you going to do, Connie?" asked Dorothy Dent. "You've gone very silent."

"The right thing. It was wrong to do what we have done with Frank and Brian."

"It was fun. Don't do anything silly."

"You've been a good friend."

It took Connie ten minutes to reach the flat in South Kensington. Walking along the corridor to the front door she watched the caretaker come out of the phone booth in the street down below. She had seen him use the phone booth more than once when she came home. Turning her key in the lock she pushed open the door. In the lounge Frederick was sitting in his armchair. The radio was on playing music. He neither looked up from his book nor said a word. Connie turned off the radio. She was standing over his chair. Without the alcohol she would have likely run out of the room. The one thing Connie hated most in life was having a scene.

"You can have your divorce, Frederick," she said, putting her hand on the back of his armchair. "I don't want any of your money. I shall get myself a job as a typist. Where I should have stayed in the first place. Marrying out of my station was always a bad idea. I was young. Stupid. Tomorrow I shall move out."

"I'm still going to sue the little bastard."

"I'm glad to hear you talk. We've had some good times. Let's both remember the good times and leave it at that."

"Has his father bought you off? To save face for his son?"

"Which father, Frederick? It seems Frank has two, neither of whom have said a word to me. I shall go as I came. Without a penny. The jewellery will stay in the box on my dressing table. It's all a mess, mostly my fault. I hope you enjoy your precious money for a long time."

"Where are you going to stay?"

"I haven't made up my mind. First, I will go to my mother. Then I will look for a job. Don't worry, I will use my maiden name again. It will be as though I never came into your life."

"All over a man who's just twenty-one. Really, Connie."

"Frank is only the symptom. You were never here. I was lonely. He gave me physical love. Made me feel young again. Made me feel wanted. Foolish me. You can't be what you are not. Neither can you. My solicitors will draw up an agreement. You will either get a divorce without a settlement or I will stay as we were the whole of this week. I will stay in this flat and say not a word to you. You in exchange for your inexpensive divorce will stop any proceedings against Frank Brigandshaw. My own life has been ruined by my marriage to you. I don't want to interfere with Frank's future. Underneath all this nonsense he's a very nice man. Not knowing who fathered you into this world is a heavy weight to bear growing up. Being different. I know. All your friends knew I was common. I am going to my room. Goodnight. The door will be locked. Have I made myself clear?"

"You're a stupid bitch."

"Probably."

"I'll sign it right now."

"What do you mean?"

"I have an agreement drawn up. Pretty much as you say. You get a divorce without dragging your precious Frank through the courts. In exchange you get nothing. You have been unfaithful, Connie. The church says a wife should remain faithful to her husband until death do us part. You broke the rules. Please go downstairs and ask the caretaker and his wife to come up. I'm sure they will be happy to witness our signatures for a small gratuity. Then it's over. You can go where you wish. You may take your jewellery. They were a gift."

"How kind of you, Frederick," Connie said sarcastically.

"I always consider myself a fair man. A man of good principle. In ten minutes this can all be over. Our lives can start again in separate directions."

"The caretaker was making a phone call from the booth in the street."

"Good. Then he's at home. Far better than involving our neighbours in our family squabble. It's all rather sordid what you have done. So there we are. Off you go. I'll have my solicitor's document laid out on the dining room table. Every page has to be signed by all four of us."

When it was over Connie went to her room. The separate room she had slept in the last week, ever since Frederick had told her what he was going to do to Frank. She was crying. Feeling sorry for herself. Completely alone.

In the morning, Connie Whitaker packed her suitcases. There was no sign of Frederick. The door to their bedroom was closed. Not so much as a note after twenty years. The man did not bother to say goodbye. The previous night, Frederick had given the caretaker a five-pound note to keep his mouth shut. On her way down to the taxi, with the taxi driver carrying her bags, the caretaker gave her a look of contempt. Without the Whitaker money behind her she was nothing.

"They say life begins at forty," she said to the taxi driver. "Now we shall find out."

With the feeling a great burden had been lifted from her shoulders, Connie gave her mother's address across the river in Lambeth. There was still money in her allowance account at the bank. Her jewellery was in her vanity case. The sun was shining. She felt young. As the realisation she was a free woman dawned, the future began to change. She was back in control of her own life. Bumping into Frank Brigandshaw in the Bond Street gallery had not been all bad. Brought her to her senses. Dorothy could cancel the lease on the Chelsea flat. If the boys had been skimming the tradesmen they too would have a little money. In her mind, she wished them well. Dorothy was right. It had been fun. And that was what life was all about.

When Frederick Whitaker heard the door close on his wife for the last time, the feelings of rage and righteous indignation had left him. He felt hollow. He had heard them talking as the suitcases were taken down to the taxi. He had stayed in the bedroom. The bedroom they had lived in for most of their married life. All the bravado had gone out of him. Truly old for the first time. Wondering what he had done.

There had been a change in her. That much he had known for

months. She was cheerful. Pleased to see him when he came home from his extended trips. The trips he had taken when he thought he no longer wanted his wife. Her company or her love. Physically he had lost interest years ago. Always the young women caught his eye. Only young girls he found in his travels brought him sexual arousal. Trying to make love to his wife became an ordeal he put off by staying away longer than he should. She had come from nothing when he married her. Over the years, the thought of his wife having an affair had never entered his mind. She was there when he came home, almost obsequious, always ready to please him. Polite and deferential to his important friends. A person they talked past, never at, smiling at her like an ornament much like any of their possessions that had been bought with money. Frederick tried to laugh. The laugh was hollow. It was ironic the caretaker witnessed their signatures on the document that got Connie out of his life without costing him half his hard-earned fortune. Before he found out about Frank Brigandshaw from the caretaker, Connie to Frederick was like anything else in his life, his interest in her fading with time. All she had been was a pretty face. For the last few years his friends no longer looked at him with envy. She was a wife like the rest of their wives. The ones who put the flowers on the table at their dinner parties at home. Like so many other possessions, he no longer bothered to look at with enthusiasm. Bluntly, he told himself, he had grown bored with her. There was nothing inside. Always the same sweet smile. No conversation of depth. She knew nothing of finances. Nothing of business. Nothing, really of life. She listened to what he said, letting it pass, deep inside her eyes a look of bewilderment, never one of understanding. Her trivial day bored him when she prattled on. Without the power of his wanting her body, his attention quickly fled from listening to her excited description of what had happened during her day.

Then he overheard the caretaker and his wife talking about him. They were laughing. Ridiculing an old man they called a fool. Talking of his wife's infidelity with a young man who paid them a quid every time the caretaker phoned to say when he was back in the flat. And when he went away again. Once he had seen Frank giving the caretaker money down the street, from the corridor of the flats. Only then did he see how young the man was, his rage taking hold of his jealousy, a jealousy that hadn't raised his ire in years. The man was a strapping youth with a ready smile. The type of leading man Frederick had seen on the stage. Not the type of man he expected to find as his wife's lover.

Finding out the rest of Frank Brigandshaw's story had been easy. The caretaker had a fondness for backing the horses. Frederick bribed him to tell him where the young man lived. The lease in Dorothy Dent's name had led to him confronting her in the Dorchester Hotel where Dorothy had thrown the truth in his face, making him drink more than was good for him. Then, by bad luck, in walked Barnaby St Clair, making Frederick fly off the handle.

Walking out of the bedroom he looked around what a few minutes ago had been their flat. Everything of Connie's had gone. She had left him not a trace. Only the last whiff of her perfume that was going out the window she had left open to air the room. Quietly, Frederick closed the window.

"So that's it," he said.

Lonely, wandering from room to room, Frederick looked for traces of his wife. It was over. He didn't know the address of her mother. Having taken his wife for granted for so long he was now on his own.

Not wishing to cry over spilt milk, Frederick bathed, shaved, dressed and went to his club. When he arrived at the East India Club the steward was opening the bar. With a large whisky in front of him, Frederick stared into the glass for his future.

"Anything wrong, sir?"

"My wife left me."

"Wish mine would. Nags me all day long. You want another one, sir?"

4

———————

After breakfast on Monday, the doorbell rang at the Chelsea flat. Frank Brigandshaw and Brian Tobin were hungover. With Frederick in town, they had thrown a party on the Saturday for their friends which ran on into Sunday. Friends had brought friends. Free drinks ensured the word spread. Half the girls they had never seen before. Many of them were young and pretty. The free booze brought the next crop of girls so they could pick what they wanted. Frank and Brian were particularly popular among the artists who liked to live in Chelsea. Most had no money. Artists always had time on their hands to go to parties. As Frank liked to say, 'life was all girls, girls, girls!'

"I'll go," said Frank. "You look terrible."

"What was her name?"

"Which one? Your bedroom resembled Piccadilly Circus, there was so much traffic."

Expecting to find one of their friends who had left something behind at the party, Frank put a grin on his face and threw open the door. On the threshold were two tall men in uniform. Both had red bands round their caps. Neither of them were smiling. The grin dropped from Frank's face. His stomach, queasy from too much alcohol the previous two days, gave an uncomfortable lurch.

"Are you Frank Sebastian Brigandshaw?"

"I am, as a matter of fact." Frank's voice was surprisingly quiet, his voice box restricted.

"We hereby serve you with your call up papers. In the envelope is a free rail pass to Aldershot Barracks. You are to report by eleven hundred hours tomorrow morning, this 22nd May, 1947. Should you not report on time you will be arrested. Our army prisons are most uncomfortable. Not a way to begin your two-year National Service. All aircraft and ships leaving the island have been given your name and the number on your passport. If you are found boarding a ship or a plane to leave the country you will be arrested. Under the National Service Act you were due to report for duty the moment you returned to England. You were then over eighteen years old and had not been granted exemption. At Aldershot you will be kitted out with a uniform after which you will complete your basic training. Do I make myself clear, Private Brigandshaw?"

"Perfectly, corporal. Aldershot Barracks by eleven o'clock tomorrow morning or I will be thrown in the cooler."

"Wisecracks lead to trouble in the army, private."

The two men were immaculately dressed, razor-sharp creases in their trousers, boots shone to look like glass, eyes with no sense of humour. They gave a smart about turn and marched away in unison, swagger sticks tucked under their left armpits at exactly ninety degrees.

Very slowly, Frank closed the door to their flat.

"Who the hell blew the whistle?" he said to Brian. "You were born in Rhodesia. Gets you out of it."

"Oh, I think they wanted you, Frank."

"Shut up smirking. If I go, the old girls won't want you in the flat."

"Why ever not? I can always find another stud from that lot on Saturday. Being kept by a rich woman beats starving in a garret. Most of the great artists in history have been kept by someone while they were painting. Van Gogh by his brother. Goes with the territory. Give Connie a chance to branch out."

"Oh, shut up! I've just been called up in the army. For two bloody years. What the hell am I going to do?"

"Report for duty on time, old son. Told you we should have gone back to hunting crocodiles. Think of the bright side. We had fun. All good things come to an end."

"Who told those goons I was here?"

"Government knows everything. Takes time to catch up. Matter of fact, I'm going back to Bulawayo. I'm a British subject. There's probably some law that can call me up. Wow, two years as a private in the army. Not a girl in sight. I heard once, they pay you four shillings a day and feed you swill from a bucket. Thirty iron beds to a barrack room. No heating in winter. It's how they turn you into a soldier of the king."

"You're enjoying this, aren't you?"

"Frank, I am. Think positive. There must be scams in the army. My vision of you in khaki uniform with your hair cropped springs to mind, old chap."

"Not even a bloody warning."

"When they want you they get you. Hadn't you better phone Connie?"

"Not with Frederick in town. You'll have to tell her. I'm stuffed."

"In more ways than one, old son."

WHEN THE MAIL was delivered to the flat the next morning, soon after Frank had begun his journey into the British Army, leaving Brian wondering what he was going to do without his friend, there was one long envelope addressed to Frank Brigandshaw. Ominously pushed through the letter box in the door, the address on the envelope was typed. Like the military policemen the previous day, no one was meant to know their address, other than friends sending them invitations to dinner parties knowing they always brought the booze.

Frank and Brian had soon found out the way to being popular was spending money among friends. Never being shy of spending it on good times. Taking the long envelope out of the wire cage attached to the inside of the front door, Brian held it with trepidation, wondering this time how he could send it on to his friend. At least, he thought, the letter was addressed to Frank so there was no requirement on his part to open the letter and find out what was inside. On the back was the printed name and address of a firm of well-known London solicitors. Had the missive been about the flat, Brian supposed it would have been addressed to both of them, or Dorothy Dent whose name appeared on the lease. The idea of running away to Rhodesia reared up again in his mind. If there was anything Brian hated most it was someone knowing something about him he did not know himself. In the bush it was the lions they had to worry about. Animals afraid of a big fire at night. The police and the letter were far more creepy.

About to go through his diary and look for Frank's replacement in the flat, Brian sat down on the couch. People were after them. Of that much he had no doubt. Then it dawned. It had to be Frederick. Frederick Whitaker had found out Frank was screwing his wife. His first thought was Dorothy. A Dorothy who only came round when Connie visited Frank. She had never given him her address or her phone number.

"You have what you want, Brian. It's better to keep our lives apart. Stop the tongues wagging. You know how nasty people can be. We don't want the tabloids tattling about Dorothy Dent and her toy boy. That's what they call you, Brian. No, we don't want that. I'll just come round with my friend and we'll all have fun together."

Like Frank, he was stuffed.

All Brian knew about his benefactor was her body, her acting career and her second husband's money. Enough for what he needed. When Frank had left with one suitcase to go to Waterloo railway station he had taken half their money as was his right. In one- and five-pound notes, Brian stashed just over five hundred pounds in an old sock, enough money to last him a year on his own. It was always Frank who thought up the scams, never himself. Brian preferred following another man's lead.

"What the hell am I going to do with myself?" he said, looking out of the window, the cold truth of life folding over him. They were a team. On his own he was nothing. At the thought he began to shiver.

An hour later, as he was making himself a cup of tea, the doorbell rang sending him into a panic. No one was expected. Frederick was in town. For a moment Brian thought of jumping out of the open window down onto the grass verge outside in front of the flats. The doorbell rang a second time. He could hear someone putting a key in the door from the outside corridor. Frozen with fright, just able to see the front door through the open door of the kitchen, Brian waited for justice to strike. They had done wrong. Vengeance was about to come at him through the door.

"Anyone at home? Frank? It's me, Connie. I've come to say goodbye. Where are you?"

"He's gone, Connie. They called him up to the army for his two years' National Service. He was going to give you a ring but Frederick's in town."

"He doesn't matter anymore. I'm giving him a divorce."

"There's a letter for Frank from a firm of solicitors."

"What's the matter, Brian? You're as white as a sheet."

"Don't worry about me."

"Show me the letter... Yes. Frederick's lawyers. Sent before I signed our little agreement. From now on, Brian, I'm as poor as a church mouse. Came round to tell Frank. You'll have to go at the end of the month."

"I can find you another toy boy. That's what Dorothy calls us."

"Wasn't there more than that, Brian?"

"I suppose so."

"We all became friends. We laughed together. Had our own private jokes. Was it only about money for you and Frank? I hope not. That would make me sad."

"Aren't you going to open the letter?"

"You do that. And read it. It won't be very nice. I'll have some of that tea while you read the letter. I'm back with my mother in Lambeth. Where I came from on the other side of the river."

"What are you going to do?"

"Learn to type again. I have found a job in a typing pool. Three hundred pounds a year in the City. Enough to live with mother. Help her a little. She hated Frederick. Wouldn't take a penny from me that came from Frederick. The cockneys are very proud people, but you're a Rhodesian. What would you know about cockney pride? Frank's turned my world upside down."

"And Frank's too. The Military Police came round yesterday. Said if he didn't report to Aldershot Barracks by eleven o'clock this morning they'd throw him in jail. About now, your Frank should be joining the army."

"Poor Frank. Was it all my fault?"

"Takes two to tango."

"I suppose it does."

"Oh, my God. They're going to sue Frank and Colonel Brigandshaw. A copy of this letter has been sent to Hastings Court. They must have posted the copy there before they posted this one. Now it makes sense."

"Why are you laughing, Brian?"

"Frank never went home. Never contacted them after we came back from Rhodesia. The copy of this letter is the first they heard of him. The colonel must have reported his son to the authorities for avoiding his National Service, to get him out of Frederick's way."

"Can we have a drink, Brian?"

"I think we should. We can raise a glass to Frank as he goes into barracks. What's going to happen, Connie?"

"Nothing. Frederick has withdrawn the case. Got what he wanted. Kept his money. You see, most people think life is just about money, Brian. It isn't. If this is the last time we ever speak to each other, remember that. There has to be friendship. Maybe not lasting love. There just has to be lasting friendship or life isn't worth a damn."

5

When Paul Crookshank flew back from America at the end of June, he went straight to his old room in Holland Park. He had paid Mrs Bigglesworth three months' rent in advance before he sailed for America. After the luxury of the small hotel in Brooklyn, where his meals were cooked for him and eaten in the residents' dining room, the two gas rings in the alcove of his room reminded Paul how much he had missed a good old-fashioned English stew. After being greeted by Mrs Bigglesworth as a long-lost friend, he had walked to the Portobello Road market where the vegetables on a Saturday afternoon were sold off cheap before they spoiled, perfect for a stew. With a bag of bones from the butcher, Paul took his prizes home and started the cooking. Frugal habits, he told himself, died hard. All the profits he had made selling antiques in America with the help of Jeanne Pétain were only on paper. The question of how much profit was going to be distributed had not yet been discussed with Harry Brigandshaw. His expenses had been paid in America along with the same salary, in dollars, he had received from the Contingency Insurance Company. All the money from the sales would go to buying more stock as quickly as possible, which was why Paul had come back to England. The problem was no longer selling. The size of the business was limited by how much stock the company could buy in England for the insatiable American market. Jeanne's knack of making an antique vase or a chair the focal point of her painting had seen the contents of the first three crates from the SS *Kentucky* sell out within a month of Paul's arrival in America. Jeanne painted the impression of a room as she foresaw it in watercolour, doing each quickly as she moved from one prospective client to another. Everything they sold had to be searched for in the old homes in England. The rest of Paul's summer was to be spent with Kenneth Grahame and the major in the five-tonne lorry touring the length and breadth of Britain, buying from the landed gentry what had been in their families for centuries. Tinus Oosthuizen had said they were doing everyone a service: willing seller, willing buyer. Paul hoped so.

Kenneth and the major were away on a trip to Scotland, using the summer months to penetrate north as far as possible. Harry Brigandshaw was at Hastings Court. Only Katherine was going to be in the Holborn office on Monday morning, giving Paul time to see his mother in the Isle of Wight and catch his breath.

On the Friday night, his clarinet in its case tucked under his arm, Paul took the Tube to Oxford Circus on his way to 101 Oxford Street and the Benjie Appleton jazz club where everything had started. In a phone call to Kenneth Grahame earlier in the week, they had arranged to meet at the club the same day Kenneth arrived back in London from his trip. Work, for Paul, would start in earnest on Monday morning.

Looking around, there was no one he knew. Kenneth had not arrived. Paul put the clarinet case on a table and sat down. Some of the band were up on the stand. The drummer waved at him.

Sitting on his own at the table waiting for the band to start playing, Paul realised for the first time since leaving New York how much he missed Jeanne. They had kept everything strictly to business. The success of the venture depended on their co-operation. Becoming lovers was out of the question.

"Hello, Paul. You look far away. Glad you got the same table. Never would have found you, the place is so packed. Haven't they started playing?"

"Not yet."

"Got your clarinet, I see. Did you take it to America?"

"There was a piano. In Jeanne Pétain's apartment. How was your trip?"

"Filled the lorry again. Everyone in this island is broke after the war. Some good stuff. Five paintings. No Reynoldses or Gainsboroughs this time, I'm afraid. Anyone you know?" said Kenneth Grahame looking around. "Thought we might bump into Beth and Nancy. Close to their flat. Here comes Appleton. Talk again at the end of the set."

It was traditional New Orleans jazz, the music Paul liked best. With his foot tapping under the table to the rhythm, his mind came back to the present, his only world the music and the people all around, a blur of sound and movement. All the tension drained out of his body. All the worry of the last weeks hoping his venture had taken off dispersed with the music. The jazz was like immersing his mind in a warm, safe haven where no one else was allowed. As the set went into its second half, Paul escaped completely into the music, unaware of anything else. Only when it stopped did he remember where he was, at a table with Kenneth Grahame, his clarinet case waiting for him unopened.

"How little time it takes to drift apart. That weekend at Hastings Court is another world. Did you see them just now, Paul? They were both looking at their men the way they once looked at us. Probably for the best. The boss's daughter and all that nonsense."

"Can't see them, Kenneth. So many couples are coming off the dance floor. Yes. Nancy. My word, she waved. I'm afraid they're not coming over. A brave new world. From one to the other. In the old days by taking her to bed I would have been expected to marry her. To spend the rest of my life with a girl who picked me up at a jazz club. Maybe the new world is better. Taking what we want and passing onto the next one. How strange. In ten years' time I probably won't remember her name."

"Beth and I stayed just friends. Whatever might have been implied. We'll remember them if the business carries on the way it's going. Memories for all the wrong reasons. Why don't we get out of here and go across the road to the pub. Unless you want to play?"

"Another day. You're right. Soured the evening. How do we ever know which is the right girl to marry?"

"We never do. There isn't one, I suppose. Most married couples I've seen make the best of what they've got. Flitting from one to the other doesn't find happiness. The major sends his regards. We've travelled thousands of miles together. He never bores me. Always has a story. What a full life that man has lived. Says he's enjoying life just as much now as when he was twenty."

"Come on. They're not coming over. Let's go before it becomes embarrassing. We only have to meet Beth's father in the office."

"We can have a good chinwag without all the noise. I'm so tired from all the travelling I don't think I could dance if I tried. Good to see you again, Paul. You never know. Maybe another time. We'll wave at them as we go out. They were going in the direction of the door to get to their table. Make everything look perfectly normal. I rather think we can both afford to waste a little money on the entrance charge now we have jobs. You were right. The Old Etonian tie still works. For the moment. The people we buy from still live in another world. The old world of a man's word is his bond. They think just because I went to Eton I can be trusted."

When they went past the table where Beth and Nancy were sitting with a group of men, the girls did not look up. Only as they were passing did Beth see who they were and smiled. Then they were gone past to the stairs that led out of the basement club.

Outside, they crossed Oxford Street and went into the pub, neither of them saying a word. Another period in Paul's life had come and gone. It made him think again of Jeanne Pétain. And her occasional lover. 'Paul, meet Rudy,' she had said. How they had met. Not much different to standing in a queue with a clarinet case waiting to go into a club.

"You want a pint of bitter, Kenneth?"

"Why ever not, old boy?"

WHILE KENNETH and Paul were drinking their pints of beer in silence, neither of them bringing up the subject of Beth and Nancy, Frank Brigandshaw was lying on his back in bed looking at the ceiling. The mattress had a lump just under the small of his back. He could feel the hard springs of the iron bed through the thin mattress. It was getting dark. Lights and music were not allowed in the hut after nine o'clock. Frank, feeling thoroughly uncomfortable, was contemplating a dilemma.

The Sunday before, the corporal in charge of giving them hell – an unhappy man with a sadistic bent, perfect for his job in an army basic training camp – had come into the hut with a smirk on his face. Sunday was the only day they were not required to march up and down the big square with the perimeter stones all painted white by some poor sod on jankers. They had all just come from the chapel, no one bothering to ask any of them if they believed in God. The chapel was multi-denominational. Zachariah Cohen had kept his mouth shut and done what he was told. Arguing with authority had a habit of leading swiftly to pain. As Corporal Snodgrass entered the hut, all thirty inmates sprang to attention.

"I am obliged to ask if any of you matriculated from school. Captain Marsden is interviewing the War Office Selection Board, after which you will go through a two-day obstacle course to find out whether you have the qualities to be an officer. If you are selected, you will be given a forty-eight-hour pass in London where the bromide we put in your tea will keep you out of trouble with the ladies. A second lieutenant, National Service, I am instructed by Captain Marsden to tell you, receives twenty-one shillings a day. More than five times your pay as a private. Those who qualify will take one step forward. Now! ... Brigandshaw and Cohen, I might have thought as much. Eight o'clock sharp in the captain's office tomorrow morning. Parade dismissed!"

In the captain's office the next morning Frank's dilemma became apparent as he stood to attention in front of the officer's desk.

"Do you have your school certificate, Brigandshaw? You must have known to apply for officer training you require proof of your education."

"I was in a hurry to report."

"Explain yourself, soldier."

Briefly, Frank described the visit of the Military Police.

"Why did you not report of your own accord?"

"I was on holiday. From Rhodesia. With my Rhodesian schoolfriend. We were at school together in Cape Town where we matriculated from the Diocesan College. A school of high reputation. Each year they are allowed to put up two of their students for a Rhodes Scholarship. Cecil Rhodes was prime minister of the Cape before the Boer War. My cousin was a Rhodes Scholar."

"What has this to do with your school certificate?"

"The certificate is likely in Cape Town. I was trying to explain that a matriculant from Bishops, as the school is better known, is welcome at Oxford. The British Army, I hope, would think the same of my qualification."

"Surely they sent it to your home?"

"Possibly. Probably. In 1944, when I had written my matric, the school allowed us to go on holiday before the end of term. Once the exams were out of the way, they had no more use for us. My family were returning to England, my mother, brothers and sister. Tobin and I decided to go to Rhodesia. His father has a ranch outside Bulawayo."

"Were you running away from being called up to go to war? The war was still on."

"I never thought of that, sir," lied Frank. "We wanted to go hunting in the bush while we waited for the results of our examination. From Bulawayo we went north to the Zambezi Valley to hunt crocodiles."

"Did you now?"

"Sort of lost touch with civilisation for a couple of years. You cut the belly skin off the croc, salt it and dry it in the sun. The Italians make the crocodile skin into shoes. When we made some money we came home on holiday. We had to shoot a lot of crocodiles to make the boat fare back to England."

"So you never received the results of your matriculation examination? You may have failed and be wasting my time to get off morning parade."

"Doubt it, sir. I was top of the class. If I'd stayed around they might have sent me to Oxford like cousin Tinus. The bush sort of gets you, sir. We were in a world of our own. Just Tobin, myself and the animals."

"Where are your parents?"

"In Surrey. We have a place in Surrey and a tobacco farm in Rhodesia."

"They must have known your results. Likely, they have your certificate of matriculation from this school I have never heard of."

"I didn't keep in contact. Sort of fell out with the family by going 'bush'. All that money on education wasted, if you see what I mean."

"Then phone them. They must be on the phone. Your father can post your certificate."

"Rather not, sir. I'll just have to stay a private."

"Give me their number. You do know your father's phone number?"

"In the book. Colonel Brigandshaw. He was Royal Flying Corps, never in the army. Air Ministry during the war. Sent the family to Cape Town out of harm's way and stayed in London himself. Intelligence."

"I'll give him a ring myself. Private Brigandshaw. There sounds more to this than meets the eye."

"There always is, sir."

"Are you a good shot?"

"I can take the eye out of a running impala at two hundred yards. We lived off the bush. Bullets were expensive and a long way to go to replenish."

"You might like to shoot for the army at Bisley. You have heard of Bisley despite living in the bush? Can't imagine many of our sharpshooters are that good."

"I have, sir. Most famous shooting range in the world. Otherwise we can write to Cape Town. Colonel Brigandshaw may not wish to help."

"What have you done?"

"I didn't come home. May I ask an impertinent question, sir?"

"Go ahead."

"Are you sure who your father is? Because I am not sure of mine. Once I left school I wanted to go out on my own. Why I did not come home. Asking my school for the certificate would be better."

"I'll ask the colonel. Yes, I know my father. He was killed in the war. Came through the first war without a scratch. He was in Singapore when the Japs came across the causeway from Malaya."

"I'm sorry, sir."

"You're lucky to have a father."

"Which one? That is the question. It's all a bit of a muddle."

Lying on his back staring at the ceiling in the half dark of dusk, Frank played it again through his mind what to do. So far, the captain had not come back to him. He was still not on the detail going up to Hornchurch for the two-day selection course. The thought of two years on four shillings a day was depressing. So far, not one scam had come to his mind to make any money. If nothing happened by Monday, he would have to phone his mother. Likely, she would tell him to go to hell.

Still translating twenty-one shillings into pints of beer in the Officers' Mess at ninepence a pint, Frank let his mind drift back to Rhodesia and their camp on the banks of the Zambezi River. They should never have left the bush. That was their mistake. As Frank dozed off to sleep he hoped the captain believed him when he had said he had not been avoiding getting his head blown off in the army when in the December he had turned eighteen he had become liable for call up. The bit about Bisley being the most famous shooting range in the world seemed to have worked. Frank, in blissful ignorance, had never heard of the place before it was mentioned by the captain. Only then did he think of Connie before he finally fell asleep.

The next day it all came together. Cohen was told he was going to WOSB at the same interview they told Frank. Bishops had returned a cable confirming his examination result. Frank never did get to ask Captain Marsden if he had phoned his parents.

For a man who had spent years living off his wits, convincing the selection panel at Hornchurch was a walk in the park. By the end of the two days and the start of two days' leave, he had been selected to go to the Officer Cadet Training Unit, back, as it turned out, at Aldershot. At the end of the course when he was commissioned it was going to give Frank pleasure making Corporal Snodgrass give him a salute.

Going straight to the flat in Chelsea, Frank rang the doorbell. Again and again. The next door neighbour finally put her head out into the corridor to see what the noise was about. In frustration, Frank had begun banging on the door.

"Oh, it's you. Your friend's gone back to Rhodesia. The flat's up for rent. What are you doing in uniform?"

"Have you seen the girls?"

"Your fancy women? The one who is an actress? Don't think we didn't know what was going on."

"Where are they?"

"You tell me, young man."

The woman stood back inside her flat and slammed her door in Frank's face.

"The late-night parties must have got to the old bag."

"I heard that!"

Smiling, Frank walked away down the corridor of the block of flats. He had two days' leave with nothing to do. Zach Cohen had gone home to his parents. 'Poor old Brian, out on his neck,' he said to himself. After two days running around an obstacle course, the bromide in the tea had worn off.

"Connie, you don't know what you're missing."

Then Frank began to whistle, feeling pleased with himself. He was going to be an officer in the army. The two years no longer looked so long.

PART 3

MAY TO AUGUST 1949 – FOR LOVE OR MONEY

1

———————

Frederick Whitaker died a friendless old man the same month Second Lieutenant Frank Brigandshaw finished his National Service. Before he died, Frederick had written his own obituary and sent it with a cheque to the *Telegraph* with confirmation of his death from the hospitals in London where he had gone to die. It was the last physical act of his life before the cancer killed him.

Over breakfast at Hastings Court, Harry Brigandshaw read the glowing obituary. He and Tina had not said a word since they sat down to table. Using the excuse of Harry's snoring they had slept in separate bedrooms for the past two years, ever since Kim went into the air force to start his National Service. With Beth in her South Kensington flat with Nancy Longhurst, Dorian at Oxford, they had been left on their own.

Harry folded the newspaper and passed it to his wife.

"He did us a favour, Tina. I've often found my worst enemies have done me the biggest favours. Frederick Whitaker has died."

"He wasn't an enemy."

"Would have been without my sending Frank into the army."

"Isn't he due out soon?"

"Out already by my calculation."

"Thank God Kim never flew. Couldn't stand another son of mine becoming a pilot. Every morning I wake up I think of Anthony. He would have been married by now. We would be grandparents with something to do. If Beth doesn't do something about her life soon she'll be on the shelf."

"She's enjoying herself. She's still friends with Paul Crookshank so I get to hear a little of what is going on. Young men can't afford to get married anymore. If they do, they both have to work and can't have children. What's the point in Beth getting married if she can't have children? Might as well have fun while she's young."

"Wish I was young again."

"Don't we all? I haven't finished reading the paper. I wonder who gets Whitaker's money. He was stinking rich. So far as I know from what was said in the City he doesn't have any close relatives. No brothers and sisters. He was the only child. His wife never had any children."

"What happened to his wife after the divorce?"

"Took a job as a typist. Still typing as far as I know. Works for an insurance company in the City I think. Once Frank was out of her life I took no further interest."

"Is Paul interested in Beth? He's got enough money to get married."

"Just good friends. She was more interested in Kenneth Grahame in the beginning."

"Has he got enough money to get married?"

"Only Paul has shares in the business. It was all his idea. The rest of them work on commission. Kenneth gets a salary."

"Doesn't his family have any money? Didn't he go to Eton?"

"Not a penny. None of my business, really."

"Would be as a son-in-law."

"Beth will marry when she's ready. It's a whole new world for the young these days. They have a language of their own. Don't understand a word of it."

"Pass me the marmalade."

"What are you going to do today?"

"Nothing. Absolutely nothing. Same as yesterday and tomorrow."

"You should find yourself a hobby," said Harry, going back to reading his newspaper, not looking at the glare he knew would be directed at him by his wife. Then he sighed. There was nothing of interest on the sports page.

"We could always go back to Rhodesia," he said, putting away the paper.

"Don't so much as think of it. Anyway, it will be ruled by blacks before long."

"Probably. The white farmers will have something to say. They've put all their lives into digging those farms out of the bush. My guess is Frank will go back to Africa. Where else is he going to go if he doesn't want to talk to us? Barnaby hasn't heard a word."

"Why should he?"

"He's the boy's biological father."

"Don't let's start that all over again."

"I'm off to the City. Have a nice day."

"You really don't listen, do you?"

THAT EVENING, while Harry Brigandshaw was trying to think of a way that would take his wife out of her constant unhappy state of mind and coming up blank, Frank Brigandshaw was having dinner with Zachariah Cohen in Zach's parents' house in Sloane Square. Mr and Mrs Cohen were on a Mediterranean cruise with four big clients of Cohen Wells, off the coast of Monte Carlo. Zach had told Frank the advertising business was all about buttering up the managing director of Cohen Wells's clients, the big London advertising agency in Fleet Street, close to the newspapers where most of the money was spent. Mr Cohen himself had told Frank half the money spent on advertising was money down the drain. That the trick was to muddy the water for the client so he never found out which half he was wasting. No one really knew which campaign was going to work until the money was spent. It was the kind of business that appealed to Frank. Getting gullible people to spend vast sums of money, not knowing what they were getting, with no risk to the agency if it flopped other than losing the account. Advertising accounts went round and round, Frank was told. So even that was not a problem. In army terms, there was no redress of grievance. No way of suing Cohen Wells for wasting their clients' money. The two of them had the large dining room to themselves, the servants having left them to their coffee and Mr Cohen's Napoleon brandy. Two old friends savouring their freedom from the army after wasting two years of their time. Frank was broke apart from the last of his army pay. All he had left was one rich friend which he was making the most of, on the principle that rubbing shoulders with money might make some rub off.

"Dad's asked me to ask you a favour, Frank. What did you think of Cook's food?"

"Perfect. Haven't eaten that well since last time I dined in this very room."

Surprised there was any favour he could do for Mr Cohen, Frank poured himself a third snifter of brandy without being asked and thought of Connie Whitaker. Or, as he admitted to himself, the death of Frederick Whitaker reported in the *Daily Telegraph* that morning.

"Why the silly sod couldn't have died two years earlier beats me."

"What are you talking about, Frank?"

"Never mind. What's the favour?" Frank was getting drunk and pulled himself together. A rich friend was never to be told about the likes of Connie Whitaker and Frank's life before going in the army.

"Your father has launched a brand of cigarettes. American and Rhodesian tobacco mixed. Selling his own tobacco straight to the public in pouches of pipe tobacco and packets of cigarettes. There was an article in the *Daily Mail* under the Horatio Wakefield byline. Your father has lived an interesting life. Growing up in Rhodesia. Famous pilot in the First World War. Twenty-three kills. I was impressed."

"What's this got to do with me? You know I don't talk to him. My own father shopped me. How they got me in the army. Who else would have told the Military Police I was back in England?"

"Did you a world of good. Didn't you enjoy the army once you got your commission?"

"No, I did not. Bloody waste of two good years."

"Father would like you to ask your father if Cohen Wells can have a shot at your father's advertising account. Cigarettes are all in the advertising. More than any other product, according to Father. The bigger the advertising spend, the bigger the sales in exactly the same proportion. Good advertising makes cigarettes a licence to print money."

"I haven't spoken to any of them since Mother left Cape Town in 1944. When I went up to Rhodesia with Brian Tobin."

"I didn't know that, Frank. That is a shame."

Deliberately, Zach moved the brandy bottle out of Frank's reach. Frank noticed his friend's attitude had changed. The smiling eyes were no longer smiling at him. Only then did Frank realise what was going on. They were using him, instead of the other way round. All along Zach had been more interested in the business potential of the father rather than the son. Containing the mirth that built up inside of him, Frank changed his tack, deliberately pushing away his balloon glass slopping with brandy. Living off his wits before going in the army had attuned Frank's mind to shift gear when the red flags went up.

"Quite an article, old boy," said Frank who had also read the piece in the *Daily Mail*. "Dad made a fortune during the war in America. Tender Meat Company is a subsidiary of Brigandshaw Oosthuizen Inc. The Oosthuizen is my cousin Tinus. Rhodes Scholar. Also a fighter pilot. They're getting big in antiques in America. The tobacco idea came from the States where we have an interest in a tobacco plantation with Cousin George in Virginia. Elephant Walk in Rhodesia is building up to be one of the largest tobacco farms in the country. With Britain short of American dollars after the war, buying Rhodesian tobacco in sterling makes sense. Tobacco is in short supply outside America. The new cigarette company should make a fortune. Guaranteed supply of raw product from the old family farm. I'm sure Tinus has thought of advertising. Some of the biggest ad firms are in the States. I could ask Tinus. He's the president of the company. He and I are good friends."

When the bottle of Napoleon brandy came back within reach, gently pushed across the table by Zach, Frank knew he had saved the conversation, along with his fruitful friendship that had started with Zach at the beginning of his National Service, the day Corporal Snodgrass told them they could apply for commissions. There was always a price for everything, Frank told himself. A price for friendship. A price for dinner in a swank townhouse in Sloane Square.

"What about your father, Frank? He's only just down the road, so to speak."

"He's not the one to speak to."

"The newspaper article seemed to think so."

"Cheers, old boy. I'll see what I can do. Don't know anything about business. Why would Father or Tinus take any notice of me?"

"All we need is an introduction. To give Cohen Wells the chance to make a presentation for an advertising campaign. Your father has nothing to lose if he doesn't like what we say. Cheers, old boy. Why don't we leave the dinner table and go into the lounge? Thought we'd go on to a nightclub."

"Can't afford nightclubs, old boy. You know what I was paid as a second lieutenant. My father has always said we children can have anything we want when we earn it ourselves."

"Evening's on Cohen Wells. If you get that introduction, you'll have earned your jolly good evening out. The night's but a pup."

"Are you joining Cohen Wells, now you are out of the army?"

"Yes, I am. You'll be doing me the favour, Frank. A favour I won't forget. Have you decided what you are going to do, yourself?"

"Not yet. I still have a little left over from the army. Plenty of time. Are there going to be any girls in this nightclub?"

"Of course there are. Lots of them, Frank. Shall we call one evening on the town a down payment, if you get my drift?"

"You really are a good friend, Zach. I don't know what I would do without you."

With the immediate crisis out of the way, Frank began to relax. He had something they wanted, which was a surprise. With luck he could string his army buddy along for weeks, if not months. Then the thought came back to him again even stronger. What had Frederick Whitaker done with his money? Had he left any to the woman who had been his wife for twenty years? All he had heard of Connie since being forced into the army was a belated letter from Brian Tobin from the Tobin family cattle ranch outside Bulawayo. Once Frank had received his commission he had written to Brian in Rhodesia, with a 'Please forward' on the envelope. Only after Brian replied did Frank find out the depth of the shit he had been in when the Military Police banged on his door. Which was how he knew his legal father had shopped him to the Military Police. How Connie had given her husband a divorce to save his neck. With all the anger at the origin of his birth again boiling up inside of him, the thought of his legal father being forced to pay money for his adultery was what rankled with him the most. From a man who had lied to him all his life, Frank wanted nothing. Feeling lost, broke and a little drunk, it was only when they reached the nightclub that Frank made up his mind. He was going to look for Connie Whitaker. Few people in Frank's life had ever done him a favour. Not even his best friend.

Zach was right. The club was full of girls. Now back in his element, his confidence returned. He was good at chatting up women. There was a group of girls out on the town. One of them Frank recognised from the parties in Chelsea, when Frederick was in their South Kensington flat keeping Connie at home.

"Why, it's Frank Brigandshaw!"

"Tessa, how are you? How goes the painting? I want you to meet a friend of mine, Zachariah Cohen."

"Where've you been? One day you were there, the next day you were gone. Where's Brian?"

"In Rhodesia. It's a long story. They called me up to the army to do National Service. King and Country. You know the stuff. Just got out. You're a sight for sore eyes, Tessa."

"So are you. These are my friends. I sold a painting. This is my treat. Zach. Can I call you Zach?"

"My friends call me Zach."

"Wonderful. We're all artists."

"Let me buy you all a drink."

"Now the man's talking. Come and sit next to me while Frank tells us what's been going on in his life. What have you done with that lovely flat of yours and Brian's in Chelsea? What parties!"

Frank, having given Tessa a wink behind Zach's back, knew his evening was under control. He and Tessa understood the business. If he couldn't get Zach an advertising account, he could get him girls. There was always a way of getting rich men to spend their money.

The Mayfair was half full. At a table away from the bar where Tessa and the girls were clustered, all their attention now on Zachariah Cohen who was buying them drinks, Frank recognised Paul Crookshank and the blighter. With them were two girls. As he had grown a moustache in the army, neither of them recognised him. Paul looked prosperous, not the man who played the clarinet in a jazz club. The Mayfair was a big jump up from the Benjie Appleton jazz club with its shilling entrance fee. On the bandstand was a quartet playing a love song with a singer. The singer wore a long black dress, with only her toes peeping out the bottom. Her shoulders were bare, her small breasts prominent. The girl could sing, whoever she was. Having found himself in better company than he expected, Frank sipped his brandy and soda sparingly. From experience, he knew it was impossible to chat up good-looking girls when drunk. All of the girls with Tessa were pretty. When Paul Crookshank stood up to dance, Frank noticed the girl with him was not even five foot tall. The girl reminded Frank of an elf. Sitting down she had looked no different to the rest of them. The blighter had stayed with his girl at the table. The last time Frank had seen the blighter he was dancing with Beth. It was a pity he had fallen out with his sister, asking which one of the two she was screwing the night he invited them to dinner. Without the slap in the face that followed he could have asked her to ask their mother to get Zach an appointment with the new tobacco company. Making enemies had never proved profitable. The small girl with Paul was exquisite. The way she used her hands on the way to the small square they called a dance floor suggested the girl was not English. English girls never used their hands when they talked. Curious, Frank asked one of the girls to dance. Tessa was still flirting with Zach, having likely worked out he was rich.

On the floor, Frank danced as close to Paul and the small girl as possible. Then he heard her accent. A strange mix of American and French.

"Aren't you Frank Brigandshaw? I work for your father now."

"Anything to do with tobacco?"

"Not much."

The dancing drew them apart.

Frank led his girl back to join the others, Paul gave him a smile as they passed his table.

"How long have you been out of the army, Frank?"

"Still on terminal leave."

"What are you doing now?"

"Nothing yet."

"You should contact Beth. She'd love to see you. Still in the same flat with Nancy. You're looking well. This is Jeanne Pétain. We work together in America. Jeanne's over here on business. Come and join us."

"Can't. I'm with an old army buddy."

"Give Beth a ring. She's in the book. Small world."

"Good to see you again, Paul."

When Frank rejoined Zachariah Cohen he was smiling. Zach was buying everyone another round of drinks.

"Shouldn't be any trouble getting you into the tobacco company. Old friend of mine at the table over there. Next to the girl with the elfin ears. She's French. Paul works for Father."

"When can you set something up?"

"Don't rush it, old chap. I'll have to put out feelers. They must have an advertising agency by now. People have loyalties. Leave it to me. Timing is everything, I'm told, in business. What my father always said. Like buying a controlling interest in the Tender Meat Company at the end of the Depression just before the war started, sending all that canned food to Europe to feed the armies. From breaking even to making a packet in months."

"I'll tell my father you're onto it."

"That's the stuff. You should buy some of Tessa's paintings before she gets too famous. Modern paintings in the offices in Cohen Wells would give it just the right amount of flair."

When the music started again, Frank asked Tessa to dance. He wanted Zach firmly on the hook.

"The family are as rich as Croesus," he told Tessa once they were on the dance floor.

"Thank you, Frank."

"You owe me a favour."

"Where are you staying?"

"I don't know after the end of the week."

"What happened to the flat?"

"Belonged to a girlfriend."

"She was never at the parties."

"Married. A bit older than me."

"And Brian?"

"Her friend was his friend. Famous actress."

"You'd better come and stay with me. There's a folding-out couch in the lounge. I share my room with Olivia. You gave us some good parties. When we get back to the bar, I'll slip a phone number in your pocket. One good deed deserves another. Good to see you. How was the army?"

"A complete waste of two years."

"Must have learned something."

"Got a commission. The pay was better. The beer ninepence a pint in the Officers' Mess."

"Sounds like you, Frank. The girl can sing."

"She can. The Mayfair's a high-class act."

Sometimes, Frank thought as he delivered Tessa back to Zach at the bar, it paid to invest a little money in people. All the booze paid for by Dorothy Dent and Connie Whitaker had not been poured down the drain after all. A cheap bed was just what he wanted for a few weeks. To give him time to get his bearings. Find out what to do to make himself some money. Which brought him back to thinking of Connie once again. All of a sudden, life had possibilities.

The next day in his old room in Soho that Frank had rented by the week, Frank tried in vain to find out what happened to Connie Whitaker. Not only had Connie disappeared off the face of the earth, so had Dorothy Dent. The nearest he got to Dorothy was being told she had gone to America. The caretakers in the South Kensington flats who had earned good money keeping Frank and Brian informed of Frederick

Whitaker's whereabouts had also vanished. Frank was told by the new caretaker Frederick had moved out of the flat at the same time as his wife.

"We don't keep track of old tenants, cock. Enough trouble keeping up with what we got. What you want to know for?"

"Never mind," Frank told the new man.

A lot had happened in two years. Every avenue he tried had him coming up against a brick wall.

Finding Paul Crookshank was a whole lot easier. The office of Brigandshaw Oosthuizen was listed in the phone book, the chances of the telephone operator knowing his voice no greater than his legal father answering the phone.

"May I speak to Mr Crookshank?"

"May I ask who is calling?"

"An old friend. I want to surprise him."

"Hold on."

"Paul? Frank Brigandshaw. How are you? How about us having some lunch, old chap?"

"Have you contacted Beth?"

"Not yet. The atmosphere was a bit strained last time she and I met. Savoy Grill at one o'clock, sound all right?"

"Why don't you come round to the office first, Frank?"

"Can't do that."

"Your father isn't in the office today or I would put you through," lied Paul.

"Talk over a good lunch."

"Not until you contact your family."

"Been too long. Old wounds are better left alone."

"Don't you ever think of your mother?"

"Sometimes."

"My father died at Dunkirk. You don't know how lucky you are. I'd love lunch with you when you've contacted Beth. Otherwise she'd have me for breakfast. I'm not getting in the middle of a family squabble. Hang on, and I'll find her number for you."

"Paul, I was hoping you and I could have lunch. Not a cat fight with my sister. One day we'll bump into each other. Let's leave it until then. And please, Paul, don't bring my sister to the Savoy. One o'clock. I'll be in the foyer of the hotel."

"Can you afford lunch for two at the Savoy?"

"Not really. I have a favour to ask. About business."

"One o'clock sharp, Frank. I'll look forward to seeing you. Quite a surprise meeting you in the Mayfair. I'll buy the lunch."

AFTER PUTTING DOWN THE PHONE, Paul sat thinking quietly for five minutes before getting up and going to the boss's office where the door was open.

"Come in, Paul. Why the big grin on your face?"

"Just had Frank on the blower."

"Frank?"

"Your Frank. We're having lunch at the Savoy. You'll join us, of course."

"Did Frank ask me?"

"No, sir."

"Then enjoy your lunch. Why did Frank want to call you?"

"Bumped into him in the Mayfair the other night. He was with a crowd of people."

"How did he look? His mother will want to know."

"Wearing a moustache. Didn't recognise him at first. A lot different to when I last saw him as a boy. You don't forget the face of a boy who socked you on the nose."

"Find out what he's doing, Paul."

"He wants a favour."

"Sounds like Frank. He never did anything without a reason. You'll find the reason is always to his benefit. So lunch today?"

"Yes, today."

"Take your time."

"YOU DON'T REMEMBER PUNCHING my nose, do you, Frank?"

"Of course I do, Paul. Why ever should I forget? Were it not for Mary Ross you would have given me a good one back. She was meant to be looking after us in the old nursery while the grown-ups were downstairs enjoying their Christmas. I was bored."

"What were we fighting about?"

"I have no idea. Let's go and have some lunch. Fact is, I don't eat much these days without a salary. The food was good in the army. I'll say that for them."

At a small table on the side of the Grillroom, they sat down opposite each other. The waiter brought them impressive menus. Frank was glad Paul was paying the bill. Having heard his change of mind on the phone at the mention of business, Frank was more confident.

"Chap I met in the army, did our officer training together, is in advertising. Specialising in mass market products. Read the story of the new cigarette company in the *Daily Mail*. Wants to have a crack at the account. Said I'd help."

"What's in it for you, Frank? Is he going to give you a job?"

"Might do. Have a few ideas in my head. Still on terminal leave. Zachariah Cohen's father owns Cohen Wells. Very successful. They say cigarette sales are in direct proportion to the advertising spend. If the money is spent properly in a well-ordered campaign it's like printing your own money."

"How did you know, Frank? There was nothing in Wakefield's article about your father bringing me back from America to run the new project. In the Mayfair I brushed you off."

"The harder I try, the luckier I get."

"We are only launching our cigarettes in England. Toasted cigarettes. British opposition to Camel. We've bought the rights of a Rhodesian company. Ridgeback will be our name in England. Non-filter. Short and strong to the taste. At first we were going to blend Rhodesian tobacco with Virginian tobacco from America. Can't get the dollars despite owning our own farm in Virginia with Harry's Cousin George. The secret of a good-tasting cigarette is in the blending, according to your father. They cook the blended tobacco in Salisbury with honey. Gives it the slightly sweet taste so smooth on the throat but strong. After the war, men like strong cigarettes."

"Who's designing the packaging?" asked Frank, ticking off the instructions he had earlier received from Zachariah Cohen in his mind.

"We haven't got that far."

"Cohen Wells have an entire design team. Packaging is very important."

"We are talking to three of London's top agents."

"Why not talk to a fourth? That's enough about business. How about a drink while we order the food? Can I tell Zach he can give you a ring, Paul? No hard feeling about the bloody nose. Why are small boys always scrapping?"

When the gin arrived, Frank raised his glass.

"To your new project, Paul. With Zach's help I'm sure it will be a great success."

"Don't you want to hear about your family?"

"Not really. When you've been lied to all your life you lose interest. My word, they've got Peking duck on the menu. Do you know, Peking duck is just about the duck's skin? Very exotic. What are you going to have to start with, old chap? This is jolly. You'd never think looking around you we'd just fought a war. Lucky I missed it. Crocodile hunting in the Zambezi Valley was far more profitable. And a lot more fun."

"Just not for the crocodiles," said Paul, not being taken in by all the chatter for one minute.

WHEN PAUL finally got back to his office feeling worse for wear, he was smiling. Harry Brigandshaw had gone home on the train to Hastings Court. The boss came in at ten in the morning, leaving Waterloo on the ten to four train, missing both ends of the rush hour. Frank was exactly like his father, proving once and for all to Paul that nature was stronger than nurture. That you were what you were the day you were born. In his travels, Paul had met the Honourable Barnaby St Clair on many occasions. Sometimes, but not always, in the company of Harry Brigandshaw. Barnaby St Clair was very much a man about town. Frank's devious mind worked on the exact same paths as his biological father. A web of words leading to a conclusion designed for his benefit. The same charm. The same smile. The exact same manipulation.

At the end of lunch and the second bottle of wine, Paul had found himself getting drunk while Frank seemed to stay as sober as a judge. Never once had Paul seen Barnaby drunk when he wanted something, mostly a new girl he had set his sights on. They were manipulators, the pair of them.

When Paul came back from his last visit to America he had asked Jeanne Pétain to come across with him to meet Major Pilkington-Jones and go out with the major and Kenneth Grahame on a succession of field trips. Trying to separate business from pleasure was the reason Paul had agreed to take on the new company in London. The evening at the Mayfair where he bumped into Frank was their first as a date, or so he thought.

"Don't be silly, Paul, we're old friends. Anyway, why the sudden change?"

"We're not in business together anymore."

"You English are so silly. What possible difference can it make? Why you live, Paul, in that one room? I help make you rich. You need a house with servants. Lots of my paintings on the walls."

"I could buy us a house in the country where you could paint all day. You wouldn't have to work."

"Are you proposing?"

"I think I am, Jeanne."

Right there and then in the Mayfair, with Kenneth and his date thankfully on the dance floor, Jeanne Pétain had burst into peals of laughter making Paul feel the size of an ant. First he had blushed. Then had come the anger at himself for being such a fool. All along for Jeanne it had just been business.

Sitting behind the desk in his office with the door closed, the wine tripping his head, it was not the lunch he was thinking about. It was Jeanne. Trying to do the right thing at the start he now saw as a mistake. The night he first played her the piano was the night he should have gone to her bed. When rejection would have only cost him a business associate. He was no good with women he liked. Only the ones that did not matter were easy. Like Nancy Longhurst, still sharing the same flat with Beth.

'You never get what you want in life if you play it straight,' he thought. Like Barnaby and Frank, father and son, you had to manipulate people. Paul had to try and be more like Frank. Care nothing of being hurt or hurting people. Then he thought of Frank's mother. Paul felt desperately sorry for Mrs Brigandshaw having a son who wanted nothing to do with her. Now that must hurt, he thought. More than Jeanne Pétain's laughter that was still ringing in his ears.

Feeling sorry for himself, Paul left the office early, taking a taxi to his room in Mrs Bigglesworth's house in Holland Park. There was a pub at the end of their cul-de-sac, hidden away among the leafy plane trees. Once he'd changed from his suit it was six o'clock and the Fox and Hounds was open. Between what Frank was doing to his mother and what Jeanne was doing to him he was feeling down and miserable. In the corner, at the end of the bar, Paul sat himself down with the intention of getting himself drunk. Jeanne was by now far on her way with the others in the old Bedford he had bought from the army after the war.

"Make them doubles, Wally," he said to the landlord. "The advantage of drinking close to home."

"Bad day, Paul?"

"Bad idea, more likely."

The next day, he would phone Zachariah Cohen and make an appointment for them to meet in Paul's office. At least Frank would get what he wanted from his night at the Mayfair. Paul drank down the double scotch and soda in three gulps. Jeanne Pétain was driving him crazy.

2

———————

While Paul was trying to drown his sorrows, finally giving up and going back to his room for a long night's sleep, Connie Whitaker was arriving home at her mother's small house in Lambeth after a hard day's work in the typing pool. Her back ached from sitting upright in front of her typewriter, the tips of her fingers numb from bashing down on the keys while listening to the headphones of her Dictaphone, the small plugs pressed into her ears. All she ever heard were men's voices dictating their letters. Connie was third in a row of six typists, passing her tray to the end of the line when she finished each of the big red plastic tubes that she fitted over her machine to play back the recording. Never once had she met one of her voices face to face. The typing pool was an assembly line. Anonymous typists for anonymous clerks in the six-storey building that housed the administration department of Lloyds Bank. After two years, her salary was still three hundred pounds a year, enough to pay half her mother's expenses and buy them a bottle of gin for the end of the week, a bottle they drank together sitting in the kitchen on Friday and Saturday nights. During the week they looked at the bottle without touching. Always Gordon's Dry Gin which they drank with a dash of orange cordial in a cocktail glass, pouring themselves their individual drinks in the stand-up kitchen cupboard Connie's mother liked to call her pantry.

"I'm home, Mum. What's for dinner?"

Connie had read Frederick's obituary in the paper and thought no more about it after the first shock from reading of his death. They were divorced, she told herself. No point in feeling sorry for him or herself. She had found in the two years since she had walked out of the South Kensington flat, it was better not to think of her previous life. Life was what she had at the moment, not what she had in the past. She had not told her mother Frederick was dead.

"A letter for you, Connie... Shepherd's pie."

"Who is it from?"

When Connie took the envelope and turned it over to look at the address on the back, a swift shaft of pain ran through her body. The letter was from the same firm of solicitors who had railroaded her through her divorce, making quite certain she would have no financial comeback on Frederick.

"When did this come?" she asked her mother.

"In the afternoon mail."

Wearily, Connie took a knife out of the drawer in the kitchen table and slit open the envelope. In her experience, letters from solicitors were never to her advantage. Especially letters from Frederick's solicitors.

"What the hell do they want now?" she said, folding open the single sheet of paper. The letter was flawlessly typed as was only to be expected. Taking her reading glasses out of her handbag that she had left on the kitchen table, Connie began to read. It was all very simple. She was the sole heir and beneficiary of Frederick George Whitaker. He had left her everything, a figure believed by the now obsequious firm of solicitors to be an estate worth in excess of three hundred thousand pounds. Silently, Connie handed the letter to her mother.

"Where are my reading glasses?"

"Here they are, Mother," said Connie taking them off the kitchen table and handing them to her.

"Blimey. The bugger's left you the lot. Can you open the gin?"

They were laughing, hugging each other until Connie began to cry.

"What's the matter, ducks? You put up with him for twenty years. You deserve a silver lining. I can't even imagine that amount of money."

AFTER SUPPER on a tray in the lounge, neither of them saying anything, Harry Brigandshaw took himself for a walk. If no one else, the dogs were happy to see him. For the first half mile past the tall cedar trees and the family graveyard, the ginger cat followed them meowing all the way. The cat neither liked going for a walk nor being left on his own. Thinking of his eldest son killed over Berlin by German ack-ack, only a plaque in the graveyard noting his passing, Harry walked on through the elm trees along the path to Headley Heath. Living with a desperately lonely and unhappy woman was the worst experience of his life. After so many years together they had nothing to say to each other. The big four-poster bed they had once shared, which had stood in the master bedroom of Hastings Court since Henry VIII was on the throne, lay unused. Since the children left, they had slept apart and lived together in silence, each with their own memories and thoughts. Even a mention of Paul Crookshank having lunch with Frank without him going along would have brought on an argument. Arguments that never reached a conclusion. Whatever Harry said to Tina was wrong.

On the heath, Harry looked for the witches' circle finding the logs still firmly in place. Sitting on the left stone in the middle Harry closed his eyes, seeking solace. The dusk was coming down on the woods below, wrapping the trees in dark shadows. The birds had started their evening chorus, telling the others where they were perching for the night. It was not like the African bush where the sun went down and darkness came in half an hour, the crickets singing in the long elephant grass in company with the birds in the trees. But it was peace with nature, the best he could get in England. After years of practice he had found it better not to think of Elephant Walk. Thinking of his mother and sister Madge on the big farm made him sad. As though his life had been taken away without proper reason. By the time he went down through the woods to the old house of his ancestors he would be feeling his way down the path, following the barks of the dogs.

Nothing came to him in the circle. A few stars had come out in the heavens. A barn owl hooted from down in the woods. No one else was left on the heath except Harry sitting on his stone in the circle.

Picking himself up from his melancholy mood, Harry began the walk home as the moon came up above the horizon. It was a night for ghosts, ghosts of his long-dead ancestors.

She was sitting in the same chair in the lounge, one standard light picking her out, an open book on her lap, staring into space. Harry sat down in his chair opposite, looking at his wife.

"Now the property prices are so low we could use some of our dollars and buy back the house in Berkeley Square. Maybe not the same one.

There would be more people for you to entertain again in London. More friends to make."

"Would you do that for me, Harry?"

"Of course I would if it will make you happy."

"It's as though my life is over now the kids are gone. They have their own lives. Don't need my help. Do you think they ever think of me?"

"Of course they do. Young people have such full lives they don't do anything about it. We're the comfort in the back of their minds. Where they will run to if they get themselves into trouble. We should be thankful they are all so independent. We always taught them to think for themselves. Grown children shouldn't run to Mother."

"They could give me a ring every now and again."

"You haven't been the best of company of late. Maybe that keeps them away. With lots more for you to do in London you'll be more cheerful with the children."

"Thank you, Harry. Do you ever think of Rhodesia where you grew up?"

"You know I do. I phone my mother once a month. Speak to Madge. We're going to bring our own tobacco to England and make our own brand of cigarettes."

"Isn't smoking bad for people?"

"Calms their nerves. Why everyone got to smoking during the war. I'm going to sell the house in Cape Town. No point in having a house there now."

"I suppose there isn't. Won't please the Coetzees. As caretakers they're lived the life of Riley since 1944. All good things come to an end."

"I'm going up to bed."

At the door, turning round to look at his wife in the lamplight looking forlorn and despondent, Harry's heart went out to her.

"I'm sorry, Tina," he said.

"What for?"

"Not being able to make you happy."

She looked through him for a long moment.

"Are you coming up?"

"Not just now."

"Did you hear the owls hooting?"

"They give me the shivers."

"Shall we try living back in London?"

"Why ever not, Harry? Why ever not?"

. . .

Oblivious to the crisis going on at home, Beth Brigandshaw was trying, without a great deal of success, to concentrate on reading her book. Beside her armchair in the lounge stood a mug of hot cocoa. From Nancy Longhurst's room came the sounds of distraction. For some months now, this had been the way things were: Beth trying to get on with her life while Nancy invited a seemingly never-ending stream of men to parade through her bedroom. She had somehow convinced herself that since she hadn't become pregnant yet, the chances were she never would.

"Have you considered you might pick up something other than a baby, Nance?"

"Who cares? You're only young once. You don't have long, Beth. Once you get a bit old you can't pick and choose. Screwing the same man every night is boring."

"What about love and a family? A home?"

"What the church and old women sell you. The jealous women without the good memories. Why is it so different? I can get it properly from a man, look at him in bed afterwards and find he doesn't turn me on anymore. Then another man walks in the door and I'm off again."

"There's a word for it, Nance. Nymphomania."

"Long may it last. Don't look like that at me, Beth, you're like some disapproving old pastor from a Victorian picture book. Fearing for my soul in the face of sin and fornication. That's what they would have called it, fornication. I call it fucking."

"Please, Nance. Someone will hear."

"We're the only two in the flat. Unless that old man next door has got his ear to the wall."

Beth, thinking of this earlier conversation, put her book down next to the mug of cocoa and listened to the grunts and groans, mixed in with the squeak of the bed springs, coming from Nancy's bedroom. Despite herself, she found the sounds arousing. It was the thought of falling pregnant that kept Beth mostly on the straight and narrow. None of the contraceptive methods she knew about held any appeal for her. Who knew what things could be like if that ever changed? London's social life would never be the same. Girls, instead of having to marry the first man that asked them, could do what they wanted. Liberated. Free. No longer beholden to men.

Not long after, Beth put down her book as a man in his early twenties came out of Nancy's bedroom. The man looked pleased with himself, then took one look at Beth and went to the door, a flush of scarlet coming to his face. Earlier, when he had gone into Nancy's bedroom, Beth was not in the flat.

Nancy opened her door. She was wearing a dressing gown and smoking a cigarette. She had the look of satisfaction written all over her face.

"I hate to say it, Nance, but you'll be growing mushrooms on those bedsheets one of these days. What was his name?"

"I have no idea. Met him in a bar."

"I'm going to bed. Exhausted just listening to you and your friend. What were you doing?"

"He was good, Beth. My God he was good. Not one ounce of fat on his whole body. Men are at their best at that age. And I'll tell you something else. I feel better than I ever felt in my life. You know something? The more you get, the more you want."

"However could I have guessed?"

"Sarcasm is the lowest form of wit. You're jealous. We'll all be dead before we know what's happened. Life's to be enjoyed. We enjoyed ourselves even if I don't know his name. Does anything else matter?"

"I heard. So likely did the dirty old man in the flat next door who leers at me when I walk down the corridor."

"It's like honey, sex. Smooth and perfect. I'm going to make myself some bacon and eggs. Want some?"

"Why not?"

"That's my girl. Did I tell you Paul Crookshank is in town? Why don't we invite him round with Kenneth Grahame? I rather fancy Kenneth."

"I thought Paul was your boyfriend. Your lover."

"That was ages ago. Paul's come back to live in England. To run a cigarette company for your dad."

"That reminds me. I haven't phoned Mum for ages. Too late now, she'll be in bed. How do you know so much what is going on?"

"When you get around as much as me, you find out everything."

"Do you ever think about getting married?"

"Whatever for? I'm having far too much fun."

"What about kids? Don't you want kids?"

"Far too much work. Kids do all the taking. None of the giving."

"And when you get old?"

"They frighten us into submission with the tag of loneliness. If you can't be happy with yourself, why should anyone else make any difference? The biological urge to fuck in all of us has put too many kids on this earth now that modern medicine brings most of them to adulthood. In the bad old days many children died young. Why parents had so many kids as insurance for their old age. Now we've got a Labour government. The welfare state. The state will look after me in my dotage. I don't need screaming kids today in the hope they'll be nice to me when I'm old. Which they won't. We're all selfish, Beth, whatever we say to the contrary... I'm going to put a sausage in the frying pan. I'm hungry. Want one?"

"How big are they? Did you buy them?"

"Small. I'll put in two. A girl has to keep her strength up."

"You didn't think of inviting your beau?"

"What for? I'm fucked. Once you fuck them they can go home. They've treated us like that down the centuries. Now it's our turn."

"You're being very coarse... I'm going to have a drink. Want one?"

"Now you're talking."

THE FOLLOWING FRIDAY, Nancy Longhurst came home from the office in a huff. Her date had cancelled.

"Phoned me at five o'clock to say he couldn't make it. Some story of staying late in the office. By then it was too late to go through my list and phone someone else to say I was free."

"You don't phone men to ask for a date?"

"Of course I do. How do you think I go out every night of the week? I've crossed Cedric Barnes off my list."

"I've an idea. Why don't we go to the Benjie Appleton jazz club? Haven't been there for ages. You're sure to pick up someone you fancy."

The idea had been in Beth's mind ever since being told Paul Crookshank was back in England. It was nice to see old friends, she told herself. Anyway, she had found him a career with her father. There would be no embarrassment if they bumped into each other. From a comment from her father, Paul had done rather well out of the deal.

"A good sweaty jive will lose us some weight," said Beth. Nancy had one of those knowing looks on her face that were meant to be annoying.

"I'm game. Can't stay at home on this Friday night. I'm not working tomorrow. It's my one Saturday off for the month. Let's have some food and off we go."

. . .

AT 101 OXFORD STREET the queue was at the stairs and out in the street. They were both wearing tight, sleeveless turtleneck sweaters as they had done the first night Beth bumped into Paul. For luck she had worn the same sweater that fitted tightly across her chest. Looking down the queue there was no one she knew waiting to go down into the basement. With luck Paul had arrived early to ask the band to let him play his clarinet.

It had begun to rain by the time they got inside. They found a table, putting their wet umbrellas underneath. Then Beth looked around. The band had not yet started playing. Benjie Appleton had not come out with his trumpet. Beth watched Nancy search the crowd for prospects, catching as many of the men's eyes as possible.

When Beth saw Paul he was coming out from behind the bandstand in company with Benjie Appleton. Instead of staying with the band Paul walked to a table and sat down. There was a girl at the table who waved her hands as she talked to a man. The man had his back to Beth. Just after Paul sat down another girl sat down just as Beth was about to wave. The woman was young and very pretty. When a third couple sat down, Beth knew there was not going to be a repeat of the evening two years ago. Paul and his friends had dates. Having built up her expectations, she felt deflated.

"You've seen him," said Nancy. "The one with his back to us must be Kenneth. Oh well, Beth. You can't win them all... Now, isn't that nice, he's seen you. Looks pleased at the surprise by the look on his face. His whole face had lit up."

"Oh, my God. It's Frank... Why are you giggling, Nancy?"

"You never answered Frank's last question. As to who was screwing who. The whole bang shoot have stood up and are coming over. I like the third man. Even from here I'll bet he's Jewish. The world smiles again, Elizabeth Brigandshaw. And the world smiles on both of us."

"He looks well."

"Which one, Beth? They all look pretty good to me."

"My brother. He must be out of the army by now. And that reminds me. I still haven't phoned my mother... Hello, Paul. What a surprise."

"Just don't slap my face in front of these people, sis."

"How are you, Frank?"

"As good as you see me. This is my army buddy, Zachariah Cohen.

Tessa my flatmate. No, that's not quite right. Tessa is an old friend allowing me to sleep on her couch. Olivia here is the flatmate. The little girl with the elfin face is Jeanne Pétain from New York. She and Paul work together for your father."

"Can't we join that table up with ours? My friend Nancy Longhurst, everyone. We were at college together. Learning how to be good secretaries. Any minute when the band starts playing we won't be able to talk. Where is your clarinet, Paul?"

"Behind the bandstand. I'm playing with them after the third set. You look well, Beth."

"What are you doing with my brother?"

"He and Zach are helping me with your father's new venture. Cigarettes. We're launching a brand of Rhodesian cigarettes on the English market. Here they go. My word, it is good to hear the band. Best jazz band in England."

For some reason Beth did not understand, there was an awkwardness between the small girl from New York and Paul. The girl looked interested in Frank, but every now and then glanced at Paul. As if she were frightened or something. Often joining people she did not know, it took her time to find out what was going on. There was nothing with Tessa or Olivia as far as she could see. The small girl had a strange mix of accents. Jeanne was an English name but it also could be French. Spelt differently. Pretending to concentrate on the music, his foot tapping to the rhythm under the table, Paul was always conscious of the girl if Beth was not wrong. A lovers' tiff? When he looked at the girl, Paul's eyes were sad. Then Beth understood. Paul Crookshank was in love with the girl who also worked for her father. Never a good idea falling in love with the staff. Or a co-worker. It was one of Beth's golden rules. Never, ever, bring the office home. It always ended with one or other changing their jobs. Deflated for the second time in one evening, Beth tried to listen to the music. The band was so loud no one was bothering to talk. That way she and Frank did not end up in a fight. My poor mother, she thought. Were all of us horrible children? Only then did she begin to scheme on how she could bring her brother and mother together again. Put a spark back into her mother's life. A spark that had gone out some time ago when Anthony was shot down over Germany. Frank looked well. The army must have been good for him. There was nothing else for her to do other than listen to the music. No one seemed to want to jive. Nancy was looking round the crowded basement. Rightly, she must have realised screwing Frank was not a good idea. Zach had his eye on Tessa.

In the break, Beth found out Tessa was a painter. That Zach was buying her paintings for his father's office. Beth was not interested in paintings or painters. The girl, Olivia, was also some kind of artist. Frank was welcome to both of them. With no attention from anyone, deliberately not drawing her brother into conversation, Beth was bored. So was Nancy by the look of her. After listening to Paul play his clarinet with the band, when he came back Beth made their excuses. Sometimes the best ideas fell flat.

"Will you excuse us, Paul? Lovely to hear you play again. So glad to hear from Father the business is doing so well. Nancy has seen friends and wants me to join them. Frank, such a nice surprise. I'll tell our mother you are looking well. Enjoy the rest of your evening."

Moments after, the band struck up again. They were not going to have a break. The regular clarinet player was back on the dais. The one who was being paid to do a job. The three girls gave Beth and Nancy distracted smiles. Mouthing her words, Beth told the men not to get up. Walking away with her arm on Nancy's elbow, out of sight behind one of the wide pillars that held up the whole building, they stopped to get their bearings.

"I haven't seen any friends! What are you doing?" Nancy said with her mouth close to Beth's ear so Beth could hear.

"Never stay where you are not wanted. Talk to you later."

Just then, a man asked Nancy to jive, bringing the smile back to her face. Another man asked Beth. When they sat down afterwards, the two men were friends. The pillar cut them off from seeing Paul and Frank. When Beth and Nancy left to go home with the two men, the other party had left. Outside, Nancy said goodnight to the man who had asked her to dance. The evening had gone flat. The two men looked puzzled and walked off.

"I'm going to wring the neck of Cedric Barnes if I ever see him again," said Nancy.

"Thanks for not going for Frank."

"We share a flat. I'm not that bloody stupid."

"What was wrong with him?" said Beth, nodding in the direction of the two men now crossing Oxford Street. The traffic had slowed down enough for them to make a dash for it.

"Can you believe it, I'm not in the mood for sex."

"Thank God for small mercies. Let's go home. We can have a good natter back in the flat."

When they reached their flat in South Kensington, before Beth had time to open the door, they could hear their phone ringing inside.

"Hurry, Beth. It's Cedric."

Beth ran inside, having fumbled the key too much in her hurry, and picked up the phone.

"Mother! What are you doing phoning this time of night? I was going to phone you tomorrow. Just saying to Nancy I owe you a call."

"Your grandmother's died. The funeral is on Monday. Can you get the day off from work to come?"

"To Rhodesia?"

"My mother, Beth. My father is devastated."

"I'll come home tomorrow."

"Kim has applied for compassionate leave from the air force. Dorian is coming down from Oxford tomorrow. We are all driving together to Corfe Castle. You don't by any chance know how to get hold of Frank? He liked my mother from a small child. Sometimes think she was the only one of us he did like."

"I've just been with Frank. I'll bring him down if I can."

"How is he?"

"Looking well. The army has done him some good. He was with Paul Crookshank. Are you all right?"

"No I am not. My mother just died."

"I'll catch the train to Leatherhead first thing in the morning."

"Phone your father from the station. He'll come and fetch you in the car."

"Poor Grandfather."

"Yes. Poor Grandfather."

"See you tomorrow, Mum."

"Just make sure you bring Frank."

"I can only try. I have Paul's phone number somewhere. He's still in the same room he rents from Mrs Bigglesworth after all these years. I'll phone Paul right now as I think he will know Frank's number."

Trying to remember that without Granny Pringle she would not be alive, Beth found Paul's phone number in her telephone book. Mrs Bigglesworth answered.

"I'm sorry to call so late. It's an emergency. A death in the family."

"I'll call him down from his room. Came in ten minutes ago."

"You are very kind. No wonder Paul has stayed with you for so long."

"Like a son to me."

While she waited, Beth thought of Granny Pringle and the few visits she had made as a child. They had never visited Hastings Court in return. Her grandfather had said he would feel uncomfortable in a big mansion, other than as a servant. She had been ten years old when she overheard her grandfather's comment. Only later, when the world and its strange habits came into focus, did Beth understand. Her mother was of a different class to her father. The system had been designed far back in the past to keep the rich in England apart, making them aloof, different to the rest of them. Which to Beth was a lot of old rot.

"Paul? It's Beth. Mrs Bigglesworth was so nice. I want Frank's phone number with Tessa and Olivia. Our grandmother has died. The funeral is on Monday. Mother wants him there."

When she dialled the second number after thanking Paul, Tessa answered the phone. Beth waited patiently for her brother to come on the line.

"You've got to be joking, sis. Only when the three of them apologise to me for the lie will I have anything to do with my family. You left in a hurry. I rather liked your Nancy."

"So you won't come to your own grandmother's funeral. She was very fond of you, Frank."

"I will mourn her on my own. I don't have to stand at her grave. She was the only nice one in the family. No sides to Granny Pringle. Genuine. Not like the rest of them pretending. Put one flower on her grave for me, Beth. Will you do that for me? Promise."

"I promise."

"Goodnight, Beth."

When Nancy handed her a stiff drink, Beth was crying.

"He's not such a bastard after all."

"By all accounts he is, darling. A genuine bastard in the right sense of the word. There aren't many who admit it these days. If I'd been Frank I'd have kept quiet like the rest of them."

"So he won't come, I gather?"

"No."

"Let's drink to your gran. Remember her life. You always said she was the best of the lot."

"I only met Granny Brigandshaw once to remember. When she

brought her father's body back from Rhodesia to Hastings Court to be buried. She went straight back again."

"Here's to your gran."

"Mum's in a state."

"Yes, I expect she is. We never expect to lose our parents, however old they are when they die."

WHEN THE CAR fetched Beth from Leatherhead railway station, her brother Dorian was driving the car. She had not seen Dorian since Christmas when the family gathered together at Hastings Court. Dorian was down from Oxford and Kim had leave from the air force.

"How did you get home so quickly?"

"On Dad's old motorcycle. I took it back to get me around the university for lectures. Easier to park than a car. Mother's in a bad shape. Father wants to go and see his mother in Rhodesia before it's too late. Aunty Madge says Granny Brigandshaw is frail but her mind is still crystal clear. Kim hasn't got back yet. Said on the phone he may take the train directly to Corfe Castle. We're all driving back the same day. Dad says Grandfather won't be able to cope with a mob after the funeral. Mother is going to drive her own car down today to help arrange the funeral. Grandfather has so many friends in Corfe Castle that are helping. There won't be a wake at the cottage. Just the funeral in the churchyard. Father wants to make a cruise out of going back to Rhodesia. So Mother will go with him. Union Castle boat to Beira round the Cape. A couple of months away with time on Elephant Walk, Grandmother and Aunty Madge. Back to Beira from Salisbury on the train and a Lloyd Triestino boat up the east coast of Africa and through the Suez canal to Venice. Then a series of trains across Europe to Calais, taking in the sights on the way. Mother hasn't been happy with her life for a long time. Dad hopes the trip will get her out of herself."

"Is she going? She hates Africa."

"They will be nine weeks on a boat. First class. Lots of people with their noses in the air. She'll go, if I know our mother."

"When do you come down from Oxford?"

"Next month. Written all the exams but two."

"How did they go?"

"I have no problem writing English. Dad's the problem now. Says BA stands for Bugger All, not a Bachelor of Arts."

"What are you going to do for a career, Dorian?"

"That's the point. Before they cart me off into the army for my National Service I want to fly to Rhodesia. To talk to Granny Brigandshaw. My tutor says the problem with most novelists is they don't have a good enough story. I have all the technical attributes after Oxford but not the story. If Granny Brigandshaw's mind is still clear as crystal I want her to tell me about Grandfather Brigandshaw, the big game hunter. Who was stamped on by the Great Elephant. Turn his life into a novel. All that roaming about the African bush without a sign of civilisation to interrupt his sanity."

"You're ahead of me, Dorian. Will Mum and Dad go on this trip?"

"I think so. Mum likes the idea I'll be on the farm with her. She hasn't seen much of any of us lately. You know, Dad thinks Robert St Clair will be at Granny Pringle's funeral. The St Clairs and the Pringles go a long way back into history, living just a few miles away from each other. By the way, where's Frank? Wasn't he meant to be coming with you?"

"He wouldn't come. You have a mind like a butterfly."

"Why not?"

"Until Mum, Dad and Barnaby St Clair admit to the lie, he doesn't want anything to do with any of us. He told me so last night. He has a point, Dorian."

"Are you going to tell that to Mum and Dad?"

"Don't be damn silly. Whatever they all did in the past is none of our business. Can you get enough story in a couple of weeks for a book?"

"I hope so. If I use my imagination. Publishers will like the idea. Especially if I get a First for English literature."

"Will you, Dorian?"

"What a silly question. Now tell me, what have you been up to of late? After Cape Town we sort of lost touch. You do know Robert St Clair is a famous novelist? He's living at Purbeck Manor with Lord St Clair, his elder brother. His son Richard is heir to the title."

"You forget, Dorian, the legitimate side of our family history. If Lucinda St Clair had not been killed by that maniac Mervyn Braithwaite, you and I would not be going to Granny Pringle's funeral. We would not have been born. Back then, Robert St Clair was our father's brother-in-law. And yes, I do know Robert writes books. I've read every one of them. If you can write one half as good as *Keeper of the Legend* you'll be doing all right."

"That does seem strange. The bullet that killed Lucinda gave us life. I'll put that idea in a book. Thank you, Beth."

"You're welcome. Now concentrate on the road or we'll end in the ditch. Are you going in the army or the air force?"

"Whatever they tell me to do. You can't argue with governments. I hope I get posted to one of the colonies. Good experiences for a writer. There are troops in Singapore and Hong Kong. Exotic places. I rather think the army has a regiment in Borneo."

"You'd better hurry and get yourself called up. Dad doesn't think the empire is going to last much longer now India has gone. They will more likely post you to Germany and the British Army on the Rhine."

"You think so? Yes, well, you're probably right. My English tutor thinks the British Empire is finished. He thinks there's going to be some kind of European Union to stop us fighting with each other. That British interests will lie in Europe and not in the colonies. Too many of the colonies are fractious, he says. Costing us money. He thinks we should give all our colonies independence and concentrate on Europe. Why I want to find out about our illustrious grandfather roaming around southern Africa before it's too late. Write it down. Save it for posterity."

"He killed elephants for a living."

"Only at the beginning. He grew to love the animals, according to Dad. Ivory hunting was what he had to do to get started."

"They all say that. Do you want a cigarette?"

"That's a bad habit."

"We grow tobacco in Rhodesia on Elephant Walk."

"Still a bad habit."

"Dad's launching a brand of cigarettes."

"So I hear. The tax man likes cigarettes. I heard somewhere the tax on cigarettes and pipe tobacco pays for Atlee's new National Health Service. Others say tobacco smoking kills you. Makes you think. Now, where was I about my books?"

Beth, switching off, let her brother talk on without listening to a word, her mind elsewhere. When they reached the big gates of Hastings Court that led into the tree-lined driveway she came back to where she was sitting in the car. All the time her brother had been talking she had thought of Paul Crookshank. There was something about him that she liked. He was loyal to people like her father and Mrs Bigglesworth.

"You weren't listening to a word."

"Of course I was, Dorian. You are going to be a great success as a novelist. Make lots of lovely money and go back to Oxford as a professor of literature."

"I didn't say that. What a good idea. Here we are. Just remember, Mother is in a state."

The dogs were the first down the steps from the long terrace of the old house, barking with excitement. The crenellated battlements looked broodily down on Beth as she stood up after patting the dogs. At the top of the steps, looking tragic, stood her mother. Behind her mother stood Mrs Craddock the old cook, and her father. Her mother was dressed for the road with a small suitcase on the steps, waiting for Beth and the return of her car.

"Leave my case in the car, Dorian. I'm going with Mum. We can both look after Grandfather."

"Oh, Beth. Will you?" said her mother. "It's such a long drive on my own. Your father wants to take me on a cruise round Africa after the funeral."

"What a lovely idea, Mother. Can we have a cup of tea before we go?"

"Have you had breakfast?"

"Cornflakes and a cup of tea. Caught the first train after my alarm went off. Hello, Mrs Craddock. Hello, Dad."

"Where's Frank?" asked her mother. "You said you could find his phone number."

"Let's not talk about Frank. He's not coming."

"To his own grandmother's funeral?"

"Yes, Mother. He asked me to put a single flower on the grave for him."

"That was big of him. Please give me a hug. I'm in need of hugging. Kim's going straight to Corfe Castle on the train on Monday from his RAF station. Somewhere in Kent. My brother Bert can't leave his business in Johannesburg for his mother's funeral. It's too far for my sister Maggie in Australia so she says. Can't afford the plane ticket. What a family. I wonder if it's worth having children. The moment they don't need looking after they take no notice of you. It's as though we mothers don't exist. All that work my mother put into bringing us up and only one out of three living children at her funeral. Dorian, you can put my suitcase in the car and leave the car where it is. Have you filled up with petrol?"

"Yes, Mother."

"Well, that's something. In this family, I'm expected to do everything."

"Give me that hug, Mum. We can talk to our hearts' content in the car. The cruise sounds wonderful. Just what you need after losing Gran. Is Grandfather going to be all right on his own?"

"Of course he isn't. But he won't come and live here even if we ask him. He's lived in that home most of his life."

"Who's going to feed him?"

"I can't be wife and daughter all at once if that's what you're suggesting. He has lots of friends. Old Mrs Battle might move into the cottage. She only has her widow's pension. I'll find someone to look after him. Damn Frank. The least he could do is come to the funeral."

"He doesn't want anything to do with us," said Beth, mentally kicking herself the moment the words were out of her mouth.

"Why ever not?" said her mother sharply.

"You know why, Mother."

In the silence that followed, Beth hugged her mother. Then they all went inside. Beth caught her father's look over her mother's shoulder. A look that said there were enough problems in the family without digging up another one.

"Was that necessary, Beth?" said her father.

"I rather think it was, Dad. But it's none of my business. The boat trip is a wonderful idea," she said, smiling to change the subject.

"We have to spend two weeks on that damn tobacco farm," said her mother.

"I'll be there, Mother." said Dorian.

"It's the only reason I'm going to the farm. Come on. We haven't all day. It's a long drive to Corfe Castle."

THE JOURNEY PROVED the longest in Beth's short life. How anyone could be so negative about life was beyond her comprehension. All the way down to Dorset it was moan, moan, moan. Her mother's stories all about herself. When Beth tried to change the subject and talk about her friends, about how much they were enjoying their lives in London, the tirade that followed was even more bitter. Beth had no idea what to say. So she listened. Or gave the good impression of listening, sympathising every now and then with her mother's woes when Beth was forced to bring her mind back to the present. Eventually, like reaching the end of a long tunnel, they arrived at the railway cottage to be greeted by her grandfather.

Her grandfather was quite the opposite. There were no tears. He wanted to talk about the wonderful things he had done with his wife. Rabbit stews with herbs from their garden that Grandmother hung to dry in the kitchen. Bottled plums in the middle of winter, the fruit from their small garden. Her grandfather was a happy man. None of that feeling sorry for himself. The two of them humoured Beth's mother as best they could. Beth's big regret by the time of the funeral in the churchyard was not having known her grandparents better. Materially they had been poor, if material wealth was judged by a motor car or a fur coat made of expensive pelts from some poor animal. For the rest they were richer than all the rich people Beth had met in all her life put together.

The churchyard was full of people from all walks of life. Lord St Clair with his elderly mother who stood at the back of the crowd not seeming to want to get in the way. Everyone knew Mr P, as everyone called him. Everyone was a genuine friend of Mrs P, now in her coffin being lowered into the old earth of England, next to the graves of so many kith and kin. As four young men let the casket down, inch by inch, cradled by two long ropes, Beth bent forward and placed a rose for Frank on the coffin. Earlier, Beth had placed her own bunch of bluebells on her grandmother's coffin, bluebells from the woods that surrounded the railway cottage where her grandmother had lived most of her long life. The rose, an early bloomer, had come from the garden of the stone-built cottage. To Dorian's delight Robert St Clair, the novelist, was at the graveside, next to her father. Robert St Clair and her father had been up at Oxford together at the turn of the century. Then it was over. Everyone moving slowly away from the churchyard, her father shaking the hand of the vicar. There was no party. No stuffing themselves with food and alcohol. The people of Corfe Castle had come to bury their friend in the shadow of the ruins of the old castle up on its hill. It had once been owned by the St Clairs, Frank's ancestors, before Cromwell knocked it down after cutting off the head of his king.

Mrs Battle had moved into the cottage to look after her grandfather the day before. The family all said goodbye, including Kim who had come down by train. On the way back, their parents went in the big car, the children in their mother's. For Beth, the difference in the two journeys was as different as chalk and cheese. They were happy. All three of them were happy. Deliberately, none of them spoke of their mother.

When they got back to Leatherhead, Dorian dropped Beth at the station. She had missed one day's work. She could not afford another. It was the last train up to Waterloo of the day.

"How did it go?" asked Nancy, when Beth walked into the flat.

"You don't want to know. My poor mother has turned into a total pain in the arse. The woman's miserable. Makes everyone else miserable. Has anyone called?"

"Paul Crookshank."

"What did he want?"

"If you ask me he wanted to take you out. We had an old lovers' chat and left it at that."

"Have you been out today?"

"Monday's my one night in. A girl has to rest sometimes. I'll make us some tea and then I'm for bed and sleep. What a weekend. You have absolutely no idea."

"Oh, I think I have. My word, it's good to be home. I just hope I don't get miserable when I grow old."

3

———————

By the end of June, Frank Brigandshaw was back in his prime. His friend Zachariah Cohen was nicely on the end of a short piece of string. It all made Frank smile watching his friend want something so badly. It was going to be Zach's way of impressing his father when Cohen Wells landed the Ridgeback account.

For weeks, Frank had kept the possibility just on the boil. Drawing Zach deeper into his web. The more Zach wanted, the more he was going to pay.

"You want a commission on the deal, Frank? You and Paul Crookshank are as thick as thieves."

"Not thieves, Zach. Old friends. I rather think he fancies my sister. How are you and Tessa getting along? Have you persuaded your father to buy some of her paintings?"

"Not yet."

"You should, you know. The price is going up. A commission of one per cent of all Cohen Wells billings for Ridgeback would be nice. I'll need it in writing with your father's signature. No more expensive than all those cruises in the Med. Introductions are like advertising these days, Zach. They cost money. The middle man has to be paid."

"We think your father's fame can be used to promote the business. Public relations is all part of the service. Free advertising in newspaper copy is the best advertising of all. People are more inclined to believe what they read in a newspaper article. All part of the Cohen Wells service. You could mention that to Paul. Tell him we explore every avenue that promotes the sale of our client's product. I've asked our design team to have a go at the cigarette packet. The one from Rhodesia Paul showed me is far too colonial. You have to be modern to catch the eye of the upwardly mobile. The ones who like to be seen with upmarket packaging when they offer a packet of cigarettes. There's a lot more to advertising than meets the eye, Frank."

"I'm sure there is. You want me to show Paul the artwork?"

"That would be nice. I don't know about one per cent. That's most of our profit at Cohen Wells."

"You can have it as you like. For less than one per cent I'm not interested. You get ten per cent of the billings from the newspapers. Ten per cent of your ten per cent sounds about right to me. Don't be greedy, Zack."

"Who told you?"

"A chap called Horatio Wakefield. You remember him, Zach? Where you read about Harry Brigandshaw and Ridgeback cigarettes in the *Daily Mail*. Old friend of the family. Bumped into him with Paul. Got chatting. He's the foreign correspondent at the *Mail*."

"Why was he writing about your father and Ridgeback cigarettes?"

"Way back, Horatio and William Smythe, then of the *Mirror*, made themselves famous writing about Harry Brigandshaw. When he disappeared in a plane crash in the Congolese jungle and reappeared three years later."

"You know everyone, Frank."

"Helps to keep in touch. William still does a programme on the BBC Overseas Service. What's going on in the world. That sort of thing. Without that story neither of them would have amounted to much. You have to get famous in this world before people take any notice of you. There are plenty of hacks. Not too many Wakefields and Smythes with their own recognisable bylines. Oh, yes, they can help with the Ridgeback story. With a little help from me, Zach. I think one per cent of total billings is generous. Don't you think?"

"I'll ask Father."

"That's the stuff. Where are we taking the girls tonight? I thought the Mayfair. A bit expensive but put it on the firm's account. All tax deductible. Did I tell you I've found out where my friend Connie Whitaker is living? If you're not quick, Zach, I'll lose interest in all this advertising business."

"Could you get Wakefield and Smythe to help?"

"I can only ask. They are pretty important these days. But for their old friend Harry Brigandshaw I don't see any problem. If they are asked by me nicely."

"Maybe I could ask Father to offer you a job in our PR department."

"Don't be silly, Zach. That would be working. For a salary. No one gets anywhere in life working for someone else."

"Shall I phone Tessa and Olivia?"

"I can phone them. I said I might call. You'd better buy those paintings. I haven't had money to give Tessa. A little something for letting me sleep on the couch."

"Are you still on the couch?"

"Of course I am. Never shit on your own doorstep. You should remember that, Zach. Why poor old Paul missed out on Jeanne Pétain."

"Is she still in England?"

"She's fallen in love with rural England and all those lovely old houses. Especially what's in them. The key to success for that company in the Brigandshaw stable is buying the goods. You got to get the stuff first before you can sell it in America. Jeanne knows what they want. Poor old Paul. Anyway, now he's after my sister. Men are so fickle. A bit like clients in business, don't you think? If you don't look after them properly."

For Frank, the game of life was all about keeping his wits concentrated in the right direction. Everyone he met was a target. A source of future revenue. The very idea of working nine to five for anyone was quite absurd.

The next afternoon, checking the address in his pocket against the number on the door, Frank rang the bell. On his face was the look of a man in full control. A smile but not expectant. A confident smile of a young man in full control of his life.

"Connie! I'll be blowed. You look absolutely wonderful."

"How did you find me? I heard they took you in the army. I suppose you'd better come in. I only just moved in as I had been living with

Mother the last two years. She didn't want to move. I presume you know Frederick left me all his money? Despite making me divorce him and leave the flat without a penny."

"That I did not know. How lovely to see you. I would have found you earlier but they gave me a commission in the army. The pay was much better. Officers are not permitted to misbehave. My naughty past was best left behind. Just got out. Free of all that protocol. My word, this is nice. What a lovely flat."

"Who told you, Frank? Don't forget I know you better than you know yourself."

"A little bird. Her name was Dorothy Dent. A friend of a friend just came over from America on business. She knew all about the actress Dorothy Dent. A friend of one friend of the friend is Genevieve the Hollywood actress. As it happens, though no one will admit to it, Genevieve and I are first cousins. Genevieve told Jeanne who told me. Dorothy gave me your address. She was so sad to hear Brian is still in Rhodesia. He's in cattle, poor chap. Working for his father. Looking for a wife. Life in the African bush without a wife is a bore. There are so few women. Why we gave up crocodile hunting."

"What do you want? You don't have a job. People with jobs don't visit the flats of ladies on a weekday."

"You are absolutely right. Is it too early for a drink?"

"Probably not."

"Good. We have lots to talk about. To catch up with. I was lucky you keep up with Dorothy. The rich usually dump their friends when the friends become poor. Which only goes to show you. My opinion of Dorothy rose accordingly."

"So Dorothy told you about Frederick's will?"

"Just a little. But honest, Connie, I was looking for you long before I knew. Ever since I got out of the army."

"How long have you been out?"

"A few weeks. Let me pour the drinks. You always liked me to pour the drinks. Poor old Frederick. After all that, he couldn't take his money with him. Just as well. Most of the wealth in the world would be sitting up in heaven. How have you been without me?"

"A working girl. Typist in a typing pool."

"Ugh. That is ugly. All day long my Connie bashing a typewriter. Sometimes you just have to wonder what life is all about."

"Are you looking for a job?"

"Whatever for? Let me get the ice out of the fridge. Here's your drink. Sit yourself down. Then we can tell each other everything. My word, you do look good. Just the right shade of lipstick."

"Just the same old Frank."

"Why ever not?"

The poor girl actually shivered when Frank handed her the drink, accidentally on purpose touching her hand. It was nice to know he was appreciated. When a person paid for something they deserved the best. Barely raising his eyebrows, sitting comfortably next to Connie, his knee touching hers, Frank lifted his glass.

"To old times," he said, keeping his eyes on Connie as he drank from his glass.

"How much gin did you put in my drink, Frank?"

"Just as I remember you liked it. Have you given up your job?"

"Of course I have. It's a weekday."

"How much did they pay you?"

"Three hundred pounds a year."

"I'm proud of you. That shows grit and character."

"Are you teasing me, Frank?"

"Why ever would I want to do that? I don't like weak people. You are not a weak person."

"What have you been doing?"

"Trying to persuade a friend of mine's father to part with his money. Zach and I are old army buddies. Would you like to meet him?"

"How old is he?"

"A bit older than me. Zach did Cambridge and a business degree before he went in the army. I introduce him to women. He has the money. I have the contacts. I'm sort of a broker."

"A pimp, Frank. That's being a pimp."

"Someone has to help. Do you want to go to bed now or a little later? Or when you've had a couple of drinks? The army was one long famine. I thought of you often, Connie. The fun we had. The fun we had in bed. Did you find anyone to replace me? Have you been to our art gallery? How is Mrs Walters? I always thought she was envious of you, Connie. Put her nose in the air but underneath I could see she was envious. She wasn't my type."

"Am I your type, Frank?"

"Of course you are. Why on earth do you think I'm here?"

"For my money."

"You cared. You came round after Frederick threatened me and Harry Brigandshaw. That's why I'm here. I read of Frederick's death in the *Telegraph*. Dorothy said he had left you some money. It could have been a thousand pounds for old times' sake for all I knew. I thought we were friends. Life is short. Before you know it you're old like my mother and no one looks at you. Never look a gift horse in the mouth, Connie. I'm here. Why do you always think I'm after something?"

"Because you are, Frank. Because a leopard never changes its spots. Cheers. It is rather nice to see you."

"Good. Now I can relax."

"That's how it all started the first time."

"I know it did. So relax, my darling. The making of love is beautiful. Why be ashamed? If two people want each other that's all that matters."

"I'm going to have a drink or two first."

"A good idea. It's been a long time. Making love should be savoured. Not rushed into. Savoured now, then and afterwards. As I savoured you when I was far away in the army."

When Connie turned to him on the couch, Frank took her hand. The palm was sweating. She was still a good-looking woman. It was all going just as he planned.

LATE THE NEXT MORNING, when Frank left Connie's new flat in Knightsbridge to go back to Chelsea, he was feeling more confident than at any other time since leaving the army. It was always better to have more than one arrow in his quiver. The crisis came when there was nothing to fall back on. It was like selling anything, Frank told himself. If you did not have to sell in a hurry it was easier to get the higher price.

Both girls were in the small flat. Tessa gave him a big smile. She was painting. The canvas stood on an easel in the big bay window with all the light. Olivia was painting next to her, standing in front of a similar easel. On the coffee table, near the couch that was Frank's bed when he pulled it out into a bed in the evenings, was the debris of a party. Empty bottles. Dirty glasses. The smell of stale booze. Ashtrays overflowing with cigarette butts soaked in lipstick.

"Ladies, what did I miss?"

"Did you find Connie?" said Tessa. "Silly question, coming home this time of day. We had a party. Zach bought two of my paintings yesterday afternoon. Or his father did. After we hung them in the Cohen Wells office, Livy and I came home and got drunk on just a fraction of the proceeds. Enough money for food, booze and six months' rent. Did you say something to Zach, Frank?"

"Why should I? Your paintings are good, Tess. They will be the ones laughing ten years down the road. If I had any money I'd buy everything in this flat as a pleasure to my eye and an investment for the future. Good for you. Time you had some luck after all the hard work you put into your paintings."

"How is she?"

"She was lonely. Moved out of her mother's home in Lambeth and bought fifty-eight years of a hundred-year lease in Knightsbridge. Frederick left her the bloody lot. She's loaded. If you ask me she was happier without the money living with her mother. It's a funny old world."

"So you cheered her up."

"Of course I did. I like Connie. Despite the age gap we understand each other. She knows I'm in the game of getting money out of people. Maybe that's a bit strong. Whatever you get in life you pay for one way or the other. You'll get more buyers with those paintings in the Cohen Wells office. It pays to advertise, so Zach keeps telling me."

"Just a pity neither of us really fancy him."

"Why ever not? His family is rich. He'll be rich in a few years."

"Money isn't everything, Frank. Come and look at this painting. Do you think it's finished?"

"You always ask me that. How am I meant to know? It's your painting. Do you feel like cooking breakfast?"

"Coming up. The cook's in a good mood today. Six months' rent for two of the paintings. Even when the rich buy a painting from a new artist they don't exactly go overboard."

WHEN JEANNE PÉTAIN went round in the evening to find the two girls painting in oils she was green with envy. The very look of the chaotic lifestyle was what she had always wanted. Paul had asked her to go with him to see Frank, knowing Tessa and Olivia were artists.

"They'll be fun for you to meet. To see what it's like to live in a garret without any money. Harry wants me to go round. He thinks he sees it as a way of helping Frank without Frank knowing. Zachariah Cohen has asked us if we mind Cohen Wells paying Frank a commission for introducing us to his agency. I'm to tell Frank we are happy to let his friend make a presentation for the Ridgeback account. The only snag is a lousy presentation. Advertising is key to launching a successful brand of cigarettes. Two of us going round will make our intentions less obvious. More casual. Frank's smart. He'd smell a rat if he thought I had an ulterior motive."

"What's the problem?"

"Frank has Harry's surname but Harry isn't his father. For years the family swept it under the carpet. Your friend Genevieve in New York knows all about not having a surname. Strange part is she and Frank are first cousins. Both are bastards in the true sense of the word. Merlin St Clair, now the Eighteenth Lord St Clair, is her father. Her mother was a barmaid Merlin met during the First World War when he was home on leave from France. During wartime, rules don't apply so much. Men back on leave, especially officers, knew that when they went back to France the chances were they'd be killed. They took whatever comfort they could find. Merlin still supports Genevieve's mother. She's a drunk. Nice flat in London. Everything she needs. She never wanted to marry and lose all the benefits from Merlin."

"And Frank. Who was his father?"

"The youngest son. A bit of a chancer as a young man. Made his own fortune in the end from scratch. Played the stock market before the '29 crash by trawling for information in the fleshpots of London. Always ahead of the market. Charming man. The ladies loved him. Bit like Frank. No, not a bit like Frank, according to Harry. Frank *is* Barnaby. The exact same man. Frank's mother and Barnaby were friends from the time they were young kids. Then lovers. Harry went away on an extended trip to the farm in Rhodesia leaving Tina and the kids behind. The old lovers got together again. *Voilà*, to quote you French. Tina still loves Barnaby according to Harry."

"Why didn't Barnaby marry this Tina in the first place?"

"The Honourable Barnaby marrying the daughter of a railway worker? He laughed at the idea. Never married, so far as I know."

"You English don't know anything about love. In France, the aristocrat with the money would set the girl up in an apartment as his mistress. Had two families. The one to carry on the line, the other to love. You English are stupid. So what's wrong with Frank?"

"He wants the three of them to admit in public to what they have done, according to Beth. I suppose the two family bit is about what Merlin did. Except he never tried to have any more kids with Esther. To Merlin, Esther and Genevieve were a gentleman's responsibility. To be paid for. Only later did he bring Genevieve home to his mother. When Genevieve was fifteen."

"So why don't Harry and Barnaby do the same? Admit what happened."

"This is England. Bastards are still frowned upon. So are the parents that fornicate. The Church of England would frown on such sinners. Not done, old boy. All that rot. Can't fornicate with the wife of a friend in polite society. I'm telling you all this so you don't put your foot in it. Only when Genevieve became famous – when Bruno Kannberg wrote her memoirs – only then did it all become public knowledge. By then, Merlin was old enough not to care what people thought."

"I will be the height of discretion. How intriguing. And now the bastard son lives in a garret with two girls, sleeping on the couch."

"Something like that."

"*Ooh là là.* Is he sleeping with both of them?"

"Neither, according to Beth."

"What's the matter with him?"

"Before he went in the army, he was living in a posh flat paid for by a married woman. How he met Tessa. When the married woman's husband was in town, the mice went out to play. Frank and his school buddy from Cape Town, Brian Tobin, threw parties for the bohemian set in Chelsea. The artists loved it. Free booze, paid for by the married woman's husband in a roundabout way. Tessa was one of the hangers-on, I suppose you can say. Now it's her turn to help Frank. All very bohemian."

"I can't wait to go round."

"I've got a bottle of Scotch and a bottle of sherry. How they like to be entertained. Tessa and Olivia prefer entertaining at home when they are painting. Again, so I'm told by Beth."

"*Chouette!*"

"You don't mind coming? I don't want the girls to get the wrong impression. That I'm after one of them."

"Really, Paul. I just don't understand you English."

. . .

WHAT SPARKED the most envy in Jeanne came when she walked forward to look over the girls' shoulders at their paintings. Tessa and Olivia weren't just living the life of painters. They were painters. Both of the canvases were good. In Jeanne's opinion, better by far than anything she had done herself in Brooklyn.

"Do you like the paintings?" asked Tessa after they were all introduced.

"Very much. I try and paint a little myself."

"Where are you from? Your accent is odd."

"New York. My family are French. I was born in France."

"I've brought us whisky and sherry. Don't you girls want a break? Frank, you can pour. I'm afraid I know nothing about paintings. Jeanne is the expert."

"Tessa sold two paintings yesterday," said Olivia, taking a good look at Paul. "To a friend of Frank's. You can pour me a whisky. Do you think this one is finished, Jeanne?"

"That's for the artist to say. Not for me to decide. I envy your lives. I wish I could live like this."

"Not when you can't pay the rent at the end of the month. So, to what do we owe the pleasure, Paul?" asked Tessa.

"I've good news for Frank. Zach's going to get a chance to make a presentation."

"Why don't you tell Zach, Paul?" said Frank. "He's the one to get excited."

"I've told him. He asked me to tell you."

"Did he now?"

"Beth sends her love."

"Does she now? You'd better give me the bottles. Beware of Greeks bearing gifts."

For a moment the two men looked at each other without saying a word.

"Who's going to pour me a sherry?" said Jeanne, smiling at Frank.

"Jeanne Pétain," said Frank. "How nice to see you again."

"The pleasure, as you English say, is all mine. Come, I'll help you find some glasses."

Soon after the top came off the bottle of whisky, people began to arrive. Tessa and Olivia had stopped painting. The easels were put up against the wall to make more room. To Jeanne, they all seemed to be artists of one kind or another. The men wore baggy corduroy trousers and loose sweaters. Two of them had beards. One of them had brought a bottle of cheap wine which everyone cheered. A girl had two loaves of bread, her friend a large chunk of Cheddar cheese wrapped in muslin cloth. When the seats were full, people sat themselves cross-legged on the floor. One of the girls sitting on the floor next to Jeanne, Jeanne sitting on Frank's sleeping couch, said she was writing a novel. She smelled of good strong soap as if she had come out of a bath. The men all thought her pretty by the way they looked at her. The girl had her eye on Frank dispensing the whisky. Jeanne thought the girl liked the whisky as much as she liked Frank. One of the bearded men had brought an old guitar. At Jeanne's suggestion, Paul went downstairs to where he had parked his car and fetched the clarinet out of the boot. One girl had a flute, someone else a recorder. The youngest of the men, a boy not out of his teens, had a keening voice that made everyone listen. The song was very sad. The boy had a club foot. Paul told Jeanne that without the club foot, the boy with the sad voice would have been in the army. When the whisky was finished they drank the cheap bottle of wine. The sherry bottle had been emptied first. Someone made a pot of tea and put it on the floor in the middle of the room. No one took any notice of it. Music flowed back and forth, Paul weaving his clarinet among the flute and the recorder. The guitar player was only good at strumming. When he tried to sing he was told to shut up. For Jeanne it was proving to be her best night in England. To make it perfect there should have been a piano so she could join in the music. Everyone knew everybody. All were friends. Every person who had come into the room had looked at the girls' paintings before joining the party. Moments in time, Jeanne thought. Moments she would keep forever in her mind. The happy moments.

Not long after the booze ran out people got up to leave.

"We'd better go, Jeanne," said Paul.

"What a lovely evening."

They began saying goodnight. Tessa and Olivia said when she was in the area she should come again.

"Bring one of your paintings, Jeanne. We want to look."

"They're in America."

"Paint one in England."

"Yes. Maybe. You are all so lucky."

"We know we are. Drive carefully, Paul. Thank you for the whisky and the sherry."

"We can see our way out. Good night, Frank."

"Good night, Paul. Sorry I bloodied your nose."

Outside in the street when Paul opened the passenger side of the car, she looked at him full in the face.

"What was the last bit about?"

"We were kids."

Jeanne kissed Paul full on the mouth before getting into the car. All the way round to the driver's side of the car, Paul held his right hand to his mouth. They drove to Jeanne's hotel off Regent Street in silence. It was a small hotel she stayed in when the Bedford lorry wasn't out on the road. It was cheap. Jeanne was always trying to save her money. Standing still, thinking of what she had done, Jeanne watched Paul drive away. Then she sighed and went inside the hotel. In her mind, she could still hear the keening sound of the boy with the club foot.

WHEN PAUL GOT HOME to Mrs Bigglesworth's house and walked up the stairs to his room he went to bed. He couldn't sleep. What did it mean? Was it just a kiss to say how much she had enjoyed her evening? By using his imagination he could still taste her mouth as he lay on his back. There was so much work to be done in the morning. Zachariah Cohen was coming round at nine o'clock with the art director of Cohen Wells. They wanted to talk before making their presentation. The meeting was important to Harry and Frank. Not sleeping would make his head woolly for the meeting in his office. Jeanne was going off in the Bedford lorry with Kenneth Grahame and the major. How the major at his age managed all the travelling was a source of wonder to Paul. The previous week, after their last trip into the country, Paul had again been invited to the Cavalry Club for a drink. The place fascinated Paul. Never once had he heard a member raising his voice. The same invisible man was in his chair every time Paul went round. Paul had yet to see the old man's face.

"I don't know how you do it, Major. That Bedford is a bone cruncher."

"Don't be silly. My bones ache anyway. What's a little bouncing up and down? Makes me feel young talking to you and Kenneth. And now the delightful Jeanne. Have you got a soft spot for her, dear boy? If only I were fifty years younger, you wouldn't stand a chance. I'm seventy now."

"You're a spring chicken," said a voice from the chair with its back to them. "Wait till you're ninety-four before you begin to complain, Bertie."

"Point taken, Lachlan."

"Does he sit in the same armchair every day?" whispered Paul, leaning forward.

"Are you here every day, Lachlan?"

"Where am I going to go? Are you two making any real money?"

"Depends what you call making real money."

"I suppose it does."

All through the night, tossing and turning, every thought in Paul's mind came back to Jeanne. He had never answered the major's question. There wasn't any point. Now she had kissed him on the mouth all he had ever wanted in life played out in front of him, his imagination running riot in the dark of his room. By the time he finally fell into a restless sleep the morning light was creeping up over the window sill and the birds were singing.

TWO WEEKS later when Jeanne came back from her trip with the major and Kenneth Grahame she had made up her mind. There was more to life than bouncing around the English countryside in an army surplus Bedford lorry making money. She had some savings. She would ask Harry Brigandshaw if she could make four trips a year prospecting for antiques. They could pay her a commission based on the difference between the price she paid for the artefact and the price it fetched in America. The incentive to buy good products at the right price would be there. She wanted to paint. Not watercolours that were thrown away the moment clients decided how they wanted their apartments decorated. Like Tessa and Olivia, she was going to become a bohemian artist living cheaply in Chelsea. Jeanne wanted to be with people where inspiration was a daily issue. Where people shared. Where a work day was truly creative and not just a means to make money. Across the Channel was Paris and the Left Bank of Paris. The antique business would provide her bread and butter. Feed her body. Painting would feed her soul. Make her satisfied with life. Not always wanting the real satisfaction, however much money flowed into the bank. All it had needed was one night in Chelsea to recognise what she was missing in life.

Frank had moved out when she called on the girls. Like so many people she had met in her life, once he had money he wanted to show it off to the world. She was told by the girls Brigandshaw Oosthuizen had signed the agreement with Cohen Wells and, at Paul's insistence, Zach had given Frank an advance on his commission. Enough to rent a small furnished flat in the right part of Knightsbridge with the right address to extend what Tessa said he was now calling his public relations business. The girls, amused but not really interested in Frank's new money, had told her that Frank considered himself on a roll.

"What have you got wrapped up in that brown paper, Jeanne? Is it one of your own paintings?"

"Did it in Scotland. I have a passion for landscapes."

"Take off the paper. Let's have a look... Oh, yes. My word. Olivia, come over here and have a look at this. Why are you wasting your time?"

"I'm not anymore. Why I came round. I need a place to stay with good light in a big bay window like that one over there."

"You won't paint landscapes in Chelsea."

"I'll paint the Thames. What's on the river. The life in Chelsea. Much the way I painted Brooklyn. Can you help me find a place dirt cheap?"

"Have you told Paul?"

"Not yet."

"The way he was looking at you the other night he's going to be upset. Another split personality. Business and playing jazz on a clarinet. You can have the couch now Frank's moved out. Someone in the crowd will have a place when they see this picture. Amongst ourselves we only accept people who are genuine artists. We don't like people acting the part."

"I'll need to get my stuff. There isn't much. I came across from America in an aeroplane. I'll leave the painting. Few ends to tie up. Be a couple of days. I'll bring some whisky."

"That's my girl. What are you going to do about our Paul?"

"I don't know."

"No one ever does until it's too late."

Outside Jeanne felt as happy as a lark. Both girls had kissed her *au revoir* on the cheek. Everything felt just right. Taking small steps she went for a walk along the bank of the river to celebrate the new start in her life. She was going to buy a black beret and put it on her head. Wear a smock covered in paint.

"What a wonderful life," she said, taking a skip. "For the first time in my life I've got what I want."

The people on the boat passing up the river waved. Jeanne waved back.

"What a lovely day," she called to them across the water.

A woman with a small dog on a leash passed by along the pavement. Jeanne stopped to pat the dog.

"What a lovely day," she said to the woman.

"It's beginning to rain," said the woman in return.

"I never noticed how lovely the rain can be when you are happy."

"Have you been drinking, young woman?"

"Only happiness."

4

———

At the same time Jeanne Pétain was tripping the light fantastic alongside the River Thames, Frank Brigandshaw was having himself a laugh. They all think me stupid, he told himself as he mentally counted his money. The girl who played the flute was sitting on the carpet at his feet at his Knightsbridge flat not two blocks from Connie Whitaker. The flat was not as expensively furnished as Connie's but it would do for the time being. Rome had not been built in a day. Amassing a fortune the size of his biological father's was going to take a little more time. Before receiving the substantial cheque from the hands of his good friend Zachariah Cohen, Frank had considered proposing to Connie. Marrying her for her money. Giving her a few good years while he got on his feet before going his own way with a nice chunk of Frederick Whitaker's money, a man who had chosen to be belligerent to himself. In addition he was hoping to get plenty more from the man Frank was sure must have been behind the large and welcome cheque from his buddy Zach. Nothing in business in Frank's short view of the matter worked that fast if the only decision had been choosing an advertising agency to run the Ridgeback account.

"Why are people so easily manipulated?"

"I don't know. You tell me, Frank."

"You want another glass of this wine? French. Pre-war vintage. Some French farmer must have hidden it from the Germans. Or been a

German sympathiser. Most of France was under a Vichy government while we battled the Germans. Sensible people. Why get in a fight unless you have to?"

"What's Vichy, Frank?"

"Leave it, Daisy. How did you get the name Daisy?"

"My mum likes daisies. They grow wild. I like that idea. Don't you think I'm a bit wild?"

"Very wild and very beautiful. Do you know this bottle of wine cost me ten shillings?"

"You've got to be kidding. I could live on ten bob for a month. Can I move in with you, Frank?"

"What about your friends in Chelsea and your painting?"

"I can paint here if I have to. If you've got so much money to pay ten bob for a bottle of wine I won't have to do any work."

"But you told me you love painting, Daisy."

"You have to say that in the crowd. They think they're the next Picasso. Or Bacon. All very modern. Most of them are kidding themselves. It's the easy way of life they like. If you haven't got money but look interesting, people with money bring things round. You remember that night at Tessa's? When Paul brought that bottle of whisky the word went round in a flash. We all had a lovely evening. I've never seen one of those pull-out couches before. Paul and his girl got entertained. We all got something for nothing. Everyone was happy. Strange a man with money can play a clarinet. I'm no good on the flute. Just looks good for a pretty girl to sit on the floor. Play a few notes on my flute. Nice, sexy little fingers. It's all for effect. This wine is good. Have you got any food I don't have to cook?"

"You know something, Daisy? You're a bit lazy."

"Of course I am."

"Did you make that dress?"

"Bought the material cheap in the Portobello Road market. I just wrap it around a bit like they do in India. Comes off quick. You want to see, Frank?"

"Not yet, Daisy. We haven't finished the bottle of wine. There's bread and a tin of sardines."

"That'll do. I'm not fussy. You want to tell me who you screwed to get this flat? It's a long way from Tessa's couch."

"First I screwed Zach my old buddy. Then I screwed Paul who played the clarinet. Then I screwed my legal father, the one I was after all the time."

"What's a legal father? They're either your dad or they're not. You mean a stepfather?"

"My real father screwed my mother when my legal father wasn't looking."

"The dirty bugger."

"And no one will admit to it. I'm going to screw all three of them financially for not admitting the truth. While having nothing to do with them. That really pisses them off."

"I'm going into the kitchen. Sounds too complicated for me."

"There's a packet of crisps in the cupboard."

"That's more like it. I never can open a tin of sardines."

"What are you good at, Daisy?"

"Fucking. You should know that. If a girl's good at fucking she doesn't have to be good at anything else."

"You'll get yourself pregnant."

"God, I hope not. I'd be a hopeless mother. But even if the worst happens, there are always ways and means."

She grinned wickedly.

"Can you open a packet of crisps?"

"I'll try. Have you got any more of that wine?"

"A whole case of it."

"We're perfectly suited. Can I spend the night?"

"That you can, Daisy. That you can."

LATER THAT EVENING, while Frank was viewing the real pleasures of life spread-eagled on top of his bed, the cloth from the Portobello Road on the carpet, Paul Crookshank was hearing from Jeanne Pétain the new plans for her life that Paul saw quickly did not include him. One kiss on the mouth. Like one swallow, did not make a summer. She was going to be a bohemian painter with all those young men around dispensing free love. Trying not to show the pain grinding his heart, Paul tried to seem enthusiastic. Everyone else had left for the night. They were alone in his office. The new design for the Ridgeback cigarette packet was lying on his desk.

"Will Mr Brigandshaw let me do a few trips? It will only be when I need the money. Until my paintings start to sell like Tessa's. She's sold three more to Cohen Wells. They really love her work."

Paul, biting his tongue, kept his mouth shut. If no one else had worked out Frank had made the sales, it was not for him to deflate Tessa's ego. Or Jeanne's, now she was pointed in the same direction.

"You can always go back to America if it doesn't work out. But won't all your hard work with the New York stores go to waste? Won't another decorator with a flair for watercolours step into your shoes and take the market? People are fickle. Their memories short. People change their allegiances very quickly. After too long away you won't have a business to go back to."

"Are you saying you'll find someone else to paint your antiques into the pictures?"

"We'll have to, Jeanne. That's business. Of course, when you come back we'll still have work for you in New York. This buying trip was more for you to show the major exactly what your American clients want. Won't you lose touch with trends? Everything changes so fast these days. After a while won't you be buying stuff they don't want? You were so on top of it in New York. Why the business took off so quickly. You were right at the heart of public taste on a daily basis."

"I'm not going back. I'm going to be a painter. You know I'm good."

"Of course you are. So are a lot of other people. New art is difficult to sell. Only when you have a name can you be sure of selling. The public like to know they're onto a good thing. Fame for a painter is often more important than talent. For any artist. Half the time, the public don't know what they're looking at. They have to be told it's good by someone who counts."

"Paul, it's what I want."

"We don't all get what we want in life. What you have in America is somewhere near what you want. You're painting almost every day."

"You don't understand."

"I think I do, Jeanne. The lifestyle is seductive. Looks good on the surface. Underneath people need money to survive."

"I hate money."

"We all do when we have it. Or we say we do. Be careful what you throw away. It took me years of hard work to get to where you got in America. You'll always be able to paint. The wonderful thing about painting or playing the piano is we can do it when we are old."

"I want to do it now. While I'm young. Will you ask Mr Brigandshaw?"

"I'm sure he will agree. We owe you a lot, Jeanne. What do you think of this new design for our packet of cigarettes?"

"You want my honest opinion?"

"That's why I asked you."

"I think it's bloody horrible. But it will sell cigarettes by sticking out in the tobacconist's."

"That's what we want. To sell our cigarettes. Not to make something beautiful."

"When you play the piano it's beautiful."

"But I can't make enough money to live off my music. Playing the piano or my clarinet. All my professional jazz musician friends have to live off the smell of stale booze and stubbed-out cigarettes."

"But they are happy. I want to be happy."

"Don't we all," said Paul, miserably. "Don't we all."

"I'm moving out of the hotel. To Tessa's. Frank's got himself a flat in Knightsbridge."

"Good for Frank. He's clever. He knows how to make money. Whether we like it or not, that's the most important part of life. Stale booze is very smelly. After a while it makes you sick."

"I'm going to show you, Paul."

"I hope you do. Just remember I will always be here for you if you need any help. It's a minefield out there. And I know all about minefields from the war in Burma."

"You're sweet."

When she got up and gave him a kiss on his mouth Paul was not sure whether he wanted to laugh or cry.

"You want a drink in the pub, Paul?"

"Not tonight. I still have work to do. Launching the brand in such a hurry is keeping me up most nights. Work, work, work. Makes the world go round."

"Do you like your work, Paul?"

"Not particularly. Who does? Some of it, maybe. There was satisfaction in getting the antique business off the ground. Turning an idea into money. I hope the cigarettes will give me the same satisfaction. I've decided to get myself a flat now I have some money. Put in a piano so I can play when I get home at night. The major found me a grand piano that will fit in a flat if the lounge is big enough. I'll miss Mrs Bigglesworth. I've promised to keep in touch."

"You will for a while."

"No, she means more to me than that. When Mother comes up from the Isle of Wight she'll have somewhere to stay. She's lonely on her own now Jeremy has gone to Rhodesia. After the navy, my brother has been a lost soul. Didn't know what to do with his life. When Harry Brigandshaw went down to visit my mother, he told Jeremy about Crown Land farms in Rhodesia for British ex- servicemen. Once you learn how to grow tobacco they sell you the land cheap, provided you can borrow money from the Land Bank to put in a crop. Jeremy was getting nowhere after Dad died in Dunkirk. He really missed Father. He was twelve years old when Dad went down with the *Seagull*. Then I went in the army and was posted to Burma. Mother's had a sad life ever since."

"You'd better get back to work."

"Have a good life, Jeanne."

"Are you saying goodbye?"

"Aren't you? Maybe it's better. Maybe it doesn't matter anymore now you are moving away from the company. I've loved you, Jeanne, since that first night I played you the piano and slept on your couch."

"Why didn't you do something about it then?"

"We were going to work together."

"I'm going to cry."

"Don't get sentimental. That will really hurt. You go and join the other artists in Chelsea if that's what you want. I'll muddle along. We all muddle along in the end. Everyone does."

Paul went back to looking at the papers on his desk, seeing nothing. When he looked up she was gone. She had left the door open. Hopefully, Paul thought, that was a good sign. Then the tears began pouring down his face to add to his misery.

THE LAST INSTRUCTION Frederick Whitaker gave his solicitor was to publish his will in the newspaper. He wanted the world to know how rich he was. How successful had been his life. He wanted people to envy his money when he was dead. It was the last touch of his money which gave him any satisfaction.

When Frank Brigandshaw read in the *Times* the figure of three hundred and nineteen thousand pounds his eyes nearly popped out of his head. He had had no idea just how rich the bastard was. He was sitting on the couch in his new flat. The *Times* had been delivered to his door. The *Times*, Frank decided, had a better ring to it than the *Telegraph* or the *Mail*. There were no pictures except at the bottom of the back page. The snob value appealed to him. Digesting the sum of money with his coffee, Frank turned his mind to Connie. The amount seen in writing looked so big. A seven-bedroom home on five acres in Surrey only cost five thousand pounds in the depressed property market after the Labour government had slapped on heavy property tax to flush out the rich. Just imagining trying to make all that money in one lifetime was beyond his wildest imagination. All the scams he could dream up in his mind could never generate so much money. So there it was, he told himself. A fortune to be picked up two blocks down the road. Now the amount of money was out in the open every male shark who fancied himself would be drooling at the mouth. Why not himself to the trough of fortune?

"Why not me?"

Working on the principle there was no time like the present, Frank went to his phone and dialled Connie's number, looking around his flat while he listened to the ring. It wasn't as good as hers, the one she and Dorothy had paid for in Chelsea, but it wasn't all bad.

"Connie? How are you? Frank."

"So you've read the paper this morning. I was rather expecting your call."

"What are you talking about? I've rented a nice flat just down the road and was about to invite you to dinner. I'm now in public relations. First big cheque came in the other day."

"What's public relations?" asked Connie, letting Frank hear the underlying disbelief in her voice.

"Introducing people. I have a lot of friends."

"I'm sure you do, Frank."

"Do you want to come to dinner tonight at the flat?"

"Why not? So you didn't read the papers?"

"What's in them that's so interesting, Connie?"

"Frederick's will. He left over three hundred thousand pounds and all of it to me."

"I thought we could get past money, you and I, now I'm on my feet."

"Are you, Frank?"

"Come and see tonight."

"Who's cooking?"

"Me, as a matter of fact. The one thing I did learn from the cook boy in Cape Town was how to cook. Before Mother employed Samson, he worked for a family of Italians who taught him all the tricks."

"What are we having?"

"Spaghetti with a delicious tomato, basil and garlic sauce. Quite Samson's speciality. And, of course, we'll have a bottle of wine."

"Do I have to get dressed up?"

"What a silly question. Of course you do. This is an exclusive dinner party for two."

"Whose flat is it really?"

"Mine, Connie. I'll show you the lease. And the deposit slip from Cohen Wells for my advance. I have so many ideas now to make my own money."

"I'm sure you do. What time?"

"Shall we say seven-thirty for eight?"

"Give me the address."

"You will be the first girl I will be entertaining in my new flat."

After the small giggle down the phone, a giggle Frank was not sure which way to take, he gave Connie his address.

With a feeling of satisfaction from a job well done, Frank picked up the paper and tried to read. They understood each other, that was what was so good. There was nothing naive about his Connie. The giggle, he decided on reflection, was a giggle of disbelief.

"How the hell did Samson make his tomato sauce? I'll have to get her drunk before we sit down to dinner. Never mind, who cares about the food? With her money I'll never have to contemplate cooking for the rest of my life."

PART 4

AUGUST TO OCTOBER 1949 – FREE LOVE

1

When Dorian Brigandshaw flew into the small airport outside Salisbury in Rhodesia for his two-week holiday before going in the army, he was not sure what to expect. His parents had sailed from Tilbury several weeks earlier. Crossing the tarmac to the small building next to the tower, Dorian was immediately conscious of being three thousand feet above sea level, the air crisp and clean. Above was a clear blue sky laced with fluffy white clouds, none of which were moving when Dorian looked up and around to get his bearings. The feel of Rhodesia was a lot different to Cape Town where he had stayed with his mother during most of the war. Behind him two black men were loading luggage from his plane onto a trolley. They were dressed in short-sleeved khaki shirts and shorts. It was a perfect day far from the drab English summer Dorian had left behind. If this, he thought, was a Rhodesian winter it was the right place to live. Putting up with the English winter for all those years, his mother had been out of her mind. Taking off his jacket and putting it over his shoulder held by his right thumb in the tag, Dorian felt jaunty. From his new perspective the Army National Service was a right royal bore. Taking in the distant bush on the edge of the airfield, all material for his book, Dorian went through the open door of the airport terminal to show his passport and pick up his luggage before deciding his next move.

"Hello, darling."

"What are you doing here, Mother? I thought I'd have to go into Salisbury and give you a ring from Meikles Hotel. How did you know which was my flight?"

"Your father. He's chatting to the airport manager. They haven't seen each other in years. We flew up from Beira yesterday. Two weeks on that damn farm and back to Beira for the rest of our cruise. I'm looking forward to seeing Egypt. The Sphinx and the Pyramids. Harry says he's going to ride a camel. Lord and Lady Chislehurst were on the boat. Such interesting people. Sat with us at the captain's table. You did know the family used to own the shipping line? Colonial Shipping was the old Pirate's company. Now it's Commonwealth Shipping. Reflects the modern trend now India has taken independence and stayed in the Commonwealth. Where's your luggage?"

"On the trolley coming in. Don't I have to show my passport? How did you get this side of the barrier?"

"Your father knows everyone. Come on. It's so lovely to see you. Harry likes talking to his mother. Madge is all right. Her children left the farm a long time ago. Married. Every girl gets married in Rhodesia no matter what they look like. Shortage of women. In the old days the 'fishing fleet', as they called them, went to India to find husbands. Now they come to Rhodesia. Lots of young ex-servicemen taking up Crown Land to farm, so Harry says. The British government want more Rhodesian tobacco so they don't have to use precious dollars to buy American tobacco. Thank God Beth is good looking and takes after me or she'd end up on some godforsaken farm in the middle of nowhere. The farms are so big. The country is empty of people, black or white. Harry says there aren't two million people in the whole damn country the size of England. You never see a friendly face outside your family from one month to the next. Now you can understand why I won't live here."

"How's the farm?"

"I have no idea."

"Are you staying on Elephant Walk?"

"Of course we are. That was part of the deal. A first-class cruise around Africa and through the Mediterranean in exchange for me staying two weeks on the farm."

"How is my grandmother?"

"Walks with a stick. Harry said she was frail. From what I can see she's as strong as an ox. Seventy-eight years old."

"I'm looking forward to talking to her. Does she know why I'm coming?"

"Harry told her. Perked up no end. Anyone wanting to talk about her Sebastian is always welcome. Quite a love story. Friends as children. Fell pregnant with Harry when she was sixteen. Then they were parted by the Pirate making her marry the eldest Brigandshaw son, not knowing she was pregnant by Seb. She'll tell you everything."

"I had no idea there was a love story." Taken aback by the revelation his grandparents were not married to each other when his father was born, Dorian was seeing more to his novel than he had first imagined.

"There's always a love story. We always remember our first true love. I know I do."

"Who was that, Mother? Wasn't it Father?"

"You don't want to know. Write your book about your grandfather. She'll only tell you half the story if she has any sense. No point rattling the skeletons in the family cupboard. It all ended happily apart from the Great Elephant killing your grandfather. Maybe it's better not to get bored with each other. To only have memories of love. Your grandmother will thank you, letting her talk about Seb. Once you get her going she never stops. Everything she ever says about him is perfect. In my life I have never met a perfect person, but that's beside the point."

"And Aunt Madge?"

"She's the glue that holds the farm together. Quite the do-gooder is Madge. There's a clinic and a school on Elephant Walk. All watched like a hawk by Madge. She wants your father to pay for Josiah Makoni to go to Fort Hare University down south. He's the son of Tembo by Princess his fourth wife. Only university in Africa that takes blacks."

"What happened to Aunt Madge's husband?"

"Barend was shot by a madman. The same man who shot your father's first wife."

"That's weird. If she hadn't died I wouldn't be alive. None of us children would be alive."

His mother gave Dorian a queer look and stopped talking. Dorian found his luggage and showed the man at the gate his passport.

"How long are you staying with us, sir?"

"Two weeks. I have to go into the Army National Service."

"Have a nice stay with us. Welcome to Rhodesia. Your first visit?"

"It is. My father grew up here on a farm."

"Thought I recognised the surname. Colonel Brigandshaw is famous in Rhodesia. I think he's over there talking to the airport manager. After the army, are you coming to live in Rhodesia?"

"No, he's not," said Tina.

"Why are you on the wrong side of the barrier, madam?"

"My husband is Colonel Brigandshaw."

"Ah. That explains it."

"You never know," said Dorian. "I may like Rhodesia. Want to come back again."

"They do say once you've been bitten by the African bug you always come back again. Something about drinking the water of the Zambezi. Does funny things to people. After that, they can't leave the place alone."

With his passport stamped, Dorian went across to his father who had broken off his conversation with the airport manager who was walking off the other way. Father and son had big grins on their faces. Then they shook hands.

"Come on, son. Back to the farm. Ralph Madgwick lent me his car to come and pick you up. Good to see you."

"How's the trip so far?"

"Wonderful. Your mother has truly enjoyed herself. Do you know we first met on a boat? The sea does something for your mother. Don't you think she looks ten years younger? Come on, I'm driving. My mother can't wait for you to arrive so she can talk about my father. I've told her all about your book. She's very excited. When do you have to go in the army?"

"The day after I get back. In two weeks' time. Do you think I can find out everything about Grandfather in two weeks?"

"That depends. You'll never know everything."

"I could always come back after the army."

"I don't think your mother would like that. Two years in the army is a long time. First you have to start writing the book. They won't give you any time during your square-bashing. That's eight weeks. Then you'll go for a commission. Just enjoy yourself on Elephant Walk. I'll show you the bush. You'll need the settings for your book. Robert St Clair always said he needed the settings in his mind. So he can see the characters as the story unfolds. If you really want to write you should spend some time with Robert and his family at Purbeck Manor. You only saw him briefly at the funeral. We can go up to the Zambezi Valley when you've had a good natter with your grandmother. What are you actually going to write about?"

"His life."

"That might be tricky."

"I'm going to call it fiction."

"You'd better. Not that I give a damn."

"What's it to do with you, Dad?" said Dorian, tongue in cheek, not wishing to tell his father what he had just heard."

"Everything. Depending on how far your grandmother goes with her story, you and I may have to sit down. For me to do some explaining. Africa was pretty wild in those days. My father got here before Rhodesia was a British Crown Colony. Got permission to hunt elephant from King Lobengula of the Matabele whose father had conquered the country from the tribes of the Shona. Mzilikazi, Lobengula's father, came up from Zululand with an army, raping and pillaging until he reached what he called Gu-Bulawayo. The place of the killings, I think it means."

"I want to take notes."

"Wait till we get back to the farm. Then you can write as many notes as you like."

"What might you have to explain?" said Dorian, amused by his father's slight discomfort.

"Let's leave that one until we have to. I'm sure your grandmother will start the story when she herself got to Africa."

"So the skeleton is still back in England?"

"I suppose so. So you've heard about a skeleton? Why don't we all have a beer at Meikles Hotel on the way through Salisbury? We're on holiday. Drinking a beer in the afternoon is allowed. Only one beer. Your grandmother knows when your plane was due to arrive. Can't disappoint Gran for a moment longer than necessary."

"Except for one beer."

"Let me carry your suitcase."

"I'm not a girl, Dad."

"How was Beth? Did you see her in London before you caught your plane?"

"She took me to the airport."

"Has she got a serious boyfriend?"

"Better ask her. Nancy is wild. I spent the night before the flight in their flat."

"You and Nancy?"

"Why ever not?"

With the thought of Nancy Longhurst rushing to his balls, Dorian reached the car a little uncomfortable. The car was a truck. A Dodge truck that Harry had imported for Ralph Madgwick from America, Harry told his son.

"Had to use some of my American dollars. You need a tough vehicle on our roads. The corrugations rattle a British saloon car to pieces in two years. Put your suitcase in the back. The cab's good for two people so you'll have to sit on the case. When Ralph takes his family from the farm to Salisbury they put a settee in the back so their kids can sit comfortably with their backs to the cab. All right until it rains. You'll meet them. They're all home from boarding school for the summer holidays, as we would say in England. Of course our summer is your winter. Faith is seventeen, Jacob fifteen. Young Becky just turned thirteen. Will you be all right in the back of the truck? Sit with your back against the cab and the wind doesn't get to you when the truck's at speed."

"You said it was a car."

"Same thing."

"I'll be fine, Dad."

On the way to Meikles Hotel all Dorian could think of was Nancy. He had been fast asleep on a mattress in the lounge when she climbed into his bed in the middle of the night, whispering for him to be quiet.

"If your sister finds out about this she'll kill me."

There was silence for a minute.

"Nancy! What are you doing?"

"What do you think I'm doing, idiot? Is there something wrong with you?... Oh, good. There isn't."

"She'll wake up."

"Her door's closed. Your Beth sleeps like a log."

Knowing when to talk and when to keep his mouth shut, Dorian had done what he was told. For most of the night. Only when the light came up did Nancy escape to the safety of her own bedroom, gently closing her door after blowing him a kiss.

When Beth got up to make a cup of tea, Dorian was feigning sleep. Only when Beth had gone to her bedroom had Dorian fallen into an exhausted sleep.

Over breakfast neither of them looked at each other. Shortly after, Beth had driven him to the airport in her car, a pre-war Austin Seven, a birthday present from their father. His father had paid for him to fly to Rhodesia. From London to their first stop in Nairobi, Dorian had slept all the way.

At Meikles Hotel, his father parked the Dodge pick-up in the road. A black man in livery greeted them at the door. The man knew his father. Dorian watched his father give the man a tip to watch the truck.

"In the old days the doorman was dressed in monkey skins round his waist and a leopard skin over his shoulder. Carried a cowhide black shield and a Zulu assegai. The old Zulu died a while ago when I was in England. He was a good friend. Now they dress the doorman like a London hotel. Takes out all the mystery of Africa. We'll have our drinks in the lounge. Don't allow women in the bar. The whole of Mashonaland meets in Meikles Hotel. When the tobacco sales are on as they are right now the farmers stay the night in the hotel after watching their tobacco sell. Kind of a tradition. Paul Crookshank's brother is here. I saw him on the floors earlier this morning before your mother and I went to the airport. You must have met his brother Paul. Paul's running my new company."

"Paul was the one who had a fight with Frank when they were kids."

"Did you see Frank?"

"Beth doesn't see Frank. Must have stolen some money. Beth says he now rents a posh flat in Knightsbridge. There's an older woman around. A much older woman. Beth wouldn't talk about it."

"I'm glad he's got a flat."

"When's he coming home?" asked Dorian.

"When you see him, ask him. He's always welcome. His mother misses him, don't you, Tina? Sit yourselves down at that table while I say hello to some people I know. Order the drinks, Dorian. Mine's a Castle. Make sure the bottle is very cold. Back in a tick."

"That's why he wanted a beer," said Dorian's mother. "Says he's been away from Rhodesia too long. Everyone seems to know your father. Make mine a gin without ice. In this country they fill the glass up with ice and then pour over the gin. Can't taste the gin. While he's off with his friends I'll tell you all about the trip."

"I can't wait to hear all your news. What are you having in the gin?"

"Angostura bitters. Pink gin. You always were a good listener, Dorian. You'll make a good writer. Good listeners remember years later what they were told. Put it into stories. Now Lady Chislehurst is about my age. She was on the stage..."

With his mind still concentrated on Nancy as it had been ever since she climbed out of his bed, Dorian let his mother prattle on about her new friend with a title. Every now and then he smiled at her. When the drinks came, Dorian left the beer in his father's bottle, next to his glass. It was still cold when his father came back and when he poured out his drink the bottle was dripping with moisture from condensation in the air.

"Cheers, son. Good to see you. So many friends I haven't seen in years. They never change, just the same. Rhodesia is just the same. This war changed nothing out here."

Trying hard to turn his mind away from Nancy's naked body, Dorian heard his father go on about how much he liked Rhodesia again, getting sour looks from his mother. They had two drinks each before going back to the truck. His father was right: once out of Salisbury, the corrugations in the dirt road were terrible, jangling every bone in his body as he bounced up and down on his case, hanging onto the side of the truck while he looked out and wondered at the beauty of the African bush. Cape Town had been tame in comparison. Once away from the few houses after leaving the centre of town, Dorian counted game on both sides of the road, dust streaming out behind the vehicle. When he reached the farm he was going to ask his father the names of the animals. There was so much for him to learn. For his book. For a good book he needed to know everything, he told himself, feeling so happy he wanted to shout at the top of his voice.

When they reached the farm an hour later, what struck Dorian was the mother. A woman of smouldering, sultry good looks that belied giving birth to a girl the age of Faith. Of the two, Mrs Madgwick was the better looking, like something out of the Arabian Nights. She had the disconcerting habit of looking straight into a man, and for the first time in two days drove out Dorian's erotic pictures of Nancy. They were all nice to look at but Mrs Madgwick was special. Dorian thought Ralph Madgwick lucky.

On the stoep, as he remembered they called the veranda in Africa from his three years in Cape Town, was seated his grandmother in a chair made of wicker. She was smiling. Kissing Aunty Madge on the cheek, Dorian went to greet his grandmother.

"So there you are."

"Yes, Gran. How are you?"

"As you see me. Old. Happy. What more can I want? So you want me to tell you the story?"

"All of it. I'm going to write a novel. One day they will make a movie out of my novel. They'll remember him forever."

"I remembered him forever. Have you been in love, Dorian?"

"No, Grandmother."

"Give me a kiss. England's so far away. I missed all of you growing up."

"You can come and live with us at Hastings Court. You remember Hastings Court?"

"Of course I do, Dorian. I was born there. Where I grew up. But here are my memories. I can't leave my memories, now can I? Every bit of the farm reminds me of Sebastian. This was our farm before Harry took it over to run as his own. It's so nice to see Harry again. Would you like a cup of tea? Florence will make us some tea. We drink tea in Africa to remind us of England. Come and let me have a good look at you."

THREE DAYS LATER, when Dorian was unable to absorb any more conversation with his grandmother, he brought a small table out of the main house and found himself a spot under a msasa tree. He could see the top of the Mazoe Dam in the distance, the rest hidden by the steep gorge. The dam was not very wide. There was a road on top connecting the two sides of the river. On the water in front of the dam, which went on into the shimmering distance surrounded by bush, was a sail boat skidding over the water. Down through the msasa trees, in among the well-kept grass and flower beds ringing the base of the trees, was the Mazoe River. Along the river was a grove of orange trees, the red dots of the ripening fruit visible to Dorian's naked eye. On the other side of the river was more bush. The dam was spilling on the one side letting water flow into the river. The main house was lived in by his grandmother and Aunty Madge. The Madgwick family had another house. Dorian counted five houses in the compound. Behind the orange grove, right on the water some distance from Dorian, was the native compound. Dorian could hear the sound of children playing. The native compound was run by Tembo. If he wished to visit the compound he required the permission of Tembo. Dorian wanted to meet Josiah who had returned from the mission school and was waiting to go to university. Aunty Madge had said Princess was very proud of her son going to Fort Hare. After two days of bullying Aunty Madge, Dorian's father had agreed to pay for all the costs of Josiah going to university. A friend of his father's in Salisbury had told his father sending blacks to university was asking for trouble. That Fort Hare was a den of black nationalism. That if blacks were educated, they would want the white man out of Africa. It was the turning point that made his father agree to pay for Josiah's university education.

"Africa can't remain a paradise for hunters and gatherers forever, Dorian. The greed of the civilised world will see to that. Better some of the locals are educated to let them look after themselves. To me, the lifestyle in a thatched hut by a river is better than a flat in London. Fish, game, a vegetable garden. What more can a man want for the perfect life?"

"Are they better off with us or without us, Dad? They have modern medicine. Better life expectancy."

"Only history will answer that question. Charles Darwin would have said it's all part of man's evolution. That you can't stop progress."

With a comfortable chair and the small table in the shade of the tree, a light breeze coming up from the direction of the river, Dorian began to work at his notes.

When Florence brought him a tray of tea at eleven o'clock he was still hard at work. Sifting all the information in his head. He wanted the human story behind all the facts. Good books, his tutor at Oxford had drummed into his head, were about people. Ordinary people placed in unusual circumstances. There was just so much for Dorian to digest. Hopefully, later, back in England, it would all make sense.

Sipping his cup of tea and looking at the scenery, Dorian stretched his back. Wild birds that sounded like ducks had flown up from the river, screaming at the dogs. When Florence came to collect the tea tray she said they were wild geese. On the other side of the river, monkeys were chattering.

When the time came to return to England, Dorian had not left Elephant Walk. Between talking to his grandmother and placating his mother there had been no time to go anywhere. His mother was jealous of the time he spent with his grandmother. The two did not like each other. Every time his mother mentioned Lady Chislehurst, which was often, Granny Brigandshaw gave her a look.

His parents were to fly to Beira the following day to board the SS *Europe* on her journey up through the Suez Canal. His father drove him alone to the airport. He could only think of Nancy Longhurst waiting for him at the other end. All thought of the army was swamped by Nancy. He had thought of writing her a letter but changed his mind. Apart from whispering to each other in bed they said nothing to each other. His father tried to explain in the truck that his mother was going through what he called a midlife crisis. Dorian thought she was bored; nothing to do anymore now all of them had left home.

When his flight took off on its first leg to Nairobi, all Dorian could think of was Nancy. His suitcase was stuffed with notes he had written under the msasa tree with the wild geese screaming at the dogs, the dogs chasing each other round the flower beds, trying to ruin his concentration. If nothing else from his trip, he had the glimmerings of a book. His grandmother had cried when he left. She was very old. Dorian wondered if he would see her again except in the book he was going to write about her life, changing the names, making it out to be fiction.

When he reached London Airport it was raining as he got off the plane. No one was at the airport to meet him. When he phoned Beth, Nancy was going out that evening.

"She goes out every evening. Why do you ask? Did you have a nice time?"

"Lovely. Mother met someone called Lady Chislehurst on the boat. Couldn't stop talking about her. Grandmother told me everything I wanted to know for the book."

"Enjoy the army."

"I'll try, Beth. Total waste of two years so far as I'm concerned. I saw Jeremy Crookshank. Told me to say hello to his brother. Can you pass that on when you see Paul?"

"If I see him, I'll tell him. Where are you staying tonight?"

"In a hotel by the station."

"You can stay here if you want. Save money."

"Not if Nancy is going out."

"What's Nancy got to do with it? ... Oh my God!"

"I'll give you a ring when I get some leave. Mum and Dad will be back in six weeks."

"Are they enjoying themselves?"

"Who knows?"

"Look after yourself. Do you want me to say something to Nancy?"

"Better not."

The next day, Dorian lined up in a queue with all the other young men to receive his first uniform. It had meant nothing to Nancy.

2

———————

The very thought of his Oxford-educated bookworm of a brother carrying a rifle on his shoulder, tickled Frank Brigandshaw pink. Twice during his lunch with Horatio Wakefield and William Smythe, compliments of Cohen Wells, he had let out an involuntary giggle.

"What's so funny, Frank?" Horatio Wakefield asked with a trace of irritation.

"Did you ever meet Dorian? A bit younger than Anthony who died in the war. Oxford degree in English literature. Plays for the village cricket side. Can't bat or bowl to save his life. My brother joined the army today. To do his square-bashing. If he's lucky, which he will be, he'll draw Corporal Snodgrass. They get the recruits at Aldershot according to the first letter of their surnames. Snodgrass will make his life bloody miserable. Especially when the corporal finds out Dorian is my brother. Once I received my commission, I walked past Snodgrass at every chance, making him salute me. Do you know, Horatio, Attlee's going to pay for his National Health Service with the help of his tax on cigarettes. Buy an extra packet of cigarettes made from choice Rhodesian tobacco paid for in sterling and help your fellow citizens to a healthy life. How does that sound? Sorry about the giggle. Every time I think of Dorian in a pair of army boots, the mirth wells up inside of me."

"I take it you don't much like your brother?"

"I love him to bits. Were either of you in the army? Of course you weren't. War correspondents. Damn dangerous I'm sure, but you never had to do your square-bashing."

"Horatio was interned by the Nazis before the war," said William.

"I'm sorry. I forgot. The picture of brother Dorian is so vivid in my mind. Do you remember Snodgrass, Zach?"

"Do I ever? Right royal bastard. Frank and I met in the army doing our square-bashing. Anyone like a brandy with their coffee? They have a good Napoleon. Anyone for a cigar? Having talked tobacco all lunchtime the least we can do is smoke a cigar with our brandy."

Frank, enjoying himself at someone else's expense, remembered Zach pulling away the brandy bottle at their private dinner in the Cohens' Sloane Square house. Now the boot was on the other foot. Which thought made him think of Dorian marching up and down in his army boots, the .303 rifle heavy on his shoulder and Snodgrass yelling. Which made him giggle.

"Life's just one big laugh."

All three round the table looked at him in silence.

"I give you Ridgeback cigarettes," said Frank, picking up his balloon glass slopping in one-hundred-year-old brandy. "A brand that everyone will know by the time my friend's advertising campaign gets into full swing. To old friends. Thank you both, Horatio and William, for answering my invitation to lunch. You are two very important people in the Brigandshaw household."

"It's always a pleasure to help Harry Brigandshaw," said Horatio. "Even if the rules of journalism are being bent just a little. My editor, Mr Glass, will appreciate the advertising revenue you tell me will flow to the *Daily Mail*. About articles praising a particular brand of cigarettes, I am not so sure. A piece on Harry Brigandshaw, mentioning his new business venture, might be worth a try. Harry is always news. That disappearing act in the Congo for nearly three years caught the public's imagination. I'll see what I can do. Maybe William can do a bit on his current affairs, like his Empire Service? Looking back on heroes from the First World War. What they are up to now. How is Harry, Frank?"

"Right now, he and his lovely wife, my mother, are on a boat trip sailing up the east coast of Africa. What a splendid lunch. Poor old Dorian."

Once again, just for good measure, Frank let out a giggle. The fat cigar in his mouth was making him feel a little ridiculous.

. . .

EIGHT WEEKS LATER, at the end of the summer, Beth drove the Austin Seven to the airport. Her parents were due in from Paris at the end of their cruise and tour of Europe. The day before, Dorian had finished his army training. They had given him a forty-eight-hour pass which he was spending with Beth.

"You go to the airport, Beth. If I hear one word of Lady Chislehurst I'll scream. Tell them I'm still in the army."

"What do I say about you failing the officer selection board?"

"Nothing. It doesn't matter. They said I don't have the right officer qualities, whatever they are. That I wasn't a leader. They asked us questions and ran us round an obstacle course for two days. You had to find a way of getting a dummy over the electrified top of the wall. The dummy was meant to be a wounded soldier. When it was my turn to be the team leader I killed the poor sod. You had a ladder, yourself and two other recruits trying to get themselves made into officers. I ended up dropping the dummy right on top. The examining officer said my wounded man would have been frizzled. After that it was all downhill. Doesn't matter. I'll get a better chance of getting to know people without my kind of snooty background. People more interesting for a book. I'm going on a course to teach me how to fix cars and trucks in the Royal Army Service Corps. The same unit that got Paul Crookshank wounded in Burma. There'll be lots of time to write. They say at the end of the three-month course they'll send us to Malta. I'll find a spot to write under a tree away from all the noise. Before I go to Malta I'll go down to Hastings Court for Christmas. We'll all be there except Frank. Is he still buggering around with Mum and Dad? Maybe he has a point. Wouldn't you be pissed off if you were lied to about who you are? What's he up to now?"

"Making money. Frank has charm when he wants to turn it on. Salesmanship is all about charm. And he's ruthless. Sell his grandmother for enough money."

"I want to finish the book before it's too late for Granny Brigandshaw to hold a copy."

"Are you that confident of finding a publisher?"

"Why ever not? I got a First in English literature at Oxford. No good, it seems, for ordering people around but it's the stuff you need to write a book."

"Keep your hands off Nancy while I go to the airport."

"What are you talking about?"

"I know Nancy. It's Saturday. She works half-day. She'll be back while I'm gone."

"Don't you trust your brother?"

"I don't trust Nancy."

When they came off the plane, her mother was chirpy. Most of the luggage had been sent on by boat and train to Hastings Court. When they were in the small car with the two overnight bags, her mother talked all the way home of a Lord and Lady Uppington. Her mother had found out soon after leaving the Port of Beira that Lady Uppington was somehow related to the Mandervilles. They had sat on the captain's table all the way to Venice. In Egypt they had got off the boat at the Port of Suez and toured the sights with Lord and Lady Uppington, picking up the boat again at Port Said. It seemed to Beth, the sun would begin to shine on Hastings Court the moment Lady Uppington insisted on paying a visit when they all got back to England.

When Beth drove the little Austin up the driveway to the old house she was sick of Lady Uppington. If nothing else, Beth told herself, it made her mother happy hobnobbing with the aristocracy. There were always small mercies. Her mother, it seemed, no longer wanted to live in London. Her parents had reached some kind of compromise, including not selling the house in Cape Town where Beth had spent most of the war. Her father said Aunty Madge liked the Bishopscourt house for holidays with her mother and her grandchildren, getting her two daughters and their families together for a holiday. When she had saved up some money, Beth fancied the idea of a holiday in the Cape. Mr and Mrs Coetzee, the caretakers, would be pleased, along with the rest of the staff. Nothing better than a permanent holiday with only the occasional guests.

When Beth got back to the flat in Kensington on the Sunday night, ready to be at work in the morning, Nancy had a smug grin on her face. Dorian had gone back to the army at the end of his leave.

"Did Dorian enjoy his leave, by any chance?"

"You have a dirty mind, Beth darling. A dirty mind. How were your parents?"

"Muddling along. Mother has a new friend. I won't bore you. I need a drink."

"Now you're talking."

"Are you going out tonight?"

"I don't think so. I phoned and cancelled."

Nancy gave her a sweet smile and went to pour the gins. With Nancy, Beth sighed to herself, nothing changed.

There were some sides of business Paul Crookshank could have done without. Telling Jeanne Pétain there was no work for her was one of them. Having criss-crossed the country in the Bedford lorry for two and a half years, they had become known. Everyone with anything worth selling knew where to come when they wanted to sell their antiques and the market was beginning to change. People had a better idea of the value of what they were selling. The new phase in the business was telling the sellers to send Brigandshaw Oosthuizen a photograph of what they were selling with a description. There was enough coming on the market through the mail and the telephone to satisfy the need in America. Kenneth Grahame with his Old Etonian tie was no longer needed to open the doors of the ancestral homes, and the major had begun to complain he was past his prime. The meeting had taken place that morning in Harry Brigandshaw's office between Harry and Paul.

"The last favour you can do that girl is to send her back to America, Paul. Romantic dreams that don't make any money have the bad habit of coming to a sticky end. No one can make money as an artist. Not in their lifetimes. Use her talent as an interior decorator and paint at weekends. You have to be cruel to be kind on this one, Paul. Everyone without talent likes the idea of living the life of the artist. It's a lazy man's way of going through life, hoping someone else will support them."

"She was counting on four trips a year."

"Well, we can't anymore. Does she have the fare back to the States? There we can help. Tinus says they need Jeanne in New York to sell the antiques. Her way of painting the rooms on canvas for the client to see is a winner. The market has changed. Selling the antiques has become more difficult with competition. When you get a good idea, other people climb on the bandwagon. Do you want me to tell her, Paul?"

"No, sir. That's my job."

"Now. Cigarettes. How's the advertising campaign shaping up?"

"We launch countrywide next week. In all the newspapers and on the radio."

"I've got my fingers crossed."

"Haven't we all?"

"Someone told me back before the war about being a success in business. Three good ideas out of five and you get rich. Two and you go bust. We're one up with the antiques for the moment. You just have to try new ideas or you start going backwards. Nothing lasts forever."

"Did you enjoy the trip?"

"My wife did. That was what counts. Two weeks on the farm just made me more nostalgic for Africa. You have to think of other people or everyone ends up unhappy. It's called give and take. Mostly I give. Or so it seems to me."

"Can't we find something for Jeanne?"

"Try selling her paintings," said Harry, sarcastically.

"I'll tell her."

"That's a good lad. We're having Lord and Lady Uppington down to the Court for the weekend. My wife can't get enough of them. They sat at the same table with us on the SS *Europe*."

"What are they like?"

"Have you heard of a bore? All they do is talk. A lot of trivia. Bores me stiff but Tina likes them. After so many years of marriage you learn to do as you're told to keep the peace."

PAUL HAD HEARD from Jeanne once since she left the hotel off Regent Street to look for her studio. To remind him of his promise to give her four buying trips a year before moving in. The flat was a room with a small bathroom and small kitchen. Tessa had found it for her. Frank, in his meetings with Paul at Cohen Wells – Frank refusing to come to Paul's office in case he bumped into his legal father – had been amused to keep Paul informed of how much Jeanne was enjoying her new bohemian life. She was painting furiously whenever the light was good enough. Making other people feel uncomfortable was Frank's specialty. Beth had said that as a kid, Frank had enjoyed pulling the legs off living insects. Pinning live butterflies through their bodies to a board to watch them flutter to death. Hearing mention of Jeanne at every chance felt to Paul like having his entrails pulled from his stomach. His obsession for Jeanne was growing. Trying to look at other women made him feel worse. She had got under his skin and wouldn't get out. She was two years older than Paul but none of that mattered.

Avoiding the issue and not phoning Tessa to get Jeanne's new phone number to tell her what he had been told to do by Harry Brigandshaw, Paul went home to his new flat. Once in the flat, Paul closed all the windows and sat down at his grand piano. It was his only way to solace himself when the waves of hopelessness poured over him. The flat was perfect for two people. On his own there was little to cherish. The piano was perfectly tuned. To purge the feeling of loss, Paul played the same medley of music, classic through to jazz, he had played the night he had slept on the sofa in Jeanne's Brooklyn flat. Playing softly, not to disturb his neighbours, Paul went on to play the music of Chopin for an hour, all to himself. Only then was he ready to pick up the phone. Olivia answered his call.

"Paul Crookshank, Olivia. Do you have Jeanne's new number?"

"She's here, Paul. Hang on."

Paul had to wait only a moment.

"How are you?" came the voice he remembered so well.

"Not too good. Bad news. Harry Brigandshaw is stopping the Bedford trips. People are coming to us now the name is known. The American market for British antiques is being flooded. They call it free enterprise."

"Is this to punish me?"

"What for?"

"Neglected love perhaps."

"Oh, Jeanne. Would I do that?" said Paul, his voice as sad as his feelings.

"There's spite in all of us. What am I going to do for money? After buying the furniture and all the paints I'm nearly broke. Never was good at saving."

"I'm sorry. Nothing I could do."

"I thought you were in charge of the company?"

"I am. I was. I'm running the cigarettes now."

"After all I did getting you off the ground in America. Charming."

"I can let you have some of my own money. Since Harry came back from his trip he's been in a foul mood. Never seen him like it before. Trouble at home, I think. He wants to go back to Africa. His wife doesn't."

"And I must pay. Absolutely charming!"

"You can move into my new flat and paint to your heart's content."

"Is it in Chelsea?"

"It could be."

"Paul, go to hell. I ask you one favour. Four miserable trips. Enough to feed me."

"We could have a drink."

"I don't want to be a housewife. I want to be a painter. Don't you understand?"

"Harry thinks you should go back to Brooklyn and your career. In America we can give you lots of work. The market has changed. We have enough product. Won't you come and see my flat? I have a piano. A grand piano. You like playing the piano."

"Where is the flat?"

"Hammersmith. Not far from Mrs Bigglesworth. Please, Jeanne. I want to see you. We have too much good together to fall out with each other. I'm going to try and sell your paintings. That was Harry's idea. How many have you finished?"

"You want to sell my paintings?"

Paul could hear a change in Jeanne's voice.

"Exactly. Tessa's sold some to Cohen Wells."

"You can come round when I have finished ten paintings."

"When will that be?"

"How do I know? You can't just paint to order. I have to feel for a painting to make it any good. I'll call you. Goodbye, Paul."

With a broad smile on his face, Paul went back to the piano. With a light heart, he crashed down on the keys. Only when a neighbour banged on the adjacent wall did he get up from the stool and pour himself a drink. However small, there was a chink of light at the end of the tunnel. He was going to see her again. When she had finished ten paintings. Even if he had to buy every one himself it would be worth it. He would tell her the names of fictitious buyers. A small white lie. Sometimes lying was better than telling the truth. Looking at his beautiful new piano, Paul imagined the elfin Jeanne sitting up on the stool. The picture in his mind made him so happy he found himself standing motionless in the middle of the room just holding his undrunk drink.

JEANNE HAD FOUND it was one thing to find the perfect studio with the perfect light, but quite another to paint. The whole build-up to the bohemian life had been too much. Even Jeanne knew she was playing a part. That her chances of being a great painter were virtually nil. Vague impressions of rooms-to-be with the right colours and the odd antique were quite different to a real canvas to hang in a gallery. Her paintings of Brooklyn were mostly watercolours that had taught her how better to go about her job as an interior decorator. A way to show the client what was in her head before money was spent painting the rooms and bringing in the new furniture, and ensuring the client got what they liked. Her impressions of rooms on quickly painted canvases had been the way to sell her interior designs.

When Jeanne walked back to her studio, the sight of all the stuff she had bought to give the place the right feel did exactly the opposite. It was all a fraud.

"Ten bloody paintings, you idiot. Take you the rest of your life. All the paint-streaked smocks and black berets don't make the artist. You need talent. Not the ability to draw and see a room with its new curtains and furniture before it's done."

Realising she was shouting when the man next door pushed open her door to see what was the matter, she sat down plonk on one of the imitation leather chairs. Everyone in the arty section of Chelsea left their doors open. It was part of the bohemian life.

"What's the matter, my little flower?"

"I can't paint. My old company told me they won't give me any work. What am I going to do, Ben? I'm a failure. Twenty-five years old, barely a cent in the bank and nothing to show for my life. I so want to be a good painter. Nothing happens. All I see are stupid damn rooms with drapes. What am I going to become?"

"You are very pretty."

"Pretty doesn't paint pictures that anyone will like. Really like. Not for me but for the painting."

"The creative spirit works in strange ways."

"Don't tell me. I can do bits of many things but none of them truly well. I can paint a bit. Dance a bit. Play the piano up to a point. I'm good at behaving like an artist."

"It will come. Being aware of being inadequate is the first step on the road to success."

"Do you think so, Ben?"

"Of course it is. I have been living this life for years. It is the way of life that counts. Who knows what is a good abstract painting? Who can really tell? The more bizarre and ridiculous, the more it sells. People buy paintings to own a part of our way of life. It makes them feel good. Takes them away from their mundane lives. For most people, life is far too ordinary. It's the image you strike of yourself that will sell your paintings. Make people talk. The bored rich collectors love to visit Chelsea. When they buy, it makes them feel important. Quite the connoisseur. Rich people like to be made to feel important. Just having money isn't enough for them. They have to be seen to have money. When they pay thousands of pounds for a Picasso, it's not for the painting. It's for how much money they can tell their friends they paid for the painting. Same with new artists. They like to be the one who boasts they found the artists. Rich people get bored. We give them a chance to amuse themselves. The greed in rich people makes them hope what they buy will be worth much more down the line because you can't mass produce a person's paintings. Come. You've got the blues. James is having a little party in his studio. Some rich people, patrons of the arts as they like to think of themselves, have been invited. The more of us who look like artists who come, the better. Gives James's studio the right atmosphere. Put on your little black beret that goes so well with your pixie ears and let's go. Never force painting. Let the painting come to you."

"You're a darling."

"I know I am. All you have to do is charm the patrons and tell them just how good James is as a painter. Your American accent will help. Give the party a rich flavour. Rich people in London think all Americans are rich. All the rich respect is money. Tell them what they want to hear. Flirt with them. Do you understand?"

With the lifestyle she so wanted slipping from her grasp, Jeanne followed Ben, this time closing the door when they left. Downstairs in the street they put up umbrellas against the rain. Walking side by side they looked what they were: artists. Ben had a long beard and hair down to his shoulders. There was a stale smell about him that said his clothes needed a good wash. Otherwise he was clean. A man of thirty-something with beautiful white teeth.

"How long have you been an artist? Is it far to James's? What do you do for money? When I have some finished I'm going to live off my paintings."

"We all say that at first."

Jeanne was cold and wished she had put on a coat in her hurry to follow Ben. Ben had a woollen scarf wrapped around his neck. He wore a pair of gloves.

"How far is it?"

"A brisk walk. Do us good. Exercise is important. Clears the artistic veins. Let's the juices flow."

"Won't it be colder when we come back?"

"Probably. If you're lucky, one of the patrons will give you a lift. Don't see why you shouldn't be lucky. Pretty lady artists are at a premium. All the patrons are men. Middle aged or a little older. They all have cars. Some have chauffeurs to drive them when they drink too much. James is famous for organising his parties, not for his paintings."

"Will there be drinks? That does sound nice for a cold October evening."

"Plenty. The patrons supply the drinks, we supply the atmosphere."

"Do they bring their wives?"

"What for? Their wives don't want to buy paintings."

"What do they do? Their wives?"

"Stay at home. Throw tea parties for their equally rich friends. Are you all right under that umbrella? I don't know your surname."

"Pétain. We are French. I was born in France, went to America as a kid."

"Wasn't he a general from the first war who sided with Hitler after the Nazis marched into Paris? Vichy, France. Who can blame him? There's always a compromise. Even in war."

"Were you in the war?"

"Not really. They thought I had a dicky heart."

"Do you?"

"Not at all. I hate wars. 'Thou shalt not kill.' Says so in the Bible. Somehow man excludes killing people in wars if they think they're justified. All wars are right. Depends which side you're on."

"You were lucky."

"My parents were bombed out. Why I can paint. Left me a little. War compensation for the house. Not enough to have a home and family but enough to exist in my little garret. Nothing like a little garret. You don't have to think. Paint a bit and look interesting, that's my motto. Better than a nagging wife and three snotty kids tied round your neck."

"They were killed?"

"Yes, they were. Sort of changed my outlook on life. Now is not a bad way of life if you don't look at the future. After that bomb hit Mum and Dad, I stopped worrying about a future. Enjoy the moment. We'll get tight as ticks, eat as much as we like and not spend a penny. What's wrong with that? All those fools who have been working in the City are still on their way home to the suburbs. Tomorrow they'll have to get up at half past six to be ready to catch the train back to London. Six days a week, most of them. Half a day Saturday and all of Sunday to go to church. What kind of life is that? Stuck in an office. During the winter they don't see the sun five days a week. Like a mole down a burrow. They're no more secure financially than we are. Say something strong or make a mistake and you're out of a job. What were you before you decided to become a painter?"

"You first, Ben."

"Bank clerk. Boring. Very boring."

"They made you cut your hair."

"And wash my clothes."

"Dear oh dear. I'm getting warm. The exercise is good. How much further?"

"Right here, Jeanne. James has his nest in the middle of these semi-detached houses. He has the floor at the top of number seven. Here is as near as we get to a true artist colony in London."

"Smart cars."

"The patrons. There's always a way of making a living. Come on, let's run the last fifty yards. I'm hungry. Last time I ate was two days ago. Now I've got plenty of room. I'm like a camel. When food and drink are there I fill up."

"Will James mind me coming?"

"I should think not. A pretty girl like you. You haven't said what you did in America."

"Interior design. Decorating people's apartments."

"Better than a clerk. If you get lost at the party come and look for me."

"I'll be all right."

"I'm sure you will. Why I brought you. I'll first introduce you to James and then look for the food."

"Have you sold a painting?"

"Not one."

"How long have you been painting?"

"Since the end of the war. A year after that damn doodlebug killed Mum and Dad. Enjoy yourself, Jeanne. Don't worry. Let life take care of itself. There you were on your own shouting at yourself and now you are going to a party."

"What's your surname, Ben?"

"Does it matter?"

The front door of number seven was wide open. A big door that had once been the entrance of a fashionable house in the reign of

George IV. The house was separated into three flats, two on either side of the stairs and one at the top. At the top of the stairs was another door, left open like the one to the street. Inside was a big room with a high ceiling. Dormer windows pushed out from the room overlooking the gardens. The gardens had fences. Like fences for chicken runs. When Jeanne looked down there were no hens in the yards. Most of the small gardens were overgrown. It was colder inside than outside. Ben had kept his scarf around his neck, his gloves on his hands. In the middle of the room, surrounded by people, was what Jeanne supposed was a sculpture. There was a small plaque at the bottom with writing Jeanne couldn't read. The sculpture was made up of metal cogs and gears gutted from old machines and welded in place. A man was standing with his head on one side, his index finger to the side of his cheek. On his face was a faraway look. A beautiful look of happiness. Most of the guests were looking at the man with the happy smile looking at the sculpture. The man, like herself, was wearing a black beret. When he saw Jeanne looking at him it broke his concentration. Jeanne turned away to look out of the nearest dormer window. On the chimney pots on the other side of the gardens was a pigeon. The pigeon was looking back at her. Jeanne wanted to close the window against the cold. Outside it was dusk. So far as she could see there was no food or drink at the party. Along the walls were paintings in beautiful frames. The paintings were all done in squares of different colours flowing into and over each other. Jeanne tried hard to see what they meant. Her watercolours of Brooklyn were far better. When she looked up, Ben was looking around for something to eat. Some of the men wore suits. The rest of the people were artists like herself. Some she had seen at Tessa's. The man with the keening tone to his singing voice was at the party.

Jeanne wandered around the room, looking at the paintings. Ben had disappeared. The man with his finger on his cheek appeared next to her. The finger was still there. Quizzical.

"My name is James. Who are you, gorgeous child? We wear the same hats. Do you like my paintings? The man with the whiskers has bought my new sculpture for three hundred pounds. The food and drink comes later."

"Ben brought me. My name is Jeanne. French-American from New York."

"How exotic. What do you paint?"

"In America, scenes of Brooklyn where I lived. In London I am waiting."

"It is always best to wait for inspiration. Come and meet Mr Chalmers. He was in munitions during the war. Made himself a fortune."

"What's the sculpture about?"

"The cogs of war. I thought he might like it. Took me a morning to stick together. Where is Ben?"

"Looking for food."

"The caterers haven't arrived. He's always hungry. Needs a woman."

"He's my nearest neighbour. Common wall to our studios."

"Do you like my paintings?"

"I think they are wonderful."

"Come on. He's very rich. I did tell you that? Hates his wife but can't get rid of her. Do you sell your paintings?"

"Not yet."

"He'll buy. If you are nice to him. Mr Chalmers has paid for the caterers. Only the best. He loves my parties. Had his eye on you the moment you walked in the door. You don't live with a man, do you?"

"No, James."

"Keep an eye on Ben. I like him. I encourage him to come to my parties. Brings such lovely people."

"Is that what it says on the plaque?"

"Yes. *The Cogs of War*. Rather appropriate. You have to catch the moment, so to speak... Mr Chalmers. Allow me to introduce the lovely Jeanne from America. There are more guests arriving. Lovely to have an open door. I must fly. Jeanne does the most beautiful paintings. You must ask permission to make her a visit. Your judgement is so valued by us artists. Such a connoisseur. Got to fly. Back in a mo. What a lovely party."

With the figure of three hundred pounds for a pile of junk ringing in her head, Jeanne pouted the best of her smiles, pronouncing her French, rather than her American accent. The old fool with the whiskers couldn't take his eyes off her. Some people had more money than sense.

"I love the arts," said Mr Chalmers. "To me, art is all that life is about. A thing of beauty is a joy forever. That sculpture will last forever don't you think?"

"I'm sure it will," said Jeanne meaning every word. "What is your first name? Mr Chalmers is a little too formal, *n'est-ce pas*?"

"You are French. Not American."

"French and American. Have you been to the States?"

"No. But I have been to Paris. You must have been to Paris?"

"As a child."

"Then I shall take you again. Do you have a studio in Chelsea?"

"Ten minutes away. I walked."

"Allow me to drive you home. It is cold outside. When all the people fill this room it will be warm. Allow me to close the window. I just love artists. You are all so interesting. Did you come with someone?"

"Not really."

"Then I shall look after you. The restaurant in Thames Street is sending up the food. Lots to drink. It will be a lovely party with you here, my dear. A French American. Do you like his paintings? So original."

"They are beautiful, Mr Chalmers."

"Call me Samuel."

"I love them, Samuel. They speak to me."

"Do your paintings speak to you, Jeanne?"

"Always. I have only just started painting in England."

"I am a patient man."

"That is good to hear. *Voilà.* Here come the caterers with the trestle tables. What a party. Is that a little piano I see in the corner?"

"Do you play?"

"Of course."

Two other middle-aged men gave her the look. Jeanne smiled back. Samuel caught the looks and the response. Three hundred pounds would give her a good living for a year. Both of the men were wearing suits and ties. One of the ties was the same tie Jeanne had seen Kenneth Grahame wear in the Bedford lorry. The party was looking swell. White cloths on the trestle tables. Fluted wine glasses. Silver cutlery. Bone china plates. The kind of set up Jeanne had seen among her rich clients in New York. The old loft became a bustle of waiters. There was a chef in a stiff white jacket, a tall white hat on his head. Ben's mouth was literally watering, making Jeanne wipe her own face to signal him what was going on. Ben was on the other side of the room next to the two men who had smiled. Jeanne thought Ben was talking about her. The men kept looking at her, making Samuel nervous. James was hovering around in his black beret, orchestrating everything, annoying the chef. Jeanne suspected both of them were prima donnas.

Looking at the small upright piano in the corner made Jeanne nostalgic for Brooklyn. Her furniture and the piano were in storage. The flat had gone to a friend with his own furniture. If it all collapsed, she still had her possessions. Samuel put a tall glass of white wine in her hand. With the wine in her hand, Jeanne went across to the piano. Striking a few of the keys to see if the piano was in tune made James come over to her, with Samuel following. Giving Samuel back her glass after giving the wine a good sip, she sat down on the small wooden stool.

"Oh darling, can you play?" asked James delighted. "Not only is she so beautiful but multi-talented. Will you play for us?"

Jeanne played Gershwin for ten minutes, while the staff of the Thames Street restaurant laid out the food. Ben was eating the rolls. People gathered around the piano. For some reason Jeanne thought of Paul. If he had seduced her right at the start things could have been different. A man had to be confident. A man like Rudy who only wanted her body. A meeting of mutual satisfaction without all the emotional complications. Paul was complicated. Wanted more than her body. Ben's imaginary wife and three kids came to her mind as she went on playing. Samuel had not moved from her side. One of the waiters came across with a bottle of French wine and filled up their glasses. Again she thought of the three hundred pounds and not having to worry Paul for a job. It was nice to know she would have one if she went back to America. All through her life Jeanne had tried never to burn her boats. To always have an escape route. Again she thought of the three hundred pounds Samuel had paid James for a piece of junk that should have stayed on the scrap heap where it had started. It made her smile. There was more to selling art than painting a picture. When she had had enough, she left the piano and went to the trestle table groaning with all the food. Ben was still stuffing his face like a camel sucking up water. She waved at him before picking up one of the bone china plates and covered it with her own food.

"Let's sit in the alcove," said Samuel.

"Why not? Have you got the wine?"

"A whole bottle. You are very beautiful."

"Thank you, Samuel. You are very generous. This is a splendid supper. You don't like the atmosphere of formal restaurants?" Jeanne thought Samuel had paid for the caterers. Or one of the other middle-aged men ogling the girls. The young girls were all artists, smiling at the older men.

"I would, alone with you. You play divinely."

"You old flatterer."

"Do you paint as well as you play the piano?"

"Of course. I'm a painter, not a piano player. Dancing and playing the piano are just for fun."

"You dance as well?"

Jeanne turned away.

"Come on," she said heading for the window. "There was a pigeon outside."

"Isn't it too dark to see?"

"Does it matter? There's a window seat."

"You have made my evening."

With the three hundred pounds for one of her paintings firmly on the hook, Jeanne led Samuel to the window seat to eat her supper. Someone was playing a guitar and singing. The man was good. So was James. Any idea of a mental block against her painting had gone out of her head. She was back on track. With or without the help of Paul Crookshank and his old army surplus five-ton Bedford truck. She was going to be a painter.

The man with the beautiful keening voice that made her sad began to sing, making most of the guests look up from their plates of food. The song was sad. Jeanne wondered if the pigeon she could no longer see was listening to the sound. The room was almost full. The moment the caterers arrived the artists living around James's flat began to drift in. The girls were all young and attractive, outnumbering the middle-aged men. The men who were artists did not seem to mind. Free food and drink was more on their minds. For a man who had been in munitions during the war, paying the bill was nothing to worry about. Jeanne had asked James on one of his circulations around the big room amongst his guests. Samuel was footing the bill. James had given her a look as if to hope she knew what was going on. For rich men, young girls were more important to their wellbeing than art. The art was to show their wives what they had been up to when they got home. Ben, happy and full of food, had sat down, a smile of contentment on his face. He was drinking wine. Jeanne hoped he knew where he had put his umbrella. No one was looking at the paintings on the walls. A man, now drunk, banged his shin on *The Cogs of War*. For a moment Jeanne thought the man was going to give the three-hundred-pound sculpture a kick. Wisely, he stopped. The wine flowed freely. When the caterers took away the trestle tables they left bottles of wine on the floor along the bottom of the walls, under the paintings that no one was looking at. The good glasses had gone. Instead, James brought out a cardboard box full of glass tumblers. The wine by then tasted just the same. When the wine was finished the crowd of artists left as quietly as they had come. Samuel said he wanted to drive Jeanne home. Jeanne had lost sight of Ben.

Later, sometime after Samuel had left her like a gentleman at her front door with her phone number written in his notebook, she was tucked up in bed thinking of what she was going to paint when she heard Ben stumble into his room next door.

The next day Ben's room was quiet. It was still drizzling. Jeanne got up and lit the paraffin heater in her flat to warm the place. The English had no idea how to live in a cold climate. Before the winter was out she would buy herself a woollen hat that pulled down over her ears. And woollen gloves like Ben's.

At ten o'clock Samuel phoned. Jeanne said she would give him a ring once the painting was finished.

"I can't wait."

If she had to sleep with him it did not matter, she rationalised with herself. She was now a bohemian. Artists needed sponsors. The whiskers would tickle her face. She would think of Rudy, or any one of her other lovers. She was happy. Getting back into her warm bed, Jeanne fell into a dreamless sleep. At lunchtime she was woken by Ben stumbling around his room next door. She was hungry despite the large plate of food she had eaten at the party. It was all a way of life. The way of life she wanted. The room, now warm from the paraffin heater, was comfortable when she got out of bed. Later, she began to paint. Not a landscape or a building. An abstract of colours with shapes that could look like faces. Whatever she did had to be different. Then it would sell to a connoisseur like Samuel.

After half an hour she threw the ruined canvas in the rubbish bin. Luckily, she had only taken out a small canvas. Outside the drizzle had stopped. A late autumn sun was shining. Putting her black beret on her head and a coat round her small body, easel and box of paints in hand, Jeanne went for a walk down to the river. She could see Battersea Power Station on the opposite side of the river. The power station was close to the river to suck in the water. It was ugly. Further upriver, under a tree away from anyone out for a walk, Jeanne put up her easel and began to paint. If Samuel did not want to buy what she was painting it was just too bad. A barge was going downriver towards the Port of London. An old man with a beard and a workman's cap waved at her. Jeanne waved back. Taking a mental picture of the man and the barge, she continued to paint. By the time the light went she had the barge on the water. The old man would come later. Feeling good with herself, she walked home. There was still no sound from next door. Later, when the phone rang, it was Samuel.

"How long is it going to take?"

"A month."

"I can't wait that long."

"To buy something beautiful you have to wait."

She wondered if she was referring to herself or her painting. Smiling, Jeanne put down the phone after telling Samuel she had to get back to work. The next day, with good light coming through her window, she painted in the old man on the barge. He was waving. On the shore she painted herself and the easel. She was waving at the old man on the barge.

Three days later, when her first painting in England was finished, she was very satisfied with herself. The feeling of satisfaction at the completion was stronger than eating the big plate of food at James's party. She asked Ben to have a look.

"Now that's embarrassing. You can paint. Most of us are frauds."

"I'm going to sell it to Samuel Chalmers for three hundred pounds."

"That's prostitution and you know it."

"I don't have to sleep with him. He's phoned me every day since the party."

"All he's got is money."

Listening to Ben, Jeanne thought he was jealous. He had still not made a pass at her. She was more comfortable with men who made passes at her so she knew where she stood.

"Do you really like my painting? You're not just stroking my feathers?"

When he looked at her again there was a difference in his eyes. Now he wanted to stroke her. She felt better. Now she knew where she stood.

Jeanne made him an omelette with herbs. The potatoes were sautéed in butter. Ben was hungry. It was nice of him to like her painting.

When Paul Crookshank phoned after Ben had left, still not having made a formal pass that slightly annoyed Jeanne, she told Paul to come round and look at her painting. She did it out of pique at Ben. To ask Paul round to satisfy her ego didn't have much point. She knew he would say he liked her painting. She hoped Ben had been genuine, not just wanting a plate of food. It was difficult sometimes to know what people were really thinking.

When Samuel phoned, now his daily habit, she said the painting was a long way from being finished. He wanted to come round. She told him that wasn't possible until she had finished. With a man, there was no better weapon than making yourself hard to get when you wanted something.

Paul, when he came round, was speechless in front of her painting of the barge on the Thames. The poor man was in love with her. Whatever she had painted would have made him look at her painting the same way. When he asked her out to dinner, she agreed. She liked his company. Later, in his new flat, she played his grand piano. It was a Bechstein. Better by far than the upright piano in James's flat she had played the night of the party. She did not tell Paul about the party. Or about Samuel.

When she got home, Paul left her at the door. They had had a lovely evening. His life was sad. She could never fall for a good man. Maybe she did not wish to fall for anyone, she told herself. She was happy as she was. Settling down with one man for the rest of her life was boring. There were many years ahead to be old and boring. She was young. Wanted fun. Wanted to live as an artist not as anyone's slave as a wife or a mother. Like Samuel, they all wanted her when she would not behave the way they wanted. Then she smiled. Maybe one day with Paul when they were older. He was only twenty-three. Needed to be having fun with the girls, not moping after her. She had heard of Paul and Nancy. There were lots of Nancys for a man of twenty-three. Next time she would tell him: at their age life had to be lived before it all slipped by forever. All the rest of those long years were for being old and responsible.

"It's going to be like my business in America," she said to herself. "When I finally want it, it won't be there." Then she sighed.

Life was tough. Always decisions. She wanted to look back in her life to a host of good memories. To have done something exciting. To be able to look back and not regret anything. It would be worse to look back and regret what she hadn't done. When it was too late. First, she would get the three hundred pounds for her painting, then she would see about what else had to be done. They were all the same in the dark. What was the difference? Always decisions. None of them right. Poor Paul, he was such a dear. If only he had seduced her that first night after playing her piano in Brooklyn there would not be a problem. After regular sex, the desire in both of them would fade. All the agony of who was feeling what would fly out the window with all the tension gone. Rather like she suspected what happened when two people got married: her man looking for some young artist wanting to sell her paintings.

To stop herself thinking she banged on the wall.

"Are you awake, Ben? Are you hungry?"

Later, when they had made love to each other, they both fell asleep in Jeanne's bed. When they woke in the morning, nothing had changed. Ben was still hungry. He did not even look at her painting. When she had made him breakfast he went back to his own room. Jeanne was smiling. He was her kind of man. No complications. They were satisfied. Both of them. The day would go on without the tension.

Later, she took her easel and box of paints back to the river. There was smoke drifting up from the Battersea station. Jeanne was not sure if what she saw was smoke from the burning coal or steam. Under her tree, the easel up, Jeanne began to paint. She was feeling good. About her life. About everything.

3

---

he Honourable Barnaby St Clair was impressed. Smithers had gone out for the newspapers. When he came back Barnaby had spread them out on his dining room table. The Ridgeback advertisements were in every paper. In the *Mirror* was an article on Harry Brigandshaw mentioning his new venture together with his background as a World War One fighter pilot. The twenty-three kills were mentioned; the disappearance during his flight down Africa in a seaplane; coming out of the jungle alone after three years. William Smythe had written the article which was placed next to a large advertisement for Ridgeback cigarettes. Horatio Wakefield had done a similar piece in the *Mail*. The cigarettes were a way for the man in the street to reward a war hero. The man in flying gear smoking a Ridgeback was leaning against the lower wing of a Sopwith Camel biplane, the inference clear: brave men smoked cigarettes. Barnaby just had to chuckle. Instead of Harry doing Frank a favour it was the other way round. Frank, the new man on the public relations block, had hit the jackpot. The introduction by Frank to Cohen Wells and the PR blitz that followed was going to make Harry Brigandshaw another fortune. The one per cent of advertising spend paid to Frank by Cohen Wells was not costing Harry a penny. The boy was a man after his own heart. It was the perfect backhander directed at himself as the boy's biological father and Tina for not telling the truth. Poor old Harry. Always trying his best to do the right thing.

Getting up from the table and the spread of newspapers, Barnaby went to the window. Across the road in Green Park there was no one sitting on the park bench. Outside it was wet and cold. The ever-present traffic up and down Piccadilly was picking up for eleven o'clock on a Tuesday morning. Barnaby had the urge to phone Frank and ask him for a drink. The boy was good. A man after his own heart.

Later, when the phone rang, it was Harry Brigandshaw. Smithers had answered the phone in the hall. With the lousy weather, Barnaby had not gone out. He could smell the waft of lunch coming through the open door of the kitchen which Smithers had left open when he went to the phone.

"Harry! What a surprise."

"What do you think of it?"

"The boy's a genius. There are some friends of mine who could do with his advice. The rather overdone bits on you next to the ad, set the tone. I almost gave him a ring. Has he made contact with you or his mother?"

"Not a word. Paul Crookshank keeps me informed. Quite a chip off the old block, Barnaby. I thought he had pulled a fast one on Cohen Wells. The other advertising companies had nothing like this to say for themselves. Every wholesale tobacconist in the country is on the phone. Katherine is overwhelmed. We're having to put in a switchboard chop-chop. Oh, my goodness. All that Rhodesian tobacco. Put the old country on its financial feet. The price of tobacco is going to go up but it's still a tiny proportion of the price of a packet of cigarettes. They were right. Frank was right. It's all in the advertising. I've agreed this morning to double the spend."

"Please Frank."

"He's taken a small office in Fleet Street. Doesn't need either of us, Barnaby. Tina's rather proud of him."

"So am I. Embarrassing, really. One minute he's sitting outside on a park bench trying to give me a hard time, next his signature is all over the newspapers. He knows that we know who put this all together. He's going to get rich under his own steam. That's the way to do it. You don't owe anyone favours."

"How you got on in the world, Barnaby."

"Exactly. I did not have to raise a finger to help. Like father like son."

"You don't think I might have set his mind in the right direction?"

"Of course you did, Harry. Where are you now?"

"In the office."

"Why don't we have lunch? We can celebrate our son."

"Are you going to give him a ring?"

"I don't think so. The fact Tina and I won't admit to our sins is the fire up his arse. The driving force. He'll have to do a lot more than this advertising campaign to make himself rich."

"How about the RAF Club? Just round the corner from you. One o'clock?"

"Splendid. They'll all be smoking Ridgeback cigarettes. I presume they are in the shops?"

"Most of them. The re-orders are coming in fast."

"Funny how life turns out."

"Why didn't you marry, Barnaby?"

"I'm too selfish, old chap. Wanted to have my cake and eat it. Too late now. How's Tina?"

"She gets moods. Misses the children."

"How's Lady Uppington?"

"They've fallen out."

"Thank God for small mercies."

FOR A MOMENT after sitting down to lunch in the ground floor dining room of the Royal Air Force Club, Barnaby looked at himself through the eyes of Harry Brigandshaw. The club was only a short walk from his townhouse. Despite the intermittent rain, the cold fresh air had done him good. His stomach was getting a paunch. His hair was largely grey and a bald patch had appeared on top. He was becoming an old man. Like Harry. Not the dashing army and flying corps officers they had been during the war. The Great War. Not the one that had just finished. Harry, like himself, was looking at an old man. Two old men about to reminisce.

Frank was passed over quickly. Two paternal old men smiling back at the trials and tribulations of youth. Both rather envious. They had done all they were going to do in life. For a moment, Barnaby wished he had more kids. He was glad to know he had Frank. All the fun without any of the responsibility. Or would that have been fun, the bringing up of the boy, he asked himself. Was there something he had missed in his life?

In his long conversation with Harry he took himself back to Palestine. Harry talked about 33 Squadron. All the reminiscing was about the happy times of the war. The people they had known and enjoyed when they were young. Laughing again at the old stories. Of Lefty Whitehead. Shaggy Cox. Willie Wentwhistle. Both talking at the same time having a jolly good time going back in their memories when life was a lot less boring.

Harry did not mention Tina. Barnaby did not say what he was doing. Ridgeback cigarettes had a brief mention taking Harry into stories of how he first met Horatio Wakefield and William Smythe, after he was taken off the ship from Africa straight to the Hospital for Tropical Diseases in Bloomsbury. He talked a lot about Lucinda, Harry's first wife and Barnaby's sister. They saw her again when she was alive. Neither mentioned the baby that had died with her. Barnaby thought about that for a moment. What he would have done with his life. How different Harry's life would have been had Mervyn Braithwaite not shot Lucinda in a mad man's orgy of imaginary vengeance, the truth of which had nothing to do with Harry or his wife.

"I often wonder what would have become of my life if Colonel Parson had been less understanding," said Barnaby. "He should have had me cashiered from the army in a cloud of ignominy. Fifty pounds was a lot of money to me in those days. Unlike most of the other officers I did not have a private income. Dad was broke. All we had by then was Purbeck Manor and a few of the surrounding acres. Merlin made money in Vickers shares. Where he got the money to invest I have no idea, looking back. Making machine guns between 1914 and 1918 was a good business. Robert wrote his novels. I lived off my wits. If Hugh Parson had been vindictive instead of paying into mess funds the fifty quid I had borrowed as mess secretary and posting me back to England so I could quietly resign my commission with so many others at the end of the war, I'd never have got on my feet. The right people in the City would never have talked to me. I told you I looked for Colonel Parsons when I made my money, to see if there was any way I could repay a good man. Never found him. Probably went to the colonies when he retired. A nice cheap place in the sun where his army pension stretched the furthest. Strange how you can owe so much to one man."

"You fought for the regiment. You were a damn good soldier from what I heard. We were young in those days. Did what we had to do for service at the moment. Being colonel of a regiment doesn't always mean playing by the rules. What makes a good officer."

"What happened to Braithwaite? Sorry, Harry. It must still hurt."

"Oh, don't worry. We all have to get over the past. He was a good commanding officer. The first for 33 Squadron. I was the second. The killing got to him. Unhinged his mind. He killed too many people. I still think about the good men I killed because my country told me to. What lives they would have had. They were all so young. Haunts me. Not a day goes by without one of those thoughts. Mervyn was shot by Tembo, immediately after killing Barend Oosthuizen, my brother-in-law and Tinus's father. They kept it out of the papers. He was a war hero. When you force young men to kill on your behalf you can't very well turn on them when the mental pressure gets too much. He was going to kill me. Tembo saved my life. I try and think of Mervyn as one of the badly wounded. The chaps with no eyesight or legs. The war killed my wife and Barend Oosthuizen. That was the truth."

"How is his son doing in America?"

"Barend would have been proud of his son. Rhodes Scholar. First-class cricketer. Now he's making us both a fortune. Antiques. Meat canning. Farming in Virginia. Tinus is marketing the crops direct to the buyers. Not losing the profit to the middle man. Best still, he has a happy marriage. Not only is your niece a good actress, she's a wonderful mother and wife."

"She was older than him."

"Does it matter?"

"I run her trust fund. From the money she made in Hollywood. She's never gone back to acting. Says she might when the kids grow up. Genevieve is very rich. Richer than her father, the Eighteenth Baron of Purbeck. Bought up all those bomb sites at the end of the war. Now the trust is developing them. They live simply. Genevieve is worried about her kids expecting to be given everything when they grow up. You did something with your inheritance from the old Pirate. Most squander what comes easily. I enjoyed making money the hard way. It might have looked easy but it wasn't. After a man makes money it always looks easy to other people. You had to keep your wits about you investing with CE Porter. We scratched each other's backs. The stock exchange is one big gambling casino. All you need is information before it becomes public. The theatre and the record business were just fun. A good hunting ground for women."

"Don't you regret not getting married? Not having kids?"

"I have Frank. Thanks to you. I'm enjoying watching his escapades. Even if he doesn't know I'm watching."

"Do you want to get closer to him?"

"Not really. How's Tina?"

"Miserable."

"That's my point. If I was married to her the misery would be my fault.

"Now it's mine," said Harry. "Why can't some people be content with their lives the way things are? She has everything. Well, not Anthony. But that's life and war. You have to move on. She's lucky to have four more healthy kids who these days seem to avoid us. They have their own lives to live, I suppose. She waits for any kind of contact from the children as if that's all that's important in her life. Maybe when she has some grandchildren. She hates being old. The men don't look at her anymore. And she doesn't have any old friends. The likes of Lady Uppington come and go. Use our hospitality. They didn't have the money they appeared to have on the boat. They were making one last splash when we met them. The old families relying on old money are being soaked by the socialists. They'll be extinct in another generation. You have to make your own money in life, not rely on other people. Inheriting money can be a blessing and a curse. I would much have preferred spending my life as a tobacco farmer in the wilds of Rhodesia. Tina likes the big city. So here we are. Only when the rains don't come does farming get on our nerves."

"Maybe we all want something else, not just our wives."

"You're right. You just have to enjoy life as you go along. A bit like Frank. You know, that advertising campaign he helped organise is far bigger than anything I could have imagined."

"You have the Midas touch, Harry. Always did. You pick the right people."

"Not consciously."

"That's why they turn out right."

"Most of it's luck. Making money is luck and timing. Why don't we take in a matinée at the Windmill? Stop us reminiscing."

"Good idea. I've nothing to do. This is pleasant. We should do it more often."

"If Tina could see us now she's spit blood."

"She can always make up with Lady Uppington."

4

———

While his legal and biological fathers were watching the chorus line at the Windmill Theatre kick up their legs, Frank was having one of his giggles. All day he had been interviewing potential receptionists in his new rented office close to those of Cohen Wells. With the money about to flow in it was all about appearances. On a nice brass plaque in black letters were his own names in bold letters, under which, in equally bold letters, was the legend, 'Public Relations Consultants'. After Frank Brigandshaw the legend read, 'and Partners'. So far no one in England had come to mind as a partner. On a nice letterhead the legend of 'partners' looked better. Gave the firm substance. Suggested more than a man and his dog. It all made Frank giggle.

After a brief deliberation with himself, the deliberation that ended with the giggle, Frank had chosen the girl with the big tits. It was, he told himself, all about appearances. All the girl had to do was answer the phone, take messages when the boss was out of the office and look pretty. A sexy girl in the outside office spoke volumes for public relations. If no one else, Zachariah Cohen would have his eye on Milly Worthington. The fact the girl had passed her school certificate and gone to secretarial college was a bonus. When Frank phoned the girl's contact number, her mother answered the phone.

"She can start at nine o'clock tomorrow morning, Mrs Worthington."

"She'll be so thrilled."

His nice desk had been delivered the previous day along with the one for reception. The phones were already installed. A friend from his square-bashing days in the army worked for the Post Office. Life, to Frank, was all about knowing people. The right sort of people who could give him some help. When the phone rang, as it had been doing ever since it was installed, Frank let it ring. Whoever it was would phone back if they wanted something. Answering his own telephone would have given the wrong appearance. The girl at Cohen Wells who ran their switchboard had his office number. People were calling. In all the Ridgeback advertising, in very small print, appeared the words Frank Brigandshaw and Partners, Public Relations Consultants alongside the name of Cohen Wells. It was Frank's idea to show both names in the newspapers. Life was a lot more simple than people made out. Not only had Frank got Cohen Wells to pay him a fee of one per cent of the ad spend, he had made them give his new firm nationwide free advertising. Which was why he needed to employ an attractive girl like his receptionist. The pull back of the bottle of cognac by Zach was a long way in the past. He, Frank, was on his way. He was going to be rich. Richer than all the rest of the family put together. A man had to be hungry.

When Connie Whitaker came round at the end of his first full day in the new office, she was suitably impressed. It was Connie who had suggested he set himself up.

"I'll give the landlord a guarantee on the lease."

"Why, Connie?"

"Because I like you. I'm not giving you money. Without a business bank account the landlords won't look at you. You require references. That knowledge comes from listening to Frederick. When you are installed you can take me out to dinner. To the Savoy. I'm not cheap."

"What would I do without you? You're the only family I've got."

"That's the nicest story you've told me."

"It's true."

"What do you want?"

"Come on, Connie. We get on with each other. I'm never bored in your company. It's a long time since we bumped into each other in Mrs Walters's gallery. I'd love to take you to supper. You'll have to dress up. I'll be in my dinner jacket. Like the first time."

"How's Brian Tobin?"

"Still in Rhodesia. I've written to him to come back to London. He and I go back a long way. We make a good team."

"Why don't we call at the gallery before going to the Savoy? She has a new exhibition."

"Will there be wine?"

"You can drop off one of your new cards. They are addressed?"

"Of course."

"I'm going to miss you, Frank, when you're a big success."

"Why should you miss me? I'll be around."

"You won't need me anymore. How life works. We all use each other. When there isn't any more to use we avoid each other."

"I hope not."

"So do I. It's a pity I'm not twenty years younger."

"This way's fine, Connie. We don't have to pretend. Don't have to take us a step further. We can be as we are."

"What are we, Frank?"

"Lovers."

"Shut up. You're going to make me cry."

At the Bond Street gallery Mrs Walters was all over Connie. She ignored Frank which made him smile at Mrs Walters. Only then did she look at them both. The effusion turned to envy, seen by Frank in the back of Mrs Walters's eyes. When she looked at him again she had lost interest in selling Connie a painting. They walked away into the gallery. People were trying to look knowledgeable. One was an artist Frank recognised from Tessa's parties. Only once while Frank kept watching him out of the corner of his eye did he stop at a painting.

"She knows you've got Frederick's money. You could see plain greed written all over her face when you arrived at the door. Then she saw we were together. She envies you, Connie. Isn't that nice? If she went to India she'd be sacred she looks so much like a cow."

"Don't be bitchy. Selling paintings is her job."

"I hate insecurity."

"You can turn on the charm."

"Hello. You like that one do you? Remember me from Tessa's? I was sleeping on the pull-out couch. This is Connie Whitaker. I'm taking her out to dinner."

Frank smiled. The last part had been for Mrs Walters. The man had been drunk the time they met. Had no idea who he was. Frank smiled across at Mrs Walters to make sure she heard he was taking Connie out to dinner.

When they reached Café Monet Frank took the same table they had sat at their first night. Only when they left the art gallery had he told her they were not going to the Savoy. Connie looked her best in the soft light with the simple candle on the table. Across the table they held hands while they ordered the food. The food was just as expensive as the Savoy.

"Are you really paying, Frank?"

"What did you think of the ads in the papers?"

"As good as anything I've seen. You had your name at the bottom I see."

"That's why supper's on me. We're going to dance. We'll make tonight some kind of anniversary."

"I don't understand you, Frank."

"Neither do I. Let's just enjoy ourselves. I like having my own money. Real money. The rest of them can all go to hell."

CONNIE HADN'T DANCED cheek to cheek since she was nineteen. Before she married Frederick. Before she climbed up into the world of money. It was the strangest thing. The evening for Frank was not about her inheriting Frederick's money. He was asking her opinion. Bouncing around his ideas for her to make comments. Using her experience. Looking for advice. The new success had changed the boy from a predator to something much more interesting. He was treating her like a partner in life, not someone to be milked for her money the way he had been before he went in the army, when she and Dorothy Dent were paying all the bills in an expensive flat for the pleasure of having two studs whenever Frederick was away. If it were not for the cheek to cheek dancing she would have felt like his surrogate mother. Being used as a proxy, without Frank realising, for the legal father he had had nothing to do with from the age of fourteen when the family ran away to South Africa to get away from the war, leaving the father to his work at the Air Ministry in London. Ever since then Frank had been on his own, his mother more concerned with her own problems than those of her children. Now she was the stand-in. Except for the cheek-to-cheek dancing.

When he took her back in the taxi she asked him in. For some reason he did not want to come in. The taxi had gone. They were standing on her doorstep.

"This isn't just about sex, Connie. I want to get that straight. So tonight I'm not coming in. Tomorrow you will come to my flat for dinner. Isn't it nice we live so close? It isn't raining so I'm going to walk home."

"Can I do the cooking?"

"Was the spaghetti that bad?"

"Let's just say I cook better than you."

When she was safely inside, his feet echoing down the corridor, she did not know what to think. She had never had any children. Or nieces or nephews. She had no experience of youth other than her own memories. And England had changed. It was a new, more liberal society where they did what they wanted. To hell with the consequences. Hedonism now rather than any responsibility for their future. The war had made them realise that a future was never certain. Everyone was now living in the present. Why had Frank changed? What did he want? Why had he treated her so nicely instead of taking her money in exchange for his physical expression of love, which before had been mere lust for both of them? At dinner, they had talked. Really talked. Not just on the surface. He was interested in her life. In her future.

"I've been thinking, Connie, what you should do with your money. You can't just leave it in the bank earning interest. There's going to be galloping inflation which will wipe out most of the money left in bank accounts. I remember my legal father always saying land was the best investment. You've always been so kind to let me talk about my business and what I'm doing to make money. I value your advice. Your experience. Apart from running around the African bush shooting crocodiles, and playing soldiers because I was given no option, I have no real experience of life. But I mustn't be selfish. Why don't you buy a nice place in the country for your mother to live in and look after? She's had a hard time. If you tell her she's doing you a favour, she won't think she's living off Frederick's money. Paul was saying that with the tax on property based on the size of the property and not its market value, the old rich are selling their estates at rock bottom prices to get out from under the new tax liabilities. In the future the land will again find its real value. Right now it's cheap. I'm getting a car for the business. Not all my prospective clients will be in London. I'll be travelling round the country. Why don't we go together? Look for a real bargain where some old family is financially deep in the manure. You have cash to offer. You can bargain a good price."

"Frederick was a stockbroker. Most of the money was in shares. Still is in shares."

"But in England. With strict exchange control you can only invest in the sterling area. The old British colonies are going to be in the past in the next ten years if the nationalists get their way. Father said a man must never fall in love with his share certificate. That pearl of wisdom I remember from before the war, when he moved some of his money to America, where everything is now booming. Before the war soaked England of all its foreign exchange."

"I've never heard you refer to him as 'Father' before."

"You know what I mean. Not a mansion, Connie. Your mother would never fall for that. I thought a farm with a solid farmhouse. Lots of fields. Some woods. Maybe by the sea. That will be worth something when England gets back on its feet. As she will, Connie. In a nice spread of land you'd have something to see for your money that wouldn't evaporate with galloping inflation."

"Who've you been talking to, Frank?"

"Zach's father. Now there's a wise old man when it comes to money. The Jews know what they're talking about. Some of the bombed out sites in London wouldn't go amiss in your portfolio."

"Why are you again talking about my money?"

"To help you, Connie. Someone has to help you that you can trust. There are too many sharks out there just waiting to pounce on a wealthy widow."

"Aren't you one of them?"

"Not anymore."

"And bomb sites in London. Whose idea was that one?"

"Paul was talking about Tinus Oosthuizen. He's married to the actress who went by the single name of Genevieve. She's a cousin of mine though she doesn't know it. My biological father put her into Central London property at the end of the war. Runs her trust fund. All the money she was paid as a Hollywood actress. She's now stinking rich, according to Paul who speaks to Tinus daily on the phone to New York. Tinus runs the American end of the family business."

"You get around, Frank."

"I keep my ears open. It pays. Why don't we do a country trip when I get my car? Get away together. If nothing else, that would be fun. I've so enjoyed this evening. You're the only person I can really talk to. Think about it. Now, let's go and dance. They're playing a nice slow number. Very romantic."

"It'll be the middle of winter by the time you get the car."

"We can wear lots of clothes. There'll be a heater in the car. The English countryside is just as beautiful when the leaves have fallen. My biological father's family have a place in Dorset. Been to Dorset but not to Purbeck Manor, which has been in the family for over twenty generations. It's in the blood. I love the countryside."

"Do I detect a romantic under all your nonsense, Frank? Let's go and dance... We'll see."

"You'll think about it?"

"Probably... The army changed you. Did you know that?"

"Probably."

They had both laughed, got up from the table and danced. Cheek to cheek.

Not sure what to make of it all, Connie undressed and got into bed. When she finally fell asleep it was the middle of the night. The traffic had died down. London was quiet.

THAT WEEKEND, Beth Brigandshaw went down to Hastings Court to see her mother. Her father had gone away on one of his business trips to America with Paul Crookshank. Nancy was spending more of her time with the new love of her life. In his flat. The South Kensington flat they shared had become lonely. On her own, it was difficult for a girl to go anywhere. To arrive at a party without any backup was embarrassing. Beth had tried it once. Left on her own in a corner with no one to talk to while they looked over the talent, Beth felt spare. She had left – quietly, so no one could see – and gone home for a good cry. She was almost twenty-five. No one in sight other than Paul. To Paul she was a family friend. His interest was still centred on the American French girl who had gone off to paint pictures in an artist's studio in Chelsea. Unrequited love. It was so stupid.

When she arrived in the second-hand Austin Seven the old house was like a morgue. Apart from her mother and old Mrs Craddock there was no one staying in the house. The servants had gone to their homes in the surrounding villages for the weekend leaving the old pile to its creaks and groans. What got to Beth most were the portraits dotted round the house in corners, watching her silently. Up the side of the stairs. All watching. All somehow familiar. All related to her going back deep in the centuries when the only way to remember a relative was to have their portrait painted. One of the faces looked just like herself. It gave her the creeps. The familiar face was four hundred years old with an Elizabethan frilled collar round her neck. She had asked her father, when the family came back from South Africa, who the woman was.

"I have no idea, Beth. She does look like you. Just shows how we live on down the centuries. Your grandmother might know."

"She's in Rhodesia. Never comes home."

"She thinks Dad still lives around her on Elephant Walk."

"All her family history is right here."

"But not her husband. She really loved him. Sad how so often great love is cut short early in life. All these old portraits need restoring. They've gone so dark."

"Not her eyes. They stare at me. It's like looking into my own soul when I look at her picture."

"You have her genes. Everything she once was you are now, Beth. It's why it's good to know who your ancestors were. Gives one a sense of belonging to more than today. I can write to your grandmother."

"There are so many portraits of the ancestors."

"I'll tell her where it is. She grew up in this house. Do you know, your grandfather put a ladder up to her window and carried us off? Both of us. We all got on a boat and Dad took us back to Africa. Young love is always the best. The love that lasts through the trials and tribulations of life."

"Don't worry Grandmother. One day when I visit Rhodesia I'll ask her myself."

"Of course, you've never been to the farm?"

"We never left Cape Town. Mother wouldn't go. She has some phobia about Elephant Walk. Something about your first wife. She says in Rhodesia the girl haunts her spirit."

"She's been reading too many novels."

When Beth found her mother she was ensconced in the cosy room, a small room in the middle of the house with a roaring fire. Her mother kept the fire burning right through the winter. With her were the cats and dogs. In the winter the cats slept most of the time, getting up to eat when they were hungry. All the dogs were lying on their sides on the carpet round the fire.

Beth went off to make them a pot of tea so as not to bother Mrs

Craddock. The woman was far too old to be carrying old silver trays loaded with cups and pots. Lifting the solid silver tray was an ordeal.

"How nice of you to visit your mother."

"Is that sarcasm, Mum?"

"Yes, I suppose it is. Even with your father at home I'm lonely in this old mausoleum of a house."

"Weren't you moving to London? Oh, that was before Lady Uppington."

"What are you talking about?" her mother said sharply. "I had a letter from my father. He and Mrs Battle are quite comfortable now they are settled down. He still misses your grandmother. What have you been up to, Beth? When are you getting married? What's wrong with that nice Paul Crookshank? I thought you had your eye on him. You're attractive. Not unlike me when I was your age. Sexy. What's the matter with you?"

"He's in love with Jeanne. Watches her with soppy eyes when I see them together. She doesn't love him. Poor Paul. He's such a dear. Can't see she isn't interested."

"They all grow up in the end. He's your age. Doing well according to Harry. Make the perfect husband and father of my grandchildren."

"Yes, Mother. Can I pour you some tea?"

"Of course you can. Just put that cat on the floor and then you can sit down. Do you know, these animals think they own the place. Have you seen Frank?"

"Paul says he's taken a flat near his girlfriend."

"So do you see Paul?" Her mother had a one-track mind when it came to her getting married. She was like a dog worrying a bone.

"We went to the Benjie Appleton jazz club last night together. Paul played a set with the band. Plays a mean clarinet. He could make a living playing jazz. Not a good one, but a living. We both like someone to go with."

"So it wasn't a date?"

"No, Mother."

Her mother gave her a look of disapproval.

"Who is Frank's girlfriend? Is she nice?"

"She's a bit older than Frank. I met her once briefly in the street."

"How old is she, Beth? I don't like the tone of your voice."

"Connie's forty-four."

"What! She's my age. Is she rich, or something?" Beth had to smile. Her mother was turning fifty-two the following week.

"Very rich. Her husband died and left her a fortune. He was much older than Connie."

"How much? Do you know how much? Just like his father at that age. We were in Africa, Johannesburg, with your Uncle Bert you've never met. Barnaby had a nose for other people's money."

"You've never admitted that before."

"Everyone knows. We all do silly things when we're young. I loved Barnaby with all my heart and soul. From a little girl. We lived close to the St Clairs."

"Why don't you tell this to Frank? Explain how it happened."

"Your father said it was better for everyone to sweep it under the carpet. You're all old enough to understand now so it doesn't matter anymore. The war changed everything. Your father was married to another woman, don't forget. He was married to Barnaby's sister."

"Why didn't you marry Barnaby?"

"His mother would have had a fit. Quite the lady of the manor."

"So you married his brother-in-law in spite."

"I fell pregnant with Anthony if you want to know. I had to marry your father. He was a gentleman. None of us are perfect, Beth. Not even our parents. Just you be careful."

"I am, Mother, don't worry. I use precautions."

"I don't know what you youngsters get up to."

"Not much different to what you and Dad got up to by the sound of it. Do you mind if I take the dogs for a walk?"

At the sound of 'walk' all four dogs lifted their heads from the carpet. Beth had had enough of her discussion with her mother.

When they had finished the tea, she got up from the fireside. Picking up the tea tray, she walked toward the door looking at the dogs. All four got up. They were wagging their tails. From behind, Beth heard her mother sigh. Life at home was always so complicated. Quietly putting the tray down on the hall table, Beth closed the door to the cosy room.

With the dogs following she headed off for a walk through the woods, picking up her coat on the way. It was two hours to lunchtime and a further interrogation. She hoped her father was enjoying the respite in America. The man was a saint. Never complained. Always did what his wife wanted whatever the cost to himself. The thought came to her, not for the first time, that she would not have been born if Lucinda St Clair had lived. Or, by the sound of it, if her mother had not fallen pregnant out of wedlock with Anthony.

After a good tramp in the cold, late autumn air, she arrived up on Headley Heath, making straight for the witches' circle. The logs were perfectly in place. Going into the circle, she sat on the rock in the middle smooth with age. For ten minutes she sat with her eyes closed, blanking her mind. When she opened them she felt better. More relaxed. The tension of London life had seeped out of her. She was smiling when she got up. Putting on her best pace she walked back towards the old house hidden among the tall cedar trees. It was better not to be late for lunch. Her poor mother. Being permanently unhappy was a terrible waste. Racking her brains for something to say that would take some of the burden of life from her mother, Beth went inside through the backdoor. The dogs were now hungry. Mrs Craddock put food in their bowls and the dogs gulped it down. When it was finished, they walked away with Beth back to the carpet in front of the fire to join the cats. The cats were still in the chairs with their eyes closed.

"Mother, I have an idea. When I drive back to London, come with me. Nancy sleeps at her boyfriend's most of the time. You can have her bedroom for a couple of days. In the evenings when I'm back from work we can go out together."

"What a lovely idea."

Her mother was smiling. Beth smiled with relief. The weekend at home wasn't going to be so bad after all.

PART 5

DECEMBER 1949 – CHRISTMAS AT THE COURT

1

———————

Dorian Brigandshaw's first book of fiction was himself. The day after finishing his basic training he became another person. Gone were the private schools, the three years at Oxford, the family with the estate in the country, the farm in the colonies, the history all the way back to 1066. Even his accent had changed. During the weeks after failing to be selected for officer training, Dorian had studied the different accents, deciding on West Country, an accent less common than the rest and familiar to himself. In his mind, preparing himself for the course in motor mechanics with the Royal Army Service Corps, he spoke with a Dorset tone.

When Dorian reached the new unit in Manchester where no one had seen him before, he tried out his new way of speech. No one blinked an eyelid. He was a country lad from a farm in the West Country, his speech almost faultless. He was one of them. Not a toffee-nosed product of some rich family with a plummy accent.

"Where you from, Dorian?"

"Corfe Castle. My dad works a farm."

"Charlie Drew. London myself. Know anything about cars?"

"Not much." Dorian had kept his soft hands in his pockets. His grandfather Pringle was the background for the man he was purporting to be. Like a good book of fiction, the character of himself, the life behind the man, had to be consistent. It was like playing a part and writing the play at the same time. He became what he appeared to others. What they saw of him, not who he was behind the face.

At the end of the course, a week before Christmas, when his hands looked like the rest of them, Dorian was told to report to Second Lieutenant Featherstonhaugh. They had left him until last. Like himself, Second Lieutenant Featherstonhaugh was a national serviceman. The platoon commander was a year younger than Dorian, at the end of his two-year service. With his cap off, Dorian came to attention in front of the man's desk.

"You're the most awful mechanic, Brigandshaw."

"Did my best, sir."

"My mother has more aptitude."

"I'm a labourer, sir."

"Bunkum. The others don't have access to your records, Brigandshaw. What's it all about?"

"Fitting in."

"Ah. Sensible. Well, you don't fit into the Service Corps, I'm afraid. Can't let you loose on your own under a bonnet. You can't even tighten a screw properly."

"I'm all fingers and thumbs."

"I said, drop the phoney accent. That's an order. The door is closed if it worries you that much. What on earth does a man do in life with a degree in English literature?"

"Bugger all, according to my father. B.A. Bugger all."

"Well, we can't keep you in the RASC. There's an army magazine they put out once a month. During the war it was to boost morale. Never read it myself. I've suggested they make you a clerk. Put you safely behind a desk. One of the chaps up in London heard you have a first from Oxford. Someone was having a laugh at your expense. Saw you try the obstacle course the time you failed the War Office Selection Board. Apparently, you're the only one from such an exalted university not to be offered the chance of a commission."

"As I said, sir. I'm all fingers and thumbs when theory goes into practice."

"Well, they want you. To help put out the army's magazine. You might even enjoy yourself. If you can write as well as you play the part of a country bumpkin, you'll be a hoot. I'm out of the Service after Christmas. Going into the City. Did you learn anything here?"

"How to enjoy people at all levels of society."

"You're good at accents. Where'd you learn the West Country one?"

"From my grandfather. He's the stationmaster at Corfe Castle railway station. Two trains in the winter. One up in the morning. One down at night."

"Now you are pulling my leg."

"Not at all. And I'm proud of him."

"Your family are aristocrats."

"Only on the side of my great-grandfather, Sir Henry Manderville."

"Well, you're out of here, Brigandshaw. I've granted you Christmas leave. Report to the War Office on the fourth of January."

"Thank you, sir."

"Don't thank me. Like you, I'm just doing what I'm told. Have a Merry Christmas."

He would miss Charlie Drew. They had become friends, Charlie trying his best to show Dorian the workings of an internal combustion engine.

"The theory, I see, Charlie. It's when I take up a spanner all hell breaks loose."

"Takes all types to make a world."

"We all have our place. That much is certain."

"What I don't understand is all them books. You a labourer on a farm. Why all them books? Never read a book in my life. Can you pass me that spanner, cock?"

KIM PICKED up Dorian from the Leatherhead railway station. Dorian was still in uniform. Regulations stated soldiers leaving their units on leave should be dressed in uniform.

"The old family estate is hopping," said Kim. "You'll have the pleasure of meeting Lady Uppington. Mother is besotted with the woman."

"Thought they had an argument? How are you, Kim? Quite the dashing young man."

"I can't say you look smart. Did you sleep in your uniform? How was the course?"

"I failed. Just don't tell Father. I'm posted as a clerk to the War Office. The army magazine."

"Sounds more your speed. It just struck me, older brother, if I was still in uniform, you'd have to give me a salute. How's the book doing?"

"Only in my head. You have to fit in. Reading was bad enough. Do you know how many people don't read?"

"Never thought about it. Dad had his old friend from his days in the Royal Flying Corps staying for Christmas with his wife. Dad met Sarah in the underground during the Blitz. She's a hoot. So's Ding-a-ling. Vic Bell. Why didn't they call him Ding-Dong? Ding-Dong Bell sounds better. Oh, and fame has come to the Court. Genevieve. She and Tinus are visiting from the States with the kids."

"Only seen her up on the screen. Maybe as a kid before she became a famous actress. Read her book. Ghostwritten by Bruno Kannberg. He was a friend of Dad's."

"How can you fail a course in motor mechanics?" asked Kim. "Any fool can take an engine apart if they have the right tools."

"Not this fool. Good to see you. Has Frank deigned to show his face for Christmas?"

"Don't be daft. Don't understand the bugger. He's still our brother, even if he has the Honourable for a father. Everyone knows."

"Maybe it would be different if it was you. I don't know what I would do if someone told me Dad wasn't my father."

"Jump in the car. We're all hoping for a white Christmas. Even the year before, the last six weeks of snow came after Christmas. We can take the toboggans down Headley Heath, like we did as kids. Some of my best memories are as a kid on a toboggan. My first ride down the slope was on Dad's back."

"It was the same for all of us. A rite of passage. Frank will remember that as well as we do. Only it turned out the ride down the hill wasn't on his father's back at all. Who else is spending Christmas?"

"Major Pilkington-Jones. Put the antique business on the road in more ways than one. Has a fund of stories."

"And Paul Crookshank? They work together."

"Spending Christmas with his mother in the Isle of Wight. His brother Jeremy is back from Rhodesia for Christmas. Been out there learning to farm for six months. Paul paid his airfare home. Close family. Their father went down off Dunkirk."

"Is Beth still soft on Paul?"

"She doesn't talk about her love life. They have quite a time in London."

"What are you doing with yourself?"

"Nothing. Can't make up my mind. There aren't many options when you come down to it."

"Aren't you going to get a degree?"

"After two years in the RAF I don't fancy going back to school. You were sensible. Took deferment and went up to Oxford right after school. Can't get my mind back into books. Anyway, what would I go for? Another Bachelor of Arts worth bugger all."

"I'm going to write books."

"They all say that. They end up teaching. Going all the way back to their school days. There's the services. Done that. The City. Don't fancy catching the train to Waterloo for the rest of my life. Or going farming in Rhodesia when all the colonies are falling apart. I mean, what does a chap do with his life?"

"You'll think of something."

"I hope so. Right now I'm bored stiff stuck at home with Mother. She has nothing to talk about but herself. Moans all day long. What are we going to do with our mother?"

"Leave her to Lady Uppington by the sound of it."

Dorian liked Kim: they were friends. It was good to have a brother that was also a friend.

When Kim parked the car in front of the house there were cars parked everywhere. People were standing on the long terrace that ran the length of the old house. It looked to Dorian like one of his mother's pre-war weekend parties. No one seemed to notice them.

Dorian followed his brother up the steps across the terrace and through the Gothic entrance. Inside, the house fires were burning in the grates. Servants, part-time and recruited from the village, were taking the buffet lunch through to the Great Hall. None of the servants were familiar. In charge, bossing everyone, was Mrs Craddock sitting in a high-backed wooden chair. Dorian gave her a kiss on the cheek in the middle of her performance. Everyone was staring at his uniform. Army privates were not expected to be so familiar with the housekeeper.

Carrying his small kitbag stuffed with books and dirty clothes, Dorian made his way through the people and climbed the stairs to his second-floor bedroom. A fire was burning in the grate. Kim had gone off somewhere.

Dorian changed out of his uniform and went back downstairs. At the bottom stood his mother with her hand on the banister. With her was a middle-aged woman. Dorian had the suspicion his mother had chosen not to see him when he was dressed in uniform.

"Hello, darling. How lovely to see you. I want you to meet my friend Lady Uppington. Dorian was up at Oxford, Mabel. First in English literature. Lady Uppington adores Shakespeare. Did you know we are related through the Mandervilles? What a lovely party, don't you think?"

"Who are all these people? How do you do, Lady Uppington? Dorian. Private Dorian Brigandshaw of His Majesty's Royal Army Service Corps."

"Friends of mine," said his mother, glaring at him while answering his question. "One or two friends of your father. He's off somewhere with Mr Bell and the major. Your sister is here. Oh, goodness, just look who's arrived. Lord and Lady Chislehurst. Can you look after yourself, Dorian?"

"I think so, Mother."

"Who picked you up at the station?"

"Kim."

"Oh, good."

A little sad, Dorian watched his mother take Lady Uppington to meet the more important new arrivals. Nothing had changed. Throwing a party, his mother was in her element. She liked living on the surface. He wondered if he ever knew the person deep inside.

Not knowing what he was meant to be doing, Dorian went off to find himself a drink. He was a stranger in his own home. They all had to be somewhere.

When Dorian found them they were in his father's study. Even Beth had found sanctuary in what was usually a men's club. The room had fireplaces burning bright at both ends. First shaking his father's hand and being given a hug, Dorian kissed his sister on the cheek.

"Nancy's pregnant, Dorian," she said sweetly in his ear.

Dorian went white as a sheet. His father was introducing him around the room. Kim had a smirk on his face. The major did not get up from his chair. With Ding-a-ling Bell was a woman of a similar age to Vic Bell. She had a nice smile and kissed him on the cheek. Dorian liked Sarah Bell immediately. The smile in her eyes was soft and inviting.

"Mother's entertaining Lady Uppington," said Dorian to his father. "Lord and Lady Chislehurst have just arrived."

"I'd better go and greet them."

"Mother has it under control."

"Good. How are you, son? How's the mechanic?"

"Not very good, I'm afraid."

Beth was smiling at him sweetly, enjoying the turmoil she knew was racing through his mind.

When they went into lunch to join the rest of the houseguests in the Great Hall with its high vaulted roof, he got his sister away from the crowd behind one of the pillars.

"How pregnant is she?"

"You're either pregnant or you're not, Dorian. She thinks about three months."

"Oh my God. Why didn't she tell me herself? That fits in perfectly."

"With what, Dorian?"

"That forty-eight-hour pass after I finished basic training. We made love in the lounge in the middle of the night. You were asleep."

"Naughty boy."

"I must be the father."

"You and the rest of Nancy's army. She admits to four lovers that weekend. Not including you, brother. She thought she was fireproof."

"What do the other chaps say? I suppose we could all chip in a bit. I get four bob a day in the army. I could give her a shilling. Oh my God. What am I going to do?"

"She's going to have an abortion."

"The army have posted me to London," said Dorian, looking relieved. "War Office."

"How convenient. You can hold Nancy's hand."

"What about the other chaps?"

"They haven't been told. For two of them, Nancy doesn't have an address."

"This all gets worse. I suppose I had better do the right thing and marry Nancy."

"She doesn't want to get married let alone take on the responsibility of a child. Come on, I'm hungry. Standing out in the cold earlier on has made me ravenous. The food's good. Mrs Craddock has laid on the works. She likes a good party. Says it gives her something to do for a change."

"What am I going to do, Beth?"

"Nothing. Absolutely nothing. We've found a reliable woman in Clapham. Then she's booking into a hospital for a D&C."

"What's a D&C?"

"You don't want details, Dorian. There's a price for everything. Nothing's free."

"Poor Nancy."

"She'll survive. Whether her mind will survive in the years to come is another matter. How long are you staying?"

"Until after Christmas. Has Nancy seen a doctor?"

"Not yet."

"I'll come and see her."

"That would be nice. Have you seen Genevieve and her two children? Tinus is as proud as a peacock. Barend's three and Hayley a year younger. Our first cousins once removed. The baby pulled down the fairy lights on the Christmas tree this morning. Genevieve had kittens."

"Is she making another film?"

"Not until her kids are grown up. She speaks with an American accent."

"And Tinus?"

"Still sounds like a Rhodesian with a clothes peg clamped to his nose."

"Are they coming back to England permanently?"

"No. They like New York. How are you, Dorian?"

"Still in shock."

"She'll be all right. Nancy has her own way of going through life."

AFTER LUNCH, Tinus Oosthuizen and Genevieve went up to their room with the children. Tinus carried Hayley on his shoulders. Barend found the big steps up the stairs difficult to climb with his short legs. Next to their bedroom was a second bedroom for the children with a connecting door. Within a minute of being put down both children were fast asleep; they had been running around all morning.

"Don't let them sleep too long or we won't sleep tonight," said Tinus, lying on top of the double bed with his hands behind his head.

"Have you noticed how yellow his face has gone?" said Genevieve.

"Uncle Harry is not well. Won't talk about it. Men never admit they are sick. It was those years with the tribe of Tutsi in the Congo if you ask my opinion. He had bilharzia. They can kill the parasite but not repair the damage. Eats the internal organs. Probably his liver, looking at the colour of his skin. The body deteriorates naturally over the years. What's left of his liver isn't enough to function properly. He's not drinking alcohol. Made me think of his liver. Asked me to be an executor to his will. Didn't like that."

"How old is Harry?"

"Sixty-two, I think. You never ask people their age. Those few years without medical attention took their toll. When he came back on the boat the doctor put him in the Hospital for Tropical Diseases in Bloomsbury. Moment the ship docked. In an ambulance. His body was full of bugs. When you live in a strange environment your body hasn't built up immunity to the new bugs. He was telling me every detail of his finances. Tina isn't interested in money just so long as she's got plenty to live on. Dorian wants to write. High finance doesn't work in that kind of brain. They think differently. Met a few of them at Oxford. Brains, all right, but different."

"Can't Kim come into the business now he is out of the RAF?"

"All he's had is school and the air force. Without saying so, Uncle Harry wants me to keep the boat on a level keel if anything happens to him."

"Do you think he's dying?"

"We're all dying slowly. From the day we're born."

"What a morbid thought... You know, that portrait at the bottom of the stairs looks just like Beth. Same eyes. Same look."

"Probably one of her great-grandmothers back a few hundred years. Some people say the only way we go on living is through our children. Why we all want to have kids."

"Two's enough, Tinus. I'm exhausted watching them all day. Where do they get all the energy? She nearly electrocuted herself under the Christmas tree. You've got to watch them all the time."

"Enjoy them while you can. Aunty Tina is miserable now her kids are gone. All she talks about to me is Anthony and the air force. Seems to bring her closer to his spirit... A fire in the grate is so nice. I wonder how many of my ancestors watched that same fire burn over the centuries? The old house likes being full of people. Wakes it up. Every fire in the place is lit."

"Purbeck Manor is going to be cold. Father only keeps a small part of the house open. With the new property taxes he can't afford to keep the whole place as it was. My grandmother is so looking forward to seeing her great-grandchildren."

"Won't she have a fright at the way they speak? You know, you sound more American than English. It's more noticeable over here."

"Tina wants me to look in on her father. There's a Mrs Battle living in the railway cottage with him. Doesn't pay rent but makes sure he's fed."

"Won't he be at the railway station tomorrow? He's the stationmaster."

"She wants me to look at the house. We can leave the kids with my father and walk along the river when it isn't raining… I'm going to take a nap while the kids are sleeping. Barend looks so angelic when he's asleep. When he's awake he wants to tear everything apart. He was sitting under the tree with Hayley when she grabbed the wires. Pulling all the Christmas paper off the presents. Having a high old time… How are we getting to the station tomorrow? My father is not much older than Harry. Why don't you ask your uncle if there is anything the matter? You two are close enough."

"He'll tell me when it's necessary."

"After all those children, my grandmother hasn't half the great-grandchildren she expected. Nothing yet from Uncle Frederick's Gwen. My cousin Richard by Uncle Robert isn't even twenty, and cousin Chuck is barely twelve."

"Haven't you forgotten Frank?"

"I always forget Frank. Before we fly back to the States, I'm going to find cousin Frank and have a word with him. He might listen to me. Why isn't he here for Christmas? His poor mother. Not a word to her since he came back to England from his crocodile hunts. We're both bastards. Anyway, what difference does it make?"

"He's making money. Own office in Fleet Street. Public relations. It was Frank's ideas and introduction that made Ridgeback cigarettes such a success. Uncle Harry wants me to launch the brand in America as every tobacconist in England is stocking them. He's the one Harry should be talking to about his money."

"But Frank isn't his son."

"It doesn't matter. You said so yourself. Harry brought him up. Harry's tickled pink Frank's making a success of his business. Frank's the only one of the boys with the money sense. He's smart. Like you, darling."

"All bastards are smart. We have to be to survive. To make people take us seriously. We can't rely on inheritance or family influence to get us on in life. We have to rely on our wits."

"Are we going to stay with your mother before we fly home?"

"Of course we are. After Christmas."

"Why didn't she come down to Purbeck Manor with us and the kids?"

"Don't be daft. She'd be like a fish out of water. She's happy with the Chelsea flat and a bottle of gin. She's happy. My mother is happy. Take her out of her environment, she'd be as miserable as sin... Do you want to put some more coal on the fire? I'm going to sleep. I ate far too much lunch. Couldn't get a part in a movie if I wanted. Far too fat."

"No you're not. You're just perfect."

"All right then. Close the door to the kids' bedroom and put some more coal on the fire. With kids around you have to take every opportunity."

"That's my girl."

2

———————

After lunch, while Tinus and Genevieve were having a rare afternoon nap, Dorian was having a talk with his father, all thought of Nancy Longhurst blown out of his mind.

"Does Mum know?"

"You and the doctors so far, Dorian. You are the eldest of the boys. You'll be the head of the family one day."

"How serious is it?"

"No one is ever quite sure. They never give you the date you're going to die."

"What is it?"

"Old age, mostly. Three years in the Congo specifically. I went back to the Hospital for Tropical Diseases. There are illnesses hidden in the African jungle they've never seen before. Monkeys, gorillas, baboons are all very similar to ourselves. We are able to pass diseases to each other. In Egypt, bilharzia is not a problem despite the Blue Nile being a host for bilharzia-carrying snails. Over the centuries, Egyptians have built up an immunity to the disease. It doesn't affect them the way it affected me, the bugs chewing away at my liver for a couple of years. I was lucky. Sometimes the bugs attack the brain. They killed the bilharzia but some of the damage was done. Without taking out my liver and having a look they can't tell how much has been eaten away. Then I drank too much which didn't help. Your mother and I like a sundowner or two together.

Left on our own with you lot away, there wasn't much to do in the evenings when I came home from London. A few drinks loosened us up. Made the evenings pleasant. We didn't get on each other's nerves with a few drinks inside us. Harmless enough, so I thought. There's always a consequence to everything we do in our lives."

"So it's just your liver. All you have to do is go off the booze."

"Not quite. Every time I get the slightest cold I can't throw it off the way I could before I went down in that damn river and the hippo clipped our float, crashing us into the riverine trees. Flu is far worse. The doctors think if I get something worse than the flu, like pneumonia, it will be the end of me."

"There are drugs. Penicillin."

"In my case, penicillin doesn't seem to work. They've never seen anything like it before. One of the doctors thinks I may have picked up more than bilharzia with my Tutsi friends."

"Is it VD?"

"No, Dorian. They did not give me a bride, if that's what you're thinking. I was a prisoner until I bribed the chief with the prospect of a supply of guns and ammunition so he could take his revenge on his Hutu neighbours. The two tribes had been enemies for centuries. I have a sad feeling my freedom came at the cost of many Hutu lives. Maybe this illness is the Hutu revenge. The Buddhist concept of my bad action coming back to haunt me. The Buddhists call it bad karma."

"But you wouldn't have come out otherwise. You would never have seen Kim."

"And all those Hutu would still be alive."

"You can't believe in all that mumbo-jumbo."

"Maybe not. But the thought of bereaved families, wives without husbands, children without fathers to bring them up, haunts me in my sleep. Why should I have been allowed to live and not them? What's so special about me, Dorian?"

"You're my father."

"Exactly. My exact point."

"Are you going to tell Mum?"

"I don't see why. It won't do her any good."

"Are you telling Beth and Kim?"

"Yes. They must know. They need time to prepare. Your mother has enough problems on her mind without me adding to them."

"What problems?"

"She's unhappy at getting old. Thinks no one is interested in her anymore. When I tell her you children have your own lives to live she thinks you're being selfish."

"I'll tell the others. We'll try harder to think of Mum."

"How's the motor mechanic?"

"He's not. They failed me. All fingers and thumbs. You always said asking Dorian to hang a picture he'd more likely nail himself to the wall. Anything mechanical I'm terrible. There's an army magazine. They've posted me to London to work on that. Still on four shillings a day."

"Like me, you won't be drinking too much. Now, what did Beth whisper in your ear that made you go as white as a sheet?"

"Not now, Dad. I've got enough to think about."

"I'm sorry. No right to pry. Just if you need help you know where to come."

"What am I going to do without you?"

"Don't cry, lad. You'll have me blubbing."

"I'm sorry."

"Life isn't about the end. About what you achieve in terms of money. It's about how you go through your life. What you made of it. All those good memories. Like you five children. The bits and pieces make up a life. Not the pilot. Not the money. Not even the farm in Rhodesia. I'm just so glad to have seen my mother and sister one more time, that I saw Africa one more time. That was important. I'm at peace with my soul. Be happy in your life, Dorian. That's all that is important. Now go and look for your mother. Beth's coming into the study next. Then Kim. We're going to all have one last, wonderful Christmas together. Despite Lady Uppington... That's better, son. Nothing like a good laugh. You promise to keep your mouth shut? Christmas is a time for celebration."

When Horatio and Janet Wakefield arrived with their two children, the lights were on in every room of the old house. Young Harry was out of the car first and up the steps to the long, balustrade terrace to look for his godfather.

"Please carry your suitcase, Bergit," said her mother.

"What about Harry?"

"Harry's looking for Harry."

"How can he look for himself, silly."

"Uncle Harry. His godfather. Your brother was named after Colonel Brigandshaw."

"Was he in the army?"

"The air force. Same as Herr von Lieberman. You were named after his wife. The nice people who saved the life of your father."

"I'm hungry."

"Come on then. I expect the children are having their supper now. If you pick up your case and hurry there might be some left for you."

"Why are all the lights on?"

"It's Christmas."

"Is there a Christmas tree?"

"Of course there is. A big one. The biggest Christmas tree in all the world. Under it you'll find presents with your name on them, darling."

With a yelp, the young girl ran up the terrace steps in front of them, bumping her suitcase.

"That worked," said Horatio, grinning. "They all want something."

"Human nature, I'm afraid... The man in the top window looking down at us is wearing a dinner jacket."

"We've just time to find our room and change for dinner."

"How do you know which is our room?"

"Same as last time. Said so on the invitation. Tina is organised. Takes a lot of time to throw a week-long bash like this. I'm hungry."

"You eat and eat and never get fat. It isn't fair. Are we staying a week?"

"Depends on Mr Glass and the newspaper."

"Oh, this is fun. I thought William and Betty were right behind us."

"Here they come. Quite like old times. There's nothing better than spending Christmas with old friends."

"Are we late for dinner?" called William Smythe.

"Seven-thirty for eight in the lounge for drinks and on to the great hall for a gala dinner. We've still time to change. Just look at all the lights. I'll bet Tina hasn't thrown a party like this since before the war."

"Come on then. Betty, you can put the kids down in the room next door."

"They won't like it."

"They'll have to. We'll take turns going up to check on them. Why does England have such a foul climate? Harry Brigandshaw says if England had a good climate there never would have been an empire. Everyone would have stayed at home. Do we know which rooms we are in?"

"You're next to us. Two rooms each. Each with connecting doors. They do that for families with children. In the old days when families visited each other on horseback they always stayed the night. Why the old mansions have so many bedrooms. In those days it was the only form of entertainment. People had to entertain each other. Shooting and fishing during the day. Fine dining and conversation at night. Being a good conversationalist was a social asset. Writers like us were always in demand. The women played instruments to entertain the other guests. All well-bred young ladies were taught to play the piano. We'll remember this Christmas. Won't be many more like it in England. Now everyone rushes around in motor cars, in too much of a hurry for the old traditions of life. The old days were more civilised. My word, there are a lot of people."

With three-year-old Patrick on his father's shoulder and Ruthy running ahead up the steps to the terrace, the two families made their way into Hastings Court.

"Welcome to my home," said Harry Brigandshaw, coming to meet them across the hall. "Saw you arrive. We keep the floodlights on until we all go to bed. How are we all? Where's young Harry?"

"Went to look for you," said Janet. "There he is. Gawping at the Christmas tree. That's the biggest Christmas tree I ever saw in my life."

"The tree is one of ours off the estate. Do you know where to find your rooms? Tina always puts people in the same rooms to make them feel at home. Familiar surroundings. I'd help with those suitcases only I'm not so good at carrying things anymore. Time stands still for no one. You go up and change. All the rooms are ready. Tina is somewhere. She's so excited everyone accepted our invitation. My word, it has been a long time we've all known each other. Must be nearly twenty years since you found me half dead in the Hospital for Tropical Diseases. 1931. Now you are both happily married with children. There are fires on in the rooms. You won't be cold. All the children are here except Frank but you know all about Frank. Quite flattering, your articles on me and the new company. Thank you both. The Ridgeback launch has been a great success. Paul Crookshank isn't here, I'm afraid. Christmas with his mother and brother in the Isle of Wight. You'd better hurry up and change. When you want food for the children ring the bell in your room. Rather, you pull the chain on the knob in the wall. Connected to a board in the maids' sitting room downstairs. It lets down a flag with the room number. They'll understand. Tina hired a small army from the village to help this week. They also make it into a bit of a party. The servants' quarters in this house are bigger than most large houses. Off you go. See you later. Really nice to see you again. I hope you're all in the party mood."

Smiling, Horatio walked up the stairs behind his wife and Betty Smythe, cocking his ear to a new sound from deep inside the old house. Reaching the top, he sensed the portraits of the Manderville ancestors had been watching his every step, the eyes seeming to follow him, his footsteps soft on the thick maroon carpet. The following eyes of so many dead people made him shiver, as if someone had walked over his grave. Down below, Harry junior was looking at every present under the Christmas tree, one by one, methodically looking for one with his name on, ignoring his mother who wanted him to follow them up to the bedrooms. Bergit was waiting for them impatiently on the landing, with her small suitcase, holding it in front of her with both hands. As Harry Brigandshaw moved across to engage his godson, Horatio realised what was making the strange noise. Somewhere, a chamber orchestra was tuning up for the night's festivities. Horatio had to give it to Harry Brigandshaw. Whatever the man did, he did it properly. There were no half measures. Like the man's attempt to fly a seaplane down Africa, hopping from lake to river in his quest to fly from Cairo to the Cape, his attempt fractured by an errant hippopotamus coming up for air at just the wrong moment, crippling the aircraft and starting his three-year stay with a tribe of Tutsi who would not let him go. The string orchestra began to play Mozart, the sound blending perfectly with the old house, the old man in the portrait nearest to Horatio seeming to smile. As Horatio paused to listen, up ahead on the landing, William's seven-year-old Ruthy joined Bergit to look down on them.

"He doesn't look well," said William from behind.

"He was likely sick when they painted him. They often wanted a portrait of themselves when they knew they were dying."

"I meant Harry," said William softly looking back down the stairs. "He has that same pallid-eyes look he had when we found him in the Bloomsbury hospital. The famous aviator back from the dead, the story of which made both of us famous. He's ill, Horatio."

"Nonsense. It's the light."

"Couldn't carry a suitcase. Every other visit he's insisted on carrying my case for me."

"That's old age. We all get there in the end."

"What's that noise?"

"Mozart. We're going to be entertained."

WHILE HORATIO and William were opening the doors to their rooms, finding the fires burning bright in the hearths, Major Pilkington-Jones and Ding-a-ling Bell had had their chinwag in front of the fire interrupted by the music, both turning their heads to the sound of Mozart. When the piece was finished, Vic Bell turned back to the major.

"How can something so beautiful come from drawing a bow over catgut? You'd think the animals' intestines would scream, not make a sound so magical that it soothes all the nerves. Then again, the purity of the sound originated in one man's head. Civilised man is such a paradox. One of us makes music like that and another invents the machine gun."

"Is it really the gut of a cat?"

"Any poor animal, I understand. So you see what I mean. Now, back where we were. You were telling me how your pith hat was given a bullet hole."

"Northwest frontier. Just before the war. Our war, not the war just finished. Damn tribesman tried to shoot me from five hundred yards. Dropped the shot perfectly, though not quite low enough, luckily for me. We British never did tame those hill tribesmen. Part of Pakistan now. The tribesmen won't like control by a central government any more than they liked us. The British Empire is collapsing. People don't like being told what's good for them anymore. You can promise the moon when you don't have the job of running the place. Keeping law and order. Building the railways. Giving the man in the street peace of mind knowing those running the country are making the right decisions, not just those that keep everybody happy. That's the trouble with democracy. Plato said it's only a tad better than a dictatorship. You get elected for five years, make a balls-up, get thrown out by the people with new promises from the next lot and the economy slides down the drain. This country is going to the dogs."

"The idea of a welfare state is laudable. Just making it work is going to be the problem. Balancing the taxes with the benefits. Everyone wants to take. No one wants to give, however generous they prefer to sound."

"Just my point. Game of ping pong if you ask me. Only the damn politicians win. A civil servant in India had his whole career to think of when he made a decision. This new breed of politicians only think from one election to another. Bloody mess."

"Winston said democracy is terrible. The only trouble was he couldn't think of a better way to govern the people."

"We're all savages. Mark my word. Now the Americans have dropped the bomb on Japan we'll all blow ourselves to pieces. Man has never, never invented a weapon he hasn't used with impunity. When a rat's in a corner it uses everything at its disposal, not caring if it dies in the process. It won't be long before we've all got the bomb, including the French and the Russians. Signed mankind's death warrant splitting the atom, if you ask my opinion."

"What can we do?"

"Nothing. When's Harry serving drinks?"

"Right now if you want one."

"Oh, there you are, Harry. Come and join us round the fire. Vic and I are getting to know each other."

"What'll you have?"

"Whisky, old chap. Found a distillery in Scotland with young Paul and young Jeanne that made the nectar of the gods. Uncivilised bunch, the Scots, but they do know how to make whisky. Where is everyone?"

"Still changing for dinner."

"Got straight into my monkey jacket and came down to find Vic sitting round the fire."

"Where's Sarah, Vic?" asked Harry Brigandshaw.

"Helping Tina. Harry and my wife met in the underground shelter during the war, Major. Took him sandwiches every night, thinking him a poor clerk in the Air Ministry with no one to look after him. Had no idea of all of this. Harry introduced us. Never been happier in my life. Luckiest man alive. Did you hear the music, Harry? Quite beautiful."

"Yes, it is. Sort of blends in with the old house. Twelve musicians from the London Symphony Orchestra. Staying in the village. They're coming every night of your stay except Christmas Day."

"Where are they?"

"In the Great Hall. The oldest part of the house. How's that for your whisky? No water or ice. I've got a good memory. In another life I'd have made a good barman."

"Aren't you having one?"

"Not just now. Fact is, I'm not drinking at the moment. Old liver playing up."

"Gives me the gout," said the major. "No pleasure without pain. 'Here's looking at you.' That's Humphrey Bogart in *Casablanca*. Is the rumour true, old boy? That Genevieve is joining us for Christmas? Isn't she married to your nephew? Seen every one of her films. Those mismatched eyes go right to my heart. Never did marry. Always being posted to some godforsaken spot. Can't take women to those kinds of places, can we?"

"She's joining us tonight. Tomorrow she goes to her father, Lord St Clair."

"Oh, yes. I read her book. Can't wait to meet a famous actress."

The clock on the mantelpiece struck seven-thirty, the prelude for the room filling up. Servants appeared with trays of drinks. Harry, smiling, greeted every one of his guests.

"Tina still organising, I'm afraid," he said to everyone as he shook their hands. Just before eight Tina Brigandshaw arrived with Sarah Bell. Both were wearing their evening dresses. Vic Bell got up and went to his wife. Harry crossed the room to stand next to Tina.

At exactly eight o'clock, Mrs Craddock, the cook, opened the door to the hallway that led to the Great Hall. The major, still watching for Genevieve, was disappointed. The girl, who for him epitomised the perfect woman, had not yet put in an appearance.

"Dinner is served, my Lords, Ladies and gentlemen."

"Thank you, Mrs Craddock," said Harry taking his wife's arm. "Follow me, everyone. Bit of a walk, I'm afraid. Old house is rather big."

Miffed at not meeting his screen idol, Major Pilkington-Jones followed the rest of them in to dinner.

WHILE THE MAJOR was daydreaming about knights of old and their perfect ladies, upstairs on the second floor Genevieve was closing the outside door to the bedroom, holding her breath. For a full minute both of them stood in the corridor, still waiting for Hayley to scream.

"We're all right, Tinus."

"Come on. We've missed the drinks. Am I hearing an orchestra playing?"

"Heard it earlier through the window. They're asleep. I hate leaving them alone in a strange room."

"I'll go up first to check on them. You look wonderful."

"Thank you, kind sir. You don't look too bad yourself. Why doesn't your uncle put more lights in the corridor?"

"When he wired the place for electricity he thought the house would burn down. Why he left out central heating. Why hot water pipes from a central furnace should cause a fire I have no idea. Harry doesn't like change."

Forcing himself not to glance at the portraits of his ancestors on his way down the staircase to the hall, Tinus smiled to himself with pleasure at the thought of his children fast asleep in the home of their ancestors.

"Will they be all right on their own?" asked Genevieve.

"The good spirits of their forebears will look over them. They'll both sleep like logs. A strange room to them but it's home. They belong here. I read a book once that said the good spirits find us in our dreams. Come and play with us. That good spirits like company in the night. They've got company by now. Happy company. All those ancestral spirits come to have a look at them. You should ask your spirits to visit you when we get to Purbeck Manor tomorrow."

"Can't we stay another day? For Harry's sake. He's been so good to both of us. There's a train to Corfe Castle every day. You think they'd come to my dreams if I let them?"

"Of course they will."

"I'm not a child."

"The child never leaves us. Just before you go to sleep, think of your ancestors. They'll come to you."

"Don't they come to you?"

"Only when I stay at Hastings Court or on Elephant Walk. I always dream of my father and grandfather, the Boer General, when I stay on the farm."

"You're serious."

"Of course I am. Mind the last step in your long dress."

"Don't you think I've put on weight with the kids?"

"Not an ounce. Do you know whose music they're playing?"

"I have no idea. Classical music was never my best suit. Even at the Hall. I did Speech and Drama at the Albert Hall. We let the musicians look after the music. If I had a guess I'd say that is Beethoven. Or Brahms. It just might be Mozart... You haven't looked at the portraits all the way down. Clever boy. I don't know why but I'm nervous. Must be all your ancestors checking me out. Don't you think somewhere back in time the St Clairs and the Mandervilles were related? Lady Uppington had Manderville ancestors so I hear. Then we'd be cousins. Kissing cousins, of course. Distant enough not to prevent us having children... What a pity. Just as we get to the door of the Great Hall, the music stops. Here we go. We'll just sneak in and find our places."

Pushing open the door, closed against the cold, Tinus let his wife go into the Great Hall first, closing the door behind him. When he turned back to the room, and the long table stretching the length of the hall from one walk-in fireplace to the other, big fires of tree trunks burning in both, the other guests began to get to their feet. The members of the orchestra, in the minstrel gallery facing Tinus at the far end of the hall, also got to their feet when they saw Genevieve. Then everyone began to clap. Uncle Harry walked down from the top of the table and offered his arm, escorting Genevieve to the place of honour on his left. On his right, also standing on her feet and clapping, was Tina. As if by arrangement, the fiddlers up in the gallery began to play 'You're the Top'. Only then did Genevieve see William Smythe looking at her as if he had just seen a ghost. Waving at everyone, and blushing, Genevieve found her place next to Uncle Harry, as she liked to call him, and sat down. Uncle Harry put a large glass of red wine in her hand. Still standing with the others, Harry waited for the last few bars of the music to stop. Then he raised his own glass.

"To Genevieve," he called to everyone.

"To Genevieve," echoed back from both sides of the sixty-foot-long oak table and down from the gallery behind. Only then did normal conversation resume as the dinner party went on its way.

"It's perfect, Uncle Harry," she whispered in his ear.

"I hope so."

"Tina," she said, leaning forward to talk across Harry. "Thank you. The welcome is overwhelming."

From across the table an old man she had never seen before was grinning at her, reminding Genevieve of a demented Cheshire cat. She smiled back at him before taking a long drink of her red wine, surveying the guests over the rim of the glass as she drank. It was good to be back in England. She had missed the place, something she had not realised while living in America. Only then did she look down the table at William and give him a wave. By now, she had hoped he would have forgotten their one-night stand in the Independence Hotel in New York. The pretty girl next to him was giving her a look that reminded Genevieve she was William's wife. There was pain in the girl's eyes, as if she knew of the one-night stand all those years ago when Genevieve was lonely in a foreign land, looking for sympathy, and found a friend in her compatriot William.

"What's the matter, darling?" asked Tinus.

"It's William. He still remembers."

"So do I the first time we made love. There's nothing wrong with good memories, even if they make me jealous." He was leaning close to Genevieve so no one else could hear.

"Are you jealous of William?"

"Of course I am. And every other man in your past. However brief."

"What about your women?"

"We don't talk of them."

"Are you sure the kids are all right?"

"Of course they are. Stop worrying."

THE MAJOR WAS NOW QUITE certain. The resemblance was uncanny. Even down to the mismatched eyes. What he had thought was a trick of the cinema was right in front of him when he looked up the table, smiling deep in his mind.

They had seated him between Sarah Bell and Lady Uppington, a pain in the arse if ever there was one. Straight away she had looked down her nose at him and told him about her uncle the general, as if sitting next to the major at dinner was a comedown for a lady of quality. The woman looked like a horse, an insult to some of the major's best friends. There had been a cavalry horse in the Boer War, up in the Transvaal, the major remembered being particularly fond of until a Boer Mauser had shot it dead under him. Listening to Lady Uppington's snobbery as she worked her way through the courses and the glasses of wine, the major would have been happy to find a Boer sniper among the guests at the table. Whenever he turned to talk to Sarah, Lady Uppington interrupted. On the other side, her husband ignored her, the lucky man. In deference to his host, the major determined to be polite.

When the coast was clear, he turned to Sarah Bell.

"Do you think, Mrs Bell, a person can reappear in your life fifty years later in the body of another person?"

"You've got me there, Major. What are you talking about?"

"Doesn't matter."

"I think your friend next to you wishes to say something."

Turning round with a smile to Lady Uppington, he switched off his mind to the present. Provided Lady Uppington was talking, she was happy. The woman liked the sound of her own voice.

Shrinking back into his own world away from the dinner party, he let his mind roam back over the years.

Her name was Bella, a first cousin on the Pilkington side of his family, his mother's side. He was a young subaltern of cavalry not long out of Sandhurst when Bella came to stay. Back many years before they had met as children before her father was posted to the Sudan. For the next ten years the John Pilkington family lived in the colonies, a series of postings that ended with the governorship of Sarawak on the mainland of Borneo. Bella had been sent to school in Australia. It was nearer than England. Unlike his brother, the major's grandfather, John Pilkington was poor and relied on his salary from the Colonial Office to bring up his small family. There was Bella and Fred. Fred had been killed in Flanders in 1915. Bella was seventeen when they both came to stay with their grandparents and the major was nineteen. The Boer War had not yet started.

For the love-struck cousins it was one long summer that lasted a week before the major was sent back to his unit after being found out by their grandfather who threatened to cut off his allowance if he ever saw Bella again. The Pilkingtons had done it before, marrying their first cousins, three times in history. The resultant inbreeding was a disaster. Two relations were in an asylum when he fell in love with Bella bringing the wrath of his grandfather down on his head. They had been caught by one of the garden boys on his grandfather's estate in Norfolk where the families were holidaying together. In the stables. Up in the loft. The boy so boggle-eyed at what he had seen, he had been unable to keep his trap shut. By the late afternoon, after tea, which the major and Bella had failed to show up for, everyone knew. It was the end of them. For the major it was pretty much the end of his life. Without an allowance in the cavalry, gaining high rank was impossible. And now, here she was across the table. His Bella. Every time Genevieve smiled at him his mind turned to water. If only they had not been caught they could have run off together. Not every child of first cousins was an imbecile. They would have been all right. They would have been happy. But caught they were in the loft, leaving both of them in the state of mind that found other people they might have married a pale reflection of what they'd had together.

Neither of them had married. When Bella was twenty-two, she had died of diphtheria.

"I'm sorry, Lady Uppington. What did you say?"

"Are you all right, Major Jones?"

"Major Pilkington-Jones. Yes, I'm all right. Thought I'd got over it. Fifty years ago. All those years ago and it hurts just the same."

"What are you talking about?"

"Love, Lady Uppington. Have you seen Genevieve's films?"

"My husband doesn't approve of the cinema. People kissing each other in public. Quite disgusting. Would you please pass the salt?"

HAVING LEFT Harry Junior and Bergit with the older children playing charades in a big room at the other end of the house, under the supervision of Mary Kingsley whose wedding Tina had organised, Horatio and Janet were enjoying their freedom. Janet had been told to not worry about her weight for once and indulge herself in the food. All around them the guests were talking and eating, drinking their wine, laughing at anything that resembled a joke. A festive party, if Horatio had ever seen one. A welcome change from the austerity of war and food rationing. Harry Brigandshaw had said that everything they ate at Hastings Court, with few exceptions, came from the surrounding estate that went with the old house. It was his only chance of farming.

"Not quite growing tobacco or maize. The bacon's ours. The beef. Lamb. Vegetables and fruit. There's something satisfying about eating your own food. Primal instinct. We were hunter gatherers not that many generations back. Then we were farmers making the supply of food more reliable. Putting down food for the winter. Bit like the grey squirrels. Man should get nervous when he has to rely on other people for his food. What is a pound note other than a piece of paper? At the moment we all have faith in a piece of paper because the Bank of England promises to pay. Once the pound sterling was backed by the equivalent in gold. Not anymore. The only real value is in a bag of maize or a cow. Something you can eat. Farmland is the real repository of wealth... Bear with an old man... I miss the farm in Rhodesia. During the war, the German U-boats tried to cut off our food supplies so everyone dug up their lawns and planted potatoes. There'll be a time when no one will know how to grow potatoes or anything else. We'll all be relying on some farmer from across the seas. I like mucking out the cow sheds.

Reminds me of my youth. My father made us do all the jobs on the farm so we'd know when the labourers were doing it right. Cousin George in Virginia said the same. Got to know what you're doing to tell someone else."

"I'd forgotten we both went to the Hall," said Janet interrupting his train of thought.

"Who are you talking about?"

"Genevieve. We both attended the Central School of Speech and Drama at the Albert Hall. I did speech therapy while Genevieve did drama. She didn't finish the course. The West End theatre found her first. Then the cinema. She looks radiant. I'm so glad they're happy. Listen to that. They're playing 'Greensleeves'. One of the orchestra has a beautiful voice. What a lovely room. The vaulted ceiling goes so high you can't see the top from here. What a Christmas we're having. Why have we been so lucky with our lives, Horatio? I'll bet the kids are enjoying themselves. A whole week without someone stuttering at me. I can't believe my luck. Harry's decided he wants to join the air force, like his godfather."

"He told me. At that age they change their minds every week. I just want to make sure he doesn't become a journalist."

"What's wrong with being a journalist?"

"You have to tell the public what they want to hear to sell newspapers. It's all about advertising and money."

"Isn't everything in life about money? I like Sarah Bell. She's so genuine. Her first husband was killed at Dunkirk. Didn't Paul Crookshank's father go down on a sailboat? He'd done umpteen trips to get the soldiers off the beaches. She's happy now. Just look at her."

ON THE OTHER side of the table, oblivious to Janet Wakefield's remark, Sarah Bell was having the time of her life. For the lady from the corner shop in her first long dress, sitting at an ancient table that had entertained for centuries under the same vaulted roof, was beyond her wildest dreams. From when she and Tom had run their tobacconist's shop off the Charing Cross Road before the war, living above the shop, she was now in a world she had only read about in books. In fairy stories when everyone was happy. Where they all lived happily ever after.

"Pinch me, Vic."

"Whatever for?"

"To make sure it's all real. That I'm here. Tom would be so proud of me. You don't mind me talking about Tom? We were two ordinary people but that didn't matter. When I met Harry on the platform of Charing Cross Tube station with the crump of German bombs all around us, I was so afraid. He told us stories of Africa to take our minds off the bombing. All lying on the floor fully clothed, covered in blankets against the cold. At night, when the German bombers came over, they turned off the power on the railway lines. Some people found shelter between the steel lines when the platform was crowded. When Harry was talking, everyone within earshot kept quiet. You could hear the German bombs and the British ack-ack and Harry's voice. He gave us all courage. I thought he was just a storyteller, making it all up. Brought him sandwiches. Harry never talked much about his family living in Cape Town. Thought he was a lonely man who told stories, with no one to look after him. Never heard of you then, Vic. Didn't know Harry's bottles of black market whisky came from you with your contacts in the Air Ministry. Now look at me. Guest of the Lord of the Manor. All those stories were true. Harry living with a tribe of savages. It all sounded too impossible to be true."

"Harry said the Tutsi were more civilised than we are in many ways. Apart from warring with the Hutu, the chief was an absolute gentleman. Never once went against his word. Never told a lie."

"What an experience. Then I find out Harry was a fighter pilot in the First World War. One of the guests said Harry had twenty-three kills to his name."

"And every one of the dead pilots haunt him. Harry hates war. He thinks we are the savages the way we kill from great distances not knowing who we're killing. There's going to be another war in Korea. Five years ago England and Russia were allies. We sent them aircraft to defend themselves against Nazi Germany. Now communism is the enemy. If there's another war with nuclear bombs we'll annihilate each other. Make the bombings of London and Berlin look like a picnic."

"Please, Vic. I'm enjoying my food... Did they really grow everything here on the estate? How did I get this lucky in my life? Two wonderful men."

"Because you are a good person. Leave the worrying to me at the Air Ministry. Enjoy yourself."

"I thought you were going to retire?"

"When they tell me. Won't be long. Then I'll help you behind the counter running the shop."

"Won't that be a comedown?"

"Not with you standing next to me."

"What are they playing now?"

"It's an old English ballad from the days when minstrels toured from one estate to the other providing the entertainment. No one knows who wrote their pieces. They go too far back. But I'll take a bet these old walls have heard this music before... I would like to have lived in those days."

"Hasn't it all been made romantic by history? None of them ever washed. There wasn't enough hot water. You couldn't just turn on the hot water tap and run yourself a bath."

"The Romans could."

"Not these old English homes. I mean, who would want a cold bath on a night like this with Jack Frost running around outside? Oh, no. I like this century. Right now. With you in my first long dress. What do you think of it, Vic?"

"It makes you look even more beautiful."

"You flatter me, sir. That's what they said in my books in those days in response to a compliment."

"Have some more wine. I can't even imagine Harry's bill from the wine merchant. A whole week of medieval luxury."

"She looks happy."

"Who?"

"His wife, Tina. Why do his kids look so miserable?"

3

———————

After the first shock of seeing Genevieve and getting a wave, William Smythe felt better. Two quick glasses of Harry Brigandshaw's expensive French wine had removed the rose-tinted spectacles from his eyes. Was that first gut-wrench love or lust, he asked himself? Had Betty seen his reflex reaction? When he looked up the table after the second glass of wine he no longer saw the same girl. The wedding of Genevieve and Tinus in America was to have been the laying of the ghost. Now, after a brief moment being caught unawares, he was back in control. Up at the top of the table was a mother of two children, another man's wife, not his. Only her films would retain the power of her youth. She had put on weight. Looked content. No longer the girl that had torn into his body and mind one night long ago in a New York hotel... Stretching for the open bottle of wine in the centre of the table, William filled up his glass.

"You still love her," snapped Betty before he could turn with the bottle and fill up her glass. "You didn't get over her by taking me to the wedding. I can't believe the way you looked at her. You've never looked at me that way."

"Oh, Betty. It was all a long time ago."

"Don't you 'Oh, Betty' me. I saw you just look at her. You can talk as much as you like, it won't make any difference. I'm going upstairs to look at our children. Have you forgotten Ruthy and Patrick the moment that woman walked in the room?"

"Are we having an argument?"

"Damn right we are. You men are all the same. You all want something else. When you've got what you want, you don't want it anymore."

"She caught me unawares. I had no idea she was in England."

"She waved at you. As if she owned you. And that smile of hers down the table. She knows she only has to flick her fingers and William comes running."

"She's happy with Tinus."

"I'm talking about you. If I wasn't in someone else's house I'd throw that glass of wine in your face and go home to my mother. With the kids."

"She was just being polite."

"Not the way you two looked at each other. Make up your mind what you want, William Smythe. I'm not playing second fiddle to anyone."

"I'll go and look at the children. I said I'd go up first. You enjoy your supper."

"Not with that woman in the same room."

Throwing her table napkin on the table next to her half-finished plate of food, Betty got up and stormed out of the room ignoring everyone.

"What was all that about?" asked Janet Wakefield sitting next to William.

"Genevieve. Why do women get so jealous?"

"She loves you. Women get jealous when they love someone and think they might lose them. Go after her."

"You're right. I'm sorry. Excuse me."

"You can tell Betty, Genevieve and Tinus are spending Christmas with her father in Dorset."

"That'll help."

"Good luck."

"It was more than ten years ago."

"The way you looked at Genevieve when she came in the room, it might have been yesterday."

"That obvious?"

"An open book."

"Just when you think your life is on an even keel something like this happens. I married Betty. Isn't that enough?"

"No, William. Go after her. With a bit of luck she'll slap your face and feel a whole lot better. It's either that or scratching out Genevieve's eyes."

"You're enjoying this, Janet. You're busting yourself not to laugh."

"One good smack across the chops should do it."

When William looked back from the door, looking from Genevieve to Janet, neither of them taking any notice, he hoped no one else at the table had overheard the argument. Then he went to look for his wife and make his amends.

"I'll never understand women," he said to the family portraits as he wearily climbed the stairs.

"I heard that, William," said Betty from where she was standing in the gloom at the top.

"I'm told by Janet to ask you to give me a fat smack across the face."

"Come and get closer. The kids are fast asleep."

"That was quick."

"I was mad at you. Ran up the stairs. Come on up then we'll go back to the dinner party. We don't want Harry or Tina to notice. Did anyone other than Janet notice?"

"She doesn't mean a thing anymore."

"Let's skip it, William. We'll only start arguing. Arguing is so pointless. Now that's just close enough."

Before William could get out of the way, Betty cracked him with a flat hand right across his face.

"Now I do feel better. Janet was right."

"Are you going back to your mother? You don't even like your mother when she tells you what to do with the kids."

"Of course not."

"Tinus and Genevieve are spending Christmas with her father and grandmother in Dorset."

"Good... Do you really love me?"

"Of course I do. You're Ruthy's mother."

"And Patrick's. Like angels sleeping. That night candle works. You can see they're all right without turning on the light. Did anyone see us?"

"All the parents of young kids go and look at their children at supper time, especially a long supper. It's expected. Harry and Tina would think there was something wrong with us if we didn't go and check on our kids."

"No wonder you're a newspaper man. You can make anything sound nice. No, I'm not arguing. That's a compliment. Don't these staring portraits up the stairs give you the creeps? Put your arm through mine. Here we go again."

Inside the Great Hall, Genevieve had left her place and was walking down the other side of the room. Timing perfect, thought William, not even daring to look at her. His face still stung. When they sat down, Janet leaned across William having looked at his face.

"Good shot, Betty."

Then they were all laughing. No one bothered to look at them. Everyone was having a good time. When the third course was put in front of them William and Betty tucked into their food, the brief argument forgotten. Likely, William thought, Genevieve had gone to look at her own children the same as any good mother.

Later, when they got up to their rooms full of good food and wine, tired and happy, they had looked at their children before falling into bed. When William woke in the dark of the night they were still in each other's arms. Kissing the sleeping Betty on the tip of her nose by the light of the moon, William fell back into sleep.

When they woke, the birds were singing. Outside, having got up to look out of the big window, William saw a light powder of snow lay on the ground. The fire in the hearth had burned low. The room was still warm. When one of the temporary servants from the village brought them in a tray of tea the day was already perfect. Better still, the kids in the next room were still asleep, not making a sound.

By the time they were dressed and went downstairs to look for some breakfast, Genevieve and Tinus with their children had gone. Harry Brigandshaw said Kim had taken them to the station for their journey down to Corfe Castle.

"Enjoy the bacon," said Harry. "I smoked it myself."

HAVING NOT much to do with his life, being a taxi driver suited Kim. At least he was contributing something to all the hard work of his mother and father. Being the youngest in the family had its compensations. Dorian had called a family meeting to discuss their father in the rebuilt horse stables later on in the day. A German bomb had knocked it down during the war when he was in Cape Town with his mother and the other children. In the car, on the way to the station, it seemed Cousin

Tinus was oblivious of the sword of Damocles hanging over his Uncle Harry's head. Kim had thought they were staying another day and had missed his breakfast in the hurry to catch the train. Genevieve and Tinus were spending Christmas at Purbeck Manor before going back to London to catch the flight for their journey home to the States. Kim wondered if Cousin Tinus would ever see his uncle again. It was better this way. There was nothing Tinus could do if what his father had told them was true. His father never made a song and dance about something so serious. The famous actress was a stunner, no doubt about that. Better they went off happy with a last good memory to look back on later in life. After Tinus's father had been killed, his uncle had taken on the job of father. They were both close to each other, more like father and son.

"Don't you want to live in England?" he asked them as he shook hands at Leatherhead railway station, their train pulling into the platform.

"You always want to go back where you came from. Sometimes it isn't possible. The kids are American. America is where we have our home and our friends. The job's exciting. England is so grey after the war. No one has much enthusiasm. The war knocked the stuffing out of England. If anywhere, the draw for me is Africa. There's some tremendous draw in all of us who have lived in Africa to want to go back again. But that's all over for the whites. The African colonies will be the next to go after India. There's going to be a clash of cultures. My people, the Afrikaners, won't take it quietly. They'll fight. As my grandfather fought the British in the Anglo-Boer War. The future lies in America. Thanks for driving us to the station, Kim. If you want a job in America you only have to give me a ring."

"I might just do that."

"A pity Frank wasn't at the party."

"Yes it was. Beth's tried to knock some sense into him and I keep out of the way. People do what they want whatever you tell them."

"Did you enjoy your two years in the RAF?"

"Not really. I didn't fly. Not enough time in two years. A few of the chaps got to fly. By the time they'd finished flying training and all the rest of it, their National Service was over. Dad won't teach me to fly. I was hoping you would one day."

"Your father was thinking of Anthony. Your father's tribute to him on the cross in the family graveyard is very moving. I gave Anthony one last farewell salute. I was lucky enough to get through the war. Anthony and my schoolfriend André Cloete, along with many of my friends, were not so lucky. The terrible price of war. You'll think of something to do with your life, Kim, don't worry. It'll come. Enjoy the rest of Christmas."

Before Kim was aware what had happened, Genevieve, star of all the films, gave him a kiss on the lips, leaving him standing looking after the train as it pulled out of the station, young Barend waving at him out of the window before someone pulled him back into the safety of the carriage. For a long moment, Kim watched the steam engine puff its way out of the station.

"I'm going to remember that kiss for the rest of my life," he said, smiling. Then he walked to the car for the drive back to Hastings Court and the meeting with Dorian and Beth in the stables.

By the time they arrived at the stables, from different directions so as not to have their mother asking questions, the sun had melted the snow on the ground. Kim was still conscious of being kissed by Genevieve. All of them were muffled up against the cold. There were no horses, just straw their father had put down to make the place look less deserted. Their father had never been a horseman, preferring to ride his old 1925 BSA motorcycle round his country lanes. With the horses killed by the German bombing no one had thought to buy any more. The milk cows lived in the cow sheds in the same line of old buildings. Luckily for the cows they had been in the fields when the bombs came down. The horses, more pampered, had been stabled for the night.

"What are we going to do?" asked Beth.

"Nothing," said Dorian. "We're all sworn to secrecy. He'll tell Mother in his own good time."

"It's awful," said Kim. "She went through this once before when Dad disappeared with his aircraft in the Congo. When the government taxed Mother into oblivion before they had to give back the death duty to Dad."

"They'll do it again," said Beth. "This time we won't be able to keep Hastings Court. With an estate like Father's they take eighty per cent."

"You're talking as if Dad's dead," said Dorian. "Dad's more important than money."

"Mother likes playing Lady of the Manor," answered Kim. "What's she going to do?"

"His American and Rhodesian estates will be taxed for death duty separately. The Americans don't criminalise a man for making money. Taking it when he's dead so he can't argue. Socialism. A great idea except when they get the money they piss it up against the wall. All the benefits are for people who don't want to work. Or the money goes to the army we shouldn't need anymore. What's the point of working hard and making money when the majority who haven't got enough take it away from you? I'm better off being fed and housed in the army with four bob a day spending money."

"If you want to be a writer, Dorian, you'd better get your ideas in reverse," said Kim. "All writers pillory the rich. You have to tell the public it's a good idea to take from the rich and give to the poor. Anyway, this family has got too much money."

"You're a fine one to talk," said Beth. "No job in sight and living at home. What are you going to do with your life?"

"I may go to America."

"And do what there?"

"Tinus said I should ring him if I run out of ideas."

"Run out of ideas! You haven't had one since you left the RAF."

"I could go farming in Rhodesia."

"Dad says they're tobacco growers, not tobacco farmers."

"What's that got to do with it?"

"The blacks want independence. They'll kick out the whites."

"Who told you that? What are they going to do without white skills and capital?"

"They'll think of something, according to the papers. Everything's changed since the war and with India getting independence."

"Do you know, eight million people have become refugees in India? Half a million have been killed in religious violence. That never happened under the British Raj."

"How do we know? They wouldn't have told us."

"The world's a mess."

"Always has been. Now, do we tell Mother or don't we?" asked Beth.

"Is that what this is about?"

"What are we going to do without Dad? He's the glue that holds us all together," said Kim.

"You didn't tell Tinus."

"Of course not... She kissed me."

"Who?"

"Genevieve. On the mouth. She has soft lips. I'm freezing. Maybe Dad won't die for a very long time. I missed my breakfast going to the station."

"It'll be lunchtime in an hour."

"Thank goodness. I think you're wrong about one thing. I read somewhere the Labour government have put death duty up to ninety per cent for the rich."

"All you think of is money," said Beth.

"What am I going to do about Nancy?" asked Dorian.

"What's the matter with Nancy?" said Kim, looking at his brother. "What's it to do with you, Dorian?"

"She's pregnant."

"Are you the father?"

"Maybe."

"That's wonderful. Dad's going to have his first grandchild... What do you mean, maybe? You either are the father or you're not."

"My friend Nancy Longhurst sleeps with lots of men," said Beth.

"Does she now?"

"Well, she certainly did."

"How are you going to find out who is the father?"

"That's the problem," said Dorian.

"I'm still a virgin."

"Congratulations," said Beth.

"There weren't any women around in the air force."

"Poor Kim. When you next come up to London I'll see what I can do. What are sisters for?"

"What about Nancy?"

"She's pregnant," said Dorian.

AFTER AN HOUR of mostly going off at a tangent, they left separately to go and look for lunch. By then all the dogs had found them, wagging their tails expecting a walk. When Kim looked back, the dogs were still sitting on their haunches outside the stables.

"A dog's life is one long hope," Kim said to no one. Surprisingly, the sun was warm on his face, the cold east wind having died down. Then he thought of the real problems. If he were to go to the States, what would happen to his mother?

When he walked round the side of the house, he found his mother in conversation with Lady Uppington. She didn't look at him. Any question of where he had been went unsaid. Inside the house, he could smell the lunch wafting through from the Great Hall. With so many houseguests, all meals other than breakfast were being eaten down the long oak table.

There was no sign of the small orchestra when Kim walked inside the old hall with its vaulted roof. Pots of food were standing on the sideboard. Under the pots were small methylated spirit burners to keep the food warm. Lifting the lid of the first pot, Kim ladled himself out a plateful. People trickled in for lunch. He had been first. To be expected, he told himself, he had not had any breakfast. Someone had put a new batch of dry tree trunks on the fires at both ends of the room. Soon after he sat himself down, the dogs found him again and sat under the table. One of them sat on his foot, keeping it warm. The food, when he ate, was delicious. No one in the air force could compete with Mrs Craddock's cooking which made him think: what would happen to Mrs Craddock if the family were forced to sell Hastings Court? So far as he remembered, Mrs Craddock had been in the house all her working life.

When Beth and Dorian came in they got their food and sat down on either side of him.

"What would happen to Mrs Craddock?"

Both his brother and sister looked at him and said nothing. When he looked up to the top of the table he saw the members of the string orchestra walking up the small steps to the minstrel gallery above. There was no sign of his father. Kim hoped he was all right. That nothing had happened to him.

4

***

When their train drew into Corfe Castle station at a little after half past three, Genevieve was looking out of the window at the ruins of the old castle brooding up on its hill. The ground outside the train was covered with snow. Standing alone in the cold on the platform was old Mr P, the stationmaster, greeting his one train of the day. When Tinus opened the door to their carriage there was no one getting off apart from themselves. Hayley had been asleep until the train jolted to a halt. Tinus got off holding Barend by the hand. Genevieve passed out the pushchair and their luggage. When the heavy carriage door was pushed shut her whole family were out in the cold. The steam engine answered the guard's whistle from the back of the train, puffing sharply as it drew out of the station on the last leg of its journey to Swanage.

"Hello, Mr P. I'm Genevieve. You may remember me from when I visited my grandparents up at the Manor when I was a girl."

The old man, snug in his heavy greatcoat, looked at her blankly without the slightest recognition, making Genevieve smile. Here, she thought, was one man who had not seen her films.

"Can we get a taxi? My father is Merlin St Clair. This is my husband, Tinus Oosthuizen. His Uncle Harry is married to your daughter where we stayed last night. Tina wants me to call on you at the cottage to make sure you are all right. I was so sorry to hear about your wife."

The old man smiled at her before loading their luggage onto his trolley.

"We'd better go in the waiting room. Good fire inside. Always have a fire to greet the train."

With their luggage safely on the trolley, the old man's Dorset accent pleasant in their ears, the family followed him down the platform to the building that made up the rest of the station. When Mr P opened the door of the small room, warm air hit them in the face. With their back to them sitting in front of the fire was one lone passenger. When the pushchair and luggage were inside with the children, Genevieve unwrapped her scarf, took off her hat and shook out her hair. She looked at Mr P again, getting no reaction. Definitely he had not watched her films.

"Why you got an American accent if your dad is Lord St Clair?"

"We live in America. I'm an actress. A film actress. Did you ever see *Robin Hood and his Merry Men*? I played Maid Marian opposite Gregory L'Amour's Robin."

"Oh, was that you? Did see that one with my wife. Gone down to Swanage we had. You sit by the fire and I'll call taxi. Charlie don't wait for train. Most time no one wants taxi. Won't take him long to come round. Village not big it isn't."

"That won't be necessary," said the man at the fire, standing up and turning round. "Hello, Genevieve. Nice to see you. Tinus, I'll be blowed. Long time no see. I've seen all your films, Genevieve. Jolly good films. You don't have to think. All these your children? My word."

"Why haven't you been to see your mother, Frank? She's worried sick."

"Not about me. I thought Grandfather would be lonely over Christmas. It's the first Christmas without Granny. Don't worry about a taxi. I came down by car. I'd love to see the old manor house. What a surprise. I'll drop Grandfather at the cottage and drive you on to Purbeck Manor. Mrs Battle makes high tea roundabout six. Lots of time. Business is so good I bought myself a brand new car. But you'd know all about that, Tinus, you working for Oosthuizen Brigandshaw in New York. How are tricks in New York? When are you going to launch Ridgeback in the States? It's all in the advertising and newspaper publicity, don't you think? Come and get warm in front of the fire before we go. Lots of time. So that's work done for the day, Grandfather. What a business. Wish I could finish before four o'clock. Had to set up an office, Tinus.

Appearances are so important."

"Congratulations on your commission in the army," said Tinus.

"Oh, that. Seems ages ago. A two-year waste of time. My friend Brian Tobin has come over from Rhodesia to join my firm, we're growing so fast. Brian and I were at Bishops. Same as you, Tinus. I rather think we were all in the same house. Didn't play cricket and rugby for the school, I'm afraid."

"Cut the bullshit, Frank," said Genevieve, wearily. "Everyone knows you and I are first cousins. That our dads are brothers."

"How can you talk about it, Genevieve? No one has talked about it at home. So far as my mother is concerned, it's a state secret. I'll just drop you at the manor house. I won't come in. Don't want to embarrass anyone do we? It's Christmastime."

"I wrote a book about my birth and career with the help of Bruno Kannberg."

"Jolly brave of you. You think I should write a book? But I'm not famous. No one would bother to read a book about silly old me. Bastards are two a penny these days."

"What are you talking about, Frank?" asked his grandfather.

"My real father isn't Harry Brigandshaw. My father is Barnaby St Clair."

"I'll be buggered. So that's what my wife and Lady St Clair were talking about when they huddled in the kitchen."

Looking from one to the other, Genevieve was glad her own nonsense was out of the way. Her mother's drinking was a bigger problem than her parents not being married. In America, no one took any notice. Life was to be lived, not looked back on, hiding all the family skeletons in the closet. Warming herself on both sides of her body in front of the fire, wrapping the scarf around her neck with her hat back on her head, she collected up the children and looked expectantly at Frank.

"I'm ready."

"Put that guard in front of the old fire and we're off. Don't worry, Genevieve. My new car has a heater. It's American. We'll have to take the bottom road to the manor house to drop off my grandfather at the cottage. You see, I know my way around. Don't look so shocked."

"Not shocked, lad. Tina and Barnaby been friends since I remember. Played as kids with no problem."

"Yes, I'm sure. In a better world they would have married. But in snobby old England we can't have that. So here I am. A love child. How I like to think of it. How do you like that idea, Genevieve? We're not bastards. We're love children. I can think of a few other names but we won't go into that. Come on. Out we all go into the cold snow. You haven't introduced me to the children. My esteemed father's nephew and niece."

"Barend after my father," said Tinus. "This is Hayley."

"What a nice name. You'll have to sit on your mummy's lap in the car."

With a strange desire to wring her cousin's neck, Genevieve followed everyone out of the door. Behind the building when they turned the corner was a brand new car.

"Nice car, cousin."

"You have to look as if you're doing well in business."

"Are you, Frank?"

"Of course. I never did like coming second best. Barend, up on your father's lap. There was a Barend at school with me. Very Afrikaans name. Of course!... Barend Oosthuizen and the famous Boer general, Martinus Oosthuizen. Learned that at school."

"The general was my grandfather," said Tinus, trying not to look irritated with Frank. "In America my son is known as Barend Oosthuizen the second. Not my idea. When I explained the name's history to my friends they christened him Barend the second."

"What a lovely little story."

The daylight had almost gone when the car pulled up in the driveway opposite the front door of Purbeck Manor, Mr P having been dropped off into the care of Mrs Battle on the way. For some reason, Frank hooted his horn as if to call the servants down to help with the luggage. The small door, in the bigger Gothic door that arched in front of the house, opened to reveal Lord St Clair and his mother. On the other side of their mother, come to greet the taxi from the station, stood Barnaby St Clair.

"Well, I'll be blowed," said Frank. "Now off you go. Why don't you pretend I'm the taxi driver? Have a lovely Christmas, all of you. Tinus, can you manage to get the cases out of the car? Better I'm off pretty quickly. Before the old cat jumps out of the bag. My word, it is a nice old house. Always wanted to see it. A bit like Hastings Court if you ask my opinion. But one big old house looks much the same as another. What's the difference? Connie says a bed's a bed whenever you sleep in it. It's how you sleep that counts, not where."

Before anyone could get down the steps from the big house, Frank drove off giving Genevieve a wave, leaving the small family stranded on the gravel pathway with their luggage.

"He was in a hurry," said Lord St Clair, giving his daughter a proprietary kiss on the cheek. "Come inside. My word it's cold tonight. Now just look at these two. My mother has been waiting patiently to see her great-grandchildren. Barend. Hayley. I'm your grandfather... Why did that chap leave his light on inside the car and drive off the driveway so fast?"

"You don't want to know."

"Must be a new taxi. Never seen the driver or the car before. When your Uncle Barnaby heard you were coming down for Christmas he said you two could mix some business with pleasure. Brought with him all the figures for your trust. He's made you a fortune. I'll be asking you for money before long," joked her father. "The rates on the old house are now prohibitive. I'll manage. Had my money in Vickers shares during the First World War. Made all the machine guns. Then in consoles. Barnaby is telling me to get back into shares before the inflation gets worse and erodes the value of money. Barnaby says the Labour government are spending more than they earn in taxes. Don't understand it all."

At the entrance to the house, the light from inside showing up his face, stood her Uncle Barnaby as if rooted to the spot. Her grandmother also looked flustered... Frank, as usual, had made his presence felt; without stepping out of his car... Genevieve gave them both a sympathetic look. No one said a word. Only then did the children take back the limelight as everyone trooped into the house, Barend and Hayley running ahead to explore.

For Frank, going away down the drive, it just couldn't get any better. The expression on his father's face was classic, the car light on his own face, the porch light on his father's. It was better than anything he had looked for, sitting on the bench in Green Park hoping his father would look at him by pulling back the curtain of the window across the street.

Taking it slowly all the way back to the cottage, he was still humming a tune when he parked the car outside his grandfather's home. For a full minute, he sat back in the seat, savouring the moment, before switching off the lights and going inside. He was hungry, the sandwiches he had taken to the station earlier in the day, long eaten.

Not surprisingly to Frank, Mr P said nothing of Genevieve's revelation. What was the point? Whoever the father, the old man was still Frank's grandfather. On the table in the kitchen, next to the wood stove, stood one of his bottles of whisky. Next to the bottle stood three clean glasses. Mrs Battle was standing over the stove, attending to the cooking. The smells permeated the room. Mrs Battle, when she could afford it, liked her tipple.

"Waited for you before we poured a drink," said his grandfather. "You want to pour, Frank? Mrs Battle says food is ready when we want it. Toad in the hole. My favourite. I miss your grandma every moment of the day but I isn't starving thanks to Mrs Battle. Pour her a good one. She deserves it, slaving over a hot stove. Come and sit down. Nasty night. You coming with me tomorrow?"

"Not tomorrow, Grandfather. Got to drive back to London."

"Not staying Christmas?"

"What about Connie? She's on her own. You have Mrs Battle to keep you company. That food smells good. I'm starving. There, Mrs Battle, how does that one look? Right up to the pretty."

"Oh, Frank, you'll have me tiddly."

"That's all right. Food's done. Why don't all of us get tight my last night? Does that cat sleep all day in front of the fire?"

"In winter... Cheers, Frank. Good you came down to see me. Why you come?"

"You're my grandfather. I like talking to you. Won't stay away so long next time."

"Bring down your Connie."

"She'd like that."

"There you go. Cheers, Grandson. May your life just get better."

"Can't get much better than today. The Honourable Barnaby came to the door. Eyes popped out of his head. The double take was as good as any present I'll get for Christmas."

The small kitchen, with the wood-fired stove and low ceiling that doubled as the front-room, was as warm as toast, the perfect place on a cold winter's night to drink neat whisky. The cat, next to the open fire-door of the stove, sat alongside an old dog with white whiskers. The eyes of the cat were shut. The old dog lay on its side. The curtains were drawn. One light hanging from the ceiling was all the light in the room.

There was no radio playing, just the soft sound of their voices against the sound of the wind outside. All of them felt secure. All of them smiled as they talked and sipped their glasses of whisky. The fact for Frank that his grandfather had taken off the collar of his shirt made the place more homely. Old Mrs Battle had a shawl over her shoulders. It was a picture of domestic content Frank knew he would remember for the rest of his life. Sitting in a wooden chair at the kitchen table with his feet stretched out to the fire, all the animosity from the earlier part of the day seeped out of him.

Not long after eating their supper, the meal his grandfather called high tea, Mrs Battle, comfortable in one of the two armchairs, nodded off. One stiff whisky had knocked her out. Frank put some more wood in the fire on the left of the stove, adjacent to the oven. The wind was now howling outside, having no effect on the stone-built house. They had both drunk two whiskies up to the 'pretty' and were sipping a third. Frank was impressed with his grandfather's capacity. There was no change in his voice.

"Good you got business of your own, Frank. My grandad said a tub has to stand on its own bottom. All this relying on other people doesn't work. Not my business but remember one thing: Harry's been good to you. Wasn't his fault. Don't take out your feeling of insecurity on him. He's a good man, Harry Brigandshaw. He may be a rich man but he's had a tough life. Fought for his life through a war. First wife shot dead standing next to him, bullet meant for Harry. Why them Rhodesians came over in the first place to fight our war beats me. Harry owed us nothing."

"He wanted revenge. His brother was killed by the Germans."

"Was it revenge or a feeling of frustration? ... She's fast asleep. Looks after me does Mrs Battle. Old people need a bit of company in the evenings."

"He could have told me himself I wasn't his son."

"Some things better not said. Life isn't all straightforward, Frank. Don't always go the way we want it. She's loved Barnaby all her life. Since they was little kids playing right here in the kitchen, it too wet outside so Barnaby end up staying night. All right as little kids. No harm in that. Oil and water don't mix when they growed up, though. She was beneath him. In Africa they was all right. Not in England. I like the class system. We are who we are. Not trying to get above ourselves. You think I'd have preferred to live in that draughty old manor house, 'stead of this? I'm content. Had a good life. Your mother always wanted what she couldn't have. No good to no one, that wanting. The more your dad pulled away, the more she wanted him. Then she met Harry. Don't let her unhappiness with life upset your own. It's all water under the bridge. Legally, Harry's your father so there ain't no stigma. None of them legal problems of not getting what's right. He treated you as a son. Give him some respect, if you can't see it in your heart to give him love, or it'll eat you away... My wife loved that dog. And that cat. Don't know what I'd do without them."

Later, alone in the bedroom that had once been his mother's room which she had shared with three of her sisters, the one survivor having emigrated to Australia, Frank looked around him. There were two sets of bunk beds opposite each other with enough room to stand up in the middle. After wars and illness, all his grandparents' efforts had come down to Maggie in Australia, who never came home, Albert in Johannesburg, a mining magnate with no time for anything other than business, and Frank's mother. Had how and where they lived as children made any difference to their lives, he asked himself. So, there was his mother. From this, to Lady of the Manor, defying the St Clairs who had snubbed her upbringing.

Confused, a little drunk, Frank turned over in the bunk and faced the wall. Then he slept, dreamlessly, right through the night, woken by Mrs Battle in the morning bringing him a hot cup of tea.

WHILE FRANK WAS DRIVING BACK to London later that morning, his Uncle Robert was watching the snow drift down. He had wiped the inside of the window. The heat from the bedroom fire had clouded the glass. The excuse for going up to his room was to write. The real reason was different. Listening to his mother argue with Barnaby about Frank was none of his business. He was better out of the way, especially when his wife Freya got in the act. His brother Merlin had made himself scarce. Chuck, his youngest son, had gone up to the room set aside for his trains. Mrs Mason, the old cook, had wisely kept her mouth shut. Genevieve, who had started it all by bringing Frank to the front door, had thought better than to argue with her Uncle Barnaby.

"Go and see him, Barnaby," his mother had said, which had started the argument. "He's your son. You know it. He knows it. We all know it. You have to go to him."

"What do I say?"

"The truth. Give him a hug. Later, talk to him with Harry. All this silence is making the problem worse. Face a problem, Barnaby. I've told you that all your life. And where are you going, Robert, sneaking away?"

"To my room, Mother. To write."

"You haven't written a word in months," said Freya.

"I can try. I won't get anywhere standing here listening to you lot argue. This is a family Christmas. We're all together except Richard who's spending his Christmas God knows where."

"What's the matter with you these days, Robert?" said Freya. "Likely Richard is in Denver with my parents."

"Then why doesn't he tell us?"

"He's travelling around America."

"That's my point. God only knows where."

"If we'd gone back to America to live we'd all be together."

"What about Chuck's schooling?"

"They do have schools in America, or had you forgotten? Chuck's American. He was born in America."

"We'll talk about it later when we're alone."

"You always say that. We came back to England at the start of the war. For you to stand shoulder to shoulder with your family. That I understood. But the war's over. A long time ago. I want to go home. My friends are in America. My family. You never think of me. It was our arrangement, Robert. When the war was over we'd go home to America. Maybe you'll write in America. Back in the cottage next to the ski slopes. Have you thought of that? I love your family. You know that. But I love my own family too. It's just not fair."

"You can visit with us in New York," said Genevieve, appalled at the strength of the bitterness pouring out of Freya.

"I'm going up to my room. It's snowing outside. You know, I think we're going to have a white Christmas."

"Oh, Robert, I'm sorry. I'm just homesick."

"I know you are."

"Don't worry about us, Robert," said his mother. "Freya is your wife. She's far more important to you than any of us. You were happy in Denver. Maybe you should go back to America before Chuck goes off to boarding school. Maybe Richard will stay permanently in America. He's half American, despite being born in England."

"He's the heir to the barony!"

"I don't think old titles are going to matter much in England anymore. The Labour government wants to abolish the House of Lords. They want a classless system, where everyone is the same with the same opportunities. They don't want someone born with a silver spoon in their mouth having an advantage. The war changed everything. It's all for the better, this levelling of society."

"There will always be a king of England."

"Maybe. The king has no power. Parliament rules the country. As it should be. No, you go back to America if it suits Freya. I'm too old to worry about what happens anyway. You two must be happy. That's what is important. But right now the problem is Frank."

"Isn't it better to let this sort itself out?"

"Not this time. That boy was goading us yesterday. Don't you agree, Genevieve?"

"Leave me out of this, Grandma. I'm sorry I let him drive us from the station. Caught me unawares. If you ask me, Frank enjoyed himself. I could wring his neck. Oh my God! What is Hayley doing now? Children! You love them but they drive you crazy."

"Say that again," said Barnaby.

"Are you coming with me to see Mr P?" asked Lady St Clair.

"No, Mother."

"Are you coming Genevieve?"

"I'll drive you, Grandma, if someone lends me a car."

"It's snowing outside," said Robert before walking out of the room.

Up in his room, playing the family argument back in his mind, Robert had to smile. His mother had only found out about Genevieve when Genevieve was in her teens.

"Family," he said again, peering through the cleared patch in the window. "It never changes. When Freya gets back to America she'll be arguing in front of her mother instead of mine."

When Robert sat down, trying to concentrate on a blank piece of paper didn't help either. Maybe Freya was right. In America new ideas would flow again. She was always right. In all their years of marriage that much he had found out.

"Why won't you talk to me?" he called to his characters, half in despair.

As had been the case for months, nothing happened. Getting up, Robert again looked out of his piece of the window. The snow was thickening on the ground. In the silence, from the far side of the old manor house, Robert heard a car start up.

"Bad weather for driving," he said to himself before crossing to his bookshelf and taking down *Keeper of the Legend*, his first book on the St Clair family history that had been followed by *Holy Knight*. When they had been made into films in America, his niece, Genevieve, now driving off in the snow, had played the heroine in both of them. The weight of the book in his hand felt good, bringing his mind back to the long years he had spent with Freya in America.

An hour later, when Freya came up to the room carrying a tray with two cups and a pot of coffee, the car he had heard had not returned.

"All right," he said. "We'll go back to America."

"Do you mean that, darling?"

"Of course I do. If it makes you happy. What would I ever do without you? We'll make this our last Christmas in England."

"Oh, Robert. I'm so happy. Won't your mother really mind?"

"Of course she will. She'll miss Chuck more than us. Where is he?"

"Playing with his trains on his own. In America he'll have lots of friends. I love Purbeck Manor but it's so isolated. So far from everyone. A big house like this needs lots of people. We can visit with them. Flying is so easy these days. Otherwise, when Chuck grows up, what are we going to do with ourselves? Now he's off on his own, I don't expect Richard thinks of his mother from one day to the other. Far more exciting things to think about. I hate getting old. Everything starts to look so pointless."

"It will be better in America."

"I hope so."

Companionably they drank their coffee together round the bedroom fire. She was right. They were getting old. Most of his life was in the past.

"My foot's itching," he said.

"Then scratch it."

"Not the good one. The one I left behind in the trenches."

"It must all seem so far away. So long ago."

"Seems like yesterday. I still wake up from nightmares. So many young lives thrown away."

"Why don't you write a book about the First World War?"

"Too many people have done that already... Don't you think they've been gone a long time? I don't like the idea of Genevieve and my mother being stranded in the snow. If they don't come back in half an hour I'm going out to look for them."

"Maybe Barnaby will go."

"I don't think so. Barnaby has avoided the issue all his life."

"Is Frank an issue?"

"He is to Barnaby. Just look at it out there," he said, getting up and looking through the window. "Hasn't snowed like this in years. It reminds me of Colorado."

"There goes a car."

"Must be Tinus in Barnaby's car. Unless the leopard has changed his spots. Why go now? Why not earlier with Genevieve and his mother?"

"Who's looking after the kids?"

"You'd better go and see."

WHILE FREYA WAS GOING to check on Genevieve's children, Genevieve was looking out of the kitchen window of Mr P's cottage at the swirling snow outside. The visibility was less than ten yards. Lady St Clair was sitting opposite Mrs Battle in front of the hot stove, the tea kettle simmering on top. The two women were talking about their families like old friends. Like Mr P, Lady St Clair had known Mrs Battle, who had lived sixty years in Corfe Castle village, most of her life.

"We're not going out in this," said Genevieve. "Poor Tinus. The kids will be driving him nuts. We'd better phone and tell them we're all right. Tinus has a vivid imagination. He'll think we're stuck on the road."

"Do them good to worry," said Lady St Clair. "Barnaby didn't worry about Frank. He doesn't worry about anyone. Even with Frank gone back to London we've now made progress. Come and sit round the fire. This room is so cosy. The manor house is full of draughts. The real question is what are we all going to do about Frank? Harry and Barnaby have to confront him together."

"Not necessarily," said Mr P. "Let him find his own way. The teapot is empty, Mrs Battle."

When Tinus arrived twenty minutes later in Barnaby's car on his own, with his fog lights on, Genevieve opened the kitchen door to find him standing on the step. He was covered in snow from head to foot.

"Hello, everyone," said Tinus, looking over Genevieve's shoulder. "Where's Frank?"

"Driving back to London," said Lady St Clair. "He has a girlfriend named Connie."

"Have a nice cup of tea," said Mrs Battle," Just making a fresh pot."

"It's snowing a blizzard outside. Barnaby wouldn't come. Borrowed his car. Tea. Wouldn't mind something stronger than tea."

"Frank brought a case of whisky," said Mr P as Tinus shut the kitchen door. "Come and sit down."

"Don't you think we should phone them?" said Genevieve.

"Let Barnaby think he's created a serious problem," said Lady St Clair. "That I'm snowed in out on the road sitting in a freezing cold car. Come and sit down. Seeing my grandson paid for the whisky, why not let us all have a drink to celebrate our families becoming related?"

WHEN BARNABY finally phoned at Merlin's insistence, the snow had stopped falling. Tinus took the call.

"Is my car all right?" asked Barnaby.

"We're drinking your son's whisky."

"What does Frank have to say for himself?"

"Nothing. He's not here. How are my kids?"

"Freya is looking after them. So there isn't a problem?"

"I'm your niece's husband. Leave me out of this one. We'll be back shortly."

"Yes, I suppose you will."

Turning from the phone that stood in a wooden stand at the back of the kitchen, he found they were all looking at him.

"Worried about his car," said Tinus.

"Children," said Lady St Clair. "Charming. Absolutely charming... We'd better go back before the snow starts again... Doesn't so much as worry one bit about his mother caught out in the snow."

When they left, the cars going off one behind the other, Mr P stood in the doorway, smiling. Then he turned round into the kitchen, closing the door against the cold.

"Can you squeeze the pot for another cup of tea, Mrs Battle? Nothing like a cup of tea with a drop of good whisky. When are that lot going to see sense? I've a mind to phone Harry."

"If you want my opinion they're best left alone. So that was the famous film star, Genevieve? My. Seen all her films. They're lovely."

ON CHRISTMAS MORNING at Hastings Court, right after a late breakfast, Harry Brigandshaw led a convoy of cars to the Norman church at

Mickleham. Everyone in the house, including the servants, had gone to the eleven o'clock service. Ruthy Wakefield, having never been inside a Norman church, ran out of the car to have a look at what her mother had told her so much about. The snow lay three inches thick on the ground and the surrounding bushes. Inside, the church was full with folding chairs down the aisles.

Holly, with bright red berries, hung down the outside of the old wooden pews. Over the altar, the sun shone a shaft of light through the coloured windows depicting the saints. There was only just enough room for everyone inside the church, with the small children sitting on the knees of their parents. With a high vaulted ceiling above, the congregation was muffled up against the cold. All the women were wearing hats. The few paraffin heaters dotted round the church made little difference to the temperature. When they stood up and sang the hymns they could see each other's breath.

All these years at Hastings Court, Harry had seen the same vicar, a man his own age. Most of his houseguests sang badly but none of that mattered. Everyone was joyful in the full spirit of Christmas, the twelfth-century church smiling down on them all. The vicar's sermon rambled on but no one, apart from the children, seemed to mind.

After an hour, they all trooped out of the church feeling spiritually stronger, the children tugging at their parents' hands. Traditionally at Hastings Court the presents under the big Christmas tree were only opened when the family returned from morning service. After the previous day of snow, the sunny sky was perfect. Harry shook the hand of the vicar at the church door and walked to the cars to lead them back to Hastings Court. Back at the house when the cars disgorged their passengers, it was the moment the children had waited for ever since the wrapped presents had gone under the tree, placed there one by one by the houseguests, each with a recipient's name on the wrapping.

With drinks served and the fires burning in the hall at the side of the stairs where the big tree stood in its full glory, the tinsel twinkling from the coloured fairy lights, presents were taken from under the tree and handed out by the givers. The ritual of present-giving lasted an hour, the children shredding the Christmas paper all over the floor, the grown-ups sipping their drinks as they watched. When every present under the tree had been given out they all went into lunch, the adults to the Great Hall, the children to the nursery. The minstrel gallery was empty, the members of the orchestra having taken themselves home for Christmas.

With the big fires burning at both ends of the old, vaulted room, Harry watched his guests tuck into his food.

ON BOXING DAY, less worried about his father, Dorian Brigandshaw got out of bed early to look at the snow. Everything outside his bedroom window, as far as he could see, was white. His father was right. It must have snowed during the night. With a glance at his small desk where *African Drums* had been started, he got ready to go out into the snow.

"It's a tradition in our family, Dorian, as you know," his father had said during the Christmas lunch. "If there's snow on the ground on Boxing Day, the head of the family takes the children to Headley Heath with the toboggans. You can take the estate truck. There are six toboggans in the house somewhere."

"Aren't you coming, Dad? You look much better."

"I feel better. No, it's your job now. Janet and Betty's children will love you forever. Those children have too much energy. They need the steam taken off in the snow. You can put Patrick on your back if William doesn't fancy a run down the slope. Give you a chance to practise for your own children. What's the matter, Dorian? Something stuck in your throat? Have a gulp of the wine. What a Christmas. Just look at everyone enjoying themselves. It makes you feel so good inside to make people happy. Your mother's on top form. Put the toboggans in the back of the truck tomorrow and have some fun. It's snow tonight, mark my words. Get up early before it starts to melt. Do you remember that first time you went down the slope at Box Hill on my back? Your mother was petrified for you. Thought you fell off. Held on tight. That was my boy. Better to take them to Headley Heath tomorrow. Not such a steep slope. Don't want any accidents."

"Why did you take me down Box Hill?"

"I was younger in those days. When you are young you don't see what might go wrong. Head first into the moment, that sort of thing. Oh, the things we do when we're young without a care in the world. How's the book coming?"

"It's started. That's something."

"You'll be competing for readers with Robert St Clair before you know where you are. Robert and I were up at Oxford together. How I met Lucinda. Everything is so long ago. Yet it all seems like yesterday. What do you think of the turkey?"

"It's perfect, Dad."

"You can thank your mother and Mrs Craddock. The bone in your throat all right now? You choked on something?"

"My girlfriend is pregnant."

"My word! Are you going to marry her?"

"I may not be the father."

"Doesn't she know?"

"Not Nancy."

"Ah, Nancy. I've heard a lot about Nancy from Beth."

"What should I do, Dad?"

"The best you can. Have you talked to her?"

"Not yet. Beth sprang it on me. It was the night before I flew to Rhodesia to meet you and Mum. I was staying with Beth in the flat."

"You seduced her in Beth's flat?"

"No, Dad. She seduced me. Along with some others now it turns out. I barely know the girl other than as Beth's flatmate."

"Just don't tell your mother. With your mother, that kind of behaviour is a sore point."

"I'll sort it out."

"Just don't run away from the problem. If you run away from problems they have a habit of coming back to haunt you. Better to face a problem head on."

Thinking of his father's illness, which he hoped was not as serious as he at first feared, he had not replied.

Preparing to get himself ready to go out into the snow, Dorian had another thought. What about Frank? Had either of his parents faced that one head on? With another twist in his stomach at the thought of Nancy Longhurst's being pregnant, Dorian left his room to look for the rest of them.

When he got downstairs young Harry Wakefield was waiting for him in the drive with the low-slung red racing toboggan Dorian had loved so much as a boy. With him was his sister Bergit.

"Where's your mum and dad?"

"They're coming. Dad's got a hangover. He and Uncle William sat up drinking in your father's den."

"Was my father drinking?"

"He'd gone to bed. They were chewing the cud together, whatever that means. Where are the rest of the toboggans? There are lots of kids who want to come."

"The snow's perfect. Kim, there you are. Is Beth coming?"

"Of course I am. William's staying in bed. Betty's bringing her kids. What a lovely day for tobogganing."

PART 6

JANUARY 1950 – THE MATING DANCE

1

***

*P*aul Crookshank's farewell party for his brother was to introduce Jeremy to girls before Jeremy flew back to Rhodesia. It was also an excuse for Paul to phone Jeanne Pétain from his Hammersmith flat.

"Oh, Paul, what a lovely idea but I can't come. Did I tell you? I sold my first English painting for three hundred pounds. There's no holding me back now. How are you, Paul?"

"So you won't need work from us after all?"

"Not at all. It's so fabulous. Enough money to live for a year and paint, paint, paint. It's so exciting."

"I was hoping you could bring round some girls to introduce to Jeremy. There aren't many eligible girls in Rhodesia. The one blight on my brother's permanent sunshine. What are you doing on Saturday?"

"I'm not sure. Samuel has something planned."

"Is Samuel your new boyfriend?"

"More a benefactor. Samuel bought my painting. Says it's so, so good."

"I'll bet he did. Who is this Samuel?"

"Samuel Chalmers. He's in some kind of high finance. Very rich. Patron of the arts. He bought a sculpture from James which was how I met him."

"Who's James?"

"An artist friend of mine. Is this some kind of inquisition, Paul? James throws the most fabulous parties for the Chelsea artists which Samuel and his rich friends pay for. The life of a working artist in London is fabulous, Paul. I'm so happy. All the artists are so natural. Not trying to be anything but what they are."

"Why don't you bring this Samuel to my party on Saturday? Kenneth will be here. The major would be here but he's spending Christmas and new year with Harry Brigandshaw at Hastings Court."

"Is it an arty party?"

"I'll be playing the piano if they want to sing."

"Probably not, then. Samuel only likes real artists."

"You don't like my piano playing?"

"It's the singalong, Paul. Must go. I'm so full of inspiration, it's fabulous."

"Are you sleeping with Samuel?" said Paul, the jealousy in him spilling over before he could regain his self-control.

"What a nasty thing to suggest, Paul Crookshank. For that I definitely won't be coming to your party. Goodbye."

Paul put down the phone and looked at his brother sitting in the armchair of Paul's flat, the gas heater burning in the grate, miffed at his rudeness to Jeanne. Paul thought through their conversation before he spoke to Jeremy.

"Well, she isn't coming. When girls are adamant they're not sleeping with someone they usually are."

"Was she your girlfriend?"

"I was hoping she was going to be my wife. French girl I met in America." Paul went to the window where he stood silently before turning round. "Well, there's only one thing to do. Phone Frank Brigandshaw. He knows all the girls in town."

"You won't marry me off in three days, Paul," Jeremy said, giving his brother a look of sympathy. "Though it would be nice to have a wife living in the bush. At night it gets lonely. Next year I become an assistant and get my own house on the farm in Macheke."

"I thought you already were an assistant?"

"Learner assistant. Big difference. In two years of being an assistant they'll make me a section manager on a bonus. Percentage of the crop. Enough to start saving for a Crown Land farm. You have to prove you know how to grow tobacco before they let you have a piece of virgin bush. The Rhodesian Land Bank help you finance your growing costs.

Owning one's own land is the ultimate goal in life. Something you can see for all your hard work. Cutting a farm out of the virgin bush is hard work but hugely rewarding. Your job is fine, Paul. Pays you a good salary. But all you've got at the end of the day is money and a rented office. There's nothing tangible to see. There's going to be a federation of Central Africa. Sir Godfrey Huggins, the prime minister, is going to combine the two Rhodesias, North and South, with Nyasaland. He wants a dominion as prosperous as Canada. Talk of damming the Zambezi River to create the biggest manmade lake in the world with generators to light the whole federation. Cheap hydroelectricity, between North and Southern Rhodesia below the Victoria Falls. The potential of unlimited water is also huge for the country. You can't imagine what we're going to have for everyone in Rhodesia. There'll be money to educate the blacks and give everyone modern medicine. Why don't you come and have a look, Paul? Owning a few thousand acres is every man's dream. Start a dynasty. Landowners. The Crookshanks have never been landowners. Has a nice ring to it."

"I admire your enthusiasm, Jeremy. But a word of warning. Aren't you going to find yourselves the last British Colonials? Harry Brigandshaw says that now India has got its independence, the black nationalists in Africa are going to want the same for themselves."

"They can't prosper without our money and expertise. Our skills. They don't farm properly. Scratch the surface and plant a few pips of maize. Run a few cows and goats. Hand to mouth farming."

"Maybe. But it won't help them if they want back their own country. There's more to life for some people than material wealth. I've heard Harry talk about the Tutsi often. Make some money in Rhodesia and bring it back to England's my advice."

"You haven't seen the place."

"Not with my eyes. But I have with my mind. Harry will talk about Rhodesia at the drop of a hat. The empire's finished, Jeremy. The French are talking about a European common market. The future is here in Europe where we belong, not stuck out on a limb in the middle of Africa where you chaps are outnumbered fifty to one."

"I want to own my own farm. With my own land as far as I can see. Staying in England, I'll be a clerk just like you, sitting in an office all day."

"It's not that bad, Jeremy. Don't you like this flat? How about the grand piano? London has its attractions. There's so much going on.

Theatre. Concerts. Jazz clubs. And people. Out in Africa you are cut off from your own tribe."

"Which is why I want to meet a nice girl. I can't do much in three days. But we could write to each other. Get on the phone to Frank. Wasn't he one of the Brigandshaw boys who bloodied your nose that Christmas we spent with Mum and Dad at Hastings Court?"

"We were kids. He's running his own publicity business. Helped us get Ridgeback off the ground. I may not be growing tobacco but I'm selling it for you. For what it's worth, the cigarette companies make far more money than the growers without any risk. We can buy tobacco from anywhere in the world. You can have a drought on your farm but it won't stop us selling our cigarettes."

"Preferably with pounds and not dollars. Within the empire."

"True. But when the empire goes, as it will, we'll still be buying tobacco from someone and selling our cigarettes. The market for cigarettes is here, Jeremy, not in Rhodesia. It's here where the money comes from. I'll give him a ring. Frank was going to stay for Christmas with his grandfather in Dorset. Let's hope he's back. He's good at introducing people. For pleasure and for business."

"Good. Get him on the phone. I'm so grateful for everything you've done for me on this trip. Mum was so sad when we left the Isle of Wight. Made me feel guilty coming up to London a few days before my flight."

"Mum also said you need a wife. She wants grandchildren. She has her friends on the Isle of Wight. She's lonely without Dad but she has her memories living where we were born."

"Why doesn't she get married again?"

"Easier said than done. Having enough trouble with you finding a wife... Frank? How are you? Paul Crookshank. Lucky to find you back. I'm throwing a party for Jeremy and need plenty of nice young girls. The marrying type this time. House and home. Kids. The broody ones. Jeremy's looking for a wife to take back to Rhodesia. In a couple of years he'll have his own tobacco farm. Big estate. Lay it on a bit, Frank. I know I can rely on you. Saturday night at eight o'clock. Everything laid on... Yes, you can bring Connie. I'd like to meet her."

"Done," said Paul when he put down the phone. "I'm going to invite Beth and Nancy. Beth Brigandshaw. There's some bad blood between Frank and the family they don't want to talk about. Frank won't go and see his parents. Stayed away ever since he returned a couple of years ago from shooting crocodiles in Africa."

"What's the problem?"

"Harry isn't Frank's father. Keep it under your hat. Tonight we're going to the Benjie Appleton jazz club in Oxford Street."

"Any girls?"

"Plenty."

"Lead on, Macduff. But you're wrong about Rhodesia. We're all going to make it work."

"I hope so. For your sake, Jeremy. And everyone else. Living hand to mouth must have its problems."

"You were right to think drought, Paul. And no food. Watching your children die of starvation. Africa is fickle. Bounteous when the rains come, cruel when they don't. In Africa, you don't prepare for a rainy day. You prepare for a drought. Building farm dams and finding ways of irrigating the lands. Stopping all the rainwater running off down the river to the Zambezi. Fresh water going into the sea off Mozambique doesn't help the inland countries like Rhodesia. The black man needs our help as much as we need his on the farms."

"Do they like working for the white man?"

"I don't know. But isn't it better than starving?"

"They survived without us for centuries. Read an article in the *Telegraph* that said the whole of mankind came out of Africa. They've found skulls of early man to prove it. Darwin's evolution. Now look at us. You want to take their land and give them a job in return."

"Can't have it both ways. No one is on the land at the moment. Teeming with game and tsetse fly. Mosquitoes. One of the big jobs is shooting out the game to get rid of the tsetse fly before we can farm. Mosquitoes you control by sleeping under nets and with white man's medicine. We all need each other in this world."

"I just hope the black man sees it that way. Let's have some supper before we go to the club. Can't be long tonight. I have to work in the morning. Even if it is in a boring old office with little to show for it."

"I wasn't getting at you, Paul. Thought it would be so nice, two brothers with farms next to each other. The whites have clubs. Tennis courts and cricket fields. Very sociable."

"You're selling too hard, Jeremy."

"Can't fault a chap for trying. Mum could join us."

"Stop. And don't give our mother ideas."

"I did mention it. She'd find a husband in Rhodesia. Women are at a premium at any age. Better than Mum living on her own for the rest of her life."

"I'm happy in England. Had enough of hot climates in Burma. England's safe. England is where we've been down the centuries. Please don't give our mother ideas."

"Why not? She needs something to look forward to."

"Let's leave it there. How big a farm are you anticipating?"

"Six thousand acres."

"That's a lot of land."

"The climate's good. Where I want to farm in Mashonaland, it's on the highveld. Fires at night in winter. Bit hot in October, but once the rains come it isn't too bad. Not like the jungles of Burma."

"You'd make a great salesman. Why don't you join me at Brigandshaw's and market our Ridgeback cigarettes? Good salary. Flat in London just like this. And lots of girls."

"Now who's selling?... Do you want me to fry the sausages?"

"You want a drink? You know what they say. When you're bored with London you're bored with life."

"Pour the drinks, brother. You know what they say in Africa? Once you've drunk the waters of the Zambezi you always want to go back again."

"Not Frank. He's happy with all the girls. That was his point. Africa didn't have any girls. Even his schoolfriend Brian Tobin has come back to London. Couldn't find any girls on his father's cattle ranch outside Bulawayo. Takes all types to make a world."

"Maybe both of them will go back again. When they've found the right girls. You only need one girl. Then you make a family and live happily ever after. Is this Jeanne the right girl for you?"

"I thought so. She wants to paint. Live the life of an artist."

"And I want to farm. Live the life of a farmer without people on top of me. My own space. No one telling me what I can and can't do. Freedom. You can do that on your own farm. No one can dictate to you when you own your own property. The Afrikaner says you need a farm big enough so you can't see your neighbour's chimney smoke."

"The African bug really has bitten you."

"Say that again. Cheers, Paul. And thanks for everything. You've been the perfect brother all my life. Dad would be proud of you, were he alive. What a waste. Wars. What a waste."

"I miss him too," said Paul, going back to look out of the window.

2

———————

When Paul reached his office the next day he was ten minutes late for work. He and Jeremy had stayed up late, preferring to talk than stay the full evening at the jazz club in Oxford Street. There were no girls they could see for Paul to introduce to Jeremy, which made talking with his brother, due to fly out on Monday, more important. Neither were sure when they would see each other again, Jeremy saying next time he came home to England he was paying for his own ticket. Paul had played one set with the band, leaving his brother standing alone while he played the clarinet. Jeremy, it seemed to Paul, was no good at chatting up strange girls. Soon after, they had decided to go home, going to bed at three in the morning. Knowing he had to work the next day, Paul had done none of the drinking. It seemed drinking what they called 'sundowners' in Africa was another long-standing habit that went on well after the sun had found its rest. To Paul's surprise, he found Tinus Oosthuizen sitting in his office, the Oosthuizen in the name of the American firm.

"Sorry I'm late. You been here long? Wasn't expecting you. Something wrong? The cigarettes were selling well yesterday. When's your flight back to New York?"

"Tomorrow. Sorry to barge in unannounced. Genevieve and the kids are with her mother in her mum's Chelsea flat. We've been staying with her father in Dorset. Drove back with Barnaby St Clair last night. We had an 'in your face' visit from Frank Brigandshaw. He was at the station when we arrived from Hastings Court. Keeping his grandfather company during the day. Gave us a lift to Purbeck Manor, dropping his grandad at the cottage on the way. His father and grandmother came to the door with Merlin. Frank made his silent point and drove off without a word. But that's not why I'm here. There's something wrong with Harry. Seriously wrong. Said if anything happened to him he wants you to be the London manager with me flying in regularly from the States. His face is yellow. Have you noticed that? Told me to tell you he won't be coming up to the office for a while. He's not telling me everything. His kids had something on their minds so I think he's told them it's serious. Tried to ask Dorian but he shied away from talking about his father. Tina doesn't know, I don't think. Harry was talking about his succession, which isn't normal for a man of sixty-two unless something is going wrong. If Anthony hadn't been killed in the war, Harry said there wouldn't be a problem. I would run Oosthuizen Brigandshaw Inc in America, Anthony would run Brigandshaw's in England. Dorian, according to Harry, has his head in the clouds. Wants to be a writer. The man's a dreamer. Failed his motor mechanics course in the army, which is more than being all fingers and thumbs. Dorian just isn't interested in anything but writing his books."

"Has Katherine been asked to bring in some tea? Jeremy and I sat up late last night nattering. Flies back to Rhodesia on Monday. If you weren't flying back tomorrow you could come to my party. My friends would be impressed meeting Genevieve. Everyone I know has seen her films... What's wrong with Kim? He's looking for a career. There are worse things than a career in marketing."

"Wants to put a haversack on his back and tour the world, so he told me. India and the Far East. Wants to find his soul in a Buddhist temple. Stay in youth hostels and cheap hotels. Says he wants a year on his own after the air force to find his own rhythm, whatever that means. The trouble with having a stinking-rich father is they don't have to make their own money. Just as well they had to do their National Service or they'd have drifted off after leaving school. Or Oxford, for Dorian. Oxford was only to teach him how to write. He'll probably be a good one. Got a First at Oxford in English literature. No, the boys are no good to Harry. He's hoping you can fill their shoes. Is there something between you and Beth? Everyone seems to think she has a soft spot for you, Paul. She's a nice girl, my cousin. A bit wild when she's under the influence of Nancy.

You'd make Harry happy if he knew that Beth was going to be all right in the future."

"What's wrong with him?" Paul had sat behind his desk, still light-headed from lack of sleep, thankful he hadn't been drinking along with Jeremy.

"If you ask me it's his liver. Why his skin turned yellow. Bilharzia from his forced stay in the Congo from his days with the Tutsi. They can kill the bug, which they did, but not repair the damage already done. He was with the Tutsi for three years... Thank you, Katherine. Put the tea on Paul's desk. Mr Brigandshaw says he won't be coming in for a while."

"He's sick?"

"That's what we're talking about. Mr Brigandshaw won't come out in the open and say as much. His skin's turned yellow. I think he's been told by the doctors he's dying."

Rattling the cups, Katherine put the tea tray down on the desk and ran out of the office. She was crying.

"They were together at the Air Ministry during the war," said Paul softly, following Katherine's departure with his eyes. "Harry made her a job. The company we now have was as much for Katherine as it was to give Harry something to do."

"Is she in love with him?"

"I think so. Unrequited love. Why there were tears. Her husband was killed by the Japs when Singapore fell in 1941. They were alone during the war at the Air Ministry. Harry consoled her loss. Nothing more. Harry couldn't be unfaithful to anyone. Not the way he's made. He and my father were friends. Why he has taken such an interest in me and Jeremy after Father went down off Dunkirk in the *Seagull*. Poor Katherine. Her life will be so lonely without Harry."

Tinus Oosthuizen left Paul Crookshank half an hour later, having discussed the possibilities of launching Ridgeback cigarettes in America, something Tinus considered problematical with the competition from Camel cigarettes, a brand that had cornered the American market. As he made his way to the Tube station and a train to Chelsea, he was playing back in his mind his conversations at Hastings Court with Harry Brigandshaw. The thought of losing his uncle was as appalling to Tinus as it was to Katherine Marshbanks.

"There's something else I should tell you, Tinus. Something I only told Anthony just before he was killed. The fortunes of families have a habit of going up and down, generation to generation. After the First World War, your father and I went on a nine-month trip together to the Skeleton Coast in South West Africa after Lucinda was killed. By then the United Nations had given South Africa a mandate to run the previously German colony. Ostensibly we were prospecting for diamonds along the miles and miles of beaches, the Atlantic pounding into the shore. My Oxford degree was in geology after I left Bishops, your old alma mater. There was talk the diamond pipes were under the sea. That the sea might wash diamonds up onto the shore and bury them in the sand. Much later De Beers found diamonds in huge quantities along that coast. Onshore and offshore. Anyway, myself and your father came up with nothing and parted ways, your father to go seek his fortune someplace else. Your father was always looking for something he never seemed to find. I stayed on alone, living off the mussels and oysters along the shore, shooting small game in the desert. The Namib Desert came right to the shore. There was the odd tuft of dune grass to feed small buck, mostly springbok. My head was so full of my dead wife, the war and the killing I still couldn't think straight. When you've shot down twenty-three enemy aircraft you know you've killed a lot of people. Saving Klaus von Lieberman's life from his burning aircraft which I had shot down in aerial combat made me realise the people I had killed in the name of King and Country were just as likely to turn out friends. Those dead men still haunt me. Thank God Klaus came through both wars. But you know all about the horrors of war."

"I have the same nightmares, Uncle Harry."

"Anyway, not long after your father went on his way I found seven diamonds in the sand. Uncut diamonds don't look like what you see on a woman's engagement finger. One of the diamonds was the size of my fist. Well, I may be exaggerating a bit. Thirty years is a long time to remember every detail. We all make our past stories that much better when we tell them again. But it was big, Tinus. Big for a diamond. When I returned to Elephant Walk, my late father's old house on the farm was in need of renovation. Among other ideas my mother wanted a larger fireplace. I suppose I could have taken the diamonds to England, sold them and spent the proceeds on high living. Without going through the war I might have done just that. Instead, I built the big stone into the mantelpiece above the fire. As a centrepiece to the stonework that made the arch over the fire. I told everyone the stone was a piece of quartz I had picked up in my travels along the Skeleton Coast. Since then, the stone turned black from the smoke curling out of the fire when the wood smoked in the hearth before the flames took hold. It's so big, no one even suggested it might be a diamond. Everyone believed my story."

"Are you sure it's a diamond?"

"Quite certain. I didn't study geology for three years at Oxford for nothing. A diamond will cut a pane of glass like nothing else. You see, the farm was doing well enough to feed everybody. A big sum of money would have given us all ideas, instead of enjoying what we had. It was a tranquil period in Rhodesia after the First World War. The surrounding bush was teeming with game. We didn't know how much land was ours. No one worried in those days. It wasn't as though we had any neighbours. We cleared and planted enough land for what we wanted. Ourselves and the labour force. Ran the cattle in the bush, dipping against ticks four times a year, sending the beef cattle to the Salisbury market when we wanted some money to buy farm equipment and put something in the bank for all of us, black and white, should next year become a drought. Most of what we needed came off the farm. A life I've longed for ever since. Grandfather leaving me all his money in England didn't improve my life, Tinus. Changed it. But life in England with all the money in the world was no better than living on a farm in the Rhodesian bush. But now I'm going off the track of why I'm telling you this story. That diamond above the fireplace, safer in the open than in any vault, is our family's insurance against a disaster. Remember where it is, Tinus, but take it only in a dire emergency. Otherwise leave it just where it is. Safe, waiting to help the family if it's ever needed."

"What do you think it's worth, Uncle Harry?"

"In today's money? Difficult to say. Depends how big a gemstone the cutters can get from the rock. Much more than the worth of this estate. I'd guess they'd get out a stone the size of the Star of Africa. And that's in the crown jewels of the King and stored in the Tower of London. Whatever the value, Tinus, it will suffice in a family emergency. When your Barend is old enough, I task you to tell him the whereabouts of my diamond. Binding him to the same conditions, you understand. You've always had my trust. Trust in a person is as valuable as any diamond. Now, if you don't mind, I'm going up to bed. I get so damn tired these days. Look after them, Tinus. I'm giving you the trust a father gives to his elder son. The trust I was once able to give to Anthony."

"Are you all right?"

"Not really. Call it old age. Call it what you like. Nothing goes on forever. Certainly not one old man's life."

By the time Tinus reached the comparative warmth of the Tube station waiting for a train, looking at the others blue in the face from the east wind that had cut into all of them above the ground, the idea of living in the warmth of Africa was at its most appealing. Spending days fighting snow, slush and an east wind with a mind to cut him in half was not so pleasant. During the days they had spent at Purbeck Manor he had always been cold. At least in New York the Americans had found ways to keep themselves warm in winter.

Later, when Tinus rang the doorbell of his mother-in-law's flat, rent paid courtesy of Lord St Clair, Genevieve's father, he was looking forward to going home to America. Esther, as was her habit, had been drinking gin since before breakfast. Luckily, the children thought their grandmother's behaviour normal, having seen her in no other state. There were more ways than one of spending a life, he told himself, as Genevieve opened the door. A nice flat, good food and a drinking companion in Joan took one hell of a lot of beating.

"How's it going?"

"She's happy so she stays with Joan. How was Paul?"

"I don't think he's interested in Beth. There's the French girl. An artist. Why do so many people want what they can't have? How is your mother?"

"I think they've gone to the pub. Mother says by never marrying my father she has all the benefits without any of the work. That old men want their wives to run after them. She has a point. Nice flat paid for. Money to eat and drink. What more do you want? She says the children were exhausting her. No one can say I haven't done my filial duty."

Tinus gave his wife a smile without saying a word, though the expression 'great minds think alike' was on his lips.

"Is she going to be drunk when she comes home? I'm thinking of the children."

"She's never actually drunk. Puts enough down her throat to keep her happy. Never has a hangover. Never sober enough. Not a care in the world, my mother. Asked her if she wanted some money and she laughed at me. Says what more can she want? A pension for life for a bit of fun when she was young and a daughter no one ever believes is hers when she tells them. Friends when she wants them. No one to answer to. No one to argue with. What she says. Says her life is better than anyone else she knows. Including Joan. Joan is always short of money. When they drink together, Mum pays the bill. I'm looking forward to going home. Without the stability of our apartment in New York, the kids are exhausting, to say nothing of Mother."

"Did you phone Frank or your Uncle Barnaby?"

"No. I'm learning to mind my own business."

"Why are the kids so quiet?"

"Oh, my God. What are they into now? On the plane I'm giving them both a sedative."

"Barend! What are you up to?" called Tinus.

"Nothing, Dad. It's Hayley. She's covered in Grandma's make-up. She looks funny. Her face is all red."

THE FOLLOWING DAY, after Tinus had restored some order to his family, flying with them back to America, his cousin Dorian was facing his own problems. After Christmas and New Year at Hastings Court, Beth had driven him back in the Austin Seven to stay the night with her in South Kensington. He was due to report to the War Office the next day. Beth had taken two days' leave to drive him up on the third. Having no money, his father having decided to give neither of the boys an allowance, telling them to work for their money like everyone else, the only place he could stay was with Beth.

"Hello, Dorian," said Nancy Longhurst as they walked in the front door. "Long time no see. Did that old car of yours actually get here, Beth? One of these days you'll be standing on the side of the road hitching a lift. Went to a party last night. New Year and again last night."

"You weren't drinking?" said Dorian.

"Of course I was."

"But you're pregnant."

"Oh, Beth. You shouldn't have told Dorian."

"Are you still pregnant?" asked Beth.

"So far so good. Do you want a drink?"

"If you are pregnant... Could I be the father?"

"Dorian, it was fun. We weren't trying to get married."

"But could I be?"

"Possibly. Obviously, what I told Beth she's told you. Relax, Dorian. There are people in London who look after these things. I did try drinking gin and sitting in a hot bath while you were away, Beth. Didn't help I'm afraid."

"You can't have an abortion," said Dorian. "I could never live with myself."

"It's my body, not yours, old chum. You were quite happy to use it when you had the chance. Far more likely to be David Haines."

"Are you going to marry him?" asked Dorian.

"Of course not. He's married with three children. Why it's likely him. Some men are more fertile than others. It's not a big deal. In a week's time, if nothing happens, a friend's given me an address in Soho. What brings you to London, Dorian? Thought you were in the army."

"I am. Posted me to London and the War Office."

"That's convenient. You can hold my hand through the abortion. Take me there and back. You owe me that much, Dorian. Now, enough of my problem. Let's have some fun."

Feeling guilty at feeling relieved, Dorian gave Nancy a smile.

"I'll do anything to help," he said lamely.

"It's life, Dorian. Now let's have a drink. Beth, were there any nice men for you at Hastings Court? Did Paul Crookshank go down?"

"Spent the Christmas with his mother. The brother came over from Rhodesia."

"Any other nice boys?"

"Not one."

"But you both had a good time?"

"Not really. My Dad told us he's dying."

"Oh, Beth. I'm so sorry. Come here and give me a hug. What's the matter with him?"

"Some disease he picked up in Africa. Mother doesn't know. Everyone else had a perfectly wonderful Christmas. We all went tobogganing in the snow. All except Father. My first ride as a child was piggybacking down Box Hill hanging onto Dad."

"Are you sure the baby isn't mine?" asked Dorian.

"We'll never know. One way or the other. Someone told me the scientists are working on a way to prove who your parents are. Years in the future. Right now, only nature knows."

"Or God."

"Dorian, I said there's nothing I can do about it. I'm a slut when it comes to men. Could have been any one of a dozen. This is my fault, not yours. I'm not going to ruin anyone else's life but my own. I'm pregnant with no idea which one of a dozen is the poor bastard's dad."

"We've got a week to think about it," said Dorian, taking her hand. "If we don't know for certain, does it matter who fathered the child?"

"Are you proposing to me, Dorian?"

"I don't know what I'm doing. I just want to do the right thing. By me, you, and whoever is inside of you."

"Have you got any money?"

"Four shillings a day as a private. But I'm writing a book. *African Drums*. The fictionalised story of my grandfather, a big game hunter in Rhodesia. He was killed by the Great Elephant. Ironic, don't you think?"

"You're a dreamer, Dorian," said Nancy, pulling away from his hand.

"I don't want your child on my conscience for the rest of my life."

"You're a very nice man," she said, smiling at him softly.

"Then pour me a drink. What with this and Father, I'm so uptight my whole body is shaking inside."

WHEN THE PHONE rang in the flat half an hour later it was Paul Crookshank. Nancy answered it.

"I've called a couple of times but no one was in, Nancy. Is Beth there?"

"She's just got back from Hastings Court. Dorian's with her."

"I'm throwing a party for my brother Jeremy before he flies back to Rhodesia this coming Saturday. Can you all come?"

"Dorian will be back in the army, unless he can get out on a Saturday night. We'd love to come. Do we bring anything?"

"Just yourselves. My flat. Beth knows the address."

Dorian, a glass of beer in his hand, looked around his sister's flat. After the first confrontation with Nancy, he had calmed down.

"Paul Crookshank," said Nancy as Dorian watched her put down the phone. "Saturday night party. You're invited, Dorian, if the army can let you out."

"More like a civilian job at the War Ministry. I'm sure I can come. We can all go together. Your lives are one long party."

"We try to have fun. You're only young once."

There were tears at the corners of Nancy's eyes. Dorian, wanting to give her a hug, sipped at his beer.

3

───────────

*F*rank Brigandshaw had phoned every girl in his book. Looking after clients was the cornerstone of his business. Eating supper in Connie's flat while Nancy Longhurst was facing her demons, Frank asked Connie to the party. Every other night they spent together going over Frank's day at work. Most times she was more helpful than Zachariah Cohen. She had an intuitive insight into what the public wanted. Frank had found advertising was all about knowing the mind of the average joe. Frank had gone on eating, looking at his plate. When he looked up at Connie in silence she was gazing at him with her lovely soft eyes that made him feel good all over. The look was more comforting than sexual. Most nights they did not make love, cuddling up in Connie's big double bed until they fell asleep, all the day's tension gone for Frank with the touch of his woman.

"Don't be silly, Frank. I can't come to your party."

"Why ever not? You'll like Paul. You like Brian Tobin. My sister Beth and brother Dorian are going to be there. Give you a chance to get to know Beth. Better than that time you two met in Kensington High Street."

"They're all half my age."

"So am I, give or take a couple of years."

"We're different. You see me differently. They'll think you've brought your mother and laugh at you. I'm only thinking of you, Frank. Here, alone, in a restaurant on our own, we're fine. It's none of anyone else's business what relationship we have with each other."

"I think Beth and Dorian would know you aren't my mother. I hate it when you say things like that. I love you, Connie. Who the hell cares what other people think?"

"I do. For your sake. We still have to live in the world of other people. Go to your party and tell me all about it when you get home. Don't let's have an argument. Connie knows what's best for both of us."

"I'm so comfortable with you."

"I know you are. We shouldn't be late tonight. You have an early meeting with a new client. A good night's sleep leaves the brain sharp in the morning. Have you on top of your job."

"I am tired. Talking with my mind racing all day takes more out of me than a day's hunting in the Zambezi Valley. Mental tiredness. Is that possible? I sleep so well next to you."

"We can play a little music on the gramophone before we go to bed."

"So you won't come with me to Paul's party?"

"No, Frank. I wouldn't know what to say to your brother and sister."

"I told Paul I'd bring you."

"That's fine. He doesn't know how old I am."

"Will you come down to Dorset in the summer and meet my grandfather?"

"Of course not. What a silly question."

"He knows about us. All about you. He started life as a railway porter. Now he's stationmaster of a one-horse village. He's the best of the lot in my family. He wouldn't care how old you are once he sees you make me happy. What are we going to do, Connie?"

"Carry on just as we are. What's wrong with it?"

"Nothing. I just want more."

"That's a common failure in people. Be thankful for what you've got."

Later, when they were cuddling in bed, Frank holding her breasts in both hands, kneading them gently as he began to fall asleep, he spoke into her ear.

"Connie, what's the lump in your breast?"

"What lump?"

"A lump that wasn't there before I went in the army. It's getting bigger."

"Nonsense, go to sleep."

"Goodnight, Connie. Please won't you come to the party?"

"No, I'm asleep."

"I want to make love."

"Go to sleep, Frank."

Smiling, Frank drifted off into the world of dreams where nothing ever quite made sense.

WHILE CONNIE WHITAKER was lying awake next to the sleeping Frank worrying about the lump in her right breast, a lump she had been aware of for months, Olivia Johnston and Tessa Handson were talking about the party. Frank had told them the reason for the party. Olivia, out of curiosity, had looked up Southern Rhodesia in the world atlas she had been given at school. They were on their own in the small Chelsea flat where once, before he got to know Zachariah Cohen's family business, Frank had slept on the couch that at night could be pulled out to make a bed. Tessa, with two of her paintings hanging in the offices of Cohen Wells, the sales a result of Frank Brigandshaw's suggestion, was always happy to hear from him. From the breakthrough of having her pictures displayed in a top London advertising agency, she had sold three more of her pictures. As Frank had said on the phone when he invited them to the party for Jeremy Crookshank, 'it paid to advertise'.

"What do you think of the idea of painting wild animals?" asked Olivia.

"You haven't even met the man yet."

"He's looking for a wife. That's good enough for me. Being a painter is all very well if you sell. You've got a patron in Cohen Wells. Poor Livy has nothing."

"It doesn't matter who pays the rent or buys the food. That was our arrangement when we took the flat together."

"You'll want something bigger than this when you're famous. You're going to be rolling in it, Tessa. Frank may be a womaniser but he never forgot a friend."

"Not anymore, Livy. That Connie has got her claws into him and it's nothing to do with money. What does a good-looking man now making money see in a woman old enough to be his mother?"

"Part of his problem is not knowing his rightful parents, I should think. He won't admit it but he misses his mother. Do they have wildlife painters in Africa? Tomorrow I'm going to paint the cat."

"Your imagination runs ahead of you, darling."

"I've got to do something. Our kind of life is fine when we're young. In the real world you need money."

"You'll sell a painting. They are good. Have faith in yourself."

"Do cat faces look like tigers?"

"They have leopards in Africa. Tigers in India."

"How do you know that?"

"Read it somewhere."

"If I put our cat in a jungle, I'll get the idea. I'll borrow the jungle from our Rousseau print."

"He never saw a real jungle in his life."

"One jungle's the same as another. Should I sleep with him on Saturday? Give him something to think about on his tobacco plantation when he's all on his own at night. Why are there no young girls in Rhodesia?"

"No one wants to go there I should think. Livy, stuck on some farm in the middle of nowhere surrounded by black people is my worst nightmare."

"Not if Jeremy is nice. We can come home for holidays. Have lots of children. They have elephants in Africa. That much I do know from school. I can paint lots of elephants sitting in the sun. Anyway, what's wrong with black people?"

"Nothing. They're just wild like an elephant that chases you up a tree and shakes it."

"Honestly! Nevertheless, I want to be shaken by Jeremy. His brother's not bad to look at. Chances are Jeremy will be good looking. Come here, Pussy. I'm going to paint you. Why haven't we given the cat a name?"

"She answers to Pussy."

"Do you want some tea? I'll go and make some. I like the sound of this Jeremy. When you go to bed on Saturday night I'll seduce him right here on the couch."

AT HALF PAST seven on the following morning, after an undisturbed night's sleep, Frank Brigandshaw drove his new car out of Connie's garage on his way to work. The street lights were still on, giving an eerie look to the yellow-tinged smog that hung over central London. Frank had taken Connie her tea in bed, eaten a bowl of cornflakes and gone before the rush hour built up. Concentrating on the business day ahead, all other thoughts were pushed to one side.

Brian Tobin, used to getting up at the crack of dawn on the ranch in Rhodesia, had beaten him to the office of Frank Brigandshaw and Partners, Public Relations Consultants, the name boldly embossed on the door. Though he was not yet a fully-fledged member of the business, Brian wishing to know first what he was talking about, their future partnership was understood. From their days as bullies at Bishops, making money out of the fear of new boys, they had come a long way together to the Fleet Street office on the third floor of a building mostly housing members of the Fourth Estate, as William Smythe liked to think of the news fraternity. They were both pleased to see each other. Milly Worthington, the receptionist with large breasts, had not yet arrived. Officially the office opened at nine-fifteen, closing at half-past five.

"I've taken two phone calls already. Ridgeback cigarettes have got the firm's name out there and no mistake. Your idea of putting our name and that of Cohen Wells at the bottom corner of the newspaper advertising worked."

"I have a nine o'clock."

"What do you want me to do today?"

"Answer the phone for the moment. I want you to be in on the nine o'clock meeting. An industrial chemist. Chap says he's invented a chemical that washes clothes clean without all the scrubbing. Says with his 'blue' the housewives won't need washboards. No more chapped hands. Sounds too good to be true. Said he's going to prove it in the kitchen where Milly makes the tea. No one has shown the slightest interest in his product so far. According to Mr Ripley, firms are only interested in manufacturing and distributing a product once it's known, once it has a guaranteed market. An inventor they've never heard of gets shown the door. I want you to be a witness to this morning's little washing ceremony."

"What's he like?"

"No idea. Only spoke on the phone. The chap's come down all the way from Liverpool to make his demonstration."

"How did he get your name?"

"From the Ridgeback ads. Read the small print at the bottom. That piece in the *Mail* by Horatio Wakefield has been widely read. Horatio called me a whizzkid at getting out new products."

"How'd you get him to write that?"

"He owes Harry Brigandshaw. Harry, through his buddy Klaus Lieberman, got Horatio out of the clutches of the Nazis before the war.

Was informed the illustrious First World War pilot would consider a little build-up for Frank a favour. You have to leverage everything in this world. Did you sleep all right?"

"Like a log."

"How's my flat?"

"How's Connie?"

"She makes me feel so comfortable. She can think. I'm a bit tired of giggling girls."

"That does surprise."

"Too much of a good thing, I suppose. Have you met Jeremy Crookshank?"

"Not yet. Dad knows the chap Jeremy works for in Macheke. We're Matabeleland. Jeremy's Mashonaland. London to Edinburgh, that kind of distance."

"Thought you whites all knew each other in Rhodesia? Bloody smog again this morning. Battersea Power Station. Without a wind, the muck spewing out of the chimneys sticks around in the fog. You can smell the sulphur or whatever it is. Don't you miss the old ranch?"

"Not with all these girls coming to Jeremy's party on Saturday."

"I suppose not. I'm going to get all this paperwork out of the way before Ripley arrives."

"I'll let you get on with it."

"And don't forget, Milly's off limits. My strictest rule of business. No buggering around in the office, or out of the office, with the staff."

"What a shame."

"Thought so myself. Do you know, a girl like that has a school certificate and has been to Secretarial College. Mostly when they look like Milly, they just wait to get married."

"She'll break some man's heart."

"More likely break your balls watching her."

"What a body."

At nine o'clock sharp, a man in his twenties walked into the office of Frank Brigandshaw and Partners, surprising Frank by his youth. Over the phone, Ralph Ripley with his Liverpudlian accent, had sounded much older.

"I thought industrial chemists were much older. Good morning. I'm

Frank Brigandshaw. Won't you come into my office? Where are you staying?"

"The cheapest room I could find. In Soho."

"The smalls in the *Evening Standard*?"

"How did you know?"

"Been there myself. When I came back from Africa, Brian and I were skint. Trying to make our money go as far as possible. Brian Tobin will be joining us for the demonstration as a witness to the great event. My receptionist hasn't arrived yet. You'll like Milly."

"Good of you to see me."

"Not at all. A man who telephones all the way from Liverpool deserves a hearing. How did you get into chemistry?"

"Liverpool College. Scholarship. Chemistry is something of an obsession. That's my trouble. I know nothing else. The ways of the commercial world quite frankly frighten me."

"Does it work?"

"I wouldn't have come all this way if it didn't, Mr Brigandshaw."

"Call me Frank. Did you do your National Service?"

"Like the rest of us. Complete waste of time. There I was with formulas screaming through my head cooking food in the kitchens. I was a cook. The army had no idea what to do with a chemist."

"At least you were cooking up something," said Frank, trying to break the ice: the man was palpably nervous, as if too much in his life depended on the outcome of the meeting.

"You're pretty young yourself. Is that your name on the door or your father's?"

"It's mine. I don't speak to my father. I haven't spoken to him since war broke out when Mother evacuated us kids to South Africa."

"That's rather sad. None of my business, of course. Don't know what I'd do without my dad. He read an article in the *Daily Mail* when he was here in London on business. Found your name in an advertisement for some cigarette. Tied the two together and told me to phone you. Dad lent me the train fare."

"I have two fathers, one legal and one natural. But I won't bore you with the details. We all have to live with our problems. I just hope that if your Ripley Blue works, as I'm going to call it, we can solve yours and make you some money. First we have to straighten out our future business relationship and sign a piece of paper which Brian will witness.

Take no notice of his funny accent. He's Rhodesian. We went to the same school in Cape Town where we met."

"Where's the piece of paper for me to sign?"

"Right here."

"Fine... Does that do it?"

"You've signed without reading what is says."

"What does it say, Frank?"

"That Frank Brigandshaw and Partners get half of everything you make out of Ripley Blue. The legal wording talks about your royalty and commission."

"Half of something is better than all of nothing. I've looked into your eyes, Mr Brigandshaw. I think I can trust you. If we can't trust our business partners there's no point in getting into business with them in the first place. I've got no money to put up front if that's what you want. Let's get that straight to start with."

"You put in the product, I put in the marketing. Why we each get half."

"Sounds fine to me."

"Except for one thing, Ralph. You've still to prove to me and Brian that Ripley Blue works. That a dirty shirt comes out of the wash clean without the use of a washboard or pummelling the dirty cloth with my hands."

"Are you going to do the washing?"

"Of course. The dirty clothes we are going to wash are mine. Over the years I've mostly had to wash my own clothes so I know what I'm doing. In Rhodesia, I washed my clothes in the Zambezi River with one eye looking out for the crocodiles. You can ask Brian. We were hunting crocodiles for their skins in the Zambezi Valley after we left school. To avoid getting in the army at the tail end of the war. When I finally came back to England the Military Police nabbed me. Funny how life goes in such strange ways. In the army I met Zachariah Cohen while doing my square-bashing."

"Cohen Wells on the Ridgeback advertisement!"

"You've got it. Without those two MPs you and I wouldn't be talking to each other. Now, give me this detergent you've come so far to prove. I've got the dirty clothes in the office kitchen... Good morning, Milly. This is Mr Ripley. We're going into the kitchen. Brian, this is Ralph Ripley. We're going to do the washing. Milly, I want you to see what we're doing. If the Ripley Blue doesn't work, there's no point in wasting any more time."

"It works, Frank," said Ralph Ripley wearily.

"Good. I like a man who believes in himself."

"How are you going to get it to market?"

"That's my problem. Let the magic wash begin."

"Have you got hot water?"

"In the kitchen sink tap."

FRANK, having worked on the principle a man would not travel all the way from Liverpool with a bum product, had made his next appointment with William Smythe for eleven o'clock. William's office, that he ran with his wife Betty, was just round the corner, all of them in among the offices and printing presses of the Fourth Estate. The square blue cube placed in hot water where it dissolved had worked wonders on Frank's dirty clothes. In his flat, Frank had smeared food remnants down the shirt along with a slosh of red wine. The shirt was filthy when he put it in the water. It was left in the hot water for three minutes, then Ralph Ripley rinsed it out three times. They were all highly impressed. Even the slosh of red wine had become a pale pink remnant. The food stains had vanished. The strong smell of body odour had gone.

"What's it cost for a sink like this of Ripley Blue hot water?"

"A fraction of a penny the way I make it. Mass production, less than half."

"Thank you, Ralph. Leave it to me. Every housewife in the country will want to use your product. The real snag with anything like this is in the marketing. Telling every housewife in the country what to buy without spending more in advertising than the product makes. You do, I presume, have a registered patent on the formula?"

"Signed and sealed."

"You can go back to Liverpool."

"How long will it take?"

Frank, smiling as he walked down Fleet Street in the direction of William Smythe's office, was mentally licking his lips.

"What can I do for you this time, Frank? What's up? Why didn't you spend Christmas at your folks'?"

"If I told you I could clean the Monday wash for every woman in England without scrubbing, what would you say?"

"Ask Betty. That's her department. The maid does the washing."

"What do you do with Ruthy and Patrick while both of you are at work?"

"You haven't answered my question."

"And I won't."

"The kids are in crèche when not at school. The maid picks them up. Why do you ask?"

"Must be expensive. More expensive later on when they go to boarding school."

"Don't tell me."

"I have an idea that will make you money. At the moment you have your *International Reporters* programme on the BBC Overseas Service. I want you to convince the BBC to give you a half-hour programme once a week dedicated to saving the housewife work in the house. To be called *Housewives' Corner*. The first labour-saving product will be Ripley Blue. My job will be to hunt down others. For placing a product in your *Housewives' Corner* you will be paid a fee by me in addition to your fee from the BBC."

"They'd never allow that."

"Then don't tell them. I won't if you won't. You'll get a lot more listeners than you now get for your political programme. I rather thought of a slot just before or after *Mrs Dale's Diary*. When Patrick turns thirteen you'll have the money to send him to Eton or Harrow, Oxford or Cambridge afterwards."

"Does Ripley Blue work?"

"One part of your job as host of *Housewives' Corner* will be to test the products before they go on the air. There are many ways of paying your fee. Call it a retainer. You're a freelance journalist. Who's to argue if they did find out? Better not, of course. I'm more worried about the housewife thinking you're selling her a product rather than giving her a tip. I have in my briefcase a dirty shirt and a cube of Ripley Blue. The detergent dissolves in hot water. Let me show you and Betty how it works."

"*Housewives' Corner*... Has a nice ring to it. How much am I going to be paid?"

"One hundred pounds an episode."

"I'm listening carefully, Frank," said William, giving Frank a lascivious smile.

"After the demo, why don't we have lunch in the Duck and Drake? On me, of course."

"If I do convince the BBC, will you go down with me to Hastings Court?"

"When my mother tells me the truth about my birth to my face."

"What about?"

"Come off it, William. Everyone connected to the family knows. The Honourable Barnaby St Clair is my biological father, but none of them will come out and admit the truth. How would you like to find out you're not your father's son? You have to know who you are. That's as important to me as breathing air. I want to be certain who I am. None of all this avoiding the issue. My parents, whichever they are, have to look me in the eye and tell me what happened. I can't be Harry Brigandshaw's son. He was in Rhodesia on an extended trip ten months before I was born. I can do the maths on my fingers. He came back to England eight months before I was born. I don't even look like my brothers or Harry Brigandshaw. Have you seen Barnaby St Clair? My Grandmother St Clair did a triple take when she first saw me in the woods around Purbeck Manor. Called me Barnaby without thinking when she came upon me by surprise. Before she recovered and remembered her son Barnaby was a young man. I was twelve years old. I can still remember the name of her dog. 'I'm sorry,' she said. Then she called 'Pinta, Pinta', and went off with the dog."

"I never looked at it from your perspective."

"Let's go and wash another one of my dirty shirts. No wonder men let their wives do the washing. Horrible job. Even with the magic cube dropped in the hot water... Hello, Betty. Would you like to see me do the washing?"

"Good morning, Frank. What are you talking about?"

"Money, darling," said William, as they moved through the reception office on their way to the small kitchen. "If what Frank says works, Patrick will be going to Eton."

"What about Ruthy?"

"Cheltenham Ladies' College. Then we are going to lunch."

Later, after the second wash of Frank's day, with a smile on both their faces, Frank and William left for the pub, a watering hole Frank knew to be frequented by journalists, the conduit for him to make his money: the more journalists he knew, the more free placement of his products' names in their articles.

It was one o'clock when they walked through the doors into the noise and the warmth. Everyone seemed to know William Smythe. Frank smiled at them along with William. It was like rubbing shoulders with money, as the old saying goes, Frank said to himself, as some of it hopefully rubs off. Being with William made the other journalists relax when they talked to Frank. In the Duck and Drake, Frank felt part of the fraternity, hobnobbing with the best of them.

"Who's the chap holding court at the other end of the bar? He's vaguely familiar?"

"Bruno Kannberg, the Hollywood scriptwriter. With him is Arthur Bumley, Bruno's editor at the *Daily Mirror* when Bruno worked for the paper. Bruno must be over here on a trip. What are you having?"

"Can they put it all on one bill?"

"I'm sure they can."

"Make mine a mild and bitter. He's got all their attention."

"Every journalist fancies himself as a film scriptwriter or a novelist. Very few do the transition. Hemingway was a journalist before he wrote books. Most novelists and playwrights don't do journalism. A journalist writes what he sees in front of him. A fiction writer puts down on paper what he sees in his head. Very different. I can only see what's in front of my nose. Don't have the imagination to do what Bruno does... He's seen me. Coming over. Wrote Genevieve's memoirs for her. He has a social climbing wife. I wonder what he's doing over here? Lives in Los Angeles last time I heard."

"My old friend William Smythe to be sure. I think the last time I saw you was in Singapore after the Japs surrendered and let me and your cousin Joe out of Changi jail."

"That was a good book of fiction you wrote around the experience. How are you, Bruno? This is Frank Brigandshaw, one of Harry's sons. Have you heard from Joe? Terrible letter writer."

"I have as a matter of fact. The other day. Cherry Blossom keeps me up with Joe's family in Singapore. She looked after me so well when I got out of that damn prisoner of war camp. I stayed with them, you remember. Making himself a fortune out of palm oil, whatever that is. I don't think it's something the ladies put in the palm of their hand and wipe on their face. How's Betty?"

"She's good. How's Gillian?"

"Much the same. We've got two kids going to the right pre-schools. Gillian's up on that sort of thing. Sally-Anne and Hunter. I had the name Hunter in a film script the time the boy was born. The names we inflict on our children!"

"You speak with an American accent?"

"Don't we all?"

"What are you doing over here, Bruno?"

"Are you a journalist, Frank?"

"No. Public relations. Have my own business. My office is just round the corner."

"Like to visit with you. How's your father? It was through your dad, William and I got to know each other. Your father had just emerged from the African jungle. Sick as a dog in hospital. William, myself and Horatio Wakefield over there talking his head off were tracking the story of your father's miraculous reappearance after everyone in England had given him up for dead... Brought the kids over to see their grandparents. Good to see you again, William. Got to go. The wolves need me. Fame has its problems."

"Come and see me," said Frank.

"Might do that."

"Everyone here knows where I am," said Frank, realising too late he was labouring a point, the last words spoken to Bruno Kannberg's back as the 'wolves' drew the Hollywood film writer into the crowd. Twice, Frank heard the word Hollywood, above the babble of voices in the pub.

"If that's the price of fame, bring it on," said Frank to William.

"Be careful what you wish for. One minute they suck up to you, next minute they tear you apart. Cheers, Frank. Here's to *Housewives' Corner*."

"You think the BBC will go for it?"

"Like you, Frank, I have my contacts. Oh yes, they'll go for it. For no other reason than it being a damn good idea... Amazing how a few beers loosens people's tongues. The noise in the bar rises in direct proportion to the number of beers drunk... Horatio. How nice of you to join us. We were all together at Hastings Court, Frank. Dorian took the kids tobogganing."

"Do you know he's sold over a million copies of *A Bowl of Cabbage Water*?" said Horatio Wakefield. "Put in an American as the leading character. Never knew there were Americans in Changi. British and Australians, a few Kiwis, but no Americans. Paid off in sales. Wherever you look now the Americans won the war. Pays to stay out of a war until it's half over. The Chinese were fighting the Japs in the thirties... How are you, Frank? Thought you'd be spending Christmas with us. Your mother threw quite some house party. String orchestra up in the minstrel gallery. Beautiful old house. So much history."

"Why did he call it *A Bowl of Cabbage Soup*?" said Frank. "Doesn't sound like the kind of subject to write a book about."

"Cabbage water, Frank. Bruno still has the craving. When his wife boils the cabbage, or any other vegetable for that matter, Bruno goes into the kitchen after supper and drinks the cabbage water out of the saucepan. In Changi they were fed rice. Only rice. When Bruno did chores in the Japanese camp commander's house, he had to clean out the kitchen and do the washing up. If he was lucky, they hadn't thrown away the vegetable water from the previous night. Bruno drank the water. Nearest he got to a vegetable for nearly three years. Now the taste of cabbage water is better than anything, so he says. I've seen him drink the damn stuff so there's no bullshit. Caught him in Janet's kitchen after a dinner party when they were over here on a promotion for his book."

"Now the title makes sense. It's so bland it has to catch your eye on the dust cover of a book."

"The cover had a lot of officious-looking Japanese soldiers in peaked hats on the sleeve. It's a good book. Wish I could write a book of fiction. That's where the money is. If it weren't for Janet's practice we'd never afford the children's education."

"Isn't she a speech therapist?" asked Frank, knowing Horatio liked to talk about his wife.

"That's right. Bottom floor of the house are the rooms of the practice. In this day and age both parents need to be earning a living. None of this housewife business waiting for hubby to come back from the office at night with the supper ready on the table. We both cook. Janet's busier than I am. Harry's a day boy at Dulwich College. Can't afford to send him away to boarding school. Bergit goes to St Paul's at the end of this year. As a day girl."

"You want a drink, Horatio?" asked William.

"Thought you'd never ask."

"Patrick's going to Eton."

"Tell me another one. William and myself live three doors away in Chelsea, Frank. We were both lucky to make some money before the war, reporting on Hitler from Germany. Danger money, you could say. Paid for our houses. Journalists don't make money. Not even freelance journos like William."

"Some of them do," said Frank, handing Horatio the pint of beer passed to him by the landlord without the landlord seemingly being asked.

"Just tell me how."

"Not here, Horatio. Maybe later. If you two are such good friends, William may well tell you himself. How about a hundred pounds for half an hour's work once a week, Horatio?"

"There's got to be a catch in it. Always is. Cheers. To Patrick getting into Eton. Why not Harrow? Janet has an appointment to Harrow to help the boys who stammer stop their stuttering. I'm sure she'd put in a good word for Patrick if Father, by some miracle, has the money. In my experience, when something sounds too good to be true it usually is. This place must be the busiest pub in London. They all feed off each other's information. Why all the London papers report the same stories at the same time."

4

While Frank was ingratiating himself with as many journalists as possible, not far away Jeanne Pétain was walking Samuel Chalmers down the Portobello Road working on a way to make money out of her art that did not rely so much on one man. There were only so many times a woman could say no without the man looking for someone else to satisfy his sexual needs. Jeanne had no illusions about Samuel. He wanted her body, not her paintings. The three hundred pounds had been to buy her, not *Man on a Barge*. If she was not careful, her sale would be a one-off never to be repeated. Certainly not at three hundred pounds. James, with his parties, gave the Patrons of the Arts a continuous supply of new and willing young girls who wanted to live as artists. It was a game for the rich. Jeanne, smiling to herself as she led Samuel down among the stalls, had her own game that she hoped would help all of them without them having to sleep with a string of dirty old men to sell their paintings. Or pimp them when it came to the likes of James and Ben.

"There are lots of perfect spots, Samuel. Look at that old shop behind the men selling antique jewellery all of which is fake. Trust me. I learned all about antiques from an old British Army major. That shop, cleared up and filled with paintings, frequented by all the Chelsea artists, would give you a permanent, important place in London Society. You'd be *the* Samuel Chalmers, the benefactor who started the Nouvelle Galerie in the Portobello Road. Look at the people walking up and down. On a Saturday you can't move, there are so many people. You'd be investing in the great and wonderful world of art and making money. Then you'd really have a good story to tell your wife. What did she think of my painting of the Thames? *Man on a Barge* has a Dutch feel to it. When I'm truly famous you'll sell it for ten thousand pounds. What we need is a permanent gallery to display the art of young artists."

"Who's going to run it, Jeanne?"

"Me."

"What do you know about running a business?"

"There's a lot you don't know about me, Samuel. All you have to do is put in a little money and tell your rich friends about the gallery. Please. Pretty please for your Jeanne."

"When are you going to let me sleep with you, Jeanne?"

"Oh, Samuel. Not in the street. Someone will hear."

"When, Jeanne? You always have an excuse. How about this afternoon at your studio?"

"Why don't we go inside and look at that shop? If we have a shop together we'll see much more of each other. More time together. More opportunities. You can't rush into things. All good things come in time. You have to be patient or you'll spoil the image."

"Do we have magic?"

"Of course we do. Now, can we go in the shop? You know all about leases. It was that little sign to let that caught my eye. For your little Jeanne. I'll be oh so grateful, Samuel."

WHEN THE LEASE on the shop was signed later that afternoon, Jeanne having used every one of her feminine wiles to make Samuel sign the papers which she had had the agent draw up the previous day without Samuel's knowledge, poor Samuel was so horny Jeanne began to feel sorry for him and suggested they have tea back at her studio.

"My wife has tickets to the theatre so I have to go. She doesn't know anything about us. Just that I bought your painting. She likes impressing her friends when she tells them her husband is a Patron of the Arts. She thinks if I do enough good work promoting unknown artists they'll give me a knighthood. She wants to be Lady Chalmers to her friends. She wants to be more than just another rich man's wife. You never know. Titles are all about money one way or the other. If I give the Tory Party a big donation and Churchill wins the next election, they'll say the knighthood was for promoting the Arts. A lie, of course. You have to have a lot of money to win an election. So much for man's free will. One man, one vote. You're now empowered because you have the vote. All that rot. You brainwash the public by spending money promoting the party and lead them by the nose. Every man has his price. Can I come round tomorrow, Jeanne?"

"Of course you can, Samuel. We'll need to open a bank account for the Nouvelle Galerie. I'll start work straight away looking for paintings and sculptures. I know such a lot of people. Tessa has two of her paintings hanging in the offices of Cohen Wells. I'm sure you've heard of Cohen Wells. Very big advertising agents. Half of all sales will go to you, Samuel. You tell your wife tonight that when this gallery is famous, as it will be, she'll be Lady Chalmers. Oh, I'm so excited. I can paint all day in the gallery. People like to see an artist at work. Like to meet the artist. I'll have two or three of the others working alongside. They can explain to the laymen what they're painting. You are just so sweet."

Knowing the immediate danger was past, Jeanne gave Samuel a luscious kiss on the mouth, a real wet one, right in the street. Then she stood back and smiled at him.

"We'll need five hundred pounds in the bank account for running expenses. You won't mind, will you, Samuel? Don't forget to tell your wife when you get home she's going to have a title... Taxi!... Here he comes, Samuel. I so like the London growler taxis. They're so quick when you want one. What are you seeing tonight?"

"I have no idea."

"In you get. Have a nice time at the theatre."

When Jeanne reached home half an hour later to tell Ben their plan had succeeded, she could still see Samuel's look of lust as he looked down inside her blouse. Jeanne no longer wore a bra when she was with Samuel. It made her nipples stand out. Deliberately, as she leaned her hands on the backdoor of the taxi to smile at Samuel, she had let her blouse fall open, giving Samuel Chalmers a good eyeful from the back seat of the cab. With that impression of soft breast and nipple in his mind, the opening of the bank account and five hundred pounds would not prove to be difficult.

"His eyes came out on stalks looking through the glass, Ben. A flash is far sexier than seeing my tits naked. He signed the lease and paid six months' rent. That agent is so sweet. Did just what we asked him. I brushed my front against the agent's bare arm yesterday. That concentrated his mind. Now we can all show our paintings. Do you have anything you want to put in the gallery?"

"Not really. I'll help you in the shop. You need people who look like they are artists. That black beret really suits you. More of the French accent and less of the American. Americans are thought by the British to be too commercial. Tell them you lived on the left bank of the Seine in Paris. Makes everything in the shop more authentic. Are you going to have to sleep with him?"

"I don't know. I'll feel so guilty if I don't. I can't keep him hanging forever."

"Why not? He's married. The man's a lecher."

"And he's rich, don't forget that. I have to have a benefactor. Olivia has yet to sell a painting. It's not easy to break in without help. Let's go round and see James. Once the word gets out, there'll be a party. I'm so high with excitement one drink will get me tipsy."

"Is it cold outside?"

"Freezing. We'll have to walk."

"What about your three hundred pounds for *The Barge*?"

"Just this once we'll take a taxi. London is just so much fun."

BEN BROWN HAD FOUND in his life it was easier to follow than to lead. The small income from his parents' inheritance paid the rent for the room next to Jeanne's studio. For the rest, he let life's bounty flow. He never pushed himself on people, preferring the flow of life to drift him along in its wake. He never worried. He never hurried. As a painter he had no illusions as to his talent. At school before the war they had taught him to draw people's faces at an early age, a knack that enabled Ben to sketch a person in half an hour with a remarkable resemblance to his subject. People liked to sit and have themselves drawn, gasping with delight when they saw what Ben had done; a portrait of themselves, the most important person in their life. When he was hungry it was Ben's sole source of income. In the street, he charged a shilling. At the Nouvelle Galerie, sitting on the pavement in a canvas chair next to the fake antique dealer, he had a mind to charge half-a-crown. Jeanne moving in next door had been a godsend. Not only did he get the occasional roll in the proverbial hay, as he so liked to think of it, she fed him a slap-up breakfast the next morning. Life, for Ben, had never been better, the painful memory of his parents' violent death fading, along with his days as a bank clerk. Ben was an only child. A boy and man who liked to watch the world go by while expending as little energy as possible. He had been blessed with a soft charm and good looks, which, along with his small monthly income from his father's trust, was everything Ben needed in life.

"You think I can charge them half-a-crown sitting out on the pavement?"

"Don't be silly, Ben. We're going to smarten you up, wash your clothes and sit you inside the Nouvelle Galerie. Five bob. How does that sound? When I want to paint outside by the river you can look after the shop."

"Will I get a salary?"

"Don't chance your luck, Ben. Lunch, maybe. We're artists, remember. Not in it for the money... You think James is at home? Should have phoned him. The Nouvelle Galerie. Has a real ring to it. We're going to trim that beard of yours. Not too much. Going to make you look like a successful artist. You'll have to smoke a pipe."

"You're quite something, Jeanne."

"I know I am. Isn't it all just so much fun?"

5

At the time Ben and Jeanne were telling James he had a gallery to display his sculptures, Nancy Longhurst was sitting in the doctor's waiting room about to find out whether she was pregnant. In her own mind there was little doubt. She was sick in the mornings, had been for weeks. She had lied to Beth and Dorian. For some time now, she had been keeping an exact record of her sexual activity and, to help with her memory, she had added the names of the men. She had missed four of her periods. According to her understanding, a woman ovulated around the middle of her menstrual cycle, the exact time, looking at her meticulous notes, she had crawled into Dorian's bed. Unless she'd caught something that made her sick in the morning and stopped her periods, she was pregnant. David Haines had been a week before Dorian and a week afterwards, as he found it difficult to get away from his wife without causing suspicion. For Nancy, it was one thing to have good sex, quite another to be the centre of a messy divorce action, herself cited as the scarlet woman.

"Mrs Longhurst? The doctor will see you now."

Clutching her diary, Nancy went in to find out her fate, something that did not take very long.

"Congratulations, Mrs Longhurst. You are pregnant. About four months by the look of you. Is this your first child?"

"Yes, doctor."

"I thought so."

"There's a problem though, doctor. I'm not married."

"The young man I'm sure will be delighted. Many marriages start with a pregnancy. You'd be surprised at just how many. Mother nature, Nancy. Nature requires us to procreate or our species will die out. It's the strongest urge in man and woman. You don't mind me calling you Nancy? For the next months we are going to be seeing a lot of each other. I like a monthly check-up. Prevention is better than cure in medicine."

"There's something I want to show you. The fact is, I kept a meticulous account of my sex life."

"How interesting."

"I was a little wild. More than one partner, if you see what I mean. Would you look at my diary for me?"

"... My goodness!"

"I'm a bit of a slut, doctor."

"These records are meticulous indeed."

"It was all part of the fun really. Something to give me a nice warm glow in my old age. My question is, doctor, who's the father?"

"The man sticks out like a sore thumb. This chap Brigandshaw is the father of your baby, Miss Longhurst. Have you known him long?"

"Just that one night."

"Nothing in life is completely certain. Nature has strange habits."

"Who else might it be?"

"I'm afraid Brigandshaw is your man. My goodness. What a predicament."

"Is four months too late?"

"What for, Miss Longhurst?"

"An abortion."

"An abortion is illegal. A criminal offence."

"Thank you, doctor. You have been most helpful."

"Be careful, Miss Longhurst. Backstreet abortions can kill you as well as your baby. I can help you with an adoption. There are many couples not so lucky as you, desperately wanting a baby they can't have. There are many more couples looking for babies than babies up for adoption. Why don't you go home and think about it? Talk to this Mr Brigandshaw."

"He's in the army doing his National Service. A private. Four shillings a day. I don't think they have quarters for privates in the army. I'm in a mess, aren't I? A right royal pickle."

"Well, thanks to Mr Atlee's Labour government your medical bills will be paid for by the NHS. Socialism. The benefits of socialism. Maybe you should talk to your parents?"

"If you knew my parents you'd know they are the last people to talk to about their daughter falling pregnant without a husband. My father would take a shotgun to every man in this diary. They think I'm a nice, innocent young girl. Luckily he won't be able to throw me out of the house as I live in a flat with a girlfriend. Who just happens to be Mr Brigandshaw's sister."

"Then talk to her, Miss Longhurst."

"I thought you were calling me, Nancy?"

"Sometimes in life, the best course of action is to tell the truth. It's just as much his baby as yours. Please make an appointment with Miss Slater at reception for a month's time."

"Do you really want to see me again?"

"Of course I do, Miss Longhurst. You're going to have a baby."

BETH BRIGANDSHAW CAME HOME from work late to find Nancy sitting in the chair next to the bottle of gin. Next to the bottle on the small table was the diary Nancy had shown the doctor.

Frowning, Beth looked from the small table and its contents to Nancy.

"You're pregnant, aren't you?"

"Saw the doctor. It's worse, Beth. It gets worse. Warned me against an abortion. If I don't want the kid, the doctor can arrange to have it adopted. There are couples who can't have children screaming for children. What a contradictory world."

"How far are you?"

"Four months."

"Isn't that too late for an abortion?"

"If I had the kid I could never give it away. I thought I was a couple of months. Hoped I was. I can't feel anything inside of me."

"I'm going to get a glass. Bloody terrible day in the office. I'm looking forward to Paul's party on Saturday. Anything to shake out my boss. He's the most demanding, ungrateful son-of-a-gun I ever worked for. Do you know that damn man never smiles... What's the notebook all about?"

"It's my diary. I want you to look at it, Beth."

"A large gin first. What's he like?"

"Who?"

"Your doctor."

"A bit self-righteous. Told me abortions are illegal."

"Why must I look at your diary?"

Quietly, after Beth had poured herself a drink, Nancy picked up the small diary and gave it to Beth.

"Look at the month of August. Right in between what should have been my periods."

"There's only one name in the middle. My brother Dorian. Are your records accurate? You said David Haines could have fathered the child among others."

"Even down to the time of sex, not just the day."

"Oh, dear. Did you show this to your doctor?"

"Dorian's the father, Beth. You're going to be an aunty. I don't know what to do. Do I have to tell Dorian?"

"Oh, yes."

"He can't do anything. He's in the army. Four bob a day. When he comes out he won't have a job. He wants to write a book. Dorian's not the type to want a mortgage and a family."

"Dorian phoned me at the office today. He's coming to Paul's party on Saturday. The army are giving him a living-out allowance. Now he's on the magazine they've made him a sergeant. He's the only NCO in the office. The rest are officers. His new commanding officer was impressed with Dorian's Oxford First in English literature. They don't have one of those working on the army magazine. If you married my brother he could move into your room. His allowance can go in the kitty. We'd have more money for the flat than we do at the moment. That way, the other person in your bedroom will be contributing to the rent."

Trying to see the funny side, Beth let out a small laugh.

"Why would Dorian want to marry me? We hardly know each other."

"You're going to have his baby. Come on. It will be fun. Think about it, Nancy. You can't have an abortion at four months, can you? Just tell Dorian. It's as much his decision as yours."

"What the doctor told me."

"Then smile, Nancy. Chin up, ducky. Have another gin."

"Should I be drinking when I'm pregnant?"

"You have for the last four months. If the poor bastard on the way isn't an alcoholic by now, a couple more gins won't make any difference."

"Poor Dorian."

"He'll look back and say it was the best thing to happen to him in his life. You're a good person, Nancy. I know that. Dorian will find that out when he really gets to know you."

"I climbed into his bed."

"Doesn't matter who did the climbing. I'm going to be an aunty. My best friend is going to be my sister-in-law. Look on the bright side. My father always says there's a reason for everything. We talk about falling instantly in love. Or is that an excuse to take off our clothes? Men are all pretty similar. They try to look different. We try to fall for the one with the best prospects. That's not selfish in a woman. She instinctively wants the best chance in life for her children. We dress that all up and call it love. It's about being looked after. Dorian called it the survival of the fittest. Dorian's a decent man. You're a decent woman. That baby inside of you is going to be lucky... What's for supper? Got to eat properly. More fruit and vegetables from now on, young lady. Lots of good sleep."

"Do you want to be a mother, Beth?"

"Of course I do. That's my purpose in life. To have kids and look after them. I think it's wonderful you are certain it's Dorian and not that David Haines. A man who cheats on his wife and children is not good husband material. If I were you, I'd show Dorian what you showed your doctor. Take him to see the man if you want to. Just make Dorian certain in his mind he's the father of your baby and all will end well. He'll do the right thing. He's my brother."

"Just because he's your brother doesn't mean he'll act like the perfect gentleman. Don't forget Frank. From what I hear of Frank, he'd laugh in my face. Tell me if I was stupid enough to get myself pregnant by a stranger it was none of his business. Most men run away from pregnant girls. They don't want any responsibility, emotional or financial."

"I'm going to look for something to cook in the kitchen."

"You're running away, Beth. I'm the one who's going to be left holding the baby."

"We'll all hold that baby. Now, who's going to tell Dorian? You or me? My father will want to know about this. Make him very happy to know he's going to have a grandchild. Neither of you can now be selfish. Other people are involved, not least the man or woman who is going to grow out of your baby."

"Will you tell him, Beth? Show him the diary. If he wants to run away I'll understand."

"Of course I will. On Saturday. At Paul Crookshank's party. Now there's a nice man. If he wasn't still besotted with that little French-American girl I'd throw my cap at him. Father says Paul's going to go a long way in business. Dad's not well. Did I tell you that? He thinks he's dying. Told us kids at Christmas. Becoming a grandfather, knowing the Brigandshaws have an heir, will make him so happy. Give him something to fight for."

"What's wrong with him?"

"Some tropical disease he picked up in the Congo that's eaten part of his liver. He's getting old. My father's had a tough life. His parents were only married years after Dad was born. Grandmother was sixteen when she fell pregnant."

"How do you know?"

"Dorian spent a couple of weeks with Grandma in Rhodesia before he joined the army. Told him the whole story. Dorian says it's the greatest love story he ever heard; why Grandma won't leave the farm in Rhodesia. Elephant Walk holds all her memories. She loved him so much before Grandfather was stomped on by an elephant. Childhood sweethearts. You see, pregnancy is just one of our destinies."

"You're a romantic."

"Of course I am. Leave Dorian to me."

"You won't force him? I don't want you to tell anyone else in your family until your brother has made up his own mind what he wants to do about the baby. I don't want him coerced or put in a corner. He must make up his own mind in his own time. Give him the chance to back off without getting emotional with me or feeling obliged."

"What are friends for? Without friends in this life we'd all get into even more trouble."

"You promise not to force him to do the right thing?"

"He's a grown man. He can make his own decisions. Can you imagine what would happen if he found out later you had given away his son? The heir to the Brigandshaw fortune? That's something you've quite forgotten. One of these days my brother is going to be a rich man, whether his books sell or not."

"I'm not after your family money."

"Of course not. But money does help. Just think of it before you rush off to Soho or wherever you found that abortionist and do something stupid. If I lost my best friend I don't know what I'd do without her."

"Should I come to the party?"

"We'll go together. Somehow I'll get Dorian on his own. Then it's up to him. Don't expect an answer on Saturday night."

JEREMY CROOKSHANK, twenty-two years old and still a virgin, was looking forward to his brother's party like nothing else. Once he boarded the flight for Rhodesia and his small, learner-assistant's, two-roomed cottage on the tobacco farm in Macheke, the likelihood of having to wait until his return to England to achieve his manhood was almost certain. The few girls in the British Crown Colony of Southern Rhodesia only looked at bachelors who owned their own farms. The assistants and managers of the farms came far down in the pecking order. A good-looking young girl in the capital, Salisbury, was priceless. In the rural areas like Macheke they were virtually unheard of. In the farming community a single, unattractive, boring girl had every bachelor's attention.

Before the first guests arrived Jeremy's expectations were at boiling point as he walked up and down his brother's Hammersmith flat while Paul played the grand piano.

"Stop pacing, brother. Everything comes to he who waits... I like the cotton slacks. Nice open shirt across the chest should grab their attention. Not sure about the haircut."

"Where are they? It's eight o'clock."

"Terrible to arrive first. I've built you up a bit, Jeremy. Some of the girls will likely think you own a farm the size of Hampstead. No, don't worry. How are they going to find out? Can't let you go home without ending in the sack."

"They'll take one look at me and laugh."

"Not at the suntan. Fading, but still impressive. Have some confidence in yourself... There's the bell. Go and answer the door. Let the floodgates open. Most of them are artists. Why I'm playing classical music. Later we'll put on the gramophone and do some dancing. More jive, these days. No one does the foxtrot anymore. You stand in front of each other and move to the music. Some fling the girls around, but don't try that without practice. Your job is to hand out the punch. That way you'll make contact with all the girls. Introduce yourself. No one does formal introductions anymore. Have a couple of stiff ones yourself. The vodka bottle is in the kitchen cupboard. Give yourself an extra slug to get you in the mood."

"Why are you laughing, Paul?"

"Because it's funny. You're like a cat on a hot tin roof."

"You've had lots of girls."

"Not as many as you think. The one I want won't come tonight. She's found herself a rich sugar-daddy."

"What's a sugar-daddy?"

"You've been in the African bush too long, old boy. An older man with a lot of money. Usually married. Hurry, that's the second ring. They're impatient to get drinking. Can't keep the customers waiting."

SMILING, watching his brother pull himself up straight before going to open the door, Paul kept on playing the piano. For a moment, before the door opened to Frank Brigandshaw and a bevy of young girls, he was envious of Jeremy's innocence; his clean, unjaundiced view of the world just before the realities of life broke over him.

Hitting the middle C with his index finger, Paul got up to greet his guests. Another night. Another London party. With a broad, welcoming grin on his face, he held out his hand to the man who, as a boy, had bloodied his nose.

Behind Frank, with a five-gallon keg of beer balanced on his shoulder, stood Zachariah Cohen. Next to Zachariah, one on each side of him, were Tessa Handson and Olivia Johnston. To Paul, it looked as if all of them had been drinking. A girl called Daisy introduced herself. Paul had met Milly Worthington in Frank's office. Frank smiled at him sweetly as Milly swept into the room.

"Who was playing Chopin?" asked Milly, taking in the room.

"You know classical music, Milly? I want you to meet my brother Jeremy. Tobacco farmer from Rhodesia."

"How exotic. Always wanted to go to darkest Africa. Frank's forever talking about his days with Brian hunting crocodiles in the Zambezi Valley. Have you shot a crocodile, Jeremy?"

"I don't like to kill animals, I'm afraid."

"I like to look at them," said Livy, getting herself into the conversation.

"Have to take the bung out of the keg and fit in the tap," said Zachariah Cohen. "You any good at that kind of job, Jeremy? Farmers are good with their hands. I'm Zach, Frank's buddy from the army. We now do business together instead of marching up and down."

"Isn't that heavy?" said Daisy. "Put it on the floor."

"Where's the music? Got to have the music. There's another bunch coming up the stairs. Nice flat, Paul. Like the piano. Did you bring the band from the jazz club?"

"Not tonight. Not enough room and too much noise. Got to think of the neighbours. Put that keg in the kitchen while I put a record on the gramophone. The latest Benjie Appleton. Can't bring the band in person but we can play their music. Great to jive to. Jeremy's pouring the drinks, everyone. Make yourselves at home. The night is but a pup. This is my brother's send-off and it's going to be a good one he'll remember on his own living in the bush. Anyone who can't drive home can catch a taxi or sleep on the floor. Tonight's the night to have fun. You're only young once. All that jazz. Make the most of it... Beth and Dorian! Come you in. Nancy! Lovely to see you. And here's the man who started me playing with the Appleton Band."

"Blimey. It's the blighter," said Frank, looking at Kenneth Grahame. "I don't believe it. You're still wearing your Old Etonian tie."

"Got to look the part, Frank" said Kenneth. "How are you? Heard you are going into the washing business."

"Who told you that? Of course, Milly. You've been seeing my secretary."

"How's it going? The new detergent?"

"Rather well, matter of fact. There's going to be a new programme on the BBC. *Housewives' Corner*. The first tip for the housewife will be the Ripley Blue. BBC fell for William Smythe's idea to help the British housewife with the chores. All the new labour-saving devices for the house. Industry is bursting with new products. You'll see."

"I'll bet we will, Frank."

"I want to hear about this," said Zachariah Cohen.

"I'll bet you do," said Frank helping Zach hand down the keg to Jeremy. "But all in good time. You scratch my back, I'll scratch yours."

"Don't you think I've scratched it enough?"

"Never enough, Zach, to satisfy me. There isn't enough money in the world to satisfy me. I want it all and then some more."

"What are you going to do with it all, Frank?" asked Beth.

"Who knows? You're never too rich. Dorian, old boy. How are you? Where's Kim?"

"On his way to India. Put a haversack on his back and went off to see the world."

"How thoroughly irresponsible."

"I thought that was more your speed, Frank?"

"Come on, you two," said Paul. "No family feuds tonight. It's a party. Have a drink, both of you... Everyone, welcome. Enjoy yourselves."

WITH THE HELP of one of the young girls who had followed him into the kitchen, Jeremy laid the small barrel of beer on its side and hit out the bung before knocking the spigot back in the hole with the wooden mallet his brother used to tenderise the meat. Putting the barrel upright next to the sink, with a pint mug under the tap attached to the spigot, he turned the small handle, letting out a gush of white froth. Then the beer flowed.

"Have you done that before?" said Livy Johnston. "That was very clever. I would have no idea what to do. What would we do without a man around? So you're the chap going to Africa? I'd love to see Africa. All the animals. Have you got a very big farm? My name is Livy. Short for Olivia."

"I don't have a farm yet. Takes five years to learn how to grow tobacco. You save up your manager's bonus and apply for a Crown Land farm. Rhodesia is mostly just bush at the moment. Vast, empty areas. The odd African village by the rivers. Teeming with game, of course. I'm Jeremy Crookshank. All that introduction at the door was a bit overwhelming."

"You're so lucky to be going back to Africa. Exciting. Little old England is so overcrowded and boring. Well, not tonight of course. All that sunshine. England's so grey after the war. Nobody has any money to really enjoy themselves. How big is your farm going to be?"

"Six thousand acres."

"Goodness! I can't imagine the size of six thousand acres. You'll be rich."

"Not really. It's virgin bush covered in msasa trees that have to be cut down and the roots stumped out before you can plough. We do it by hand."

"Who does it by hand?"

"The blacks. They're coming from all over central Africa to the white farms for jobs. Some bring their families. They build their own pole and dagga huts and thatch them with grass. We give them food rations every week we bring out from Salisbury in the truck. That's the capital of Southern Rhodesia. Named after Lord Salisbury who was Prime Minister of England when the town was laid out by Rhodes's pioneers. The blacks get paid on the top of their food rations, of course. It's my idea to put a school on my farm so the kids can get an education and be taught English. There are so many different languages in Africa that the blacks from the different tribes can't even speak to each other. We have a mixed language of all the tribes with bits of English called Fanagalo, or something like that. When they all speak English it will be much easier. I'm going to build a small school with a football pitch next to a cricket field. Bring electricity onto the farm. Pump water from the river to the African huts so they have running water. Put in proper loos. At the moment they all use the forest. There's so much to do. There's talk of damming the Zambezi River for hydroelectricity. With our skills and their labour there's no telling what we can all do. Just needs a lot of money and a lot of work. I like the idea of building something worthwhile with my life."

"It sounds so wonderful."

"I've got to hand out the punch."

"Can I help you, Jeremy?"

"Would you? That's super. If they want beer, give them a glass and tell them it's here in the kitchen. Do you want an extra sling of vodka in your punch? There's a bottle in that cupboard."

"I love vodka. It's so Russian. This is going to be some party."

It seemed to Dorian, Nancy was avoiding him. His relief mingled with his guilt. She had, he hoped, had her abortion without his help. Or better still, the panic inflicted on him at Christmas by Beth had been a storm in a teacup and Nancy had never been pregnant. Once, across the room while drinking the beer he had got for himself from the barrel, he thought she was looking his way, her look tinged with pain. But when his eyes sought out hers, they looked away. Next to Nancy, drinking her punch, his sister watched him over the rim of her glass with a look of quizzical speculation.

As the room quickly filled up, the party spilling into the hallway and the kitchen, it was more difficult for him to work out what was going on. By the time the music was jamming, with everyone trying to dance, Dorian thought he was off the hook. If nothing else, the incident had made him invest in packets of Durex, so that when the opportunity presented itself again it wouldn't end in a mess.

The week for Dorian had gone well. From the inside of trucks and cars he had no wish to understand, he was back with words, in an environment he liked and understood. All morning he had been looking for a place to rent with his living-out allowance. It had to be quiet with a bed, desk and gas ring to cook. And cheap. With luck, his two years in the army would not, after all, be a complete waste of time. His work in the War Office, helping to edit the magazine, required no imagination, let alone a continuing line of thought to interrupt those on his book. The small army pay, the way it was going, would let him write his first major novel without having to concentrate on making a living. Failing his course in motor mechanics had been a blessing in disguise. As he drank his beer, standing in a corner by himself, the ideas for *African Drums* flowed through his mind. Having never met his Brigandshaw grandfather he could now see him in his mind. He was smiling from the pictures in his head, far away in his dream, when Beth jogged his arm, spilling some of his beer.

"Sorry, Dorian... You and I have to talk, I'm afraid."

"What about?" said Dorian, feeling suddenly cold all over.

"Nancy. She's pregnant. Four months pregnant. She kept a diary of her sexual moments. Her doctor agrees the child can only be yours. Congratulations. You're going to be a father."

"What are you talking about?"

"Four months. Almost five. Too long for an abortion even if she wanted one. Think about it. You could move into the flat... Have you found somewhere to stay?"

"Not yet."

"I'm sure Dad would help out with money... No, I haven't told anyone."

"Why's Nancy been avoiding me?"

"She wants you to make up your own mind, without any pressure."

"About what?"

"What to do."

"I now get eight shillings a day as an acting sergeant. What do you expect me to do?"

"The right thing, Dorian."

"It wasn't my fault."

"Probably not, but that doesn't alter the fact you are going to be a father."

"I'm going to get drunk."

"You do that. You know my phone number. I rather like the idea of my best friend as my sister-in-law."

"You think I'm going to marry her?"

"I don't know, Dorian. That's all up to you. Just bear in mind there's another person involved."

"That's what I thought. More than one person by the sound of it."

"I'm talking about my niece or nephew."

"She had dozens of lovers."

"You can see the diary. Together we can go to Nancy's doctor with it. He'll explain how nature works. Think about it."

"Does she expect me to talk to her now?"

"Not now. Sleep on it. You can get drunk tonight. How's the new job?"

"That bit's all right. I was just thinking how well my life was going. I want to get on with *African Drums*... Where are you going?"

"To get another drink. Enjoy the party. Seems Livy's latched onto Jeremy. Life's so much fun."

When she left him alone, Dorian's first instinct was to run for the door, find sanctuary in a bar far from the problem and get drunk by himself. All the storyline in his head had been blown away, the pleasant months writing his book at the army's expense a lost hope. Instead, he sank back like a cornered rat. The rest of the party went on around him, his life-changing drama only known to himself. When he looked in his beer mug it was empty. Feeling furtive, Dorian slunk back into the kitchen, put his mug under the barrel at an angle and turned on the beer. No one noticed him. The kitchen was empty of people. Jeremy had taken the punch bowl out into the lounge where Dorian could see him through the open door ladling out drinks. Some of the guests had brought bottles of spirits which were on the table next to the gramophone. Somewhere, in among the crowd, was Nancy with his child in her stomach. Cursed with an imagination, Dorian began to think of a name for the child.

After the second and third pint of beer, still standing in his corner, Dorian began to feel better. She was an educated girl and certainly sexy. The idea of sleeping with her again rushed into his head, swamping his fear.

Frank came up to him and tried to make conversation. Frank's problem with their parents now looked different. Like for a character in his book, he was thinking about what it was like to be in Frank's position, making his previous opinions of his brother feel like those of a sanctimonious hypocrite. For a moment, quickly controlled, he almost told Frank about his problem.

"So how's life, Frank?" said Dorian, trying to be nonchalant. "You seem to be doing well for yourself. Paul said you were bringing your girlfriend, Connie."

"She didn't want to come. Has Beth been talking to you?"

"What about, Frank?" asked Dorian, his situation immediately back at the forefront of his mind.

"Connie. She met Connie once in the street near her flat. Connie's a bit older than me."

"How much?" Thankfully they were not talking about his problem. Dorian tried to relax.

"Twenty years. A bit more actually."

"That's the age of Mother!"

"Not quite."

"Isn't she a bit old for you?"

"Snag is, I love her. We get on so well. Can sit next to each other on the couch reading our books in perfect harmony. Never had that before. Certainly not at home in Cape Town. There was never any peace. We were always niggling each other... Of course, we'd never have any kids. Connie thinks I'll leave her when she's a bit older... What's the matter, Dorian? Something wrong? ... Love's strange. Sort of creeps up on you. I don't know what I'd do without Connie. She's my lover and my muse. Anything goes wrong in business, I ask Connie. Her husband was much older than her. Died and left her a fortune. At first I was after her money. Now it's nothing to do with her money. I just like being with her. She makes me so calm. Happy. For the first time in my life I'm happy."

"Have you talked to her about the question hanging over your parentage?"

"Things like that don't matter anymore. Or not as much. Makes them all look petty. All they had to do all those years ago was tell me the truth... Are you enjoying Zach's beer? Much prefer draught beer. The stuff in the bottles is too fizzy. Zach pretty much does what I tell him."

"So why wouldn't she come to the party?"

"Says she's too old. That she'd embarrass me in front of my friends. I don't even see her age anymore. Nothing but Connie. All I see is Connie."

"Were you drinking before you got here?" Listening to his brother sounding so nice had never happened before.

"We all were. Can't come to a party sober. Nice to see you again,

Dorian. Hear you're going to be living in London. We must have a drink together, on our own. Whatever the truth, we still have the same mother. Look after yourself, Dorian. Don't do anything I wouldn't do."

"You're getting mellow in your old age, Frank."

"I suppose so. It's Connie. She's so good for me. If it wasn't for Zach and the money he pays me I'd go home to her now. Our flats are very close. Nice and cosy. You never thought you'd see me as a stay at home kind of chap. Love changes all, Dorian."

Dorian watched his brother drift back into the party smiling at everyone and thought life really did have its twists. If he was writing a book about Frank he would say the man had found an outlet for his unrequited love for their mother. That all the years of Frank's rejection had found a home in Connie.

By the time the party got into full swing, with most people drinking standing up, there being nowhere left to sit, Livy had realised she was not the only girl with her sights set on Jeremy Crookshank. To ensure his brother had the greatest chance of finding himself a girl at the party, Paul, Livy concluded, had spread the word far and wide. The exotic background, the chance of finding a potentially rich husband, had pushed Livy into stiff competition. Her dream of living the life of luxury, with servants at her beck and call, was quickly receding. Not only was the man's background and desire for a wife fascinating, he was also, like his brother Paul, good looking. The tight shirt over his chest showed strength with a pair of broad shoulders. The slacks were tight round his buttocks, his backside firm and enticing. Jeremy Crookshank, despite his baby looks, was a catch for any girl with limited prospects. In the art circle of James and his friends, there was no one with substance, no one with a future. All of them, in the end, would be looking for jobs as clerks or worse, spending the last three quarters of their lives in drudgery with any poor girl foolish enough to become their wives. The arty crowd were for the moment. The likes of Jeremy, so rarely found in Livy's circle, were for the future, an exciting life of luxury that wouldn't fizzle once the bloom of youth had flown out the window. One day, in the not too distant future, *The Cogs of War*, James Coghlan's sculpture which he had sold to some fool for three hundred pounds, would, in Livy's humble opinion, end up on the scrap heap where it had started...along with the likes of James Coghlan. Livy, aware she only had a few more years to play her cards right for a comfortable future, racked her brains as to how she could cut young Jeremy out of the pack, take him home and screw him so well he'd never forget, his hormones falling over themselves to make her his and only his forever. Having always enjoyed a good fight, Livy launched back into the competition.

"Come and dance, Jeremy. This is a nice slow one. Leave the ladle in the punch bowl. You don't have to act the host anymore."

Having got him onto the crowded patch of parquet flooring where the carpet had once been, Livy sidled sweetly into his arms before getting close and personal, moving her crotch in time to the music just touching the front of his pants. Having got his complete attention, Livy gave a solid push into his manhood, pulling back with a smile up into his face when she had made her point. Neither of them said a word. Neither of them needed to.

"Oh, look," she said, knowing full well he was hoping for more. "There's Tessa waving at us. Come on. She's a hoot. She's got a new man in tow. Let's go and talk to them."

"Can't we go on dancing?"

"You can have another dance later."

"Can I?"

"I'll make it very special. You just don't know how special, Jeremy. Don't let yourself be carried away by all these girls. It's the right one that counts. We artists know how to enjoy ourselves. Share the happiness, so to speak... If you are very good, later, much later, we can go back to my flat and I'll show you my paintings. I'm good, Jeremy. You'll see." The sudden look of lust in Jeremy's eyes told her he had understood her *double entendre*.

"Will you really show me tonight? I fly back on Monday. I don't have much time."

"Let's enjoy the party. Tessa and I have shared a flat for ages. It's not very big. Two rooms. When we're alone we share the one bedroom. I'm going to be sleeping on the pull-out couch tonight by the way she's looking at her new man. Have you ever slept on a pull-out couch, Jeremy?"

"I don't think so."

"There's always a first time. Now, come over with me to Tessa. If she's too absorbed in her new man you can tell me all about Rhodesia. Do people paint the wild animals in Africa? Make them look all fierce? I'd love to do that. Lions and tigers," she said, making the mistake about tigers in Africa deliberately.

"We have lions and leopards in Rhodesia."

"Tell me. Tell me all about it. I could listen to you talk all night."

Thinking what to do with her painting *Pussy Cat*, in case Jeremy jumped to the right conclusion when they got back to the Chelsea flat – that she was hunting him like any predator – Livy led him by the hand across the room. The picture of the ginger cat, with a background of tropical foliage copied out of a book of Rousseau paintings she had borrowed from the library, stood on the easel in the big bay window of their lounge, staring at everyone who walked in the flat. For a first try at painting wildlife, Tessa had said it wasn't that bad. In her excitement to get to the party Livy had forgotten to put the painting away. Somehow, she told herself, she would talk her way round it. But first she would have to get him drunk so he wouldn't notice it was a domestic cat in her painting. But not too drunk. She wanted him to remember every detail back on his farm in Rhodesia. In Livy's mind, they were going to write letters across the ocean to each other, Livy slipping him sexy thoughts every other paragraph, until his sexual desire got the better of him and made him send her money for a nice boat trip out to Rhodesia, and all the sunset colours of red and orange of an African sunset that would be her perfect future. To keep his mind on her she stroked the palm of his hand with her fingertip. Time was short. It was nearly Sunday. The day after, he was gone.

As the booze sank in, the girls grew bolder to Dorian. Struck rigid by panic in his corner, he had only moved out to replenish his beer from the keg. He had seen Nancy twice on the dance floor, looking to have not a care in the world. He was making himself drunk, no longer able to get to the door through the throng of people to make his escape. His legs felt like they were made of lead. It was all very well thinking about the child but what about him? His life had not started. To go into marriage with a perfect stranger might solve their problems but not his. He had not so much as once in his life thought of marriage. The idea of being told what to do all day by some woman was appalling. Beth had started in on him. If Nancy was her best friend she would be the same. He would end up a hen-pecked husband supplying the family's money for the rest of his life. He had watched his own mother boss his father around. She always had her own way down to keeping Frank's identity a secret. Knowing when his parents married and when Anthony had been born, led him to believe he was being led into a similar trap. They could all tell him until they were blue in the face he was the father but how could he ever be sure Nancy wasn't lying? In a corner, everyone lied to save their skin. It was part of human nature. Part of self-preservation, the strongest sense in mankind. He was an eligible man. His father was rich. Nancy would know. Maybe Beth had told Nancy their father was dying. That soon he was going to have enough money to bring up a whole tribe of kids. David Haines, by all accounts, was married. Had his own children. He was no good as the fall guy. But could Beth do such a thing to her own brother? With everything inside his head, the party going on around without him, it all went round and round, chased by the beer.

"Don't you want to dance, Dorian?"

"Do I know you?"

"Does it matter? Beth told me to come and dig you out of your corner. We don't have to dance properly. There isn't enough room. I've never seen so much drink at a party. No food but plenty of drink. Typical bottle party. What have they put in the punch? Kicks like a mule. Oh well, tomorrow's Sunday. What's the matter, Dorian? I've been watching you in your corner. Beth says you're in the army. Lucky we girls don't have to do National Service. My name is Mandy. Come and dance. Put your beer glass in the kitchen. It's empty. When we've had a dance you can tell me why you've been standing all alone in the corner. Come on. I won't take no for an answer. What a party Paul's throwing. Beth fancies Paul. Did you know that? Where's his French girl? Or is she American? Why do we always want what we can't have? Do you have a girlfriend, Dorian?"

His feet still like lead, Dorian let himself be led out of the corner in among the people. Then he began to dance, swaying in time with the music. Mandy was pretty. Like so many of the girls. If he married Nancy, he told himself, all this would be over. He would be a responsible, married man with a family before he had had any fun. Not like Kim off on his trip to India, the whole world at his feet, the whole world his oyster. When the dance was over he was going to pour himself a shot of whisky. On top of the beer, he hoped that would do the trick. With enough drink inside him the very idea of doing the right thing by Nancy would fade into oblivion.

"You dance well, Mandy."

"That's better. Now you're enjoying yourself. Why were you standing all alone in the corner?"

"You don't want to know. Neither do I. Do you drink whisky, Mandy?"

"I can try."

FROM THE OTHER side of the room, both with half-full glasses of punch in their hands, Nancy and Beth, without seeming to be looking, watched Dorian dance.

"Who's he dancing with?" asked Nancy.

"Don't know her name. She's all over him."

"Did you tell him?"

"More than an hour ago."

"Did he understand?"

"Couldn't have made myself clearer."

"I've tried a couple of times to catch his eye but he won't look at me. Men are bastards."

"Bad phrasing, Nancy."

"It's worse now he knows and is going to do nothing. He's clutching that damn girl right into him. What was he doing in the corner so long?"

"Thinking. My brother is a thinker. Did you know he got a First in English literature at Oxford University?"

"Probably. Is it any good to him? Can you make any money out of a degree in English literature?"

"Got him a better job in the army. From private to acting sergeant. Doubled his pay."

"Bully for him. What's he getting now?"

"Eight shillings a day plus living-out allowance. The rest in his new office are officers. He wants to write a novel. A bestseller."

"Don't we all... He's ignoring me, Beth. Last time he was going to take me to the abortionist."

"I told him that was too late."

"What did he say?"

"Please, Nancy. If he wants to talk he'll come over. You wanted to give him some space."

"He's had an hour of space. How am I going to bring up a kid on my own? On a secretary's salary? If your dad didn't pay some of the rent we'd never afford the flat. Kids are expensive. Prams and cots. Baby clothes."

"What about your parents?"

"Don't be ridiculous. That French girl hasn't come. Why don't you leave me alone in my misery and go and talk to Paul? You know, that brother of his isn't half bad looking. What a waste running to Africa. I wonder what Livy's up to?"

"Paul's not interested in me. I'm the boss's daughter. Far too complicated for Paul. I thought he was going to play the piano."

"They'd all rather be dancing. Can't dance to a piano. I feel sick."

"You've drunk too much."

"I don't think so. I get morning sickness at night. Or maybe tonight it's fear at the thought of being left on my own to support a baby. What am I to do, Beth?"

"Right now, I don't know. Maybe give him time to let it sink in. In the morning he'll act differently."

"Why? In the morning he'll have convinced himself the kid isn't his. I did lie to begin with about all my lovers. Damn it, I wish I'd never climbed into his bed. You know, you can't win."

"You'll have to have the baby adopted. Think about it, Nance. If Dorian isn't going to do anything, it's your only chance… Paul's coming over. We'd better stop talking about your baby."

"Doesn't stop me thinking. You're right, Beth. It isn't your problem. You're not the one who's pregnant… Hello, Paul. Lovely party. Where did all these people come from?"

"Don't ask me. Half of them I don't know."

"Who's Dorian dancing with?" asked Beth.

"Oh, that's Mandy."

"What does she do?"

"She's an artist. Dorian will like an artist. Have something in common. He once told me his English tutor said a writer paints with words. They're both in the same kind of business… What's the matter with Nancy? Why'd she suddenly run off? I was going to ask her to dance."

"Don't you want to dance with me, Paul?"

"Of course, Beth. Come on. Last time we danced was at the Benjie Appleton jazz club."

"Where's your American?"

"She didn't want to come. Why's Frank in such a good mood? These days he's positively charming."

"Maybe he's in love."

"Didn't bring his girlfriend."

"Who's Frank's girlfriend, Paul?"

"A girl called Connie."

"Connie! She's the age of my mother."

"Someone's making him happy. Just look at him. All smiles. Hasn't made a snide comment all evening."

ONCE THE TWO men were talking about Rhodesia, Livy gave Tessa the signal they should go to the loo, with the door locked, both looking at their make-up in the same mirror, they could talk.

"Who's the new man?" asked Livy.

"You didn't bring me in here to ask me who he is. Why are we here, Livy?"

"You've got to go back to the flat first. I want you to hide *Pussy Cat*. I forgot in my hurry. He's quite delicious, Tessa. So young and innocent. I'm going to bang him so hard he'll never forget me. Do you know, I think the poor man's a virgin? Six thousand acres. Do you have any idea how big that is? If he sees my painting and the cat he'll put two and two together. See, I've been working on painting African wildlife."

"The cat isn't exactly wildlife, Livy. The poor thing's never been out of the flat since we got her."

"But he'll see what I'm doing. 'Tis my ulterior motive."

"What is your ulterior motive, Livy?" asked Tessa sweetly.

"I'm going to marry him, see. He's going back to Africa the day after tomorrow."

"It'll soon be after midnight. Then he'll be going back tomorrow. Not the day after."

"You're enjoying this. I need your help. I'd help you snag a man if you were in the same boat."

"There's a problem. I'm not coming home tonight. He wants me to go back to his place so we can spend all Sunday together."

"Can't you take him to our place first? Say you need something. Something you've left at home."

"But I haven't. I don't want to ruin my chances because of the cat. How's he going to know the cat is in your painting?"

"He'll be able to see. I'm not that bad a painter. You said yourself it wasn't that bad. And hide the book of Rousseau paintings. I think I left it on the coffee table... Hang on! We won't be long."

"What are you doing in there?" came a voice through the door.

"Having a pee."

"I'm going to pee my pants."

"Just hang on... Tessa, if he puts two and two together and sees I've started painting wildlife he'll never send me the boat ticket. I'm going to really make him randy. He must think it's love, not me looking for an eligible husband. He's so charming. So innocent. Please, Tessa. Go home first and clear the decks. I'll do anything for you. This is my one big chance. I've only got tonight to put the hook in. It's got to go in deep without any afterthoughts about my premeditation to let it slip out when he gets back to Rhodesia. He has a cottage on his own. No social life, let alone any girls."

"Sounds ghastly."

"We'll have lots of kids and servants."

"I'm going to piss through the keyhole!"

"Don't be vulgar!"

"What are you two doing in there?"

"Who is it?"

"Frank, you idiots. Don't you recognise my voice? I know you two. You're up to something."

"Please, Frank. This is important."

"So is having a piss, Livy. I've drunk half Zach's barrel of beer."

"Just hold it in a bit longer."

"You men are all the same," said Livy, unlocking the door. "You're too impatient... Frank! Can't you wait for us to get out of the loo?"

"No, darling, I can't, when a man's got to piss, man's got to piss. Lovely party... Close the bloody door. I don't want the whole party watching me."

FEELING agitated after Livy went off with Tessa, Jeremy had kept his eye on the door of the loo, only half listening to what Mike Sorrell was saying. It had never happened to him before. A girl had asked him to see her etchings... Unless it was all a joke. His brother Paul's idea of pulling his leg. For the life of him Jeremy could not see what Livy thought she was going to get out of him. He had heard of older women seducing young men in search of their youth. Livy was about his own age. As good-looking a girl as anyone in the room. What did she want from him, he asked himself, knowing there was nothing he could give. Thinking of what she had said to him on the dance floor broke him out in a cold sweat. He had never made love. What did he do? How did he start anything? The chances were a young girl like Livy was a virgin like himself. They would both fumble and feel embarrassed with each other, ruining everything.

When Jeremy saw Frank trying to get in the loo he expected Livy and Tessa to come out. Two other people were lining up. There was only one loo in the flat. All the beer drinking was creating a problem. Thinking of it had made him want to go himself, compounding his feeling of uncertainty. When Frank didn't get in the door, his need to go had increased. He had seen Frank crossing his legs, trying to hold it in.

Jeremy began to sweat properly. The record had stopped, people moving off the piece of dance floor. More of the men headed for the loo. Everyone was talking loudly from all the drink. The door had opened, letting Frank run into the loo, leaving it open. Jeremy could see Frank's look of relief on his face. In a rush, Jeremy made for the loo, pushing past Livy as she and Tessa went back to the party, barely closing the door behind them.

"Got to go, Frank. Got to go. Don't mind me. Oh my, that's better."

"Can you move over, Jeremy, I'm bursting," said Zachariah Cohen, who had followed him in before the door closed. "Once the music stops you want to pee."

"Someone close the bloody door," said Frank. "Can't a man pee in peace?"

"It's closed, Frank. Relax. There's only one toilet. Kenneth Grahame is disgusting. He's gone to have a piddle in the bathroom basin next door. Couldn't hold it in any longer. What do girls do in the toilet? When you got to go you got to go. You can't rush out of a flat in London and do it on the street."

"Had to do that once," said Frank, still relieving himself. "Move over, Jeremy. Three can piss at once."

Jeremy, turning round, was pleased to see the door was closed. Someone, probably his brother, had started the music again. Jeremy washed his hands in the small basin and went out to look for Livy. She took his hand and pulled him back on the dance floor, folding into his arms. Neither of them tried to dance. They swayed to the music. For some reason when she pressed against him nothing happened.

"Relax, Jeremy. Everything's going to turn out fine. We've got the flat to ourselves. Tessa's going home with Mike Sorrell. There's a bottle of sherry at home. Have you got enough money for a taxi?"

"I'll borrow some from Paul."

"That's the idea. There isn't any rush. There are plenty of growler taxis in Hammersmith on a Saturday night once the West End theatres come out."

"How much is the taxi?"

"Borrow a quid. You can always give it back if it's too much. You'll need a taxi back in the morning. Or you can catch the Tube... Are you all right, Jeremy?"

"I'm not sure. This has never happened to me before."

"You're not, are you?"

Blushing scarlet to the roots of his hair, Jeremy hoped she hadn't seen his embarrassment. To hide his red face he had pulled Livy as close as possible. When he felt her press into him down below he had an instant erection.

"That's better," said Livy. "My, oh, my."

NANCY, left on her own while Beth danced with Paul, felt abandoned. She watched Beth flirting with Paul. The girl with Dorian was all over him. If they had any problems they weren't interested in hers. Lonely in a room full of people, she began to feel sorry for herself. Did anyone give a damn what happened to her and the baby, kept screaming in her head. Putting it simply, she told herself, it wasn't their problem. The drink wasn't helping either, however much she poured down her throat. With no wish to dance or talk to anyone and hear how much they were enjoying themselves at the party, she went to find her coat among the pile on the bed in Paul's bedroom. A drunk was asleep on the floor. No one took any notice as she left, all too absorbed with themselves to notice. Dorian had his arms right round the girl. He had his back to her as she went to the door. She looked at her watch. The Tubes were still running. She'd go home to the flat and have a good cry on her own and eat a box of chocolates.

It was freezing cold in the corridor outside Paul's flat. The noise from the music was not as bad as she had thought it would be.

Downstairs, out in the street, it was raining sleet, the mix of snow and rain pushed in her face by the wind. She pulled her coat closer together against the cold. There wasn't a taxi in sight had she wanted one. The theatres had yet to come out. The street lights looked as cold as she felt. After two hours of drinking she was stone-cold sober. Her fear of being left alone in the world with her baby had sobered her up. Not sure whether to walk the block to the Tube station and save the taxi fare, Nancy hesitated, standing alone on the pavement. From upstairs she could still hear the music from the party.

"Want a lift home, Nancy? Kensington is on my way. My new flat's in Knightsbridge."

"Frank! You gave me a fright."

"Did my bit for Paul and Jeremy. Olivia Johnston is all over Jeremy. If Jeremy doesn't get his oats tonight he'll likely die a virgin. Never seen a girl make it so obvious. She must want to live in Africa. We all have our quirks. Come on. My car's that one across the road standing under the lamp post. Why are you leaving so early?"

"Why are you leaving so early, Frank?"

"Connie didn't want to come to the party, said she was too old. And you, Nancy? Never seen you go home early from a party on your own before."

"I'm pregnant."

"Now that is something. Come on. There's a heater in the car. Your cute little nose is turning blue."

"Aren't you going to ask who is the father?"

"None of my business, Nancy. That much I've learned in life the hard way. To mind my own business."

He took her by the elbow and led her across the street, putting her in the car before going round to the driver's side and letting himself in. The car started immediately.

"Takes a little time for the heater to warm up."

"The car's new. I can smell the leather. Never been in a car with leather before."

All the way from Hammersmith to South Kensington, the temperature in the car rising to a pleasant warmth, neither of them spoke. There was a radio in the new car, something else Nancy had never before experienced. Frank dropped her opposite her block of flats.

"Do you want me to come up, Nancy?"

"No. Better not. I'll start blubbing. I have a full box of chocolates upstairs."

"Does Beth know?"

"Beth knows everything. Thanks for the lift, Frank. Didn't realise how cold it was going to be outside on my own."

"Look after yourself... Are you going to have the baby?"

"I'm not absolutely sure. There's someone I have to talk to."

"The father. That's the stuff. Men like to have all the fun and take none of the responsibility."

"The abortionist. There's a woman in Clapham."

"If you want any help you know my number. Just in case I'll give you one of my business cards. You can either phone me at the office or the flat."

"You're not the bastard I thought you were."

"That much I am, Nancy. That much I am. Illegitimate kids are just down my street of understanding."

Without thinking, Nancy leaned across in the car and kissed Frank on the cheek. She had put his card in her coat pocket. Then she got out of the car and ran across to her building. As she pushed open the door she heard Frank's car swish past on its way to Knightsbridge.

Upstairs, when she let herself in, the flat was as cold as charity. Nancy lit the gas fire, still wearing her coat. When the room had warmed up a little she found the box of chocolates and took off her coat which was still damp from the sleet. Frank had been kind to her. Life wasn't so bad after all. Slowly, enjoying them one by one, Nancy began to eat her way through the box of chocolates, sitting in front of the hissing fire.

BETH HAD WATCHED Nancy leave the party not knowing what to do. Dorian still had himself wrapped round Mandy on the dance floor. Bringing her mind back to Paul, she smiled up into his face. The music was too loud to have a conversation. His arms around her felt nice. There was a twinkle of speculation in Paul's eyes as he looked back at her. They stopped dancing briefly while Paul went to the gramophone and turned over the record. When it started again the music wasn't so loud.

"After eleven I always turn down the music. At twelve it stops. You have to think of other people. You want to dance again, Beth?"

"Why not?"

"Most of them will be going home soon to catch the last Tubes. Did you bring your little car?"

"My Austin Seven is parked in the street at the back. Should be safe. How many others have cars?"

"Not many. Your brother Dorian is leaving with Mandy. The beer barrel is empty. The whisky bottles are empty. Just fruit left in the punch bowl. People go home when the booze runs out. You'll see."

"Are people that obvious?"

"No one will care when they're drunk."

"How's your French girl?"

"She's American... You know my mistake? I didn't go to bed with her when she gave me the first and only opportunity. You just can't win with women. Treat them like a lady with a little respect and they think something's wrong with you. She wants to be an artist."

"You want to play jazz."

"But not for a living. You have to have money to get through life. Romantic dreams are all very well up to a point. Someone has to work to make the money to pay the bills. Half the artists Frank invited tonight are spongers. Too lazy to get a proper job. The art bit's a façade to give them something to show for their lives. Something to talk about and sound interesting. None of them are serious. Jeanne likes the bohemian way of life of an artist. Don't we all? When they get back to Chelsea someone will be having another party. They drift around."

"Aren't you being cynical?"

"Probably. I'm sorry... There goes Jeremy with my pound note. Oh well. That was what it was all about."

"What was it all about, Paul?"

"Getting my brother laid before he went back to Rhodesia. Livy latched onto him like a limpet. She's one of the artists. Probably thinks Jeremy's a rich farmer with a big estate in Africa. Silly girl. Jeremy says it will take him ten to twenty years to establish his own farm. He'll have to cut it out of the virgin bush. Put in roads. Dams. Build a house. Put up curing barns. Grading sheds. Workshops. You name it. He's hard working, my brother. I just hope Rhodesia lasts long enough for him to enjoy what he's going to build. I'd hate to see him put in all that hard work for nothing. There's a swell of African nationalism building up across Africa when you look below the surface. Can't blame them."

"Better than painting pictures that never get sold. Let's dance. I'm tired of other people's problems. No matter how hard you try, you can't do anything for them. People have to work out their own lives. Often, when you interfere in what you think is their best interest, it backfires. You don't help and if it's bad enough you lose a friend. I just try and listen. Tell them what they want to hear. What else can you do?"

"What are you talking about, Beth?"

"Nancy. She's pregnant. She's over four months pregnant and right now will be sitting on her own in the flat contemplating an abortion which at five months is dangerous. She went home on her own when we were dancing. And no. Don't ask who is the father. It's far too complicated... You're right. People are starting to leave. Did you know there's a drunk asleep on your bedroom floor?"

"A man or a girl?"

"I think it's a man. Long hair. Face like an angel."

"Someone will pick him up and take him home. The artists look after each other. They're a tight community. Not a bad life while it lasts."

They danced quietly before Beth asked the question uppermost in her mind.

"Do you love her, Paul?"

"Probably not. We always want most what we can't have."

"Why don't you take me out to dinner?"

"Bit late tonight."

"Be serious. I'm serious."

"I work for your father. He wouldn't approve. Never mix business with pleasure. I've heard your father say that more than once... Now look at them. Like a stampede. Funny how at bottle parties where we contribute our own bottles no one says goodbye to the host. Oh well. It was all for Jeremy. All night I've been wiping the top of the piano to stop the wet glasses leaving marks on the woodwork."

"It's a lovely piano. You've changed the subject. We can go Dutch. Then you won't have to tell my father we went on a date... I'd better go with the rest of them."

"Why don't you stay? You've got a car. We can make some tea and I'll play the piano."

"The place is going to be a mess."

"It always is at the end of a party."

"I'd love some tea. What happened to Frank?"

"He went home early. To Connie."

THE SLEET HAD TURNED to snow when the taxi reached Chelsea. Jeremy had never before been invited up to a girl's flat.

"It's number twenty-seven," said Livy, jumping first out of the taxi. "I'll run upstairs while you pay the taxi man."

"Do you really want me to come up, Livy?"

"Of course I do, silly. I want to turn the lamp on in the lounge and not flood the place with overhead light when you come in. Much more romantic. Number twenty-seven. Don't be long."

Watching Livy go into the building, her overcoat flecked with flakes of snow, Jeremy wondered what would happen to him in the middle of the night when he paid off the taxi and she wouldn't answer her door. He had little idea where he was. All the drink had fuddled his brain.

"Six shillings, guv. Don't keep the lady waiting."

"You think I should go up?"

"Tell you what, cock, I'll wait five minutes."

"Will you? Oh that's good of you. I don't know London. Come from a party."

"Dropped a fare from Drury Lane in Hammersmith. You's tonight's bonus, so to speak. Get on with it."

With the change from Paul's pound note in his pocket, Jeremy walked into the building. There was no one to ask how to find flat twenty-seven. The ground-floor corridor had numbers that started with one. In the middle of the corridor was a flight of stairs with an arrow to the floors above. Jeremy climbed the stairs. At the second-floor landing Livy was waiting. Down the dark corridor a door was open, dim light spilling into the night.

"Come on, Jeremy. It's cold. Why's the taxi waiting?"

"I wasn't sure."

"Come on, silly. I found the bottle of sherry and turned on the gas fire."

"I've never done this before."

Inside with the front door closed there was one standard lamp on in the lounge. The couch had been pulled out into a bed. In the bay window stood two easels. Over one was draped a length of black silk cloth. The top of the other was empty, its painting propped against the forked foot of the easel. A ginger cat was making itself comfortable in front of the gas fire.

"Let me take your coat?"

Without his coat and for something to do, Jeremy stroked the cat. The cat purred. Livy game him a glass of sherry.

"Let's sit on the bed."

"What's hidden behind the black cloth on that easel?"

"My new painting. I never let anyone see what I'm doing until it's finished. Isn't this cosy? We've got the flat all to ourselves. I hope you're not hungry as there isn't any food. Domestically, we're terrible. There's half a bottle of sherry to get us in the mood."

"I've had too much to drink already, Livy. I drank too much at the party."

"What are you doing?"

Jeremy had walked over to look out of the window into the street. "Seeing if he waited."

"Come and sit down with me on the bed."

"Do you have any music?"

"We don't need any music."

"What are you doing?"

"Taking off my clothes. Have you ever seen a girl in her panties before, Jeremy? I never wear a bra. You can take off your trousers before you sit on the bed. Then they won't crease when we get into bed. It's nice and warm under the blankets."

Jeremy, his eyes transfixed, watched Livy take off the rest of her clothes. When he got into bed she pulled him close to her. She put her hand inside his underpants and then got on top of him. She was very wet. When she put him inside of her it all happened at once. Beside the bed he knocked over his glass of sherry.

They lay back in the dim light. The cat had taken no notice.

"In half an hour we'll do it again, Jeremy. Was that nice for you?"

"It was wonderful."

"Good. Come closer. My, oh, my. It's coming up again. We've got the whole night ahead of us."

"Should I turn out the light?"

"Don't you want to see me?"

"Of course I do. Oh, Livy. You're wonderful. I'll never be able to forget you when I'm back in Rhodesia."

"Why would you ever want to forget me, darling?"

"Won't Tessa walk in?"

"Not tonight. Tonight it's just you and me."

"I wish I wasn't going back."

"When you've got some money you can send me a boat ticket."

"Would you come out to Rhodesia?"

"I'd go anywhere for you. Slowly, Jeremy... That's better... Oh, that's much better."

. . .

WHEN THE LAST guest had left, Paul checked the bedroom. The drunk had gone, along with the overcoats. When Paul felt the counterpane it was damp from the coats. Someone had left a half-empty glass half under the bed. In the glass was the stub of a cigarette.

"They've wet the bed," he said through the door to Beth in the lounge.

"I know Kenneth Grahame used the hand basin in the bathroom but that's really disgusting."

"The coats, Beth. From the sleet. When they took off their coats and put them on my bed their coats were wet. I'm going to have to open the window and let in some air. They've smoked in here. The drunk's gone."

"Has it wet right through the bed?"

"I don't think so. Just the counterpane."

"You think Jeremy is staying out for the night?"

"Looks like it. Good old Livy. Strange how he'll be so far away from all this in a couple of days... How's the tea coming along?"

"I have a condition for making the tea. I want you to play me the piano."

"What about Nancy all on her own at home in the flat?"

"Half an hour. With luck she'll be asleep when I get back. I can deal with the crisis better in the morning. What a mess in here. Fag ends in every saucer. Even in the slop-bowl under Zach's barrel of beer."

"You throw a party and take your chances. I hope your car starts. It's damn cold outside through the open window."

"I'll have to stay the night if the old jalopy won't start. We were the only two still sober. How many sugars?"

"None. Got used to not having sugar in my tea during the war. You really want me to take you to dinner? How about Friday? I don't work this Saturday."

"Neither do I. Where are you taking me?"

"We're taking each other, don't forget... So that was another Saturday night," said Paul, walking back into the lounge. "It's nice on our own. Kind of peaceful after all the noise and people. What kind of music do you want?"

"Gershwin. I love Gershwin at this time of night... Paul, this is just so nice. The two of us. No one else to think about. I wish I could play the piano. Could you teach me?"

"You have to start young to play properly. I'll teach you *Chopsticks.*

Come over here and sit with me on the piano stool... Wow. Good old Jeremy. The things we do for family."

"You can say that again... I'll just sit next to you while you play some Gershwin. Let all the tension run out. I can relax with you. Don't have to play a part. I hate having to play up to people... You play beautifully."

"Thank you, Beth. Without music I don't know what I would do in life. It speaks to me of everything that isn't material."

Quietly, gently, Paul played the piano while their pot of tea on the tray began to go cold.

WHEN BETH WENT HOME, the car having started, she was smiling. She had the feeling, deep inside, her life was about to turn out right. When she got home Nancy was in her bedroom fast asleep. On the coffee table in front of the cold gas fire was a box of chocolates. Beth looked inside the debris of chocolate paper. Not even one.

"We all have our therapy, Nancy," she said happily on her way to bed. For a full five minutes she lay warming up under the blankets, thinking of Paul. When she fell asleep and dreamed, someone was playing the piano in a crowded room.

PART 7

APRIL TO MAY 1950 – DINNER FOR TWO

1

———————

It was make or break night for Jeanne Pétain's Nouvelle Galerie. Outside, the first daffodils of spring had bloomed in the wooden flower box that ran the length of the pavement in front of the shop. Flower baskets hung from the metal arms Ben Brown had screwed into the outside wall above the window. In the baskets were crocuses and snowdrops that James Coghlan had brought from the nursery in Kew Gardens. The three hundred invitations had been written out by Tessa Handson and Livy Johnston and posted the week before. The list, provided by Samuel Chalmers, included every rich art buyer in London and the Home Counties. Samuel's wine merchant had supplied the fine wines, Fortnum & Mason the array of breads and cheeses. The fake antique jewellery seller had been given a flower to put in his hat and his barrow had been moved to the edge of the pavement. Inside around the walls were the last paintings Jeanne had collected of Chelsea's bohemia, each with an individual light directed at the canvas. On the floor, on pedestals, she had placed five sculptures. Below each was a price tag beyond Jeanne's wildest expectations. The paintings, like the sculptures, were exorbitantly priced. On three of the paintings, two of them the most expensive, were small red dots on the frames, the paintings ostensibly having been sold. Between the sculptures, on tables covered in white tablecloths, was the lavish display of cheese and wines. Handpicked by Jeanne, ready to hand round the trays of fluted wine glasses filled with vintage French wines, were the prettiest girls from James Coghlan's arty parties. By six o'clock, the time the exhibition was due to open, Jeanne and Ben were ready to welcome the guests. By seven o'clock not a soul had opened the door to the gallery.

"I'm going to have a drink," said Jeanne, her nerves making her small hands clammy. "Where's Samuel? At least Samuel could have come."

"The exhibition is open all evening," said James, handing Jeanne a glass of white wine. "Said so on the invitations you all wrote out so carefully. Be patient. The gallery looks beautiful. My sculpture is magnificent."

"If they come they won't buy at these prices, James."

"Samuel was right. The rich only appreciate sky-high prices for art. Otherwise they have no means of judging its value. They have no idea what is good or bad art, only what it's worth. The most expensive pieces will go first. Do I look all right?"

"The very picture of a Chelsea artist."

"Good," said James, preening himself. "Let's enjoy our glass of wine. Calm you all down. The trick is to always look confident. To make the rich feel we artists are doing them a favour by inviting them into our world. You have to sell everything, my little Jeanne. Even art. Even love. A rich man likes to feel his money has bought him something. A beautiful woman. A beautiful painting. They all like to feel important. A fool and his money are easily parted. You'll see tonight. They'll come. All their friends have been invited. Can't do to miss something so important. Have these red-dotted paintings been sold?"

"Not one of them. Samuel's idea."

"How is Samuel?"

"He's still on the hook, if that's what you mean. Won't be if tonight turns out a fiasco. I suppose then I'll have to sleep with him."

"The things we have to do for art... Everyone, lift your glass to the gods. I give you a toast. To the Nouvelle Galerie, to our little Jeanne."

BARNABY ST CLAIR, not a man with the slightest interest in the arts but bored with his day, arrived at eight o'clock. He was impressed. Artists, mostly pretty young females, were all over the place. Handing his invitation to a girl who could not be more than five feet tall, his eyes roamed the gallery looking at the talent. Smiling at his luck, Barnaby put his hand out to take a glass of wine from the tray offered to him by one of the girls, his boredom gone. The small girl reading his invitation smiled up at him.

"Welcome, Mr St Clair. You wouldn't by any chance be a relation of Mr Harry Brigandshaw of Hastings Court? He mentioned a brother-in-law by the name of Barnaby St Clair."

"Is he here?"

"He's not very well, I understand. I worked for him for a while. Buying antiques which we shipped to America. You must know Mr Chalmers?"

Giving her a smile but no answer, his mind on the rest of the room, Barnaby walked forward taking a piece of cheese off a plate from the table as he went. Two of the elderly men in the room he knew but chose to ignore. Businessmen with too much money bored him. Taking note Harry was not well, he reminded himself to give him a ring. Vaguely, as was expected from him at an art exhibition, Barnaby wandered around looking at the paintings on the walls, sipping his wine and munching his cheese. One of the paintings caught his eye due to its incongruity. A ginger cat, much like the one he had at home that slept on the windowsill most of the day with its eyes open, stared at him out of a tropical forest. On a whim, Barnaby raised his finger to a man with a beard and hair down to his shoulders.

"I'll take that one, young man. Send it to the address on my card. My man Smithers will give you a cheque... The painting doesn't have a name."

"All great art finds its name later, Mr St Clair," said James Coghlan.

"I'll try and remember that. Which one is the artist?"

To Barnaby's surprise, the man pointed out one of the young girls who had caught his eye when he entered the room. Barnaby walked across.

"Are you Livy Johnston? I've just bought your painting. Maybe when it's delivered to my house you'd like to be the one to accept my cheque? Made out to the gallery, of course. They have to get their commission. Why is that cat painted in a tropical forest?"

"I'm going to Africa next week. To be married, I hope. I want to be a wildlife painter."

"Well, that cat looks like mine. I wish you luck in Africa."

Losing interest in a girl about to go to Africa, Barnaby became annoyed with his impulsive purchase. He was bored. When he was bored he did silly things he always regretted afterwards. Having lost his appetite for wine and cheese, Barnaby made for the door. As he reached it a young man came in with a middle-aged woman on his arm. When the man stared at him it was like looking at himself in the mirror.

"Don't I know you?" said Barnaby.

"Not as well as you should."

The man brushed past him holding firmly to the woman's arm. Only when the man was inside the gallery, Barnaby left holding the door looking back at him, did he realise who it was.

"I'll be buggered if that wasn't Frank."

With a smirk on his face, Barnaby walked out into the street to hail a taxi.

"Want some jewellery for your missus, guv?" said the street seller. "Best antiques."

"Piss off. Why are you wearing a flower in your hat?"

"It's spring, guv. How about this one? Only a couple of quid."

"All right. What is it?"

"Georgian."

"Georgian my ass. Here's a quid."

"Thanks, guv."

"Good position you've got out here on the pavement. Taxi! Taxi!"

With the piece of worthless jewellery in his pocket, Barnaby got into the cab.

"What a night. You know a good bar, cabbie?"

"Plenty."

When Barnaby looked back at the gallery, his son Frank was standing outside on the pavement looking after him down the street.

FEELING SECURE IN HIS BUSINESS, Frank had left Connie with a glass of wine and gone to look for his father. By the time he got outside, a taxi had pulled up to the kerb. His father was opening the door and getting inside with his back to Frank. Only when the taxi pulled away did his father turn round and see him by the light of the doorway. Their eyes had met in a moment of understanding.

When Frank went back to find Connie she was sitting on a chair. The glass of wine was smashed next to her on the floor. Her face was contorted with pain. Forgetting all about Barnaby St Clair being driven off in the taxi, Frank ran across to her.

"What's the matter, darling? Are you all right?"

"I have a terrible pain in my side. Can you go and get the car? I need a doctor and a hospital. Do you know how to get to St Mary's?"

"What is it, Connie?"

"I'm dying, Frank. I was going away next week to join my mother in the house I bought for her in Cornwall."

"Come on. Don't talk. Can you give me directions?... Does anyone know how to get to St Mary's Hospital?" said Frank, raising his voice above the murmur of polite conversation.

"Yes," said one of the girls. "I was a nurse at St Mary's before I decided to become an artist. Is your mother all right?"

"No she's not. And she's not my mother. Can you come with us? Don't I know you?"

"You should, Frank. I'm Daisy."

"Of course. Give me a hand. Do they know you at St Mary's, Connie? This is Daisy. She's going to help. Daisy was a nurse."

"Who was the man, Frank?"

"My father. My real father. I was going to give him a piece of my mind. Daisy, stay with Connie while I go and get the car. Have you got anything to take?"

"I've taken a pain killer. I'm sorry, Frank."

"You're not going to Cornwall. I'll tell you that much. It was the lump, wasn't it? I'll be five minutes at the most."

"Don't make a fuss. I was so looking forward to seeing your friends' exhibition. I'm sorry about the glass on the floor."

Frank, unable to think straight, his eyes misting, pain racking his body, ran out of the gallery to fetch the car. His Connie was dying. Connie had said she was dying.

THE SECOND PAINTING sold at half-past eight for six hundred pounds. The third for nine hundred five minutes later. The photographer from *Tatler* magazine had arrived, tipped off by Frank Brigandshaw the previous day that big names in business were buying the paintings of up-and-coming artists for headspinning prices. Samuel Chalmers had arrived with four of his friends. The photographer took pictures of each benefactor standing with the artist in front of the painting with its newly placed red dot sticker on the frame. The rich buyers looked pleased with themselves, the prize of their pictures in *Tatler* worth more to them than the paintings. The gallery began to fill up. The noise level grew from a polite hum to the voluble chatter of people as Jeanne's guests drank more of the wine. She was smiling with relief.

"You're making money, Samuel," she whispered into his ear in passing, the need for sleeping with the man fast fading.

A second photographer arrived from the *Daily Mail* looking for Frank Brigandshaw. Jeanne's agreement to give Frank ten per cent of the night's sales was paying off. The agreement had been signed earlier in the week in the offices of Frank Brigandshaw and Partners.

"I only get paid when I deliver, Jeanne. I put my money where my mouth is. Too many people in public relations make promises they never keep. If it doesn't work I don't get paid a penny. People want to be seen to be rich benefactors of young artists. It's a double whammy. The old fart buying the painting gets his name and face in the paper. So does our young artist, giving whoever it is recognition and establishing a benchmark price for their painting. It's much easier to sell an artist's second painting when the first has sold for a good price. We play to the old farts' egos. They all want to be famous. I've asked Horatio Wakefield to send along a photographer from the *Mail*. Two of the social magazines will be there. With Samuel's list of potential buyers and the media stroking their feathers you're going to have a night to remember. Oh, and I hope you don't mind. I've invited Paul Crookshank. He's going out with my sister. Beth's rather keen on him. Can you do me a favour? The rumour has it you and Paul were an item back in New York. Try not to smile at him. Give him the impression you and Ben are in bed with each other."

"But we are... Every now and again."

"Good girl. I'm bringing Connie. You'll like Connie. A lot of the things I do in business are Connie's ideas. Experience. Experience in life is everything."

With so much going on, Jeanne had not seen Connie drop her wine glass. Or go off with Frank and Daisy. They had been introduced briefly at the door before Frank chased off after the Honourable Barnaby St Clair.

"Where's Frank?" Jeanne asked James who had closed the sales on all three paintings.

"His woman wasn't feeling well. Daisy went with them to the hospital... Isn't it all so wonderful? Got to go. That chap looks interested in my sculpture."

"Is it serious?"

"I have no idea... Here she comes. Why don't you ask Daisy? I can see her outside through the window getting out of a taxi."

LIVY STOOD next to the painting of her pussy cat, her mind in a turmoil, as the man took her photograph. Everything had compounded in a matter of minutes.

"Hello, I'm Walter Featherstone-Wallace of the *Tatler*. James has told me your painting has been sold to the Honourable Barnaby St Clair, son of the seventeenth Baron St Clair of Purbeck and brother of the eighteenth Lord St Clair. My word. What a story for my magazine. Will you stand next to your painting with that nice red sticker for a photograph? I'd have asked Mr St Clair to stand on the other side but James said he left after buying your painting. What a wonderful painting. Worth every penny of the four hundred pounds. Now, do you prefer me to write of you as Livy or Olivia? Olivia has more snob appeal I should think. Now let's see. A little to the right, Olivia. Look at your painting please. That's it. You'll be in next month's edition of *Tatler*. Did you know the St Clairs are one of England's oldest titled families? They came over from Normandy with William the Conqueror. Just what our readers want to read. A beautiful young artist, if you don't mind me saying, selling her painting to the British aristocracy. They have a country seat in Dorset. Been there for centuries. One of the brothers is a famous novelist. *Keeper of the Legend* and *Holy Knight* tell the St Clair story. Made today's family famous... The first of the St Clairs built Corfe Castle before Oliver Cromwell knocked it down after winning the Civil War. Roundheads and Cavaliers. What a piece I'm going to write. You've a good chance of your painting hanging in Purbeck Manor. This is a real break for you, Olivia. Once this gets out your work is truly going to be in demand. A painting needs a history. Something for the public to catch hold of. I hope you have lots more like this to sell. What a career for a young girl... Just one more shot if you don't mind. Got to get it just right... Thank you, Olivia. That's wonderful. The place is really filling up. Why don't we drink a glass of wine together? James told me the cheeses have come from Fortnum & Mason. Divine. You're such a lucky girl. The Honourable Barnaby St Clair. Very rich. Made all his money before the stock market crash in 1929. But enough of that. What I want to hear about is you. Your plans. What are you going to do in your life now you are going to be a famous young artist? Are you married? Do you have a boyfriend?"

"No, I'm single. Free as a bird."

"How wonderful. Would you care for a glass of this very expensive French red wine from Bordeaux? Or a German hock?"

"The white please, Walter."

"You can call me Walt."

After one sip of his wine, Walt went off in pursuit of another painting James was signalling had just been sold, leaving Livy to her turmoil. Half an hour before she was about to take a boat trip out to Rhodesia to join Jeremy Crookshank in his cottage on the farm in Macheke. Now she was not so sure... Poor Jeremy. All those letters week after week to build up his desire. Now, having received the boat ticket, she was no longer sure... Four hundred pounds. Like Tessa, she was rich. A successful artist. The need to chase off to Africa to find her future was gone. Her future was right in front of her, in the Nouvelle Galerie. She had made it as an artist. She could see what she wanted without needing the help of a man... With a grin on her face similar to the one on *Pussy Cat*'s face in the painting, Livy went off to find Tessa and tell her about Walter Featherstone-Wallace, the photographer who was about to make both her and her paintings famous... Poor Jeremy. Life really did have its twists and turns. Poor man. He'd never forgive her. One minute you were going one way, the next you weren't. Life for Livy was all about opportunities. And taking them when they came along... He'd find someone else. They always did. All those children she was going to have in Rhodesia just wouldn't be born. The chance of life for everyone was just that small.

Searching the room for Tessa slowly with her eyes, Livy sipped on her wine. The German hock, as Walt had promised, was wonderful. She was going to be famous after all.

PAUL CROOKSHANK ARRIVED with the letter from Beth's father to Frank in his pocket. They were all summoned to Hastings Court on the Sunday. Kim, still on his journey through the Himalayas, was in the Kingdom of Bhutan, the only one of the children unable to attend. Beth had handed Paul the letter in the Kensington flat when he picked her up to go to the exhibition.

"He won't take it from me. You do business with him, Paul. Make him come. This is not an invitation, it's a summons. Dad would like you to be with us on Sunday. Dorian keeps office hours during the week like everyone else in London, so I'm driving him down."

"What's it all about? Never had your father demand attendance before. He always asked me if a visit was convenient. What's the matter, Beth? What's Frank done this time to make you so upset?"

"Dad will tell you himself on Sunday. Are you sure Frank is going to be at the gallery?"

"He's organised the press. Jeanne's public relations consultant. You have to invite the right people and make the best of your opportunities. He'll be there. He's bringing Connie."

"What is it with this Connie?"

"Life turns in strange ways. Let's say Connie Whitaker is the best thing to happen in Frank's recent life. If this invitation on Sunday is so important, I'll give it to Connie to give to Frank."

"Do you mind seeing Jeanne?"

"Of course not. I've learned never to fall out with people who were once important to me."

"So she isn't anymore?"

"No, Beth. There's you and me. That's all that matters now. If tonight is a success for Jeanne, the last chance of her being near my life is over. She won't want work from us buying antiques. Or selling them if she is forced by lack of money to go back to America."

When they pushed open the door, Paul having bought a fake piece of antique jewellery for Beth from a man sporting a flower in his hat, the first person he saw was Jeanne.

"This is nice, Paul. Tonight is very special for me. Make or break, so to speak. Hello, Beth. Nice to see you two together. Grab a glass of wine. We've sold three paintings so far tonight."

"Where's Frank? I don't see him."

"Something's wrong with the woman he came with. She dropped her glass on the floor after Frank went outside looking for someone. Ask Daisy. She went with them in Frank's car to the hospital. Daisy, you remember Paul?"

"Is Frank coming back?" asked Paul.

"I hope not," said Daisy.

"Is there something wrong with Connie?"

"I left them at the hospital and caught a taxi."

Daisy, pushing her way through, picked a glass of wine off the table and drank it down.

"What was all that about?" asked Beth.

"I'll go and see Frank tomorrow in his office to give him the letter... Just look at these prices! Well, I can't afford one, despite my bonus this year. Let's go and get ourselves some wine. The place is filling up. I'll give it to you, Jeanne. When you do something, you do it properly."

Walking further into the gallery, Paul stopped in front of a table laden with food and picked himself a piece of cheese which he put in his mouth before handing Beth a glass of wine. Then he waved at Zachariah Cohen and Brian Tobin across the room before starting a tour of the paintings, happy his friends in Chelsea were having a successful evening.

"It's always so difficult to make a living out of art," he said. "The red dots tell you the painting's been sold. Let's go across and talk to Tessa and Livy. They will know what's happened to Frank, and Connie."

BEN BROWN, never one to count money, picked up a bottle of wine and two glasses and went outside where the spring night was surprisingly warm. Next to the barrow with the fake antique jewellery Stan kept a fire going in a bucket punched with holes. After all the people inside trying to impress, Stan was a breath of fresh air. Often since the gallery opened Ben had made his pitch outside on the pavement next to Stan, as much for someone to talk to as to attract customers for his sketches.

"They're too full of themselves in there, Stan. How can anyone throw so much money around... You done any good? Want a glass of wine? You and I could live for a month on the price of this bottle of wine. All snob value. They sniff the bloody wine and look all knowledgeable. As if the bloody smell makes any difference. You get drunk on wine. That's what it's for... My taste's a pint of bitter... Never look a gift horse in the mouth. There are so many bottles open on the table they won't notice this one. Why are people such frauds?"

"You're asking the wrong person there, old cock. Stan the antiques jewellery seller my foot. All this stuff's made in Hong Kong... Rather partial to a glass of wine. More kick than beer. Now, a good scotch, that's my tipple when I got money like tonight. Two good sales I done. More to come. Come and stand round the fire. You like the flower in my hat, Ben? Tells them it's all about spring. The patter, you see. Got to have the patter... Thanks, cock. To your health, not your wealth unless you're giving it to me... How you lot doing inside?"

"Working like a charm. Fleecing the rich. Jeanne's got it just right. Before she tried painting to make a living Jeanne was in business in New York. Don't know how she's done it tonight. To me it's plain stealing."

"Isn't it all, Ben? How money goes round. Everyone in business stealing from everyone else. But it's fun. I get a kick out of selling for a quid what cost me sixpence... Tell me, Ben, what makes you artists grow hair down to your shoulders and not bother to shave?"

"Image. All part of the image. That's what they're buying inside, Stan."

"Can you get me some of that food? I'm starving."

"Hang on. Hold the bottle of wine while I go inside. Us two are going to have a party."

Behind Ben, more cars and taxis were pulling up to the gallery. Jeanne was waving at him to come inside. Free wine and food came at a price, he told himself. Turning back to Stan, who was pouring himself a second glass of wine from the bottle Ben had left in his hand, he gave a gesture that said he was wanted inside.

"You should be chatting to the clients, not drinking my wine with Stan," snapped Jeanne to Ben's surprise. "You have to work like the rest of us. You don't get anything for nothing in this world."

Realising his days of free love and free food were about to be over, Ben mentally shrugged. The money got to all of them in the end... Going across to the table, he picked up a plate of cheese. Jeanne now had her back to him. Making a dash for the door, he took it outside.

"Enjoy the cheese and the wine. Got to go inside. I have a bad feeling my days of free parties have just come to an end."

HAD she looked at Paul it would not have made any difference, Jeanne told herself, annoyed she had snapped at Ben. She had used Ben Brown every bit as much as he had used her. She had the bad habit of sleeping with the men that meant nothing to her and keeping the ones that did matter at arm's length. Looking at Paul and Beth together as they talked to Livy and Tessa, Jeanne wondered if Beth and Paul were sleeping with each other. Paul was looking at Beth the way he had once looked at her. Why hadn't Paul taken advantage of her that first night in her Brooklyn apartment like the rest of them when opportunity knocked at their door?

Surprised to find herself jealous of another woman, she turned to greet the next guest, covering the feeling of loss inside her with an outward smile on her face.

"I'm sorry, Ben," she said when the new people walked away to look at the paintings. "You go and have a drink with Stan. That fire of his does look inviting."

"Doesn't matter. I can always natter to Stan in the morning. I'll go and mingle. The place is getting crowded. Anyway, here comes Samuel."

When Ben walked away, to do his job by mingling with the invited guests talking about the paintings, she found herself alone with Samuel.

"You haven't gone back on your promise this time, I hope? When the exhibition is over we go back to your flat. You promised. No wheedling out of it this time."

"Of course, Samuel. It's what we agreed. Your list of friends made all this possible. Why don't you bring me a glass of wine? I can't leave the door. Three paintings sold."

"Once the word gets round, you'll have a very successful gallery. All thanks to me."

Jeanne shuddered while Samuel Chalmers walked across to the table to fetch her wine. The man was smirking. Licking his lips. Whether she liked it or not, this time there was no getting away from sleeping with the damn man. He had fulfilled his part of the bargain. Now it was her turn to pay the bill. Her mother had told her from when she was a child the most simple truth of life. 'Darling, there's no pleasure without pain. Remember that as you go through life. Sometimes we do things to get on in life. Especially you'll find that when you become a woman. You are lucky, my little Jeanne. You are going to be pretty. Pretty girls always get more than the ugly ones. We all have regrets. Regrets are part of life. It's what comes after the regret that counts. Sometimes you just have to close your eyes.' Jeanne watched Samuel return wearing the same look of lecherous ownership that made her shudder.

"Here's your wine. You looked far away. To our success, Jeanne."

"To our success, Samuel."

"I've waited a long time."

"I know you have. So have I for this. I'm sure it will all be worth it."

"I hope so. Tonight's the night... What a lot of wealthy people. What's Ben doing out in the cold?"

"Standing round the fire. He and Stan have become good friends."

"Now there's a friendship that won't do him any good."

"Oh, I don't know. They like each other. Look at them laughing."

Drinking her wine, Jeanne came to a conclusion. Like her mother said, she would just have to close her eyes.

PAUL'S last letter from his brother in Rhodesia had been all about Livy. What they were going to do with their lives together. How many children they were going to have. Jeremy had sounded so positive, Paul had wished some of the positive thinking would rub off on himself. Make his mind up... From such a short meeting, so much had come from the letters Jeremy and Livy had written to each other. All in just three months. For Jeremy, everything was just right... Livy. Rhodesia. Farming. The land he was going to own... There had not been a negative thought in Jeremy's letter telling Paul he had sent Livy the money for her boat ticket from the London docks to Beira. Jeremy wrote he had borrowed from three of his friends against the small bonus he was due when the tobacco crop went into Salisbury to be sold on the auction floors in June. Apparently, the price of tobacco was sky high which meant Ridgeback cigarettes would make a slightly lower profit than he and Harry Brigandshaw had calculated. Jeremy had given him the date of Livy's sailing, asking him to take her to the boat to make sure everything went right.

"You must be looking forward to your trip to Africa next week, Livy."

"Oh, Paul. I was going to tell you. I can't go next month. I just sold a painting. Four hundred pounds. Isn't it wonderful?"

"My word, Livy. You could have paid for your ticket by yourself with that kind of windfall. How exciting for you to have such a big nest egg to go into your marriage."

"I haven't bought the ticket yet, Paul... *Tatler* have taken my picture. Some English aristocrat has bought my painting. I'm so excited I can barely think."

"But you are going to Jeremy next week?"

"I'm sure I am. Just need some time to think. Don't you think we've rushed into everything just a little? I mean, we only knew each other a couple of days. Jeremy will understand. He's such a darling... Look, there's Walt waving at me. He took my picture. Says I'm going to be a famous artist. You two go on talking to Tessa. Back in a minute... Isn't it wonderful?"

Only then did Paul see Jeanne watching him as his brother's fiancé walked away to talk to the man called Walt. With his mind still on Jeremy he did notice Jeanne's look was the same as it had been in New York after he had not taken advantage of her the night he stayed in her flat. She was with an old man he took to be Samuel Chalmers. The proprietary look on the man's face told Paul that Jeanne Pétain was now his possession. He had his hand firmly on her elbow. If that man was her lover she was welcome to him, thought Paul, trying to look away. The man was rich. It made Paul look at Jeanne with a new understanding.

"Are you all right, Paul?" Beth asked.

"I am now... Tessa, what do you think? Is Livy going out to Rhodesia? With four hundred pounds it appears she doesn't need my brother quite so much. Who's Walt?"

"She's a butterfly. Always has been. Why we get on so well. Neither of us stay too long at anything. I thought until tonight her painting was just another phase... Will you excuse me? I'd better go and talk to Zach. They still have my paintings on the wall in Cohen Wells. He's such a darling, Zach... Oh, and there's Brian Tobin, Frank's partner coming to talk to him. Do you know Brian, Beth, from the days he went to school in Cape Town with your brother?"

"Yes. I just hope he's changed. They were school bullies in those days."

When they were left alone with their thoughts, Paul took Beth's hand.

"At least we two have each other," he said to her. "I'll go and see Frank first thing in the morning. He's not a bully anymore with Connie teaching him how to live... Why are people so fickle? She's going to dump my poor brother. Mark my words. For her, surrounded by new people, it won't matter. For Jeremy on his own it will be devastating. Maybe I should take a trip to Rhodesia when the tobacco auctions open in Salisbury? Tell Jeremy how it really was. Give him some comfort... Oh well. At least he lost his virginity. These things usually happen for the right reason. I don't think a London girl would enjoy a life isolated on some African farm. The romance is better than reality. He'd be better marrying some farmer's daughter when he has his own farm. Just lucky she didn't get pregnant, I suppose. Can we go, Beth? I've had enough of this place. Jeanne's left her post at the door to go off with Samuel. We can slip away. There's a new restaurant I want to show you. Hope you're hungry."

"Are you really going out to Rhodesia? We could go together. I know my grandmother would love to see me."

"Maybe. There's so much work for me to do in London now Ridgeback has taken off. Like everyone else, Jeremy will have to paddle his own canoe."

"We can go one way by boat to Cape Town and fly from Cape Town to Salisbury. An official honeymoon."

"Goodness me, Beth! Are you proposing to me?"

"What would you say?"

"I'd have to ask your father first."

"You can ask him on Sunday."

"Now there's an idea... Are you serious?"

"Never more serious in my life. I want kids, Paul. Looking at Nancy has made me broody. Like Nancy I'm twenty-five. Nice age to have kids."

"What's Dorian going to do about Nancy?"

"I have no idea. Why don't you ask him on Sunday."

"What with Frank and now Dorian... Aren't you passing the buck?"

"I can't force either of them to do anything. They're my brothers. You can ask them a question and walk away."

"Not if I'm their brother-in-law."

"Wait until Sunday. Dad may refuse you my hand in marriage. Think you're after the boss's daughter."

"Oh, Beth. Will he think that?" said Paul, feigning shock.

"I hope not... Don't look like that. Don't be daft. You're right, I'm hungry. Let's go find that restaurant."

FOUR MORE PAINTINGS sold in quick succession, distracting Jeanne from Paul's early departure. Samuel was delighted, more interested in looking at her than the cheques. Only Livy's painting had not been accompanied by a cheque. Just a calling card where the painting was to be delivered in Piccadilly against a four-hundred-pound cheque.

The photographers from the *Tatler* and *Daily Mail* were having a field day leaving Livy looking around for the next person to tell she had sold a painting. Within a minute of Walter Featherstone-Wallace leaving her side a man in his sixties, old enough to be Livy's grandfather, was chatting her up, Livy all smiles. Being successful was contagious, it seemed to Jeanne.

Samuel couldn't keep the grin off his face, making Jeanne feel sick inside and causing her to have a mind flash of her apartment in Brooklyn where she was still paying the rent. Another of her mother's little homilies came to mind as Samuel stroked her bare arm: 'Never burn your boats, darling. Always have a bolt bole. Always have a little money away from everything where no one else can see it. Even when you are married!' Pulling away from Samuel to take a cheque from Ben – selling his first painting had left an expression of relief on his face – she whispered in Ben's ear. The touch of Samuel's hand on her bare arm had given her the creeps.

"I'm about to do a Connie and pass out on the floor."

"Is there something wrong with you, Jeanne?" whispered Ben in alarm.

"Of course not. The old goat wants its oats."

"Oh, dear. Crunch time. I'll stay close to you."

"Paintings, Ben. Sell another painting. How did you do that?"

"A trick I just learned from Stan. Said three people were already after the painting while the poor man was trying to work out just what he was looking at. Told him the artist was famous. That modern art was going to be worth a fortune once Britain was back on its feet."

"Samuel! Please. I'm talking to Ben. This is business."

"Are you sure?"

"Of course I am. What do you mean?"

"I don't want Ben coming back with us just because he lives next door."

"Sorry, got to go... James has sold another one."

"You won't go back on your word?"

"Stop begging, Samuel. It doesn't become you."

"Does Ben know about our bargain?"

"I have no idea. Why don't you ask Ben while I talk to James? One of these days in the not too distant future our James, long hair, beard and all, is going to be a rich man. Just be nice to everyone, Samuel."

Giving him a wet kiss on the mouth to concentrate his mind, Jeanne walked away to talk to James. With her back to Samuel she wiped the taste from her mouth with the back of her hand. By hook or by crook, she promised herself, she was going to have her cake and eat it. A besotted man, kept on the hook, rarely threw away the chance, however small, of getting her into the sack. Looking at her watch, Jeanne decided to have her fainting fit just before ten... The man was turning her stomach. Even with her eyes closed he might make her vomit. The last look of contempt from Paul had made her see what she was about to do to herself. If the worst came to the worst she could always go back to

America. She would never be able to afford to live the life of an artist in New York. The old life would be frustrating, art losing out to money. But sacrificing her pride to a Samuel Chalmers was suddenly just out of the question.

BORED WITH LISTENING to uninteresting old men trying to look down her blouse, Livy drifted across to talk to Brian Tobin and Zachariah Cohen.

"I sold one, Zach."

"Good for you. Why wasn't the cat in an English garden?"

"All the tropical foliage made the painting more interesting."

"You remember, Brian? Works with Frank."

"Of course. How are you, Brian?"

"Heard you're going out to Rhodesia to be a tobacco farmer's wife? Brave girl. Tried working for my father on the cattle ranch outside Bulawayo. Nearly drove me nuts. What little social life was with the same old people. No young people except for kids. They say the only crop that never fails in Rhodesia is the children. They have black nannies to look after the kids of course. In the tobacco-growing areas of Mashonaland where you're going the men talk tobacco, the women babies and servants. You want to tear your hair out. Nothing but trivia all day long. On their own they read books and drink. Not good books. Mills & Boon. Trivial love stories of perfect men in perfect marriages. Takes their minds off reality."

"Are you trying to put me off, Brian?" said Livy, getting her back up: there was something about Brian she didn't like.

"Just warning you, Livy. The grass is never greener on the other side of the fence, if you'll excuse my cliché. Luckily Frank wrote and offered me a job in public relations here in London. We were at school together in Cape Town. If you can amuse yourself ninety-five per cent of the time it's a life full of sunshine. Lots and lots of sunshine. Jeremy will be out in the lands during the day. They have their lunch and breakfast taken out to them in the fields. Too far to come back to the house. He'll be dog tired when he comes in. Sundowners on the stoep, supper and straight to bed exhausted by working in the sun all day. Monday to Saturday. Sunday you'll go to the club. Hope you play tennis. More sundowners and a *braai*, that's a barbeque, with the other farmers and their wives. You'll have plenty of time to paint, Livy. All day long. With all the servants you won't have to raise a finger in the house. Once a year you'll take the kids to Beira for a holiday by the sea. Indian Ocean. Not bad. Mozambique is very colonial. Good Portuguese food for a change. Then back to the farm for another year of making a baby. Ask my mother. She'll tell you. All Mum does now is drink. On her own. No one else to drink with until Dad comes back from riding the ranch. On a motorcycle. Don't use horses anymore. I rode round and round the bloody bush checking on the cows. Day after day. The only part of a cow I ever want to see again is a piece of steak on my plate... You're a brave girl, Livy. You'll probably be rich, have a beautiful house and a swimming pool, and go out of your mind."

"Leave her alone, Brian," said Zach. "The girl's going to get married. She's in love with Jeremy. Love transcends all, don't you know that?"

"Sorry to pour cold water. I'm just so glad to be back in London. You have no idea. If I never see the African bush again in my life I'll be happy."

"London can be boring if you don't have money," said Livy, Brian's picture of Africa compounding the problems in her mind.

"You've got a bit now. Enjoy it... Why is everything so always about money? How long did you know Jeremy when he was in England?"

"Two days. We've written a lot of letters to each other since."

"I'll bet you did... Can I get you another glass of wine? What an exhibition. Never seen so many people in an art gallery before. Jeanne Pétain must be proud of herself. We only helped with the press. Did Walt get a good photograph of you and the painting? I can always have a word with him if he didn't do enough. Good pictures are so important."

"He took quite enough shots, thank you. No, I've had enough wine... Will you both excuse me?"

BEN, mildly amused at the oldest trick in the world when a woman wanted to get out of something, caught up with Livy as she walked away from Brian Tobin.

"She's going to faint, Livy. Jeanne. She's reached the point of no return with dirty Samuel. He's positively drooling with lustful expectation, the perfect picture of a dirty old man."

"She wouldn't do it."

"A deal's a deal. When she passes out we must all rush over to help. Keep an eye on her. Why are you suddenly so glum? Four hundred quid less the gallery's forty per cent isn't to be sneezed at."

"Brian. He's a pig. Likes to knock everything down. I had a nice idea in my mind of a life in Rhodesia. Should I go, Ben? I said I would. How can I get out of it? I mean, I'm now a real artist."

"Follow your heart. Better to say no now than make both of you miserable. It was fun while it lasted. For both of you. I wasn't going to interfere but Africa is a long way from your life here... Do you think if I sock him in the gob, he'd call the police? He's the kind that would. The very look of him leering at Jeanne makes me clench my fist. Now she's in it deep. I can't imagine what will happen to the Nouvelle Galerie and all of our money if Samuel pulls out. They talk about a woman scorned. Wait till you see what a rich man can do."

"A woman can always say no."

"Not if she wants the Nouvelle Galerie to go on making money. Blokes like that can turn off the tap as easy as they turn it on. Don't like being crossed, ruthless bastards. How most of his lot made their money in the first place, being ruthless. You don't make their kind of money without hurting people."

"Fainting may help tonight. Not tomorrow. Poor Jeanne. She wanted this life so much. If Samuel closes the gallery it'll affect all of us. James looks as pleased as punch. I think he's just sold his own sculpture."

"Why don't you throw yourself at Samuel? Save the day, Livy... I'm only kidding."

"He's only got eyes for Jeanne, thank goodness. We all have our dreams."

"Are you going out to Rhodesia?"

"I've told Paul I haven't bought the boat ticket. Next thing I know he'll tell Jeremy."

"Make up your mind... Tell James she's going to faint. They're beginning to drift away. The party's almost over."

"Can't we run it on our own without Samuel?"

"Who knows?"

"Frank will help. We still have the list of clients. Can he run around telling people she reneged on a deal? He's a married man. If we all stick together we can help... Look, you're right. He's sold it. What's it meant to be this time?

"What a night. Without Jeanne none of this could have happened. I'd better warn James and the others. What Jeanne does affects all of us."

. . .

WHEN JAMES COGHLAN joined Jeanne just before closing he wasn't smiling, despite having sold *One Finger to Heaven*, his sculpture of a six-foot metal finger pointing at the sky. Samuel had gone off to get his car.

"Don't do it, Jeanne. You talked all of us into this. We've all worked hard. Don't let the side down. Ben and Livy are worried they'll never sell another painting if the Nouvelle Galerie closes down. I know Samuel. I introduced him to you don't forget. There's always a price to pay for everything. If you pull out now we'll all lose out. These are your friends. Ever since he bought your painting of *Man on a Barge* it was you he was after. Indulge him. What's a bit of bad sex to help your friends? You want to be the artist. Through history artists have had to have rich sponsors. Mozart. Van Gogh."

"Mozart didn't have to sleep with the King of Bavaria, or whoever it was. And Van Gogh got a pittance from his brother. He wants me to be his mistress. One night in the hay won't satisfy Samuel."

"Why take it this far if you didn't intend carrying through with it? It's not fair on the rest of us. Kid him along, Jeanne. Grin and bear it. Think of England."

"I'm American."

"Of course you are."

"He just touched me on the arm. Made my skin crawl."

"A bit late now. Anyway, trying a faint on the floor won't help. The rest of us will just laugh."

"Will you, James?"

"They all know. You told Ben. Ben told Livy. Made us all giggle."

"So you won't help me?"

"How can we? You got us all into this. You can't pull out now. Everyone through life has to prostitute themselves to get what they want every now and again. Life is all about winning. To win we tell white lies and cheat when it suits us. Didn't you sometimes cheat at school when it was really necessary? Tell your parents lies? Tell a man you have your period just because you don't want to sleep with him but enjoyed the dinner he just paid for?"

"I've done that to Samuel a couple of times. He's been keeping a diary of my cycle, so he says. Won't work again."

"Neither will passing out on the floor. You'll have to come round again. Do what you promised. For all of us artists."

"Are we real artists, James?"

"They paid real money for us tonight. That's all that counts. They think we are artists. A lot of life is a confidence trick. Making something out to be what it isn't... He's coming back, Jeanne. I can see him parking his car right outside. Don't let us down. Don't let down your friends. What's sex if in return you get all this? When you've nailed it all down you'll be able to move away from Samuel... He isn't that bad."

"You don't have to sleep with him."

"Then do it for America... Or France... Or your friends. We all have such a good time together. Ben won't mind. I asked him."

"That really makes me happy," said Jeanne, sarcastically.

"It's the oldest dilemma in history. Sensible women marry the man with the money... Smile, Jeanne... To be or not to be."

"You really can mangle your Shakespeare. I don't think Hamlet had the problem of turning himself into a prostitute. Even a male prostitute."

"Then try. One more into the breach, dear friends! Henry the Fifth."

"James, you're incorrigible."

"Just trying to help. Here he comes through the door."

FEELING the pangs of carnal jealousy, Ben Brown watched Jeanne get in the car. She had given him the key to lock the door when everyone had gone. There was a look of resignation on her face. With James watching her closely, she had not tried her trick of passing out on the floor. When the car drove off there was nothing he could do other than wait for everyone to go before locking the door to the gallery. Neither Livy nor James were smiling when they left. Stan had gone, along with his barrow, pushed down the street to a lock-up garage where most of the vendors kept their goods. The top folded down on the barrow and safely locked up the fake jewellery. Most evenings on his way home to Chelsea at the end of the day's trading, Ben helped Stan push his barrow.

Slightly disillusioned, despite having sold one of the paintings and earning himself a fiver in commission, Ben looked at his watch. He saw there was time for a pint so he went to the pub down the road, calculating the time of the last Tube train back to Chelsea. The coals in Stan's bucket fire had died down to a soft red glow when Ben looked back at the darkened gallery.

When the train doors opened and let him out at Chelsea, two pints of beer later, Samuel's car was parked in the street. Hunching his shoulders, Ben went inside the building he shared with Jeanne and the others. All of them had self-contained apartments. Ben's was one room with a gas ring to cook on and boil a kettle for his tea.

Inside his room Ben could hear them talking next door. They were having an argument. Ben heard a noise through the wall that sounded like a flat hand slapping a face. Immediately afterwards came a dull thump, followed by a thud of someone hitting the floor. Only then did he hear Jeanne scream. She was still yelling when Ben got to her door and pushed it open. Jeanne had not properly closed the door. Samuel was standing over the small figure of Jeanne. Her dress was open, her panties down to her knees. Samuel turned to look at Ben with a look of surprise on his face that turned to annoyance.

"Bugger off, Ben. She can't have it both ways."

Ben hit him hard straight in the face, knocking Samuel over the top of Jeanne and into the wall. Samuel looked up at him and said nothing, getting to his feet. Jeanne was crying on the floor.

"I'm going to call the police," said Ben.

"You wouldn't dare."

"If you so much as threaten Jeanne or the Nouvelle Galerie I'll have Frank Brigandshaw put this in every London paper after I go to the cops... Did he rape you, Jeanne?"

"Not yet."

"Then here's the thank you for helping Jeanne, Mr Chalmers. Leave everything at the gallery as it is and don't come back. From tonight's sales we have enough money to pay back your loan."

"She's a cock teaser."

"Probably. And you're an old fool who should know better. Go home to your wife, Samuel."

"All right. You promise you won't say anything to anyone?"

"The bastard hit me in the face," said Jeanne, recovering from her tears, a glimmer of hope registering behind her eyes as she looked at Ben.

"You two are even, I'd say," said Ben. "Let's leave it at that. Getting even for a punch in the face won't help anyone. He didn't rape you. Your face is going to be sore for a few days but it will get better."

"You've broken one of my teeth."

"Good. I've also cut open my right fist. When you're out of here, Samuel, I'm going to scrub my knuckles with Dettol to clean out your shit."

Watching Samuel get on his knees and use the sofa to pull himself up on his feet, Ben waited, the blood dripping from the gash in his hand.

When Samuel left, Ben closed the door and turned the key in the lock. Then he went to the window and watched Samuel down below in the street get into his car.

"Are you okay, Jeanne?" Jeanne was still sitting on the floor.

"No I'm not... You're pouring blood all over my carpet."

Jeanne was now shaking from shock. Blood and all, Ben wrapped his arm round the girl by kneeling down on the floor. Only then did they laugh.

"You couldn't have planned it better," said Ben, feeling Jeanne's shivers.

"No, Ben. That one I didn't plan... He'd had a lot of wine to drink..."

"Have you got enough money to pay him back?"

"I hope so. Let me have a look at your hand."

"It's your face I'm worried about. You won't be going outside the flat for a day or two. By tomorrow, your face is going to turn black and blue."

"Thank God you came home."

"Where else was I going to go?"

"Hold me, Ben."

2

———————

When Paul Crookshank walked into Frank Brigandshaw's office the next day at eleven o'clock, Frank looked terrible. Katherine had made the appointment with Milly, receptionist to receptionist. Paul gave Frank the letter from Harry Brigandshaw and sat down. When he looked up, the letter was still on the blotter, unopened.

"She's dying, Paul. My Connie is dying. They found a lump in her breast that should have been looked at a year ago. The cancer has spread right through her body. When we got to St Mary's last night they gave her morphine. Put her in a private room. Just as well she has Frederick's money... Why didn't she tell me? They've been treating her at St Mary's for weeks as an outpatient. What am I going to do without her?"

"Can't they do anything?"

"I spoke to the doctor. There's nothing they can do at this stage of the cancer. They've put an extra bed in Connie's room for me. They think I'm her son. When I say I'm her lover they smile at me. I don't know which way to turn. There's so much work here. Brian won't be up to speed for some time. At present he isn't very good with people... How did it go for Jeanne last night? I couldn't come back. Couldn't leave Connie. This morning they had to drug her up to the eyeballs against the pain. Didn't know I was still in the room. Haven't slept a wink all night. I must look terrible. No time to change before my eight o'clock this morning with Ralph Ripley. God knows what he must have thought of me. What's wrong with the Ridgeback campaign today, Paul? Shouldn't say it to a client but I'm not focusing."

"I came to give you the letter, Frank. You'll have to open it. I'm sorry. They want to see you at Hastings Court. Something of a royal command."

"What's going on?"

"Open and read Harry's letter."

Speaking softly had caught Frank's attention. Paul watched him read the letter, putting it down on his desk and looking up at Paul with a puzzled expression.

"He's going to Rhodesia on his own," said Frank. "Not coming back. Wants to see me before he goes. Why isn't he coming back? Can't leave Connie alone in the hospital. Sorry, Paul. You'll just have to tell him I can't come on Sunday. How can I? Connie in so much pain is far more important."

"Not this time, Frank. Harry is going to Elephant Walk to die. Wants to die in Africa. Be buried on the farm next to Lucinda and their unborn child. His liver's just about packed up. You owe him this much for bringing you up. He's always accepted you as his son."

"What's going to happen to Mother?"

"She's been told to stay in England. Harry wants to do this on his own. They say his liver is down to thirty per cent of its function. Wants to see his mother and sister. Then die at home. You know he always wanted to go back and live in Rhodesia. It was your mother who insisted they stay in England. You can explain to Connie. Or if she's so doped it won't matter. Harry wants me at the meeting. You, Beth and Dorian. Kim's somewhere in Bhutan. Had a letter of introduction to the King of Bhutan. Harry's spoken to your father on the phone and told him to look after your mother when he's gone. Made Barnaby promise. It was all a mess, I suppose. Your mother has loved Barnaby St Clair all her life. All the social nonsense in England when they were young stopped your father thinking of your mother as a wife. He'll look after your mother. Harry told him he owes him that much for bringing you up. You see, they couldn't tell you when you were a child. There were too many complications for you at school. Even in Cape Town. People like to know their children are making friends with socially acceptable children. The church has to take some of the blame. They frown rather badly on adultery. Well, maybe blame is the wrong word. You see, it was for your sake no one said anything. In a few years it won't matter. England is changing its ideas on the sanctity of marriage, for good or bad. The church always wanted to protect the children. Why it frowns on divorce. I don't think the Catholics even now will marry someone who has been divorced. So saying nothing was the right thing to do… You'll be coming with us on Sunday, Frank. We're all driving down together. I'll leave Beth and Dorian and drive you straight back to Connie after you've made your peace with Harry. He's a good man. One of the few good men in the world. I'll pick you up at St Mary's Hospital at eight o'clock on Sunday morning. If Connie is able to talk to me I'll tell her why you have to go. She'll make you go, Frank. Connie is also one of those rare good people. Eight o'clock. I'm not going to take any argument this time. Last time we argued we were kids and you bloodied my nose. This time we're not going to fight. There's nothing to fight about. If you don't come with me you'll regret not coming for the rest of your life. You can't blame your mother's indiscretion on Harry Brigandshaw."

"I'll come," said Frank at length.

"Do I have your word of honour, Frank?"

"I'll be waiting downstairs in the lobby of the hospital. You don't have to burden Connie. Straight there and straight back?"

"On my honour."

"Thank you, Paul. What a mess I've made of my life. What a mess we all make of our lives."

"Yes. I'm trying not to. I'm going to ask Harry on Sunday if I can marry Beth."

"I'm glad for you both. May your lives together be fruitful and happy. I envy you, Paul. You're not so complicated as the rest of us."

"Don't you believe it. Under the bravado we're all pretty much the same. We all came down the same line of life, generation to generation. All making the same mistakes. Sunday, Frank. I hope your Connie isn't suffering too much pain."

"I'm going to miss her so much."

"She'll be in your head for the rest of your life. Don't forget that. Your luck was knowing Connie. She's changed you, Frank. For the better."

BY LUNCHTIME, when Livy Johnston called at the Brigandshaw offices in Holborn she had changed her mind three times since breakfast.

"He's gone to have lunch with the major," said Katherine. "You can sit down and wait, Miss Johnston. Mr Crookshank doesn't linger over lunch.

It's the major's birthday. The major says at seventy-two, every birthday has a little more significance. Maybe I can help you. Mr Brigandshaw and myself started this office just after the war. During the war I was his secretary at the Air Ministry after Oliver was killed in Singapore in 1941. Oliver was my husband."

"I'm so sorry... I don't think you can help. It's about his brother."

"Such a nice boy. Did you know he's going to be married?"

Livy had smiled at Katherine and sat down at reception to wait. What she wanted was someone to make up her mind. After returning from the Portobello Road to their flat in Chelsea, she and Tessa had sat up talking half the night.

"You can't change your direction after selling one painting. Anyway, you haven't yet been paid. You and James are to present the Honourable Barnaby St Clair's card with the painting to his man Smithers and hopefully pick up a cheque. Men can be just as fickle as women... Don't let Brian Tobin put you off. I can think of a lot worse ways to live than in a big house with a swimming pool permanently in the sun. The fact Jeremy will be working all day is a bonus. Who needs a husband underfoot all day long? And as for a house full of servants! Be sensible, Livy. Think of your future. You're not getting any younger. None of us are. You have to nail down the right man when you are young. A man who will provide for you and your children. The practical things in life are far more important than all the emotion. Anyway, if Jeanne isn't giving Samuel what he wants right now it will be all over... Now you see it, now you don't... Jeremy wants a wife. A wife is permanent. The life of an artist is hand to mouth. One in a thousand painters finally makes a living out of their art. Go and buy your ticket and get on the boat. Stop changing your mind. If you blow this chance, Livy Johnston, you'll never have another one as good. You've had the part of your life playing the Chelsea artist. Put it in the memory bank and go out to Rhodesia."

"Do you think a British colony in the middle of Africa can last?"

"Oh, Livy. Stop putting up obstacles. Who knows what's going to happen to any of us in life? My father said after the first war there would never be another one. Then look what happened to the poor Jews and millions of Russians. To say nothing of London being bombed night after night."

"Do you think Paul can help me make up my mind?"

"You can only ask him. Why don't you go to his office?"

"I know nothing about Jeremy."

"There you go again. Anyway, who knows anything about anybody? Everyone I know is changing their mind. My worry right now, along with James and Ben, is Jeanne. That gallery has the smack of permanency for all of us."

"That's what I'm saying. I can now make my living painting."

"Go and see Paul. See if he can talk some sense into you. I'm going to bed. We're just going round and round in the same circle."

"Will you come out to Rhodesia to visit me?"

"Of course I will. You can introduce me to a rich tobacco farmer."

"What a wonderful idea."

"Go to bed, Livy. One dream at a time."

THE CAVALRY CLUB was quieter than usual for Paul. When he asked the major why the staff were so quiet, Major Pilkington-Jones leaned across the lunch table, motioning with his hand for Paul to lean close to him.

"They found Lachlan in his chair on Monday morning when they cleaned the room. When they locked up the previous night the steward had called his name. The man got no reply and couldn't see Lachlan's bald head. The cleaning girl found him. Dead at ninety-six. Been a member of the club for seventy-eight years from when he first received his commission. No one ever recollects a longer standing member. Went to sleep in his chair and never woke up. Hope I'll be so lucky. I'd invite him to my birthday lunch. Lachlan made me feel young. That I still had a future."

"I never saw his face," said Paul. "Only heard his voice. I'm getting married to Beth. Without your help at the Contingency Insurance Company helping me buy antiques none of this would have happened. I'd still be a junior insurance clerk. Thank you, Major."

"Thank you, Paul. You've given me a new lease on life. You, Jeanne and Kenneth Grahame. Old men like the company of young people. We're the past, you're the future. Without a future there isn't much point, I suppose... I recommend the roast beef with a good claret. Now, tell me what's been happening at Brigandshaw's, here in London and New York. Poor old Lachlan. He rather liked a slice of roast beef or two with a glass of claret. Lived through the British Empire at its height. You'll see the flame of empire go out, Paul. We'll be just another small European country in your lifetime with the British Empire but a memory."

"Will it make any difference?"

"Probably not."

When Paul reached his office at a quarter past two there was a note from Livy on his desk saying she was going to the offices of the Union Castle Shipping line to buy her ticket on the *Carnarvon Castle* the next week, asking Paul to take her to Tilbury Docks and see her off to Rhodesia.

"We had a good chat while you were lunching with the major," said Katherine.

"You convinced her to go?"

"No, Paul. She convinced herself... There's a call coming through at three o'clock from America. The monthly sales figures for Ridgeback cigarettes are on your desk. They're rather good. Congratulations."

"Thank you, Katherine. Without you I'd be lost."

WITH THE ONE-WAY boat ticket in her shoulder bag, Livy walked up Oxford Street on her way to the Marble Arch tube station feeling better in herself. They had given her a berth in a two-berth cabin with a girl her own age. The girl, a Miss Lavington, was going out to be married. The man behind the counter in Union Castle had been the clerk to Miss Lavington when she had bought her ticket.

"You've left it very late. The boat sails from Tilbury on Wednesday. I can give you a single berth for one hundred and sixty pounds."

"I only have one hundred pounds for a ticket. My fiancé in his letter said that would be enough."

"Miss Lavington's friend changed her mind. Cancelled her ticket. The cancellation lets you have the last one in a double berth for one hundred pounds."

"I slept in a dormitory at school. Give me the ticket. I'll have ten pounds left to spend on the boat."

"Six weeks from London to Beira. I'm sure you'll have a wonderful trip on the *Carnarvon Castle*."

Having come down after all her excitement from the night before, Livy was certain the buyer had forgotten all about her painting, having given James his calling card on the spur of the moment. If she and Jeremy didn't like each other she would have to get a job in Salisbury. A six-week free boat trip calling at every port on the way wasn't to be sneezed at, she told herself, the butterflies fluttering in her stomach.

When she opened the door to the studio flat she shared with Tessa she was feeling elated at having finally made up her mind.

"There you are, Livy," said James Coghlan. "We're going to be late."

"What for, James?"

"Our five o'clock appointment to see the Honourable Barnaby St Clair with your painting to collect our cheque. Walter Featherstone-Wallace is meeting us at the house in Piccadilly. When I told Mr St Clair on the phone you'd be there for a photograph with him to go in the *Tatler*, he deigned to remember who I am. Quite a trick, bringing the press. Frank Brigandshaw's idea when he heard the name of the buyer. Seems he knows Mr St Clair. Told me to mention the names on the phone when I made the appointment. I explained Frank Brigandshaw and Partners are our publicity consultants at the Nouvelle Galerie... Now, how do you look? Let me see."

"I'm going to Rhodesia on Wednesday, James."

"We'll talk about that when we have the cheque. There's more to selling paintings than meets the eye. For a moment he was going to renege on the deal. Whatever happened to a man's word being his bond? Don't know what the world's come to after the war. Promiscuity. Free love. No one giving a damn about the future. Isn't it wonderful?"

"Have you seen Jeanne today?"

"She's fine in spirit but not in face. Ben punched Samuel. Lovely story. Anyway, Jeanne is off the hook and so are we. There is so much light at the end of the tunnel it's blinding me. Now be a good girl and change that dress into something a little more sexy. A cheque in the hand, you know... Appearances, Livy. All about appearances. We're going to make you famous. What a lovely little life we're all going to have."

"I'm going, James. I'm serious. I've paid for the ticket."

"Even more reason to collect your money. If you don't like it when you get to Rhodesia you can catch another boat up the east coast of Africa and home to Chelsea. Through the Suez Canal. Kind of story that is good for publicity. Now hurry. We don't want to keep a member of one of England's oldest families waiting... Isn't it all so lovely? Spring is in the air... Dear Jeanne. Such a lovely girl."

3

____

*D*orian Brigandshaw was the last on Paul's list to be picked up the following Sunday. Somewhere behind Holland Park the church bells were ringing for early communion. There were people in the street dressed for church, prayer books in their hands, men in suits, women wearing big hats. Dorian had a cheap room he rented in a run-down row of Victorian terraced houses, the paint peeling off, pigeons cooing on the old slate roofs. Beth had not seen Dorian since the New Year. In the street, the plane trees were sprouting lime-green leaves, giving the place hope. Frank, sitting in the back of the car, had not said a word after being picked up at St Mary's Hospital. Connie was worse, still heavily sedated with morphine.

"You go and see him, Frank," Connie had said to both of them from her hospital bed. "I'll be all right. Don't look so glum. It's life. Make peace with him. You'll feel better."

Checking Frank in the rear mirror, Paul started the car and the journey to Hastings Court. In his breast pocket was a letter to Harry Brigandshaw asking him for his daughter's hand in marriage. Paul thought it better that way. In case the cat got his tongue. Some important words were easier said on paper, he had decided, before sitting down at his desk to write his letter.

"How's Nancy, Beth?" said Dorian, taking Paul's thoughts away from Frank and the letter in his pocket. "When did she have her abortion? She never asked for my help. Thought it better to say nothing. She had someone to go to in Clapham."

"She's still pregnant, Dorian. Next month. Round about the middle of next month you are going to be a father. You can tell Dad when you get home. Cheer him up."

"Oh, my word. Not hearing from her I thought this was all over."

"You were running away, Dorian."

"I've been so busy."

"Don't make excuses."

"What am I going to do? I'm in the army."

"Whatever you do won't alter the fact next month you're going to have a son or a daughter. A living being. Part of your flesh. However the poor little bastard was made... No offence, Frank... Why don't you talk to Dorian, Frank? First-hand knowledge kind of approach."

"Congratulations, Dorian," said Frank sarcastically, smiling for the first time as Paul watched him in the rear-view mirror. "Love 'em and leave 'em, Dorian."

"It was a one-night stand."

"It worked. You only need one night."

"I barely know the girl."

"Bugger the girl. What about the child? You don't have to marry the girl. Just look after the kid. How do you know it's yours?"

"How's Connie, Frank?" asked Dorian.

"She's terrible. Dying. Don't change the subject."

"We are certain, Frank," said Beth.

"Think of the kid, Dorian. It takes one poke to make a baby. One bit of fun. The bastard has to live the rest of his life without his father. How'd you like that?"

Paul, watching them both in the mirror, kept his mouth shut. There were enough sparks flying without his help.

"Put your foot on it, Paul," said Frank. "I'm in a hurry."

For the rest of the journey down to Surrey none of them said a word. In the front seats, Paul and Beth held hands with Paul keeping one hand on the wheel. When he changed gears, Beth put her hand on his knee. At least they were going to be happy with their lives, he promised himself. Which was something.

When they turned up past the gate house into the long driveway towards the old mansion with its crenellated battlements, the sun was shining.

· · ·

HARRY BRIGANDSHAW, not feeling his best, watched the car roll up the driveway and park in front of the terrace down below facing the Gothic doors to the Manderville house that had been his maternal grandfather's family seat back through so many centuries. The terrace ran the length of the house with steps leading up from the gravel driveway. Frank was the first to get out of the car and walk up the steps to where Harry was standing, his hand on the balustrade to keep him steady. They hugged for a long moment before Frank pulled back to look at him, still holding his shoulders. Neither of them said a word. There was nothing to say.

"Your mother's somewhere around, Frank. Lovely day. Nice to see the sunshine in England. Paul told me he's taking you back. We can all have a good breakfast together before you go. Mrs Craddock is cooking it now. Why don't you go into the kitchen and say hello? Mrs Craddock has had a soft spot for you since you were a child. I'm sorry to hear about Connie. From what Paul tells me she sounds a wonderful lady."

"Are you all right?"

"Not really... Hello, Beth. Dorian, good to see you again. Thanks for bringing them, Paul. What's this? I haven't got my glasses."

"You can read it when I'm gone, sir. It's about your daughter."

"So what have you been up to, Dorian? How's the army? Not really the army, I suppose. Good practice for your writing. How are you coming along with *African Drums*? Have you had any time to write? Had a letter the other day from Josiah Makoni. He mentioned you. Why don't we all go inside? Josiah said your advice about going to university has helped him settle into Fort Hare. He was thanking me again for putting him through university. He's going to go a long way in life. Tembo and Princess must be so proud of him. So nice to help someone who appreciates what's being done for him. South Africa's Fort Hare isn't exactly Oxford but he'll get a degree recognised in Africa. They only take black people at Fort Hare. He's reading PPE. Philosophy, politics and economics. Same degree as your Cousin Tinus. Tinus wanted to fly over from New York to be with us today. Told Paul to tell him not to come. He has his own family to look after... Beth, is this letter what I hope it's about? Do you agree with what's in it?"

"I've no idea what it says."

"That dazzling smile tells me you are lying. Good... I'm flying out of London tomorrow. Ding-a-ling is taking me to the airport. Vic Bell and I went through the war together. Makes it easier. Just good to see you all, my children. And that includes you, Frank. You mean just as much to me as the rest of them. Haven't been able to contact Kim for weeks. He's here in spirit if not in person. As is Anthony. So long ago lost over Berlin but he is always in my thoughts... Come on. Don't like standing up too long these days. Dorian, can you give me a hand? Oh, and no sentimental nonsense today. It's a celebration. Of the luck in a good life that gave me five wonderful children all perfect to me. If you have as good a life as mine, you'll be as happy as I am right now. A mother and father that loved us children. Grandfather Manderville to talk to on the farm after Dad was killed by the elephant. A friend beyond friend in my brother-in-law, Barend, despite all his pain in life. Family. Children. That's what it's all about... Now it's a bit early but how about a glass of sherry in the lounge when Frank comes back from visiting Mrs Craddock? Thank you. Both of you. Two shoulders to lean on are better than one. I don't seem to have any strength."

"Where's Mum?" asked Beth, her voice choking.

"She's in one of her states, I'm afraid. Your mother was never very good at handling emotion. Go and look for her, Beth. She'll talk to you. You'll all have to look after her for me when I've gone. You see, I have to go home. To Africa. Elephant Walk is my home. This was the home of both my grandfathers in turn. But it wasn't mine. I want to watch the African sun go down again. Smell the wild sage in the bush. Hear the calls of the wild. Africa is in my blood... It's time for me to go home."

THE SMELL of bacon cooking drew Frank down the corridor. Mrs Craddock must have heard the car and started the breakfast, he told himself. It was cold in the corridor. Frank was cold deep inside. The man he had called his father most of his life was a shadow of the man Frank remembered. His skin was yellow, hanging off his face. The body he had hugged, that of a skeleton. Twice in one day, Frank had looked into the eyes of death.

Numb, unable to think coherently, he stumbled into the kitchen, a place that had once been for him a sanctuary with the cook, Mrs Craddock.

"Hello, Mrs Craddock. That smells good."

"Frank! Oh, Frank. How lovely to see you again."

"And you... Where's my mother?"

"Here, Frank. Good of you to find the time to pay us a visit."

"I don't have the energy to argue with you, Mother. You look well."

"I don't feel it. I'm being abandoned. He never loved me, you know. Put up with me, of course. I was pregnant with Anthony when I got to Elephant Walk. Being the gentleman, he married me. Did me a favour, I suppose. We had an affair on the boat. Just a physical affair. There wasn't anyone else I fancied on the SS *Corfe Castle*. Anyway, Harry Brigandshaw was rich. You take what you find in life, Frank. Your father had dumped me by then."

Mrs Craddock, looking up at his mother, left the room, the bacon still sizzling in the frying pan, the gas left on.

"Why does he want to leave me now?" went on his mother. "Just shows. When you're no longer attractive to men you're of no interest. I'm an old woman. I hate being an old woman. No one even looks at me anymore."

"You've upset Mrs Craddock."

"He's upset me. Why does nobody think of me? No one cares a damn about me anymore. Beth and Dorian up in London. Kim, God knows where. Not even a phone call or a letter. As for you... Didn't you ever think of my feelings? You're all so damn selfish. Here you are, walking into the kitchen as if you hadn't stayed away from me all these years, and to see Mrs Craddock."

"Stop feeling sorry for yourself, Mother. You are not the only person with a problem. The person I love most in the world is dying. No, not the man you first told me was my father. Connie is dying. Can't you sometimes think of other people? Think of me for a change. You never so much as tried to look for me in London. Why must I be the one to apologise to you? You were married to the man who just hugged me on the terrace. A man I now know loves me. You didn't even care about him, you selfish bitch."

"How dare you say that to me! I'm your mother."

"Then act like my mother. I will be going straight back to London. Goodbye... The bacon's burning."

"Frank! Frank! Come back."

"No, Mother. I'm going to have breakfast with the others, if you'll let Mrs Craddock back in the kitchen. Have a glass of sherry with them before breakfast. I thought the problem was my real father and the man outside. It wasn't. The problem was you."

"I'll tell your father what you've just said to me."

"Which one, Mother dear?"

"It wasn't my fault."

"That's what they all say. What people always tell me. It's not my fault. Don't give me that crap. How can this one be my fault?"

"You're alive. Isn't that enough?"

"Not at the moment."

"Don't run away again, Frank. Please. I'm sorry."

"We're all sorry. Everyone is sorry. So bloody sorry. Well, I'm not."

"I'm still your mother. You can't run away from that. Half of you is me. I'll make Barnaby come and see you. I loved that man like you love this woman. Is that a crime? All my life I've loved your father. All my whole damn, miserable life. Please hug me, Frank. I'm so alone. We'll go and see him together."

"The bacon's burning."

Not looking back, Frank walked out of the kitchen to find Mrs Craddock in tears in the corridor.

"I'm sorry, Mrs Craddock. It wasn't my fault."

"Go back to her, Frank."

"I can't."

Like the child he had once been, Frank ran away down the corridor away from his ghosts.

BETH PICKED up the phone in the hall after it rang and rang. Paul and Dorian had helped her father into a chair by the fire in the lounge and given him a glass of sherry.

"Hastings Court residence."

"May I speak to Mr Brigandshaw?"

"He's resting at the moment. Who is speaking?"

"Doctor Matthew Hull of St Mary's Hospital."

"Do you want Frank Brigandshaw?"

"His mother has taken a turn for the worse. Please tell him to hurry."

"When I find him I'll give him your message. He's somewhere in the house."

"She's calling for him. I'm not sure if she understands. I've been injecting her with morphine for the pain."

Running down the hall towards the kitchen, Beth met Frank running the other way.

"Did you hear the phone, Frank? It was for you. Doctor Hull. He wants you back at St Mary's as soon as possible. You can forget breakfast, both of you. Paul will understand."

"I'm not hungry. Where's Paul?"

"In the lounge."

"I can take the car. You can both catch the train tonight."

Beth, in a dither as to what to do, watched her brother run into the lounge and come back with the keys to Paul's car. Then she heard the car go off down the driveway on its way to London.

"He didn't have to rush off like that," said her mother, coming down the hall.

"Hello, Mum. We're in the lounge with Father. The hospital rang. Connie's taken a turn for the worse."

"I thought he was running from me. We had an argument in the kitchen."

"Come and have a glass of sherry."

"Before breakfast?"

"Everything is upside down today."

"When's your father going?"

"Didn't he tell you?... Tomorrow. Vic Bell is coming down from London to take him to the airport."

"My whole life has fallen apart."

"You still have us, Mum. We're not going away."

"Frank's gone."

"He'll come back. It's Connie he's mad at for being sick. They think she's his mother at the hospital. We'll all work something out."

"Will you come and visit me?"

"Of course I will. We all will. When's Kim coming home?"

"Only he knows, Beth. Not so much as a postcard for the last month. I worry he's sick."

"He had a letter of introduction to the King of Bhutan. He'll be fine. Just come and have a glass of sherry. Smile. We're all trying to smile. I want the memory of today to last forever. A good memory. None of us must spoil it... Frank will be at the hospital in less than two hours. They hugged. They really hugged. They both made peace with each other."

DORIAN WATCHED his mother walk into the lounge without greeting him. She was glaring at his father. Earlier Frank had burst into the room, taken Paul's car keys, shaken hands with Dorian's father sitting in his chair and run out again saying Connie had taken a turn for the worse.

"Beth says you are going on this idiotic journey tomorrow. You're not well enough. This is your home, Harry. I'm your wife. I'm the one to look after you."

"My mother and Madge will do just fine. My sister started a clinic on the farm. Don't worry. I'm going home. Vic's coming down to drive me to the airport. We've argued about this quite enough. Please. Not anymore and not in front of the children. Have a glass of sherry."

"We haven't even had breakfast yet."

"Why not? This is a breakfast party. Beth and Paul are getting married. We'll drink a toast to them. What a lovely send off. The first of my children to get married. And to the son of a good friend of mine. God bless your father's memory, Paul. Frank has a good heart, running back like that to Connie. Makes me proud of him... What are we eating for breakfast?"

"We burned the bacon so Mrs Craddock is cooking sausages. Well, if it isn't Dorian," his mother said, finally turning to look at him. "The army, I presume, takes up all your time?"

"Hello, Mother. I have very little money as a national serviceman to gallivant around."

"You could ask your father for the train fare."

"I don't like asking money from Dad. You are always the one who says you can have anything you want when you earn it yourself."

"Don't throw that back in my face, I was talking about the children of rich parents who don't bother to work for a living sponging off their parents."

"Tina, please don't let's argue," said his father. "I want this to be a happy day."

"I'm so upset, Harry. You're going. What am I going to do without you?"

"The children will look after you. Dorian, give your mother that glass of sherry. You've been very quiet. Is there anything the matter?"

"A girl I had sex with is going to have a baby. Beth's friend, Nancy. I was staying with them before I joined the army magazine."

"We don't want all the lurid details, son. Are you the father, Dorian?"

"Yes, Dad."

"Wonderful. Before I die I'm going to become a grandfather. The Brigandshaw name goes on. That's the best news I've had for a long while. Nancy's a lovely girl. A bit wild by all reports. Motherhood will calm her down. It does for all the girls. Ask your mother."

The look his mother gave his father made Dorian sad, adding to the turmoil in his mind.

"But what do I do?" he asked unhappily.

"Marry her of course." His father was looking at him with deep sympathy. "When's the baby due?"

"Middle of next month."

"A registry office, Dorian. Not a church. The church has the hope of the bride being pure at her wedding. Eight months pregnant would be a little obvious. Registry office. Special licence. Two witnesses. I'm sure Paul and Beth will help you out."

"But I don't know the girl."

"Then get to know her, Dorian. Under all the nonsense we're all much the same. Now, you lot can all stand up while I propose the toast. To Beth and Paul. To Dorian and Nancy... What are you going to call the child, Dorian?"

"Dad, you're laughing."

"Of course I'm laughing. I'm happy for all of you. Now raise your sherry glasses to the happy couples."

Trying his best to smile with the rest of them, Dorian took one sip of his sherry. It was all very well being given advice, he thought. The problem was carrying it out. The rest of his life depended on making the right decision. To say nothing of Nancy and the child. To reach the end of a life and still be arguing wasn't what he had in mind. It seemed to Dorian his father was going home to Elephant Walk for a last bit of peace and quiet. If he and Nancy came to arguing and bickering he'd never write a book in his life.

When they all trooped into the morning room for breakfast, Paul and himself helping his father up onto his feet, he still had no idea what he was going to do.

4

At the end of May, Barnaby St Clair left Lord's Cricket Ground to walk the three miles to his townhouse in Piccadilly feeling pleased with himself. The Bedser twins had bowled out Middlesex for a paltry one hundred and ninety runs in the first innings leaving Surrey well on top. Alec Bedser had taken six wickets for sixty-four runs, Eric three for sixty-eight. There was barely a cloud in the sky as he walked around Marble Arch into Park Lane. The birds were singing in Hyde Park. At fifty-three he had never felt better walking briskly, enjoying his constitutional, the furled umbrella in his right hand jauntily held as he marched under the trees beside the park. On the one side of what Barnaby thought of as the big London square that included his home was Hyde Park. On the other, Green Park. It was like living in the country.

Turning into Piccadilly down the Old Park Lane, past the Royal Air Force Club he had lunched in many times with Harry Brigandshaw, past the Cavalry Club, he arrived home feeling hungry for his supper. A good walk had done him good. Using his latch key, Barnaby let himself into his house. Smithers would be up in his room. There was no point in disturbing him until he called for his dinner. As usual, the whisky decanter was set out on the silver tray with the soda syphon on the sideboard. Next to the decanter stood a heavy crystal glass ready for his use. Everything was as he liked it. As it had been for years. Being a creature of habit suited him admirably. He had in life exactly what he wanted, when he wanted and how he wanted. If, sometimes, he was a little bored with life, his daily routine, administered by Smithers, made up for it. He was a bachelor. Had been all his life. And proud of it. None of these nagging wives for Barnaby St Clair, he always told himself. He could do just what he wanted. No one to ask. No one else to consider. If it was all a little selfish Barnaby didn't care. It was how he liked it.

Having smiled at the painted cat among the foliage on the wall just inside the door as he came in, and seeing his ginger cat asleep on his chair, Barnaby thought briefly of the pretty artist who with half an army had delivered the painting, making sure he paid up his four hundred pounds. It was a pity she had gone to Rhodesia. The young girl was just his type.

"Win some, lose some," he said to the cat as he poured himself a drink. There were plenty more young girls in London looking for money; life truly had been good to him.

Barnaby picked up the cat, put it on the floor where it glared at him, and sat down in his chair to savour the day's cricket while sipping his whisky. To his annoyance, the front door bell interrupted his thoughts. With luck, whoever it was at the door would be sent packing by Smithers who knew after a day at the cricket he was not to be disturbed.

The doorbell stopped ringing and Barnaby went back to mulling over the day's cricket.

"Ah, Smithers. What's for supper? Bowled them out for a hundred and ninety. Between Alec's fast bowling and Eric's spinners, Middlesex were all over the place."

"A young man wants to see you."

"Tell him I'm not here."

"He was sitting in the park and saw you come home, sir."

"Did he now?... You'd better bring another glass. Ask the young man to come in."

"Lamb chops, sir. With mint sauce and mashed potatoes."

"Plenty of chops. I'm hungry. Walked six miles today."

"Very good for you, sir. How many chops? They are rather big."

"Make it four. With a nice green salad."

"Very well."

Barnaby, with a smirk on his face, waited for Frank Brigandshaw to be shown into his lounge. Who else could it be sitting in the park on a summer's evening waiting for him to come home.

"Would you like a drink, old chap?" he said as his son walked through the door into his home for the first time. "I've been rather expecting you this last month."

Smithers put a second glass on the tray before leaving them alone.

"What have you got?"

"Whisky."

"Yes, I could drink a whisky and soda. No ice, thank you. Brian Tobin drinks his whisky soaked in ice. Ruins the flavour."

"Harry Brigandshaw phoned me before he left for Rhodesia. I'm glad you paid him a visit. Why don't you sit down, Frank? Take the weight off the old feet. Middlesex were all out for a hundred and ninety. Do you follow the cricket?"

"Tinus Oosthuizen taught me to bat left-handed for some reason. Never any good."

"Of course. He played for Oxford."

"It's my mother I'm here about."

"Have a drink first... What do you want me to do?"

"Be nice to her. You've known each other all your lives. She can't stay alone at Hastings Court. She wants to leave the place, find a flat in London. I hoped you could help. I'm afraid my mother and I don't get on very well with each other."

"I was sorry to read about Connie Whitaker. So young to die... Sit down, Frank."

"Beth and Dorian have their own lives to lead. Mother's pretty much on her own."

"We all do. Have any of you heard from Rhodesia?"

"Beth had a phone call in the flat. The sun has made him feel better. She spoke to Grandmother and Aunty Madge."

"I'm glad. He loves Elephant Walk. Africa was Harry's first love. There are good places to live and good places to die. Somebody told me that. He'll be happy now... Was she in a great deal of pain?"

"They drugged her with morphine. She smiled at me. Just smiled. Never talked at the end... Can we change the subject?"

"I'm sorry... How's business?"

"I don't really care. I don't really care about anything. That's the problem."

"You'll get over it. Grief fades. You'll remember only the good parts in a few years' time."

"I hope so... Could you take my mother to lunch or something?"

"I could try."

"If you talked about the old times in Salisbury and Johannesburg together when you were young it might help. She's so miserable in herself."

"I'd like to hear about you, Frank. What you've done in your life. What you are going to be doing with the years ahead of you. We've a lot to catch up on... How does that look? Not too much soda?"

"The colour's just fine... I liked Livy's painting where you've hung it on the wall in the hall. First thing I saw."

"Reminded me of the ginger over there."

"They do look alike. She's on her way to Rhodesia."

"Hope it all works out for her."

"She was very pleased with her part of your four hundred pounds."

"Then my 'spur of the moment' wasn't all wasted. Would you come for some supper? Lamb chops, I'm afraid."

"Thank you. I don't think I've eaten today."

"Cheers, Frank. Nice to see you after all these years."

Then they laughed together as Barnaby rang the bell to tell Smithers there were two for dinner.

~

PRINCIPAL CHARACTERS

~

The Brigandshaws
Harry — Central character of *Treason If You Lose*
Tina — Harry's wife, formerly Tina Pringle
Anthony — Harry and Tina's eldest son killed in the Second World War
Beth — Harry and Tina's only daughter
Frank — Central character of *Horns of Dilemma* and Tina's illegitimate son but recognised as Harry's
Dorian — Harry and Tina's second eldest son
Kim — Harry and Tina's youngest son
Sir Henry Manderville — Harry's maternal grandfather who lived on Elephant Walk
Emily — Harry's mother who lives on Elephant Walk

The Oosthuizens
Madge — Harry's younger sister and wife of Barend
Tinus — Madge's son and Harry's much-loved nephew
Genevieve — Tinus's wife and Merlin St Clair's illegitimate daughter
Barend and Hayley — Tinus and Genevieve's children

The St Clairs
Merlin — Eighteenth Baron of Purbeck, Lord St Clair
Robert — Merlin's younger brother
Barnaby — Youngest son of Lord and Lady St Clair and father of Frank Brigandshaw
Freya — Robert's American wife
Richard and Chuck (Charles) — Robert and Freya's children
Lady St Clair — Mother to Merlin, Robert and Barnaby

The Wakefields
Horatio — Journalist at the *Daily Mail*
Janet Bray — Horatio's wife
Harry and Bergit — Horatio and Janet's children named after Harry Brigandshaw and Bergit von Lieberman

The Smythes
William — Freelance foreign correspondent and host on the British Overseas Service
Betty — William's wife
Ruthy and Patrick — William and Betty's children

Other Principal Characters
Ben Brown — Jeanne Pétain's neighbour where the Chelsea artists live
Benjie Appleton — Jazz band leader
Brian Tobin — Frank Brigandshaw's best friend from school
Connie (Constance) Whitaker — Frank Brigandshaw's close confidante and lover
Frederick Whitaker — Connie's much older and spiteful husband
Freddie Marble — A trombone player
James Coghlan — A sculptor who lives in the Chelsea district
Jeanne Pétain — A French-American interior decorator and artist
Jeremy Crookshank — Paul Crookshank's younger brother
Kenneth Grahame — A friend recruited by Paul Crookshank to work in his antique business
Major Pilkington-Jones — The major helps Paul Crookshank set up his antique business
Mrs Craddock — The cook at Hastings Court
Nancy Longhurst — Beth's promiscuous best friend and, like Beth, a secretary
Olivia Johnston — An artist friend of Frank Brigandshaw
Paul Crookshank — The eldest son of Phillip Crookshank who was killed in the Second World War
Smithers — Barnaby St Clair's gentleman's gentleman
Tessa Handson — An artist friend of Frank Brigandshaw
Vic 'Ding-a-ling' Bell — Harry's World War Two adjutant and friend
Zachariah Cohen — Frank's army friend

ACKNOWLEDGEMENTS

With grateful thanks to our *VIP First Readers* for reading *Horns of Dilemma* prior to its official launch date. They have been fabulous in picking up errors and typos helping us to ensure that your own reading experience of *Horns of Dilemma* has been the best possible. Their time and commitment is particularly appreciated.

Alan McConnochie (South Africa)
Hilary Jenkins (South Africa)
Derek Tippell (Portugal)
Marcellé Archer (South Africa)

Thank you.
Kamba Publishing

DEAR READER

~

Reviews are the most powerful tools in our kitty when it comes to getting attention for Peter's books. This is where you can come in, as by providing an honest review you will help bring them to the attention of other readers.

If you enjoyed reading *Horns of Dilemma* and have five minutes to spare, we would really appreciate a review (it can be as short as you like). Your help in spreading the word and keeping Peter's work alive is gratefully received.

Please post your review on the retailer site where you purchased this book.

Thank you so much.
Heather Stretch (Peter's daughter)

LADY COME HOME (BOOK EIGHT)
CONTINUE YOUR JOURNEY WITH THE BRIGANDSHAWS

She left home for a husband. But she fell in love with Africa…

With a fiancé waiting in Africa, and a one-way ticket in hand, artist Livy Johnston boards a steamer ship at the port of London. A tantalizingly future awaits, and Livy is exuberant with a lust for life. So much so, that when she catches the eye of a fellow passenger, she embarks on a shipboard romance. Surely one last fling wouldn't hurt…

Arriving in Rhodesia, Livy quickly makes new friends, who waste no time exposing her to the nightlife of colonial society. But what of Jeremy, her fiancé? When the life he offers turns out to be nothing like what she envisaged, Livy embarks on a safari to the Zambezi River. Camping on the shores, she passionately paints the winding river. Lost in the beauty of Africa, she creates a nostalgic painting never meant to be sold.

Confused and disillusioned, Livy begins to question where she really belongs. Harry Brigandshaw's damning words have become a portent of things to come in Africa. Should she listen to them now? Or follow her heart's desire…